The Devious Husband

SIERRA AND XAVIER'S STORY

THE WINDSORS

CATHARINA MAURA

Content Warnings

This book contains many sensitive themes, and reader discretion is advised. Please find a non-exhaustive list of content warnings on the author's website: www.catharinamaura.com/warnings

This one is for those who learned the hard way that while words can be wielded as weapons, the things we leave unsaid can leave deeper scars.

Take your chances.

Follow your heart.

It might just lead you to a life better than you dared dream of.

Contents

One

SIERRA

"I can't believe that asshole," I snap as I storm into my best friend's office. She raises a brow and slowly looks up from the drawing tablet on her desk, her pencil still in hand.

"Let me guess," Raven, my best friend and sister-in-law, says. "Xavier Kingston did something entirely unforgivable... for the second time this week?"

I cross my arms and scowl at her as I sit down, my eyes roaming over the beautiful studio she's created, designs and fabrics strewn all around. Even her mess looks artistic, and I have no idea how she does it.

"He hacked into my computer and stole my design plans for his new theatre," I begin to explain, regaling her with yet another tale of my nemesis's obnoxiousness. "He didn't even try to change them — he left every last detail as I designed it, almost like he's mocking me, telling me that there isn't a single thing I can do about it if he wants to steal my ideas."

Raven's eyes widen as I thrust my phone in her face, replaying the interview Xavier did with *The Herald*, of all newspapers. "*Oh wow,*" she murmurs when Xavier proudly showcases the design of his new theatre, her eyes wide.

I've seen him show off my work as though it's *his* on three different morning shows and every newspaper imaginable in the last twenty-four hours, and each time I see his stupid smirk, my anger burns a little fiercer.

"That's... Sierra, you worked on those designs for *months*. How could he even have gotten his hands on them?"

I sigh and run a hand through my long, dark hair. "I don't know," I tell her, feeling a lot more defeated than I'd care to admit. "Silas reviewed all of our security measures, and there's no way he physically broke in. We can't actually find any evidence of a cyber security breach either, but how else could he have done it? Somehow, he hacked into my computer."

Raven stares at me that way she does sometimes, like there's something on her mind, but she isn't sure she should voice her thoughts. "What?" I ask, narrowing my eyes.

"I'm just trying to figure out why he'd suddenly steal your design plans. I was under the impression that you'd both put your feud behind yourselves — was I wrong?"

I sigh and look out the window, my heart heavy. From the moment my older brother Dion introduced me to his best friend, Xavier, I've disliked him. That dislike grew into full-blown hatred throughout the years, as we became business rivals. My hatred for Xavier was further fueled by each of his attempts to interfere with every major business decision I've made, more often than not sabotaging me under the guise of looking after me in Dion's absence. I don't understand how Dion doesn't see it. Xavier Kingston is the devil in disguise, yet somehow, my sweet older brother thinks the world of him.

"It's been over three years since we last truly butted heads over anything," I tell Raven, my stomach twisting in an unfamiliar way. Xavier stopped messing with me as much as he used to when Dion moved back home from London, but I should've known the tentative peace between us wouldn't last.

"So why now?" Raven ponders. "Those designs are clearly yours. I've watched you draw them up myself. It's almost like —"

"—Like he's provoking me," I snap. "That damned asshole is provoking me, going on live television with my designs, claiming them as his own, and being showered in praise while he's at it. It was bad enough that he announced the opening of his theatre right as I was about to acquire one myself, and now he blatantly steals my designs for said theatre? He seems to think that us treating each other civilly for a while means he can suddenly get away with murder. He's wrong."

Raven tucks her long dark hair behind her ear and smiles, her eyes twinkling. "I was going to say that it's almost like he *misses* you. You haven't been attending any public events that you knew he'd be at, and for the last six months, you've been pulling out of every project he's claimed an interest in. There was a time when you'd never go a week without seeing each other, even if it was only in boardrooms."

I draw a shallow breath, my treacherous heart beating a little faster. "Don't be ridiculous," I admonish, my tone weaker than I'd have liked. The mere thought of Xavier *missing me* makes me feel a little funny. "He's too preoccupied with *Valeria* to even spare me a second thought, hence my confusion about his latest actions." My voice drips with disdain as I say the name.

Valeria appeared on his arm years ago, and she's attended countless events as his plus one ever since. I'd never seen him with a woman before then, and there hasn't been anyone else since her. The way he dotes on her is sickening. While I'm always subjected to the most vicious parts of him, all he ever directs her way is pure adoration, like he hangs onto her every word. Xavier looks at Valeria like she can do no wrong, and each time something she says makes him laugh, I find myself staring at him, wondering why he seems like an entirely different person around her.

"He's always refused to comment when asked about her, Sierra, and I just don't believe that he's dating her. If he were, he'd just have said so. Besides, I've never seen the two of them act in any way that could be described as intimate."

I roll my eyes at her naivety. "Haven't you seen the article *The Herald* published, about how he supposedly commissioned ten different jewelry pieces from Laurier?" I ask, an emotion I can't quite identify twisting my stomach. "Apparently, just the gemstones and diamonds are worth twenty million in total. You don't do that kind of thing for just any woman." I rise to my feet and begin to pace, my emotions in turmoil. "I don't even understand how he managed to so much as speak to Laurier. Regardless of his notoriety and money, Laurier was one of few people I didn't think he had access to. Money isn't enough to get an appointment, so how the hell did he buy *ten* pieces when I can barely get Laurier to make me one a year?"

Raven looks over her left shoulder and clears her throat. "I don't know," she murmurs, her voice a little shaky. "Maybe he called in a favor? Who knows?"

I raise a brow, suddenly feeling like I'm missing something. "Who would be dumb enough to make a deal with the devil?"

My gorgeous best friend laughs, her whole face lighting up. "Who, indeed," she says, amusement dancing in her eyes. "You know? For someone who claims to hate Xavier Kingston, you're awfully concerned with how he's spending his money and who he spends his time with. If I didn't know better, I'd say you're jealous. In fact, I'd go so far as to say that you've stopped going to events you know he'll be at so you don't have to see him with her."

I part my lips in denial, pure outrage rushing through me. "I'm simply surprised he's got time for corporate espionage," I retort, running a hand through my hair in frustration. "I've been trying to be the better person, and you know it, Rave. I tried my best to stop reacting to his bullshit, but he must've known that I'd never let *this* slide. Those designs meant a lot to me."

Raven nods, a knowing glint in her eyes. "Yeah, I bet he knew exactly what he was doing."

I grit my teeth and glance down at my red nails, a bespoke color my other sister-in-law, Celeste, gave me. "That piece of trash," I mutter under my breath, my blood boiling as I think back to his smug smile as he showcased my designs on the news this morning. "I'm going to make him regret so much as setting eyes on my drawings. If he wants war, I'll give it to him."

Two

SIERRA

My heart is pounding in my chest as I park my car in a secluded area at the back of the Kingston compound, right by a little gap in the thick hedges that surround the property. For years now, I've used this tiny weakness in the Kingstons' security measures to break in and enter Xavier's house, and each time I park here, I'm certain they'll have fixed their lax security, only to breathe a sigh of relief when I find they haven't.

I grin to myself as I glance down at my all-black outfit — a pair of black leggings, a black tee, black leather thigh-high boots, and of course, black gloves. I'm not silly enough to leave fingerprints, after all.

I inhale deeply before I try to shimmy through the gap in the hedge like I have so many times before, staying as quiet as possible. It never gets any less nerve-racking, and each time I do this, I'm certain I'll find Xavier or one of his brothers standing at the other end. Or worse — his security staff, who would definitely detain me. I've done some wild things throughout the years, in my many attempts to sabotage Xavier, and I know from experience that my brothers will happily leave me in jail for the night if I get arrested for breaking and entering, even if it's just to teach me a lesson.

I smirk to myself when I make it through undetected, my gaze roaming over the vast terrain ahead of me. Much like my own family, the Kingstons also all live on one huge gated piece of land, with each sibling having a separate part to themselves. The hedge I entered through places me near Xavier's back garden, and my heart begins to race as I slowly make my way toward the building I'm aiming for tonight — his garage.

Xavier is nothing if not cocky, and with a bit of luck, he's left his garage unlocked like he's occasionally done in the past. He seems to think that he's so untouchable that he doesn't need extensive security, and for the most part, it's true. The Kingstons aren't just billionaires — they're deeply entrenched in politics and law enforcement too. What money can't buy them, their connections do. No one but me would be crazy enough to break into a Kingston property, and thank God for it, because tonight's mission would've been near-impossible otherwise.

I glance over my shoulder furtively as I jog up to the huge glass structure, trying my best to watch out for cameras or other security measures and finding none. My heart pounds wildly as my fingers wrap around the cold metal door handle, and I hold my breath for a beat. The door opens with ease, and I huff in disbelief. "What an *idiot*," I murmur under my breath as I carefully pull the door open just enough to slip through.

I pause at the entrance, my eyes roaming over the endless rows of ridiculously expensive and rare supercars. There aren't a lot of things Xavier cares about, other than getting on my last nerve every chance he's got, but his cars definitely rank high on the list of things he adores. He won't appreciate anyone messing with them.

The biggest smile spreads across my face, pure glee lightening my mood as I imagine his sour expression when he walks in tomorrow morning to find he's unable to drive any of his beloved cars. I can't help but chuckle as I grab the pocket knife I sharpened especially for tonight and kneel by the tires of the car closest to me.

A soft hiss fills the room as air slowly leaves the tire, and it deflates. Xavier has more than enough money, and the cost of replacing his tires won't even register for him, but it'll positively impact the countless car repair centers he'll have to employ to fix all the damage I'm about to do.

Normally I'd have gone for a tit-for-tat approach, and I'd have tried to steal one of his projects or designs in return for the one I lost, but somehow, this feels a lot more satisfying. This time I'm much more agitated, and I can't quite tell why.

Is it because it's been so long since we truly came for each other's throats like this? Because I thought we'd moved past it and could treat each other civilly? Or is it something else? I can't figure out why I'm so *hurt*. It isn't the first time either of us stole the other's design or project, but this time, I haven't done anything to him to deserve it, like I would have in the past. Maybe it's all in my head, but I can't help but feel like Xavier is telling me that he doesn't give a damn about my hard work, or my feelings — except he isn't actually bothering to say it to my face because I'm simply not worth a second thought.

I bite down on my lip as I work my way through his cars, my heart aching. Until he showed up at a charity event with Valeria on his arm, our feud had kind of been *fun*. We often went too far in our attempts to sabotage each other, but there was some sort of mutual respect. Neither of us would admit it, but we both kept a tally and gave in to each other to keep things fair, resulting in both of us ending up with half of the projects we both fought over. This time, it feels different.

I sigh as I make my way to the last car, a matte black supercar that's been placed on a round platform. It wasn't here the last time I snuck in, and I've never seen Xavier drive this car before. I frown when I don't recognize the make. It's clearly bespoke and incredibly expensive, and for a split-second, I hesitate, before I jam my knife into the back tire.

An alarm instantly goes off, and all lights turn on, causing me to jump up in shock. I whirl around as metal barriers begin to close outside the windows, nearly trapping me inside, and I rush over to the exit, my stomach turning.

Just as I reach the door, the alarm cuts off, and the lights suddenly dim again. I'm breathing hard as I try to figure out what's going on, my eyes zeroing in on the flashing screen by the door. *Mrs. Kingston Protocol*, it reads, and moments later, the metal barrier begins to rise, leaving the room as it was before I set off the alarm. I stare at the screen for a second longer before I rush out, my thoughts a mess.

Three

SIERRA

I clench my phone and lean back in my desk chair as I stare at the article my sister-in-law, Faye, forwarded this morning. **XAVIER KINGSTON SPOTTED DRIVING A YET TO BE RELEASED WINDSOR MOTORS SUPERCAR.** My blood boils as I click on the video, Xavier's irritatingly handsome face filling my screen.

"You've never driven a Windsor Motors car before, Mr. Kingston," the reporter from The Herald says, looking annoyingly flustered as she smiles at him.

He smirks and glances over his shoulder, taking a moment to caress the hood of his new car with the tip of his finger before he turns to face the reporter again. His eyes are filled with a mixture of amusement and provocation — a unique blend he's always reserved for *me*. "I had no choice," he explains, an enticing chuckle leaving his lips. "My sweet kitten got her claws into all my other cars, so I had no choice but to buy a car I thought she might leave untouched."

The reporter's eyes widen. "Well, Windsor Motors cars are definitely robust," she says, trying to mask her obvious confusion.

"They sure are," he replies, his eyes blazing. "I'm honored Lexington Windsor entrusted me with it several weeks before the car's official release date. I can't wait to find out what my darling kitten will think of this car, since she seemed to dislike my others."

"The thought of you having a cute little kitten is incredibly endearing, Mr. Kingston. It certainly isn't what I'd have expected."

"I'm not sure cute is the right word to describe my kitten," he says, laughing with far too much glee for a man who found all of his favorite toys damaged this morning. "Fierce, perhaps. Beautiful, for sure."

"That piece of shit," I say through gritted teeth as I swipe the article away, *fuming*. I hate that he's right too — I'd never damage a Windsor Motors car. I'm seething as I stare out the window, my mind endlessly replaying how he referred to me as his sweet kitten on national TV. He's unhinged, that's for sure. Unhinged and *insufferable*.

He knows I hate that stupid nickname, which is exactly why he insists on using it. Before today, he'd never used it in earshot of anyone else, though. It started as a nearly-missed whisper when I danced with him at a charity gala eight years ago, and it turned into a taunt in empty hallways and boardrooms. "*Kitten*," I repeat in my quiet office. He thinks I'm small and inconsequential, an unruly *pet*.

I'm seeing red as I call my brother, the CEO of Windsor Motors. He instantly declines my call, which doesn't surprise me in the slightest. He must've known I'd be furious if he sold a car to *Xavier Kingston,* and he did it anyway. All of my brothers know I can't stand Xavier. I've made it a point to complain loudly about all of his attempts to sabotage me. They always seem to know I had it coming but being the good brothers they are, they have always my back, so how the hell did Xavier get his hands on that car?

SIERRA

> Call me back right now, or I'm calling Raya instead.

I smirk to myself when I notice my brother has read my text.

Each and every single one of my brothers are complete suckers for their wives, and sadly for them, my sisters-in-law all love me dearly. There is no threat that works better than telling my brothers I'll call their wives when they get on my nerves.

I chuckle when Lex calls me within a minute of reading my text, clearly having calculated the odds and deciding he's better off facing me directly. "H-hello?" he says, sounding surprisingly nervous when his demeanor is always calm and playful.

"How could you?" I snap.

"I'm sorry," Lex instantly says, thankfully not bothering to put up an act. "I owed him a favor, Sierra. Honestly, I'm surprised this is how he collected it. All he wanted was to *buy* the car early. Didn't even ask to have it for free. There was honestly no reason to say no."

"You owed him a favor?" I ask, confused. Why would my sweet older brother owe that devil a favor? There isn't much of anything my brothers can't accomplish themselves, so why would he ever have needed Xavier's help?

"You still should've said no," I argue. "Now it looks like the Windsors and Kingstons are friendly with each other, and who knows how he plans to capitalize on that? He can't be trusted."

Lexington laughs, clearly not understanding how grave his error is. "It's fine, sis. I promise."

Before I can even refute his words, my office door swings open, and a familiar-looking man walks in, my assistant on his heels. "Forget it. I'll talk to you later," I tell Lex, before ending the call.

I raise a brow at Xavier's assistant, Sam, and he smirks at me unapologetically, like he didn't just force his way into my office. "Ms. Windsor," he says, bowing his head. "Such a pleasure to see you again."

"I'd say the feeling is mutual, but we both know I'd be lying," I reply, before throwing my assistant, Claire, a reassuring smile. She looks distraught, even though she knows there's no stopping Sam when he's been sent on a mission by Xavier. This isn't the first time he's stormed into my office unannounced and uninvited, after all.

"You wound me, Ms. Windsor," Sam says, throwing his hand over his chest dramatically.

I sigh and cross my arms. "What brings you here, Sam?" His eyes begin to light up, and I hold up my hand. "And spare me the theatrics, please."

Sam's smile drops, and he hands over a black envelope with a gold seal on it. My heart begins to beat a touch faster when I recognize my name written in gold, in Xavier's handwriting. "Mr. Kingston requested that I deliver this to you, Ms. Windsor."

I take it from him, but before I even have a chance to push it through my paper shredder, Sam tenses, his expression sobering. "He also told me he'd fire me if I didn't ensure you read his letter."

"*What?*" I ask, hesitating as I hold the envelope an inch above the shredder. "He would never fire you," I begin to say, but truthfully, I'm not so sure. Xavier is erratic, after all.

"Have mercy on me, Ms. Windsor. If you choose to shred it after reading it, then so be it, but please... please help me keep my job."

Damn him. I grit my teeth as I grab my letter opener and slice the letter open, pure fury radiating off me when I realize it's an invitation to the grand opening of the theatre he stole my designs for — Artemis. "He can't be serious."

Sam looks down at his feet, but I could've sworn that for a split second, I saw a hint of a smile on his face. "There's more, Ms. Windsor," he says, his tone pleading. I'm so furious that I'm shaking as I reach for the handwritten letter, gold ink glittering on the black page.

My sweet Kitten,

Surely you didn't think you'd get away with damaging my precious car collection? You, of all people, know me better than that.

In return for the damage you did, I took something

of yours. Dance with me tonight, and I'll consider giving it back. I won't even mind if you blatantly and purposely step on my feet — after all, I've greatly missed the way you keep me on my toes.

Yours,
XK

Surely he's joking? He stole *my* designs, yet he claims I'm the one in the wrong? "He's delusional," I whisper as I begin to wonder what he possibly could've taken. The possibilities are endless when it comes to him. "Completely and utterly out of his mind."

Sam smiles. "I'm afraid so, Ms. Windsor," he says, before stepping back. "I'll see you tonight," he adds, and I stare at Sam as he walks out, his smile far too smug for someone whose job was supposedly on the line mere minutes ago.

Four

SIERRA

My heart is racing as I step out of the car wearing a red bespoke *Raven Windsor Couture* gown, paired with lipstick in the same shade. It has a slit from mid-thigh all the way down, and a gorgeously cut sweetheart neckline. It's a dress that's supposed to make me feel confident as I step into my enemy's lair, but somehow, I can't shake my nerves.

My eyes widen as I walk into the grand theatre room tonight's party is being held in, pure fury stealing away my anxiety. Everything is exactly as I'd imagined it, right down to the three-tier chandeliers and the beautiful ceiling roses. *That rotten pile of poop.* He clearly spared no expense, duplicating my vision right down to the last detail, and he's been showered with undeserved praise because of it. *God, I hate him.*

My hand trembles ever so slightly as I grab a glass of champagne off a tray and thank the server, my thoughts in disarray. Why is he suddenly provoking me again after a ceasefire that lasted over two years, and what did he take from me? It's been months since I last saw Xavier in person, and I'm not sure what to think of his recent behavior. I don't understand what his motive is, but I know Xavier Kingston well enough to know he's got one.

"Sierra Windsor?"

I look up to find a familiar man walking up to me. His mid-length brown curly hair bounces just a touch with each step he takes toward me, and his smile lights up his blue eyes. "Graham Thorne," I say, smiling involuntarily.

He grins as he pulls me into a hug, holding me tightly for a moment before stepping back, his eyes roaming over my face. "I haven't seen you in years," he says, his tone as kind as I remember it.

Graham and I are childhood friends who were frequently forced into each other's orbits by my grandmother and his parents. We always knew we'd both end up working in real estate, by virtue of our families' companies, and because of it, we were strongly encouraged to become friends. We were really close, growing up. "I'm not the one who decided to work in the Mediterranean for years," I tell him, my tone teasing. "I can't believe you left me!"

He smirks at me and begins to reply when a hush falls over the room. I don't even have to look to know who just walked in. Xavier Kingston has always had that effect on people, and I'm not sure he even realizes it.

Graham and I both turn, and my heart tightens when I find him walking into the room with Valeria on his arm. They look incredible together in their matching black outfits, both of their auras exuding class and power. I hate that he's still so handsome, that I still can't look away when he walks into a room. That dark hair, his sharp cheekbones, and that stubble I can't help but want to touch... I suppose it makes sense for the devil to come in an enticing package. Makes it easier to trick unsuspecting souls.

"Her beauty perfectly complements his allure," Graham remarks, and I tighten my grip on my champagne glass as my eyes zero in on the diamond necklace she's wearing. I haven't been able to get the article The Herald published out of my mind, and a dark emotion I can't quite identify rushes through me as I watch her jewelry sparkle underneath the chandeliers I chose. Before I can catch myself, my eyes trail to her ring finger, and something heavy unknots in my stomach when I find it empty. Chances are that at least one of the pieces of jewelry Xavier commissioned from Laurier was an engagement ring, and Xavier's alarm system clearly stated *Mrs. Kingston.* Raven's words ring through my mind, and I bite down on my lip as I push aside the hope that comes with them. She seemed so certain that they aren't dating, and she was right to say that though they're often together, they've never seemed intimate, but I'm not really sure what to believe.

I grit my teeth and begin to wonder why I even came here at all, only to freeze in place when I feel Xavier's eyes on mine. He stops walking, and Valeria looks over her shoulder, following his gaze. She smiles at me so sweetly that I instantly feel guilty for the faint and entirely irrational animosity I feel toward her. I lower my head for a moment before turning toward Graham, not wanting to look too closely at Xavier.

"I guess the rumors are true," Graham says, smiling at me knowingly.

"What rumors?" I ask, my tone sharper than I'd intended.

"That the rivalry between Xavier and you is the fiercest the industry has ever witnessed."

I roll my eyes and put my champagne glass down. "He's an unscrupulous asshole," I mutter. I'm tempted to tell Graham about my design plans, and how everything around us was once my grandest vision, but for some reason, I bite my tongue.

Other than my sisters-in-law, no one knows about any of the things Xavier and I have done to each other throughout the years. Everyone knows that we fiercely compete for the same projects, but no one knows just how far we've gone in our attempts to sabotage each other. I'm not even sure why we've always kept our antics under wraps when either of us could've gotten the authorities involved and permanently put an end to our rivalry.

"An unscrupulous asshole, huh?" Graham repeats, looking amused. "I see you're still a sore loser."

I gape at him in pure outrage, and he bursts out laughing.

"What did you just say?" I ask, biting back my smile. Graham is one of very few people that I could always be completely myself with. He's never been intimidated by the Windsor surname and everything that comes with it. In a world filled with pretense and fake friends, he's always been a breath of fresh air.

"Oh, come on," he says, laughing. "He's far from unscrupulous. The man spends a lot of his spare time building schools, hospitals, and public housing for the vulnerable — all with his own money."

I groan and bury a hand in my hair. No one knows him like I do. Everyone sees his charitable heart and his kindness, but they don't know it's all a facade. "Xavier Kingston is the devil is disguise," I tell him, only to notice Graham looking past me, wide-eyed.

"*Sierra.*"

My heart instantly begins to race at the sound of Xavier's voice, and I look over my shoulder to find his dark eyes filled with the kind of intensity that makes it hard to look away. He smiles in that way he always does when he sees me, his expression a blend of provocation and amusement. "Care to dance with the devil?"

I narrow my eyes as I turn to face him. *Of course* he'd catch me badmouthing him, and *of course* he wouldn't turn a blind eye. I'm tempted to reject the hand he's holding out for me, but if I did that, I'd never get answers to the question that led me here. What did he take from me?

I grit my teeth as I place my hand on top of his, ignoring the little thrill that runs down my spine as I do so. Something akin to relief flashes through Xavier's eyes as he pulls me onto the dance floor and against his chest in one smooth move. "I wasn't sure you'd come, Kitten."

I narrow my eyes and purposely step on his toes. "You left me no choice. I'm here, and we're on the dance floor, so tell me what you took from me."

He looks at the band for a few moments, and just like that, *Por una Cabeza* begins to play. Xavier smirks at me as we both take our positions for the tango, like we've done so many times before. He requests this exact song every time we find ourselves at the same formal events, and though I'd never admit it to him, I've come to consider the song *ours*.

"There is always a choice," he tells me as we dance around the room, our bodies moving together far better than they should. I'm not a short woman, but in his arms, I feel tiny. "And you chose me."

My leg hooks around his, our eyes locking. "Coercion and choice are vastly different concepts, Xavier. Though I understand that might be hard for you to grasp."

We're both breathing hard as we move together, neither of us looking away from the other. "I've always loved the way you say my name."

My eyes widen a fraction, and my heart skips a beat. "Tell me what you stole."

He smirks, his eyes roaming over my dress and lingering on my chest. "You look dazzling, my darling kitten, but you're not glittering as much as I'd expected."

I pause in his arms, something hot and dark unfurling in my stomach. "Your date looks far more dazzling," I reply, jealousy taking control of my actions, my words.

He stares at me, something akin to amusement in his eyes. "Valeria, you mean? I'll be sure to convey your kind compliment to her."

I push away from him, coming to my senses. How does he always do this to me? I'm convinced Xavier Kingston was born to aggravate me. He pushes my buttons like no one else has ever been able to, and I never should've agreed to dance with him in the first place.

I push against his chest and step away. "I don't know what you took from me, but I strongly recommend you return it before I find out what it is, or so help me God, you'll rue the day you broke our truce by stealing my design plans."

He smirks at me in that way he does, like I'm some kind of damn pet of his. "I won't return what I took until I get what I want, Sierra. Not a day sooner."

For a moment, I'm tempted to ask him what it is he wants, but I know better than to pay these silly games with him.

Never again.

Never in a million years will I let Xavier Kingston occupy all my thoughts again.

Five

XAVIER

I glance at my watch as I rush into my office building for my monthly board meeting with my brothers and parents. "You're late," my father says, his expression unreadable.

"Probably too busy messing with Sierra," Hunter says.

I glare at my younger brother, unable to help myself. Ever since *The Herald* reported that Sierra was seen at his nightclub several months ago, he's been trying to get on my nerves by mentioning her every chance he gets. He claims it isn't true, but they've been reporting on how she allegedly went into his office with him, and how great of a couple the two of them would be. That stupid newspaper has no idea how close I've gotten to just buying their entire office building and flattening it.

"Did you see this, Mom?" Elijah asks, tipping his head toward the screen behind me. Instantly, a picture of Sierra and me dancing the tango appears, and I groan.

"That's a wonderful photo," my mother replies, her eyes glittering.

"When will we get to meet your girlfriend, Xavier?" Dad asks. "I feel like I've been hearing about her for an eternity now."

Zach bursts out laughing and shakes his head. "Sierra Windsor? His *girlfriend*? Maybe in his wildest dreams. She *hates* him."

I run a hand through my hair and sigh. "She doesn't hate me," I retort, my voice weak. My response only elicits more laughter from my brothers, and my parents glance at each other, doing that thing they always do — communicating silently. I've never witnessed it in anyone but them, but at times, I'm certain they can read each other's minds.

"She can't stand you," Hunter says, grinning. "She likes me just fine, though."

"Shut up," I tell him, annoyed I let him get under my skin. All of my sources tell me she's never really spoken to him for more than a few minutes, and I doubt she'd even recognize him if she ran into him, but it still gets on my nerves. "Are we here to talk about my love life, or our company's performance?"

"Love life is overstating it a little bit, don't you think?" Elijah jokes.

"I'd much rather talk about *your* performance — or lack there-of," Zach adds.

Dad chokes back a laugh, and I let my eyes fall closed. "You're all fucking insufferable."

"Insufferable?" Hunter repeats. "Did Sierra teach you that word?"

I glance at Mom, silently pleading for help, and she sighs as she rises to her feet. "Enough," she says, her voice soft but firm. My brothers all instantly straighten in their seats, their smiles melting away.

"You," she says, pointing at Zachary, "are the mayor of a city that was named after us, and this is how you behave?" I smirk at him, pleased she's standing up for me. "Elijah, you should be especially ashamed of yourself. You're the head of a private intelligence agency, and here you are, abusing your powers and showcasing your brother's private affairs." She points at the screen, and he rushes to disconnect his laptop. "And Hunter? You'd better stop humoring these reporters just to provoke your brother and start focusing on composing and recording some new songs. You're wasting your talent in that godforsaken club of yours, and if you keep this up, I'm taking it away altogether."

"Must be nice," Hunter mutters under his breath as he crosses his arms, his expression sullen. "Being Mom's favorite child."

I shake my head and connect my laptop to the screen so I can pull up our monthly figures. We all know who the real favorite child is, and it isn't me. "We're up 13% year to date across our holdings," I begin to explain, glad Mom got this meeting back on track.

While my siblings and I all do vastly different things, all our different endeavors are simply different entities of the King Group, and we all report directly to our parents. I handle all our real estate, Zach handles politics and our family's image, Elijah is in charge of maintaining some of our old ties and using them to take down some of the worst threats to our family before they materialize, and Hunter... well, he's the only one of us with real otherworldly talent. Why he hasn't picked up his guitar in years is a mystery to us all, but I'm certain he won't be able to stay away forever.

"Our aim is a thirty percent rise," Dad reminds me, his gaze roaming over our figures. He begins to dissect our performance, giving each of my brothers and me pointers on where to cut costs, and where to invest further. He's never said it, but I know guilt and self blame still keep him up at night. He's worked himself to the bone to ensure we'd thrive in ethical and legal ways, transforming himself and our family virtually overnight in hopes it'd make a difference.

"Good job this month, kids," Mom says as the meeting concludes. Normally, my parents leave quickly, and my brothers and I end up having a couple of glasses of whiskey while we catch up, but judging by the way Mom ushers them out today, it's clear she has something to say to me.

My brothers all throw me pitiful glances as they leave the room. They know as well as I do that it's never good when our parents want to have a word with any of us. After all, they rarely interfere in our private lives, and the only times they say anything at all about the way we run our businesses is in this monthly meeting.

I raise a brow when Dad follows my brothers out, and all of a sudden, I feel like a teenager again, having gotten caught doing something I shouldn't have been. "So," Mom says, pushing the door closed behind Dad. She turns to face me, a deceptive smile on her face. "Sierra Windsor, huh?"

"No," I say, rising to my feet. "I'm not talking to you about her."

Mom crosses her arms and leans back against the door, ensuring I can't just walk out. "I suppose I could just go speak to her myself."

I sit down slowly. "What is it you want to know?" I ask cautiously, and Mom smiles.

"I would like to know what your intentions are, Xavier. I didn't raise a bully — but that's exactly what you seem to be. I didn't mind it when your feud was mutual and it seemed playful, but now? You took her designs, and she looked devastated when she walked into that party. That's not how you treat a woman you care about. Your feud is only acceptable if she's enjoying it too."

How could she possibly know that? I'm tempted to tell her that Sierra *slashed* all my tires shortly after, but I know that isn't what my mother needs to hear. "Mom," I murmur, wringing my hands. It doesn't matter how old my brothers and I get, or how much we accomplish. Our mother has this way of making us all feel like we're five years old all over again.

"Your intentions, Xavier. If they're anything but honorable, Sierra slashing your tires will be the least you'll have to contend with."

"How..." I shake my head and sigh. *Elijah*, no doubt. Fucking tattletale. "Mom," I say, taking a deep breath. "If things go the way I hope they will, I intend to make Sierra my wife."

Six

SIERRA

I keep rereading the same paragraph in my romance novel and silently curse Xavier for ruining my favorite hobby for me. All evening I've been trying to read, and all evening, I haven't stopped wondering what Xavier stole from me. Three years ago, I swore I was done with him and our stupid feud, only to become embroiled in his schemes again.

I never should've retaliated when he stole my design plans, and I shouldn't have gone to his opening party. I *definitely* never should have danced with him. My heart beats a little faster as I think back to the way his body felt against mine, and the way he looked at me as we moved so perfectly in-sync. Each time we dance together, he makes me forget why I hate him, and then he opens his damn mouth.

I clench my jaw as his whispered words come to mind, and all of a sudden, they make sense. *You look dazzling, my darling kitten, but you're not glittering as much as I'd expected.* I slam my book shut, and my heart begins to pound as I rush through my walk-in wardrobe, toward a hidden panel that slides open when I push against the Windsor family crest, my fingerprints registering. My heart drops as I walk into my hidden safe and find all of my most expensive necklaces missing, the displays showcasing vastly different designs.

I gasp as I take a step closer and recognize them for what they are: seven extremely expensive Laurier designs that I've never seen before. My stomach somersaults when I notice the little notes in front of each design, and I raise a brow in confusion.

"What the hell?" I mutter as I take in the pieces of paper that look like a cut-up ransom note, all of them in slightly different sizes, and all of them on sepia paper. Did he cut these out of a newspaper? My hand trembles as I lift the first two pieces and study them. *Dear kitten*, they read, and judging by the font and the size of the text, I strongly suspect he cut this out of a novel.

"What a barbaric, inhumane thing to do," I mutter as I begin to reassemble the pieces in an attempt to figure out what the note is supposed to say. I'm so distraught by the fact that he seems to have cut pages out of *books*, like some kind of psychopath, that it takes me a moment to comprehend what the message is.

Dear Kitten, please know that I wish it were my hands on your skin each time you wear these necklaces.

I stare at it wide-eyed and raise my fingers to my neck, my heart hammering in my chest. Is he *threatening* me? Does he want me to wear these necklaces and imagine him choking the life out of me for annoying him just a touch too much? "He's crazy," I mutter to myself. "I've driven him completely crazy."

I can't figure out the meaning of this. If he wanted to gift me jewelry, he'd just have done so, though I can't imagine Xavier Kingston ever giving *me* a present. No, this isn't a gift, or he wouldn't have stolen my jewelry and left that creepy note. It isn't even in his handwriting, nor is it signed, so even if I did report it, there isn't anything pointing toward him, other than it being

Laurier jewelry, which he reportedly recently commissioned. I know him well enough to know he won't leave traces, and even if I could pin this theft on him, he'd simply walk away unscathed. His brother is the mayor, after all.

I'm frazzled as I begin to take inventory of what exactly he took in an attempt to figure out his motive, only to realize he stole one piece he never should've touched — a diamond and emerald heirloom piece my grandmother gifted me when Raven married Ares. Each Windsor bride is given a heirloom Laurier piece shortly after their wedding day, but my grandmother gave me mine on the same day Raven received hers. She rightfully didn't think I'd be patient enough to wait for it, and I've carefully stored it ever since I received it, only for Xavier Kingston to steal it. "*Damn it.*"

If he hadn't taken that specific piece, I'd likely have let his unhinged behavior slide. After all, the value of the items he left me likely matches or exceeds what he took. But *this*? If my grandmother ever finds out I lost something so precious, she'd be beyond disappointed in me. I need to retrieve it before she ever finds out it was missing.

"*Xavier Kingston,*" I mutter under my breath as I grab my car keys and storm out of my house. He had to have known that necklace meant something to me. I don't know how, but somehow, he must've known. This can't have been a coincidence, and I just don't understand how he continues to get under my skin like this. How does he know which buttons to push to *infuriate* me, and why does he keep coming after me when I tried and *succeeded* in being the better person for so long?

Whatever unspoken ceasefire existed between us ends nows, permanently. I don't know how he managed to get into the Windsor estate, let alone inside my home, but he should've known better than to break into what should've been a highly secure vault and taking something my grandmother gave me.

I'm fuming as I park in front of his office building, pure adrenaline rushing through me as I sneak around the back, to a private entrance Xavier thinks I don't know about. I once bribed our head

CATHARINA MAURA

of security, Silas Sinclair, to hack into Xavier's system and give me his entrance codes. Xavier, being the cocky asshole he is, never changes them.

I breathe a sigh of relief when the door unlocks, revealing a hallway with an elevator at the end that leads straight to Xavier's office, where he's hidden his most secure safe. I'm certain that's where he'd have put my jewelry, but even if he hasn't there'll be something in there that I can use as leverage.

Nerves rush through me as I enter the elevator and keep my head down, realizing I rushed into this without the usual preparation. Normally I'd have worn a wig and a hoodie, along with gloves and actual shoes, instead of the fuzzy house slippers I stormed out in. I'd have carried my usual mischief bag, filled with tools that help me both break in and do some decent damage — instead, I'm armed with nothing but my knowledge of Xavier and a whole lot of guts that have suddenly failed me at the thought of Xavier's office not being empty when the elevator doors open.

I exhale shakily and step into his office carefully, suddenly far more nervous than I'd anticipated. I'm trembling as I push against a painting and watch it swing open to reveal a large safe. "Please," I whisper, hoping his code is still the same. 8502, as always. I'm sure it has some kind of sentimental value since he uses the code frequently, but I haven't been able to figure it out. I've only just begun to turn the lock when alarms begin to blare, and I turn around, panicked.

"Who are you!" a patrol guard shouts, illuminating the room with his flashlight, and I rush over to the elevator, only to find it locked.

Seven

XAVIER

"Kitten," I murmur, trying my hardest not to smile at the fire blazing in her eyes as she sits behind bars, for the second time since I've known her. "You really do seem to think you have nine lives, don't you?"

She glares at me and crosses her arms, not realizing it just makes her look even more beautiful, even more provocative. The way she unknowingly pushes her breasts up in that black tank top she's wearing is a sight for sore eyes. "I see you've come to gloat," Sierra says, pouting just slightly.

I smirk, I can't help it. "You do realize it's *my* office you tried to break into, right? Who else would they have called?"

"They should have called *Raven*, like I asked them to."

I tut mockingly, loving the way it riles her up. Her eyes begin to sparkle dangerously, and her cheeks flush beautifully. "You haven't learned your lesson from the last time you got arrested for breaking into my office, have you? Do you need a reminder, sweetheart?"

Her breath hitches, and her expression shifts, becoming disarmed and a little shy at the mention of that evening. She'd

29

broken in with Valentina, her sister-in-law, who, at the time, was still her brother's secretary. They'd gotten caught and arrested, resulting in Luca bailing Val out — but much to Sierra's absolute horror, he left his little sister to me.

"Hardly," she says, looking away. "That night was one I've regretted ever since, and the last thing I need is a reminder of it."

My chest clenches painfully, and my smile slips. Right. Of course she regrets it. Why else would she have distanced herself from me shortly after I kissed her for the very first time.

"Let her go," I tell the officers behind me, feeling oddly defeated. "But leave the handcuffs on."

Sierra's eyes snap to mine, and the way she blushes does something to me, makes me a little hopeful when I know better. "Gotta protect myself from your claws, sweetheart," I tell her, loving the outrage on her face.

She storms past me, indignation oozing off her in waves, and I sigh as I stare at her for a few moments, taking in her curves and her long, dark hair that just about hits her waist. She pauses and looks over her shoulder when she notices I haven't moved, and I smile, realizing that I'm just as completely and utterly *fucked* as I've ever been when it comes to her. She doesn't even need to say anything for me to follow her, and she has absolutely no idea how much power she holds over me.

"I see you got your tires fixed," she says sourly when she finds my town limousine and my driver waiting for us.

I bite back a smile as I hold my car door open for her. "Which is exactly why you aren't getting out of those cuffs anytime soon."

She rolls her eyes as she gets into my car, and I join her, ensuring we're facing each other as I pull the door closed behind us. Sierra inhales sharply when I lean in to put her seatbelt on for her, her eyes roaming over my face and lingering on my lips. It isn't until the car is in motion that I snap out of my daze and click her seatbelt into place. She blushes, and just like that, my wounded heart recovers.

I smirk as I pull my tie loose, noting the way her expression shifts just slightly when I pull it off. For a moment, I could swear I saw longing in those gorgeous emerald eyes, but then her expression hardens. "I was right, wasn't I? You hid my jewelry in your office."

She still knows me so well. "I'll trade you a truth for a truth. I've got a question for you. Answer it, and I'll tell you whether or not you were right."

Sierra narrows her eyes and throws her head back a little as she slips her foot out of her cute fuzzy slipper and presses it against my chest, pushing me flush against my seat. "Just because I'm handcuffed doesn't mean I can't forcibly make you talk, Xavier."

I bite down on my lip as she slides her foot up and presses against my throat lightly. "Oh yeah?" I murmur, my voice huskier than I'd intended.

Sierra gasps when I grab her ankle and turn my face to bite her leg. "W-what are you doing?"

"What do you think? You presented me with a snack, so I'm taking a bite."

"Xavier!" she admonishes as I suck down on her skin and mark her just above her ankle. "You... you're completely unhinged!"

"You say that like it's new information, when you were the one who drove me crazy." I smirk and undo my seatbelt before leaning in and working my way up her leg, my teeth grazing over her soft leggings.

"Tell me, Kitten. Did you like the gifts I sent you?"

Her breath hitches when I kneel in front of her and drape her leg over my shoulder. She's never looked more beautiful, and I love having her eyes on me like that. "T-That's your question?"

"Answer me." My lips hover over her inner thigh, and she squirms, her breath coming out in little pants.

"You should give your jewelry to that girl you keep bringing to parties with you. Valentine. Valerie. Whatever," she breathes, her voice faltering when I kiss her thigh. Our eyes lock, and she tries her best to glare at me, but the clear desire in her beautiful emerald eyes negates the effect she's going for.

I chuckle, loving the way she can't quite keep from moving her hips just slightly. "Valeria," I correct her, loving how unnecessary jealous she is. It's the only real indication she's ever given me that she cares, and I know I need to tell her the truth, but I revel in these little bits of hope she gives me every time she's jealous. "Her name is *Valeria*, and she can buy her own jewelry," I say, dragging my nose over her inner thigh, so fucking close to her pussy that I could lean in and taste her if not for those damn leggings she's wearing. "You're the only one I'll ever buy jewelry for, Sierra. Only you."

She squirms, her breathing shallow as I softly kiss her right between her legs, loving the soft moan she can't quite conceal. Sierra watches me, cautious relief in her eyes as she tries to determine what to make of my words, and I smile to myself as I kiss her again, loving the way I can feel her push her body against my mouth subtly, involuntarily. "If I... if I wear what you gave me," she says, her voice thick with lust. "If I do that, will you give me back what you stole?"

"I'll think about it," I murmur as we pull up in front of my house, my eyes on hers. I've never seen her look so tormented, and fuck, I think this is my favorite look on her of all.

Eight

SIERRA

My heart is pounding wildly as I follow Xavier into his living room, my hands still bound behind my back. I have no idea what I'm even doing here. Why can't I ever walk away when it comes to him, even when I know it's the right thing to do? This is exactly why I've just avoided him altogether for so long. Nothing good ever comes from being around him.

"I have a feeling you know this place as well as I do, so make yourself comfortable," he says, and I rattle my handcuffs, reminding him that I'm still cuffed like some kind of criminal. It just makes him laugh, and I stare at him, caught off-guard. I completely and utterly despise how handsome he looks when he laughs, and it has always irritated me that he's got dimples. It's just so *unfair*. Dimples are meant for adorable and kind human beings, not this piece of shit.

I throw him my filthiest, deadliest glare, and he grins as he walks up to me. Xavier places his index finger under my chin, and I narrow my eyes at him. "Aw," he says. "Is my little kitten angry? You're so adorable when you glare at me like that."

"God, I hate you," I mutter, my eyes dropping to his mouth. I bite down on my lip to keep my thoughts in check, but all of a sudden, I can't help but wonder if he still tastes like cinnamon. It's messing with me to stand here with him, the circumstances so similar to that night all those years ago, when he bailed me out after I'd gotten caught breaking into his office. Then, too, we ended up here.

"No, you don't," he retorts, his gaze roaming over my face hungrily. "You wouldn't be here if you did."

"Debatable. I'm quite prone to ill-thought out decisions, hence my current outfit and the handcuffs."

"Perhaps so, but only ever when it pertains to *me*," he says, his voice soft as he grabs my waist and pulls me closer, until my body is flush against his. My heart begins to race, and I draw a steadying breath, trying my best to ignore the rush of desire he's making me feel. "I occupy all your thoughts, don't I? How much time did you spend thinking about me in an attempt to figure out where I hid your jewelry?"

We're both breathing hard, his body heat seeping into my skin as we look into each other's eyes. "I don't think of you at all," I tell him, refusing to acknowledge that things had gotten so dire that he managed to steal my attention away from a brand new romance novel I'd been waiting months for.

His eyes flash, and then he leans in, his lips brushing over my ear. "Liar," he whispers, his breath tickling my skin. A shiver runs down my spine, and Xavier must feel me responding to him, because he laughs, the sound husky and so damn sexy.

A soft moan escapes my lips when he kisses me just below my ear, and I subconsciously tilt my head, allowing him better access. "You think of me all the time, Kitten," he claims, his teeth grazing over a sensitive part of my neck. "You think of me every time you decide not to attend an event at the very last second, because you'd just found out I'd be there." His hand wraps into my hair, and he kisses my neck, his touch featherlight. "You think of me each time you pull out of a property auction or retract a development proposal."

"I don't," I whisper, my voice as weak as my resolve.

Xavier chuckles and pulls back to look at me, his gaze affectionate. "Then I'd better make sure I give you something to think about, hmm?" He gently brushes his thumb over my lips, his gaze searching. My heart instantly begins to race, my entire body reacting to the desire in his eyes. When he looks at me that way, all rhyme and reason disappears, leaving me craving the one thing I shouldn't.

"Tell me to stop," he whispers, tilting his head as he leans in until his lips are hovering over mine. My heart thunders in my chest, longing making me lightheaded, desperate. "If you tell me you don't want me to kiss you, I'll take those handcuffs off and let you go." I tilt my hips just a touch, needing to feel more of him, and he smiles as he kisses he edge of my mouth. "You can't, can you?"

"Xavier," I whisper, my voice tinged with need as I turn my face just slightly, so my lips brush against his. His breath hitches, and he hesitates for a split second, before his lips come crashing against mine. I moan when he deepens our kiss instantly, almost like he's just as aware as I am that this moment won't last, that it's a lapse in judgment we'll soon correct.

I rise to my tiptoes, needing him closer, and he pushes his hips against me harder. It's maddening to know he wants me this badly, and I yank my handcuffs apart, wishing I could touch him. Xavier grunts when I pull my lips off his and move them to his neck next, my teeth sinking into his skin softly, my thoughts ruled by desire. His grip tightens on my hair when I suck down on his neck, an irrational sense of possessiveness washing over me as I leave a mark.

"*Fuck*," he moans, and I move my lips a little lower, doing it all over again as Xavier reaches around me, his movements urgent as he takes off my handcuffs. "I need your hands on me, Kitten," he tells me, and I oblige the moment the cuffs hit the ground. My hands thread into his hair, and he moves his lips back to mine, kissing me with the same desperation I'm feeling.

He walks me backwards slowly, until I hit the wall. "What are we doing?" I whisper against his mouth, before kissing him all over again, my self-restraint non-existent.

Xavier pushes his hips into me before he grabs my waist and lifts me up against the wall, his hands moving to my thighs as my ankles lock behind his back. "Giving in," he replies, driving his erection into me with the same kind of need I'm feeling. My arms wrap around his neck, and he moans against my mouth when I grab his hair. "*Sierra.*" My name is a plea on his lips, a wish, one I can't help but want to fulfill.

My fingers brush over the buttons of his shirt, and I begin to undo them, loving the feel of his skin against my palm. He moans deep in his throat and slides his hands to my ass, squeezing as he rolls his hips. He's breathing hard, and I grin against his mouth when his shirt falls open, revealing his wide chest and rock hard abs. Xavier looks into my eyes as I slide his shirt off his shoulders, only to startle at the sound of a door slamming.

"Xave!" a female voice calls, and Xavier puts me down in a rush, his eyes wide with panic. He pulls his shirt closed and rushes to button up, every hint of desire replaced by something akin to terror. Before I can even fully process what's going on, Valeria walks into the living room, an oven dish in her hands.

"I brought you some linguine and—" her voice trails off when she notices me standing in Xavier's living room, and her eyes go wide as she stumbles back, the oven dish slipping from her hands and shattering into pieces on the floor.

Nine

I decline Xavier's call for the seventeenth's time today and try my hardest to focus on my work, but every few minutes, I'm reminded of last night. I stood to the side and watched as Xavier rushed up to Valeria and took off his shirt, using it to clean up the pasta that'd gotten on her feet. I've never seen him so concerned, and I've never felt more like a fool as I walked out quietly.

My phone rings again, and I turn it off altogether. I sigh and bury my face in my hands, my heart heavy. When Raven said that she didn't think he was dating Valeria, I'd secretly hoped she was right, but I should've known better. My stomach turns as I think back to that look in Valeria's eyes when she spotted me, and I instantly feel disgusted with myself. I've never been the kind of person that'd knowingly hurt another woman, and in any case, I'm not after a cheap fling. I've always wanted more than that.

My heart begins to ache as my mind drifts to my five older brothers and my sisters-in-law, each of them uniquely perfect for their spouse. I want *that*. I want the kind of intimacy they have, where one person always knows what the other is thinking, without any words being exchanged at all. For as long as I can remember, I've wanted my own *happily ever after*, and I should've known that getting involved with Xavier Kingston is a surefire way to ensure I'll never have it.

I stare out the window as I begin to wonder when it'll be my turn. Just like my siblings, I'll end up in a marriage arranged by my grandmother, and I can't help but wonder... will the man she chooses for me captivate me? Would he be able to *finally* make me stop thinking about Xavier Kingston?

"Sierra?" Claire says, snapping me out of my thoughts. I look up to find my sweet assistant hovering by the door, looking nervous. "There's a Mr. Graham Thorne here to see you. I told him that your schedule is packed, but he insisted that I let you know he's here."

I smile involuntarily and nod. "Let him in," I tell her. "He's a friend, Claire. Please add him to my approved visitor list."

Her shoulders sag in relief, and she smiles sweetly. Claire has been with me for so many years, but she's still exactly the same person she was when I first hired her. Honest, hardworking, and loyal. She's one of my best paid employees and one of the people I depend on most, but she's never let it get to her head. I doubt she realizes just how rare it is to meet people like her, who are truly earnest. Unlike Xavier damn Kingston.

"Sierra!" Graham says as he walks into my office wearing the biggest smile.

I rise to my feet and walk around my desk to hug him, my mood instantly lifted. He squeezes me tightly before letting go, and I grin up at him. "What brings you here? I wasn't expecting you at all!"

"It's work, I'm afraid," he tells me, holding up his briefcase. "My parents insist that I work with you. Apparently, you've become quite the industry titan."

I raise a brow, intrigued, and he hands me a folder detailing a development plan for a shopping mall that's been on my radar for a while. "You think we should jointly acquire and develop this?" I ask, holding up the folder. "I guess if we work together, we could make it work, but you should know that this is a plot of land that—"

"—that Xavier Kingston has his eye on. I know." Graham smiles at me. "If you wanted to, I reckon you could win this bid all by yourself, but it's a high-risk acquisition since the area hasn't been developed yet."

I nod as I begin to mentally run the numbers. "I'm not sure..." I murmur. I wouldn't even have considered it at all if it hadn't been Graham asking me. He's always been sensible, and from what I understand, he's grown his family's overseas holdings at a higher rate than anyone thought possible. I have no doubt he'll do amazing things here too, now that he's back home. I don't stand to lose much by working with him, but this specific project... it's not one I'm sure I want to get involved in, considering how badly Xavier wants it.

"I think you should let me take you out for dinner so I can ply you with good food and drinks as I make my case."

I chuckle as I grab my purse. "You had me at food," I admit. "Besides, I've been meaning to call you so we could catch up properly, and I'd much prefer to do that in person."

"Perfect, because I really want to go to The Renegade."

I miss a step, and Graham wraps his arm around my waist. "What?" I ask, my voice strained.

"The Renegade," Graham repeats, frowning.

I nod slowly and gesture toward my door, uncertain whether I should make an excuse. The last thing I want to do today is visit Xavier's best-known restaurant, one he often frequents himself, but I don't want to try to explain myself. Besides, I might never admit it, but the food is really great. They have every single one of my favorite dishes on the menu, and each of them is done to perfection.

"You're practically buzzing with excitement," I say as Graham and I walk into the restaurant. He hasn't stopped talking about all the things he wants to try from the moment we left my office, and I'm starting to suspect that going out for dinner was his main objective. It's such a Graham thing to do. He's always been such a foodie, and he was the one who introduced me to some of my favorite dishes that I might never have tried otherwise.

"Welcome to The Renegade," one of the servers says, a big smile on her face.

I smile back at her apologetically and glance at her name tag. "We don't have a reservation, Jane, but we were hoping you'd have a table for two available for us?"

Her smile slips a little, her eyes widening. "Ms. Windsor?" she asks, her tone uncertain.

"Wow, you're famous, huh?" Graham murmurs, knocking his shoulder against mine. I can't help but blush and shake my head. I'm not at all well-known, unlike Raven, who is both a designer and a supermodel, or even my other sister-in-law, Faye, who is a famous concert pianist. Just like the rest of my family, I'm frequently featured in both business and gossip magazines, but not to the extent that I'd be recognized at a restaurant.

Jane clears her throat and smiles brightly. "Please, allow me to lead you to your table," she says, and I nod, a little confused by her reaction to me.

"Definitely famous," Graham whispers when she leads us to a secluded table by the window, overlooking the city.

It isn't the view I'm looking at, though. How could I, when Xavier Kingston sits at the table next to ours, Valeria seated in front of him, his hand covering hers over the table? He laughs at something she says, and I tear my eyes off him, my hatred for him burning hotter than ever before.

Ten

XAVIER

"Xave?" Valeria says, snapping me out of my thoughts. I look up at her and realize I've completely missed what she was saying. I haven't been able to stop thinking about Sierra, and the way she felt against me, the way she tasted. My sweet kitten has no idea how long I've waited to kiss her again, how many times I've fantasized about it, how *patient* I've been.

"Xavier?"

I blink and smile at Valeria apologetically. "I'm sorry, V. I didn't get much sleep last night."

She shakes her head and sighs. "Have you spoken to Sierra?" she asks, her tone cautious.

I look out the window, taking in the skyline just outside of my restaurant. "She's been ignoring my calls. She's doing what she's always done — jumping on the first excuse to run away from this thing between us."

"You're such an idiot," she snaps, pure rage flickering through my sweet sister's eyes, and it catches me off-guard. "From her point of view, you took her home and kissed her, and then rushed over to *another woman* who walked into your house uninvited and unannounced. I know you're not as stupid as you look, so don't tell me *she's* the one that's running away."

I run a hand through my hair, trying my best not to let on just how much V's outburst shocks me. I didn't think I'd ever get to experience my sister's eyes flashing like that again. Hell, there was a time when I didn't think I'd ever even get to see her again.

Valeria left home when she was twenty, not wanting anything to do with the way our family conducted our business, and instead of stopping her, I let her go. If I'd followed my instincts and stopped her from leaving, she'd never have gone missing without a trace. That's on me, and I'll never forgive myself for it.

We searched for her for years, only to find her on our doorstep one night, bruised and broken, her clothes drenched in blood. She hasn't been herself ever since, and she's mostly kept to herself, requesting that we help her stay hidden, her identity kept secret. It's clear she's scared, and until we know what she's running from, we're abiding by her wishes.

"Why are you smiling like that?" Valeria asks, her tone icy. "If you think this is funny, you deserve everything Sierra has ever put you through a thousand times over, and I won't have even an ounce of sympathy for you when she strikes next."

"I'm just happy you seem so... spirited. I'm proud of you, you know?" I tell her, my heart aching as I wrap my hand over hers and squeeze gently.

I've been able to convince her to attend a few highly secure events with me, just so she'll slowly become accustomed to being in crowds again, and with each passing day, she unveils more parts of herself that we all thought we'd lost forever. I didn't think I'd experience her snapping at me over anything ever again, though.

"Xave, I could walk in a straight line and you'd be proud of me," she says, her tone teasing.

I can't help but laugh and look away, only to spot bright emerald eyes that I'd recognize anywhere. "Sierra," I whisper.

Our eyes lock, but she acts like she doesn't even see me as she turns away and sits down at the table next to ours, her undivided attention on the man she's with — *Graham Thorne.* Is that why she's been declining my calls? Not because she misunderstood my relationship with Valeria, but because *I* misunderstood *her* relationship with Graham fucking Thorne? I thought he'd been standing a little too close to her at the party, and the way she'd laughed with him seemed a little too intimate, but I was certain I was just seeing things.

"Think before you act," Valeria urges, and I unlock my jaws. I didn't even realize I'd been glaring at them.

"Bold of you to assume I'm capable of thinking straight when she's near," I mutter as I rise to my feet. My sister audibly sighs as I close the distance between our table and theirs. "Sierra," I say, my tone filled with venom I don't truly feel — never toward her. "A word, please?"

She looks up, seemingly disinterested, but her eyes give her away. There's anger in them, but there's pain too. Valeria was right. I fucked up. "*No,*" she replies, her tone sharp.

"Please," I beg, my voice breaking.

Something shift in her expression, and her fiery eyes soften. She sighs and throws Graham a sweet smile before slipping out of her seat wordlessly. Much to my surprise, she follows me out quietly.

"What do you want?" she asks the moment the restaurant manager's office door closes behind me. She sounds tired, not a hint of her usual provocation in her voice, almost like dealing with me is a minor inconvenience.

She leans back against the closed door, her expression betraying her impatience, like she wants me to just get to the point so she can go back to Graham. Blinding jealousy takes hold of me as I cage her in against the door with my forearms, barely an inch between us. "Did you bring him here on purpose?" I ask, my voice strained. "You're in *my* restaurant. Tonight, of all nights, when I'm here."

Her eyes flash the way they do when I've infuriated her, but instead of the tirade I'd expected, she merely inhales deeply, her shoulders sagging. "No, Xavier," she says, her voice soft, her tone defeated. "It's a coincidence. How could I have known where you'd be?"

I place my index finger under her chin and force her to face me. She's never this restrained when we're alone. Normally she'd already have turned the tables and put me in my place. Sierra grabs my wrist, and for a moment, I'm certain she's about to push my hand away, but she merely holds it in place, our eyes locked.

"Tell me why you're here with Graham Thorne," I ask, my voice barely above a whisper. Her eyes roam over my face, searching, but what for I'm not certain.

She hesitates, and my heart begins to race. "Same reason you're here with *her*, I'd warrant."

"Just a friendly, completely platonic, non-romantic dinner, then?"

She raises a brow mockingly and part her lips, a sharp retort no doubt on the tip of her tongue, but then she snaps her mouth closed and nods. "Sure."

"Sierra," I warn. "There isn't much that I won't let slide when it comes to you, but there are lines you shouldn't cross. Eat with him if you'd like, but you're leaving with *me* after. I'll drive you home myself."

Her eyes soften just a touch — anyone but me would've missed it. My heart skips a beat when she gently cups my cheek, her eyes roaming over my face with a hint of the same longing she showed me when I kissed her. "Xavier," she whispers, leaning in until her lips brush over my ear. "Go to hell."

She pushes against my chest and walks away, leaving me staring after her. "I'm already *in* hell," I whisper, knowing I have no right to stop her.

Eleven

Sierra

I glance at the folder in my hands one last time before I step out of my car, my mind made up. I've deprived myself of some great business opportunities in the last couple of years, all because I've been avoiding Xavier.

"Sierra," Graham says as I walk into the building the auction is being held at. He smiles at me sweetly, a pleased look in his eyes. "I wasn't sure you'd come."

I raise a brow and shake my head. "I promised you I would, didn't I?"

Graham nods, his gaze searching. "I suppose you did."

Did he truly think I wouldn't show up today after we crafted this proposal together? He leads me toward the boardroom, and I can't help but overthink his reaction. What signal have I been sending the industry by walking away from purchases the moment I knew Xavier was interested in something? Have I made myself, and thereby my family and business, look weak?

"Ready?" Graham asks, pausing in front of the door.

I hesitate when I hear Xavier's voice through the door, his

words muffled. It's been so long since I faced him head-on at an auction, and truthfully, I don't want to walk into that room. I don't want to compete with him the way we used to, when nothing feels the same anymore. There is no friendly rivalry anymore — just bitterness and a plethora of other feelings I don't quite understand.

"Ready," I murmur, before pulling the door open and walking in, Graham by my side. All five people in the room look up, and though I feel his gaze burning on my skin, I try my hardest not to look at Xavier. I'm done acknowledging his presence, but I'm done avoiding him too.

"*Sierra Windsor*," says Lena, the owner of the plot of land the mall is being built on. She sounds equal parts surprised and impressed, and the way she smiles at me tells me I'm at an advantage here, though why, I'm not quite sure. "I didn't realize you were interested in this development."

I smile at her as Graham pulls out a chair for me, and I sit down. "I am," I tell her, before glancing at Graham. "*We* are."

A hush falls over the room, and at last, I look up, into those captivating brown eyes that haunt me at night. "We?" Xavier repeats, his tone filled with indignation.

It hurts to look at him, and I try my best to remain unaffected as I look away, not bothering to answer. Graham, however, smirks as he leans back in his seat and places his hands on the table, his pinky brushing against mine.

"Sierra and I decided to join hands on this project," he confirms. "Our offer will be a joint offer, and both of our resources will be put toward this development."

Xavier stares at our hands with clenched jaws, his eyes zeroing in on where they're touching just slightly, and I can't help but wonder what's going through his mind. He claimed his dinner with Valeria was platonic and non-romantic, but considering the way he was holding her hand, I just don't believe him. I've ignored too many red flags when it comes to him, when I know better.

I'm snapped out of my thoughts when a man I don't recognize whistles, shakes his head, and rises to his feet. "I can't compete with that," he says, walking out the door without a word. Silence falls over the room, until another man rises and walks out, and another, until Xavier, Lena, Graham, and I are the only ones left in the room.

"Well," Lena says, her expression incredulous. "I suppose that makes sense. Staying would've been a waste of their time, after all. However, since the decision now comes down to just two offers, I'd like to see your development plans. As you all know, I inherited this land from my father, and it's important to me that it's developed by someone who understood his vision. Rather than giving it to the highest bidder, I'd like to hear your plans."

I nod and rise to my feet, well-prepared for this scenario. Unfortunately, I know Xavier is too. We've both been in too many situations where what should've been a simple auction turned into a test of faith.

Xavier's eyes roam over the blouse I'm wearing and down to my pencil skirt, only to travel all the way up again, slowly, his gaze caressing every inch of my body. I suspect he does it to distract me and throw me off my game, but he's sorely mistaken if he thinks that's all it takes.

He watches me carefully as I give my presentation, highlighting everything I know about Lena's father and all the little details I knew he would've wanted, that I'd ensure we'd have. It's all knowledge Xavier can't possibly possess, and he must know he's at a disadvantage.

His expression tells me he's trying to work something out — why I'm here so unexpectedly, no doubt. Knowing him, he's mentally calculating the odds of still walking away victorious, but there is no way I'll let that happen. I throw him a sugary sweet smile as I retake my seat next to Graham, who gently knocks his shoulder against mine, his eyes blazing with pride.

Xavier's expression is tumultuous as he begins his presentation. "As usual, Ms. Windsor's proposal is thorough, well-structured, and perfectly tailored to your late father's wishes," he says, surprising me. I raise a brow, and he smirks. "However, I bring experience to the table that she simply does not have. The only other mall the Windsors own was one they acquired, but I'm well versed in building them from the ground up."

I lean back in my seat, irritation running down my spine as I cross my arms and decide to give him a taste of his own medicine. My eyes slowly roam over the three-piece suit he's wearing, and I take my time studying the way it doesn't at all hide his muscular arms. For a moment, I'm reminded of how he looked with his shirt hanging off his shoulders, his abs on display and pure lust in his eyes. Fierce longing rushes through me, and all of a sudden, my memory becomes so vivid that I can almost feel his lips on mine again.

"Mr. Kingston?" Lena says.

I blink and drag my eyes back up to his, only to find him staring at me, his cheeks rosy and an adorable disarmed expression on his face. He must've stopped speaking in the last couple of minutes and not even realized it. "I..." he stammers, running a hand through his thick hair. It makes me feel so incredibly powerful to throw him off like that, and just like that, I'm reminded why I've always loved messing with him.

"I'll give the project to all three of you," Lena says. We all instantly begin to protest, but she shakes her head. "It's a take it or leave it offer."

Xavier stares up at the ceiling and sighs. "We'll take it," he and I say at the same time. Our eyes lock, and something passes between us. Graham nods and slips his hand around the back of my chair, and I turn to look at him. He smiles reassuringly, indicating that he's still on board too.

"Wonderful. I'll have the paperwork drawn up. In the meantime, please work on one cohesive plan, and present it to me next week." She rises to her feet, throws us all a polite smile, and walks out, leaving the three of us alone.

Xavier just inhales deeply and glances at the arm Graham draped over the back of my chair, before looking into my eyes. "We need to talk."

His jaw begins to tick when Graham wraps his hand around my shoulder. "Indeed," Graham replies. "If she wants a new proposal by next week, we'd better start working on it straight away. We'll need to get our strategies aligned."

Xavier musses up his hair, his eyes never leaving mine. "I don't want this collaboration leaking until the papers are signed, so our meeting must be held at a completely confidential location."

"Well, there's no time like the present," Graham says, his tone far less friendly than before. "We'll let you lead the way."

Twelve

XAVIER

"Your house, really?" Sierra says, her tone a little bitter as both she and Graham follow me in, almost like she's reminded of what happened the last time she was here.

I hesitate and look over my shoulder, my expression earnest. "We needed a private location, and this works just fine. You know as well as I do that deals as big as this one have to remain confidential until the ink is dry."

She locks her jaws and throws me a hateful little look before walking down the foyer, toward my living room. I wonder if she realizes how telling it is that she knows exactly where to go. Judging by his sour, forced smile, Graham has certainly noticed.

I smirk at him and follow Sierra. I haven't stopped thinking about her having dinner with him, and the way he's been behaving around her today. His touches are subtle, but they're there, and she isn't pulling away.

In all the years we've known each other, neither Sierra nor I have been in a relationship. Hell, I've never even seen her act remotely flirtatious with anyone, and she's always quick to step away and set boundaries when a man treats her with too much familiarity, so why has she been letting Graham get away with his little touches? I can't shake the feeling that something is going on between them, and the thought of that doesn't sit well with me.

I raise a brow and bite back a pleased smile when Graham and I walk into my living room, and I find Sierra standing next to my liquor cabinet, a glass of cabernet in her hand. She has no idea that I don't even like red wine, does she? I bought that bottle for her, in the unlikely event she'd ever come over.

"Please don't drop wine on the sofa," I tell her, my voice soft. "My mother chose it for me, and she loves coming over to read on it. Pretty sure she doesn't even come here for me — just the comfy sofa. Mom's a clean freak, so she'd be upset if it got ruined."

Sierra looks disarmed as she lifts her face. "Your mother loves to read?"

I smile. "Almost as much as you do."

She stares at me like I've grown two heads, and I wonder what she finds so surprising — that I know about her obsession with romance novels, or that she has something in common with my mother. Hell, she might just be surprised I *have* a mother and didn't just spawn from the depths of hell. "Your mother is Mrs. Kingston," she says, her voice soft, like she's talking more to herself than to me, and instantly know what she's referring to.

The Mrs. Kingston Protocol — a protocol that's enacted the moment Sierra steps foot on any of my properties. She has no idea just how robust my security is, and just how many security personnel are on site and purposely stepping away when she breaks in. The Mrs. Kingston protocol allows her to do whatever she wants without setting off any of my alarms, and it always makes Elijah's day when she breaks in. There's nothing he loves more than replaying the security footage from our spy cams in our monthly meetings. If not for the guard that had already been patrolling the office when she was on her way up, she might just have gotten away with her jewelry last time.

"So, how do we merge both of our development plans into

something Lena will approve of?" Graham asks, sitting down. "As a starting point, tell us which parts of your proposal are non-negotiable for you, and we'll do the same. We don't have much time at all. By the end of this meeting, we need to be on the same page." His expression is carefully blank, but I notice the way he looks between Sierra and me, and I wonder what he sees.

Sierra nods and carefully places her glass on my coffee table before sitting down next to Graham. Her thigh brushes against his, and Graham's shoulders relax. What the fuck is going on here? My sofa is big enough to seat five people, so why the fuck would she choose to sit right next to him?

I sit down in the armchair opposite them with my laptop and force myself to work my way through all the documents I've compiled for this project. I take my time telling them which aspects are most important to me, and which my firm is best positioned to handle in terms of strengths, but it's near impossible to stay focused when Graham wraps his arm around the back of my sofa, his thumb touching Sierra's shoulder.

Why the fuck does he keep doing that? It's inappropriate, and I don't understand why she's letting him. I've seen her put countless men in their place for behaving like that with her, so why is she okay with him doing it? He turns his laptop toward her to show her something when it's their turn to determine their priorities, and she nods, her head far too close to his. "What about this?" he asks, and she leans in further to take a closer look at his screen.

"I'm not sure," she says, reaching over to click on something before placing her hand on his thigh. She leaves it there as she begins to read what's on his screen, and my heart squeezes painfully. It's one thing for him to touch her in little ways, but it's something else for her to reciprocate.

I rise to my feet and walk over to my drinks cabinet to pour myself a glass of whiskey, even if it's just so I have something to keep my hands busy with. I ran a background check on Graham after I saw them together at dinner, and it came back squeaky clean. Even worse, it revealed the deep ties between their families, and their years-long friendship. Was she waiting for him to come back home? Did they stay in touch while he was living overseas?

"Oh, it should be down the hallway, on the right," I hear Sierra say, and Graham tenses for a moment, before he rises from his seat and walks toward my guest bathroom.

I knock back my glass of whiskey when Sierra rises to her feet too, her deep emerald eyes unreadable tonight. "You don't usually drink," she remarks, her eyes zeroing in on my whiskey glass. "Even at events, I very rarely see you drink."

I smile to myself as I think about the monthly poker nights I attend with her brothers, which she has no idea about. One night of drinking with the Windsor brothers is enough for a whole month. "You don't know me as well as you think you do, Sierra."

She raises her brow and places her glass down on the counter inside my liquor cabinet. "Clearly," she murmurs, and I bite down on my lip, certain it's Valeria she's referring to but unsure how to address the situation. I'm terrified of saying the wrong thing and putting Valeria at risk again. If I tell her that V is my sister, I need to tell her the whole story, so she understands why it's information she has to keep to herself, or I'll need to have her sign a non-disclosure agreement. Now isn't the right time to discuss it, and I'm honestly not even sure I'm capable of telling her the full truth at all.

Even so, I can't help myself as I step forward and wrap my hand around her waist, pulling her against me. "Tell me, Kitten... why the fuck are you letting him touch you?"

She places her palm against my chest, her eyes on mine. For a moment, I'm certain she'll push me away, but she merely stares at me, her expression conflicted. "Why shouldn't I?" she asks. "He's nice, and he's one of few people who truly know me and still like me for who I am. I think there could be something there, if I let it."

"I thought you didn't want to be with anyone until your grandmother chose your match, because it'd just be a waste of your time?"

Her eyes widen, and it's clear I've finally truly managed to shock her. "I changed my mind," she says, her tone resolute. "I don't want to wait anymore. I'm going to write my own story and marry a man of my choosing."

Thirteen

XAVIER

I try my best to be sly as I walk into one of the gardens in Zane's observatory, still as terrified of getting caught by Sierra as I've always been. For years, I've hidden my friendship with her brothers, knowing she'd do whatever she could to put an end to it if she realized just how much I learn about her by attending every month.

More than once, the Windsor brothers have unknowingly given me a competitive advantage against her, and they've told me countless stories about her childhood that she definitely wouldn't want me to know. Over the years, they've become brothers to me too, and though they couldn't possibly know it, they were the ones who kept me going when dealing with Valeria's absence became too much.

I'm not even sure how we became this close. It was mostly Dion's doing, but Ares was the one who continued to invite me when Dion moved overseas. Even as my rivalry with Sierra reached new heights, the invites never stopped coming, until eventually, invites were no longer necessary. I wonder if he knew how much I needed those monthly poker nights, if he saw something no one else did.

"You're late," Lex says as he sets up the portable poker table he invented for our poker nights.

"Weird," Ares remarks. "You're usually very punctual."

Zane takes a long, hard look at me and sighs. "Whiskey?" he asks.

I nod, and Luca pulls out my chair for me. "What has our sister done this time?" he asks, his sympathetic tone at odds with the amusement on his face. "I thought you guys were done with your little feud, but that look in your eyes tells me she's done something crazy again."

Normally I'd fill them in on the shit she pulled while leaving out some key details, such as what I did to deserve it, but today I don't have it in me.

"I doubt she did anything," Lex says, thrusting his phone in Luca's face. "She's been too busy parading around town with Graham. I have to say, they look pretty damn good together."

"Graham fucking Thorne," I mutter, before knocking back my whiskey. Sierra has been avoiding all my calls and every attempt to be alone with her after business meetings, and all the while, I've had to watch her sit next to Graham and laugh with him. Two weeks of that, and I'm at my breaking point.

"I reckon Grandma would actually allow it, you know?" Zane says. "If Sierra went to Grams and told her she wants to marry Graham, I think Grandma would let her. After what she did to me, she won't risk telling Sierra no when they know each other so well and are clearly a good match."

I stare at them in pure fucking disbelief. "How the fuck are they a good match?" I ask, my tone aggressive. "He doesn't fucking know her. Since when is working in the same industry equivalent to knowing someone?"

Ares smiles at me and shrugs. "Well, they *are* childhood friends."

I glance at the photo on Lex's screen, and pure fury rushes through me. They were captured walking out of a restaurant, and he's got one arm wrapped tightly around her while he holds up an umbrella above their heads. "Does she look like a child to you?" I snap. "He knew her when they were kids, but he doesn't know who she's become, what shaped her, what makes her tick."

"Still," Luca says. "It's clear they like each other, and there's plenty of time for them to get to know each other on a different level once they're married. A merger between both companies would fulfill Grandma's criteria. I think she'll go for it."

"I quite like Graham," Lex says. "It'd be nice to have him as a brother-in-law." He knocks his shoulder against mine then. "We'll have an extra poker player, Xave. Wouldn't that be nice?"

"There's no space," I say dumbly. "This table was designed for the six of us."

Lex smiles and nods excitedly. "Oh, you think I should already start designing a new table? That's a great idea. Best to be proactive about that kind of thing."

"Stop it," Dion tells Lex, punching his shoulder.

I look at my best friend in surprise, but he merely shakes his head and starts to deal the cards. I never told him how I feel about his sister, and considering the way Sierra and I have treated each other over the years, he'd probably never expect it.

I'm not even sure why we became such bitter rivals, but I'm certain the root cause of it was something I did unknowingly. In part, I think I kept our rivalry going because I knew she wouldn't really let me into her life any other way, and it provided a much needed escape for me.

Besides, for as long as I've known her, she's been waiting for the husband her grandmother will eventually choose for her, and she hasn't been interested in anyone else. So I waited, and I did everything I could to make sure her grandmother would consider me, but it's still not enough. It might never be.

"You okay?" Dion asks. "We've played three rounds and you haven't said a single word other than *call* or *fold*."

"Yeah, what's going on with you, Xavier?" Ares asks, putting his cards down. He looks at me the way he sometimes looks at his younger brothers, like he knows exactly what's going on but is waiting for me to tell him.

I stare at my cards and place them down, showcasing my Royal Flush. I don't even bother collecting my winnings, though. No, there's something far more important I want. "I'm ready to collect all the favors you've all come to owe me throughout the years," I say. "Every single one of them, at once."

Ares crosses his arms and leans back, a knowing look in his eyes. "And what, pray tell, is it you want?"

I take a deep breath, knowing full well there's every chance I won't walk out of this room in one piece if I say what I need to, but I risk it anyway. "I would like to marry your sister, and I will need all of your support to make it happen."

I expected backlash, maybe a broken nose, but instead, I'm met with five smiles. "About damn time," Zane says, grinning as he and his brothers reach for their wallets, taking out wads of cash, and I raise a brow in surprise when it ends up mostly in Dion and Ares's hands.

"We'd all been wondering how long it'd take you to collect your favors," Dion explains, shrugging. "Ares bet it'd be this month, and that you'd use them to win Sierra's hand in marriage. I lost because I thought you'd have done it a month ago, but thankfully I did get your rationale right."

"You knew," I murmur, my shoulders sagging in relief.

Lex chuckles, and Luca shakes his head. "Xavier, we've known for far longer than you could possibly know," Zane tells me. "Why did you think we kept inviting you to our poker nights?"

Lex refills my whiskey glass and throws me an amused look. "That seat at the table has always been yours, Xavier. It always will be, provided you can win over both our grandmother and sister."

"And that, my dear future brothers-in-law, is where you come in."

Fourteen

XAVIER

"I should've brought the Lex-board," Lexington says nervously.

"Shut the fuck up about that damn whiteboard," Zane snaps, sounding equally on edge as the six of us stare up at Anne Windsor's home.

"Sierra is at the office and stuck in a meeting, so we have at least a solid hour. Even in the unlikely event that she caught wind of you being on the Windsor Estate, she wouldn't be able to get here anytime soon," Ares says, his tone reassuring.

Luca nods. "Our grandmother is... tough. Stepping into her home is different to sneaking into ours for poker night, and honestly, I'm not sure we can keep this from Sierra. If this gets back to her, it could backfire majorly."

"Regardless," Dion says. "We've got your back. I'm not gonna lie, not even the five of us combined can control the outcome of what's about to happen, but we'll do what we can. Though she'd never admit it, Sierra stopped being herself when you two stopped sabotaging each other. She smiled less and began to read more, like she needed an escape more than she used to. You bring out something in her that no one else can, Xavier, and it wouldn't surprise me if Grandma knows it."

Lex places his hand on my shoulder. "None of us were sure about you until you two stopped fighting and Sierra lost her spark. Ultimately, Sierra's happiness is what we care about most, and we're willing to entrust you with it."

"You know I'll do everything in my power to make her happy, don't you?"

Dion claps my back and smiles menacingly. "If, for even one single second, I doubt that you are, we'll have words."

Words. Knowing Dion, very few words will be exchanged if he thinks I'm mistreating his sister. Honestly, I'm a little surprised I didn't see it sooner. She's their little angel, and had anyone else messed with her, they'd have found themselves tied up in a warehouse until they swore to never look at her again. I should've realized they knew about my feelings for her when they not only continued to let me get away with all kinds of shit, but they kept inviting me into their homes too.

I inhale deeply and nod. "Let's do this," I say, my voice betraying my nerves.

The Windsor boys throw me varying reassuring looks and lead the way through Anne Windsor's house, toward her sitting room. "Grandma," Ares says.

She merely smiles as she takes the six of us in, not a hint of surprise or confusion in her expression as she sits on her sofa with crossed ankles, her hands folded in her lap. The cream-colored pantsuit she's wearing only enhances her authority, and at last, I begin to understand why she's always commanded so much respect from everyone who knows her.

"Xavier Kingston," she says, tipping her head toward the sofa opposite her. "I see you've brought reinforcements. Sit, boys."

We all follow her command and sit down. From the moment I made up my mind, I've been rehearsing what I'd say, only to find myself at a loss for words now that the time has come. "I'm here to present you with an offer," I begin to say, terrified of saying the wrong thing and losing my one chance with Sierra forever.

"No," Anne says. "You're here to steal my beloved granddaughter from me."

My eyes widen, and heat spreads across my face. My surprise must be evident, because she laughs and holds out her hand. I stare at her for a moment too long before I hand over the folder I brought, detailing my business plan.

"I... I'm offering a merger," I tell her, sounding a little less confident than before. I didn't think she'd see through me so quickly. I thought I'd catch her by surprise and make her an offer she couldn't refuse, but I'm starting to think she's several steps ahead of me.

"I was rather surprised you were able to grow your company into one I could not ignore, one my granddaughter had to be cautious of, when we've never had real competition in the industry before. I've been wondering why you kept trying so hard, even after you'd virtually dominated the industry," she says, never looking up from the documents in her hands.

Fuck. I clear my throat and hand her another document. "You are correct to assume that I offer a merger in return for your granddaughter's hand in marriage," I tell her. "I'm here today to reassure you it's a good match in all respects. This merger will turn our company into a formidable force. Though there is significant overlap due to the similarity in some of our acquisitions, there is also plenty of synergy. My portfolio contains malls, amusement parks, and airports — three areas in which Windsor Estate does not yet dominate. Sierra, on the other hand, owns a lot of hospitality and residential real estate. Our portfolios would complement each other's."

"Indeed," Anne says. "In the last three years, you've been exceedingly strategic in your acquisitions. Which begs the question, why now?"

I hesitate, unsure how to answer. "I have grown my company to its fullest extent, and I believe both Sierra and I have grown weary of competing when we could be collaborating."

"Perhaps so, but in that case, the offer need not come with a marriage agreement. Tell me the truth, Mr. Kingston. Does this have anything to do with my granddaughter suddenly being seen around town with Graham Thorne, when she's never formally dated anyone before?"

I contemplate the various answers I can give her, hyperaware that all five of Sierra's brothers are in the room with me, by my own stupid request, no less. "Yes," I answer truthfully.

Lex chuckles, and I don't have to look over my shoulder to recognize the sound of money exchanging hands. Assholes.

"Very well," Anne says, completely unfazed. "Then answer this, Xavier Kingston. Do you love my granddaughter?"

Instantly, every hint of laughter and amusement makes way for deafening silence, and my heart begins to race. "I don't know if it's love, but I can't imagine marrying anyone but her."

She considers me for a few moments. "Your feelings for her, whatever they may be, do not mean you are entitled to hers in return," she tells me, her tone disapproving. "You could love her with all you have, and she might never reciprocate those feelings. Do you wish to marry her regardless?"

"I do." I know Sierra doesn't have feelings for me, but even so, I want her to be my wife. I want a chance to show her that I can give her the kind of marriage each of her siblings have, if she'll just give us a chance.

"And if, after three years of marriage, you cannot make her happy, do you agree to let her go?"

My entire body reacts to the question, and the word *no* rests at the tip of my tongue. The thought of having her and then letting her go doesn't sit well with me, but realistically, I know that if I can't make her love me after three years of marriage, it'd never happen. "I would set her free, so she can find what I couldn't give her."

She nods, but she doesn't look convinced. "What do you think of this, boys?"

They speak up one by one, surprising me with their answers.

"I approve," Ares says. "He knows her better than Sierra realizes. If anyone can keep up with her, it's him."

"I approve too," Luca says. "Sierra doesn't realize it, but he brings out the best in her. No one has ever been able to keep her on her toes or push her to do better, but he does."

"I agree," Dion says, and I turn to look at my best friend. "For years, I've watched him quietly protect her without ever being overbearing or enforcing his own agenda. He's always offered her invisible support, never shaking her sense of independence or undermining her strength and business prowess."

"I'm inclined to approve their match too," Zane says. "They've danced around each other for years. He says he's not certain it's love, but speaking from experience, nothing else could possibly keep a man like him so enthralled with a woman he isn't in a relationship with, one he claims to not even like."

Lex chuckles and throws me an amused look. "He has my approval too. There are very few men that wouldn't be intimidated by Sierra, but he's one of them. She'll be able to just be herself with him, without having to fear she'll overshadow him. Sierra needs that — someone who appreciates her strong personality."

"Very well," Anne says. "In that case, you have my approval too, Xavier."

My shoulders sag in relief, and she smiles at me reassuringly in a way that's so reminiscent of Sierra that I stare at her a moment too long, suddenly realizing just how much of an impact the woman in front of me must've had on my future wife.

"She won't react well to this," she says, her smile slipping. "She'll fight the decision with everything she's got, and I wouldn't put it past her to find some kind of loophole. If anyone can do it, it'd be her." She sighs and tucks a strands of her shoulder-length hair behind her ear. "It's best if you leave this to me, Xavier. Let me be the bad guy, or she'll never give you a chance. Under no circumstances are you to let her know that this marriage is your idea — she'd hold it against you. If it comes from me, she'll accept it."

I nod hesitantly, unsure what she has in mind but well aware that her expression spells trouble. After all, it's the exact way Sierra looks right before she does something completely unhinged.

Fifteen

SIERRA

My heart is hammering in my chest as I grab one of my grandmother's chocolate chip cookies. She asked us all to gather for an announcement, and considering the huge mountain of cookies on the kitchen counter, I have a feeling I know exactly what this is about. Raven snatches my cookie out of my hand and stuffs as much as she can into her mouth before I can even take a bite, and I can't help but smile.

There are at least fifty cookies here, so I know she did that to distract me from the inevitable. "You don't need to worry about me so much, you know?" The last thing I want is for my best friend to worry about something we can't control. She always cares so much, and I don't want this to keep her up at night.

"How could I not be worried?" she asks as she hands me back half of her cookie. I force a smile before taking a bite, wishing I could find the right words to reassure her.

"How do you feel?" Faye asks carefully. I smile at my tiny sweet sister-in-law, unsure how to answer her. She's probably one of few who truly get it — after all, out of all my sisters-in-law, she's the only one who knew she'd be in an arranged marriage from a young age. Though our circumstances are vastly different, she understands why I never wanted to date anyone. It wouldn't have mattered, since my fate was sealed anyway.

"Nervous, I'd bet," Celeste says, throwing me a reassuring look. "Whoever it is, and whatever happens, just know that life has a way of working itself out. What's meant to be, will be."

I smile at her, taking her words to heart. She'd know — she and Zane grew up as rivals, fell in love, only to fall apart tragically before they were forced into an arranged marriage none of us thought would work out. "I really hope so. I just have a bad feeling about it."

Raya, our newest sister-in-law, joins us and shakes her head. "How bad could it be?" she asks. "Grandma would never let you marry someone that isn't right for you."

"How bad could it be?" I repeat. "Lex literally showed up in your classroom as your professor and hid that he knew you were arranged to be married."

She bites back a laugh and nods. "And even so, it worked out, didn't it? Celeste is right. What's meant to be, will be."

Grandma crosses her arms, and the boys instantly stop mocking Lex about how he said he'd never be whipped, only to become just as bad as all my other brothers the moment he married Raya. It reminds me that *that's* what I want. A husband who adores me, and the kind of happiness all my siblings have found. I've waited so long for it, and now that it's my turn, I'm nervous beyond words.

"I'm certain you can all guess why I've gathered you here today," Grandma says, her eyes roaming over all of us with a hint of pride in them.

Raven bumps her shoulder against mine, and I can't help but blush. Maybe the girls are right, and this is the start of something amazing. For so long, I'd been looking forward to this exact moment. When did that change?

"Sierra, sweetheart," Grandma says in that sweet tone she reserves for my sisters-in-law and me. "Your engagement has been finalized."

I take a deep breath and nod, my heart uneasy. "Who is it?" I ask, my voice trembling.

Grandma hesitates, which is entirely uncharacteristic of her. She looks down, and then she faces me head-on, her expression unyielding. "You'll be marrying Xavier Kingston."

My expression must convey my utter horror, because my brothers all chuckle at my expense, earning themselves glares from my sisters-in-law.

"Combining his real estate empire with ours would result in us jointly becoming the biggest real estate firm the world has ever seen," she explains, and though it makes sense, I just can't quite comprehend it. "It'll be the biggest merger we've ever done as a family."

I put down the cookie I was holding and shake my head. "Absolutely not," I declare, pure hatred rushing through me. "I'm not marrying Xavier. Just disown me, Grandma. I'll move out tomorrow. I can get my bags packed today."

Not in a million years will I marry that rotten man. The only good thing about him is his looks, and I'll be damned if I sleep with the devil, let alone marry him.

"You will," Val says softly, much to my surprise. "You'll marry him." The betrayal stings — I'd expected all my sisters-in-law to be on my side.

"Over my dead body," I snap.

"Well," Grandma says, sighing. "As it turns out, it may well be over mine."

Grandma grabs a set of papers from the kitchen counter and slides them toward me, her expression resigned. "I know you're not ready, sweetheart," she says. "I've waited for as long as I could, because I wanted to spend as much time as possible with my little girl. But Sierra, my time is up."

My hands begin to shake as I unfold the documents, fearing what I'll find. I've never seen Grandma look at me that way — with such regret and heartache. I read the words over and over, but no matter how badly I wish they would, they don't change. I look up with tears in my eyes, my heart breaking. "Colon cancer?" I ask, my voice breaking. It can't be. Is this a ruse, an attempt to convince me to marry Xavier?

"I accompanied her to the doctor this morning," Val murmurs. "She brought me with her because she didn't think any of us would believe her otherwise. It's true, Sierra."

Grandma's gaze moves around the room, a sweet smile on her face. She looks at us like it's the last time, like she wants to memorize every last detail about it, and it breaks my heart.

"How long have you known?" Lex asks, his voice hoarse, devoid of his usual lightheartedness.

"About a year. I'm old, Lex. I've accepted that my time has come, and I don't want to spend the few months I have left becoming even sicker and frailer from chemotherapy. It's okay, truly."

She's been sick for a year, and none of us knew? How much has she been through all by herself, suffering silently? I bite down on my lip in an attempt to hold back my tears, but they fall anyway. I was so young when a plane crash took our parents from us that I barely remember them. Grandma is the one who raised me, and I can't lose her. She's everything to me — my role model, my only parent figure, and my biggest supporter. I'm not sure who I even am without her cookies, her laughter, our weekly family dinners.

"I know you think you hate him," Grandma says, her voice filled with understanding. "But he'll love you like you deserve to be loved, Sierra. Xavier will protect you, and he'll continue to be by your side when I'm no longer able to. I know you don't want to marry him, but sweetheart... this is my last wish."

Sixteen

Xavier

"Explain that discrepancy to me," I tell my team, pointing at the slide they presented to me.

Farhana, my CTO, instantly begins to type furiously. "That doesn't look right to me," she agrees.

Mitch, my CFO, leans in to look at Farhana's screen. "Let me recalculate that," he says, his voice trembling. "I have no idea how this could have happened."

"How the hell did none of you spot this when I noticed the figures couldn't be right at a glance? I've told you countless times how important this project is — especially as it's a joint one with Windsor Real Estate and Thorne Developments. These kinds of elementary mistakes make us look bad not just in front of the client, but in front of our peers, our *competitors*. No one is leaving this room until these figures are resolved and these slides are presentable."

As if on cue, the doors to my conference room swing open. "I'm afraid I can't just let you enter," Sam says, his voice frantic, but there's no stopping my future wife.

Sierra walks in, her beautiful eyes tinged red, like she's been crying. My heart wrenches as I rise from my seat, the implication clear. She found out about our engagement, and she isn't just unhappy about it, she's devastated. For once, she's caught me entirely off guard. I didn't think she'd respond well to the news, but I never expected it to make her *sad*.

"Sierra," I say, nodding politely, my tone mellow, cautious.

Her eyes roam over my board members, and her cheeks turn beautifully rosy. "I'm sorry, Mr. Kingston," Sam says. "I told her to wait, but the meeting lasted longer than expected, and she thought I was just stall—"

"— you made her wait?" I ask, my tone carrying a hint of danger. He should know better than to make Sierra wait, but then again, she's never walked into my office during office hours. She's only ever broken in, wreaking havoc for me to find the next day.

"Xavier," she says, her tone weary and lacking its usual fire.

"Get out."

She recoils and I instantly realize she misunderstood. "I need to speak to—"

"— all of you, get out," I repeat, glancing at my board members. "I need a word with Ms. Windsor, in private. You have until tomorrow to sort out the figures we just discussed."

My team all breathe a sigh of relief, no doubt grateful for the reprieve. The door closes behind Farhana, and I take a step toward my fiancée. Her breath hitches when I come to a stop in front of her, leaving nothing but an inch between our bodies. I thought she might step back, but she faces me head-on, her expression unwavering.

"Why did it have to be you?" she whispers, sounding pained.

I thought she might try to convince me to speak to her grandmother and end our engagement — I did not expect quiet acceptance. I push down a hint of panic and try my best not to overthink my response. "Why *not* me? This merger would make our joint company unstoppable, and though you might not want to acknowledge it, we're better off working *with* each other, instead of against each other."

"You'd marry me for the sake of your business? Xavier, you already have over half the market share. There's no need—"

"I want more," I say, knowing full well she'll misunderstand. She always does.

Sierra turns her back to me and runs a hand through her hair, her face tipped up toward the ceiling. I've never seen her look quite so *helpless*. It isn't a look I like on her, and I fucking hate that I'm the cause of it. "I'll marry you," she says, turning to face me, her expression crestfallen. "If that's what my grandmother wants, I'll do it, but I hope you know it'll never be a conventional marriage."

I raise a brow and lean back against my conference table. "What does that mean?"

"We'll pretend in front of our families, and we'll show them exactly what they want to see, but behind closed doors, I don't want anything to do with you."

I smirk despite the way my heart aches. "Sure didn't look like that when you wrapped your legs around me, your lips on mine."

Her eyes flash, that fire I've gotten used to making her emerald irises sparkle. She steps forward and places her hand on my chest, anger radiating off her. "If we're to be married, I expect you to adhere to some rules."

"What rules?" I ask, wrapping my hand around her wrist, keeping it in place.

"I expect discretion from you. Don't let your flings into the home you share with me, don't get caught cheating on me, and don't tell anyone about our marriage. If my grandmother sets the same rules for us as she did for my brothers, we'll only have to be married for three years. You can manage those three simple rules for three years, can't you?"

I stare at her wide-eyed and shake my head, a humorless laugh escaping my throat as barely contained rage takes hold of me. "Discretion, you say?" I grab her waist, catching her off guard as I turn us around and lift her onto the table. My hands move to her thighs, and she gasps as I push her legs apart to stand between them, her skirt riding up. "Kingston men don't cheat," I tell her, my grip tight. "There won't be any need for *discretion*, Sierra. I won't look at anyone but you, won't touch anyone but you. For as long as you're my wife, I'll be loyal and faithful to you, and I expect the same in return."

She searches my face, and I'm certain I see a flicker of hope in her gorgeous eyes. "Don't pretend you're actually going to stay away from Valeria, and I won't pretend I'll stay away from Graham."

I clench my jaws, my thumbs brushing over her soft skin in an attempt to control my temper. "I don't know what's going on between you and him, but it ends now. Don't fucking test me on this. The only bed you'll find yourself in is *mine*, Sierra."

"I'll never want you," she snaps. "Not in a million years."

I cup the back of her neck, my thumb brushing over her pulse point. "Then I'll wait a million years and a day, Kitten. I'll wait forever if I need to, so long as you understand that you're *mine* as much as I'm yours."

"So not at all then," she says, and my heart twists painfully when I recognize the pain in her eyes.

I sigh and drop my forehead to hers. "I get how it looks. Truly, I do. But I swear to you that you're entirely wrong about Valeria. It isn't what you think, and quite frankly, the mere insinuation is sickening."

She pulls back a little to look at me, betrayal written all over her face. "I don't know what to think anymore. How am I supposed to believe your words when your actions continue to tell me otherwise?"

I thread a hand through her hair and force her to face me. "Fuck the past and everything you think you know," I snap. "Fuck every goddamn misconception you insist on having, and *listen* to me. I will never, ever, cheat on you. I am yours, and yours only, Sierra, whether you like it or not."

Seventeen

SIERRA

I sigh as I glance over the wedding plans Celeste sent me. I refused to engage in any of the planning, but I did make one request — to hold the wedding right at the centre of the elaborate maze at my family's estate, with no one but our closest family present. It's bound to piss Xavier off when he learns of the location, and that'll just make my day. Apparently, he gave us free rein to do whatever we want, and my sisters-in-law are doing all they can to romanticize it, none of them willing to admit that he cares even less than I do.

I look up in surprise when Graham walks into my office, and he sighs as he approaches my desk. "Did you forget about our resource allocation meeting?"

"I'm so sorry," I tell him, quickly clicking away all the wedding stuff before I rise from my seat. "It completely slipped my mind!"

Our project hasn't been high on my list of priorities, not in light of the hospital appointments I've attended with Grandma, and my upcoming wedding. I bite down on my lip as I glance at my office door, my heart beating a little faster at the thought of seeing Xavier again, even if it's only for a business meeting I'd forgotten about entirely.

Since we signed our contract with Lena we only have a meeting once a month, so I haven't seen him since we last discussed our marriage in his office, and I'm not too sure what to expect now that we're technically engaged.

"What's wrong?" Graham asks, reaching for me. He gently pushes my hair behind my ear, and I instantly feel guilty, my mind replaying the lies I threw at Xavier in anger. *Don't pretend you're actually going to stay away from Valeria, and I won't pretend I'll stay away from Graham.* I don't even know why I said it, when there's absolutely nothing but friendship between Graham and me. I suppose I did it to get on his nerves, and to make myself feel a little less pathetic.

"Nothing is wrong," I lie. Graham cups my cheek, and I lean into his touch. I need to tell him, but I don't know how. I can barely believe I'll have to marry Xavier Kingston, and acknowledging it feels impossible.

"How do I make it better?" he asks, his voice soft. Graham and I have been hanging out a bit more frequently, and it's been so refreshing to have a friend that isn't also one of my family members. He looks at me like he really sees me, and I need it now more than ever before. He's unlike Xavier, who reserves all his chivalry for Valeria, never extending so much as a kind word to me.

Just as I'm about to answer, my office door opens, and Xavier walks in. He tenses when he catches sight of us, and Graham reluctantly pulls his hand back. For a few moments, Xavier and I just stare at each other, neither of us quite sure how to act around each other now.

I take a step away from Graham and gesture toward the sofa in the corner of my office. "Let's get started." I sigh and run a hand through my hair, annoyed with myself for forgetting about this meeting. If I'd remembered, I could've just cancelled it. I'm not ready to be in the same space as Xavier, especially not with the lies I told standing between us.

I'm nervous as I sit down, and Xavier doesn't hesitate to sit down next to me, his thigh pressed against mine and the hand on his knee brushing against the hem of my pencil skirt. I shift away a little, but he just moves with me, ensuring our bodies are pressed against each other no matter what I do.

"We've already agreed to equally split the budget three ways, but we need to determine what each firm's strengths are, to ensure we capitalize on synergies between our companies," I tell them, hoping to just get this meeting over and done with.

Xavier barely says a word as Graham and I begin to assign different parts of the project to our own firms, and I can't help but wonder what he's thinking about. I've spent the last few days analyzing everything he's said to me, trying my best to figure him out.

For years, I've witnessed him catering to Valeria, going as far as carrying her out after long nights because her feet seemed to hurt. He's carefully kept her out of the media and by his side, protecting her from the gossip and slander my family and I are often subjected to, yet he wants me to believe she isn't someone I need to worry about. Maybe I truly am crazy, because for some reason, I want to put my faith in him.

"You both seem distracted," Graham remarks. "What are your thoughts on this allocation?"

"I apologize," Xavier says, running a hand through his hair. "Can we reschedule? I don't think either Sierra or I will be able to focus today. There is something else she and I need to discuss privately first."

"Privately?" Graham repeats, a hint of irritation in his eyes.

I sigh and rise to my feet. "He's right, Graham. I'm sorry. Can we reconvene early next week?"

He looks between the two of us, confusion written all over his face. "I— yeah. Sure. Of course." He stares at me for a few moments, and I throw him an apologetic look, unsure how to explain. Graham sighs before walking out reluctantly, and my shoulders sag in relief when the door falls closed behind him.

"What was that?" Xavier asks. I turn my back to him, but he grabs my wrist and pulls me onto his lap. I gasp and straighten in his embrace, but my protests die on the tip of my tongue when I see the look in his eyes. "What did I walk in on, Sierra? Why the fuck was he touching your face like that?"

I place my hand against his chest, his heart beating wildly against my palm. "It was nothing," I promise him, my voice not as confident as I'd have liked it to be.

He cups my face, his thumb swiping over the part Graham touched, almost like he believes that'll brush away any remnant of his touch. "Maybe I haven't been clear enough," he says, his voice soft. "You're *mine*, Sierra Windsor. You can avoid me all you want, but there's no avoiding this marriage. I'm being as patient as I can be, Kitten, but you crossed a line today. You never should've let him touch you at all."

He forces me to face him, and I'm captivated by his tumultuous dark eyes. "Maybe keeping up this act for our families won't be that hard after all. You almost had me fooled, Xavier."

"You were born to frustrate the fuck out of me, weren't you?" he asks, his voice pained.

I smirk and slide my hand up his chest, around the back of his neck. "Yes," I whisper. "You really should think twice before making me your wife. I won't mind if you leave me at the altar."

He chuckles, the sound husky. "You have no idea just how many times I've thought about it," he whispers, his gaze roaming over my face. "No clue at all."

Eighteen

SIERRA

"You're not mad at me, are you?" Grandma asks as I stand on a platform in Raven's bridal boutique, wearing a stunning dress she designed for me long before my engagement was even announced. It's far from done, and it's already the most beautiful dress I've ever seen.

"I could never be mad at you, Grams," I tell her as I twirl for her, showing off my dress. I accompanied her to the hospital this morning, and I've been trying to keep my heartbreak hidden ever since. I know how much this dress fitting means to her, and I don't want to ruin it by crying, but all I can think about is that I'm losing her, and this is one of the last monumental memories I'll get to make with her.

Grandma smiles as her eyes roam over my wedding gown, and for one single moment, my mind involuntarily drifts to Xavier. What would he think if he saw me in this dress? Judging by the way he kissed me, I'd say that he's at least a little bit attracted to me, but could he have meant it when he told me he's mine, and mine only? I've never felt more conflicted, more scared of the future.

"Sweetheart," Grandma says. "Everything is going to be okay. You trust me, don't you?"

"I do," I reply cautiously. "But you don't know him the way I do, Grandma." Raven looks up from my wedding gown design on her drawing tablet and shoots me a warning look, but I ignore it. "That humble philanthropic persona he portrays at events is all just a sham. He's ruthless, unyielding, and dare I say it, *unscrupulous*."

"Ah," Grandma says, her eyes twinkling. "A match made in heaven."

I gape at her, and she laughs, the sound weaker than it used to be. She's grown so frail, and I'd noticed it, but I'd dismissed it. Even now, despite all the hospital appointments I've accompanied her at, I find it hard to believe that my sweet grandmother is sick. I keep waiting for someone to tell me that there's a cure, or there's been a misunderstanding and she was misdiagnosed, but it's all been to no avail.

"Are you calling *me* unscrupulous? I'm nothing like him!"

"Yeah, right," Raven mutters as she approaches me with even more pins. She's in full concentration mode, but clearly not even my wedding gown is enough to make her keep her commentary at bay. I narrow my eyes at her, but she merely smiles the way Grandma does. "God, it's surreal to see you in this dress. We've been working on this design for years," she murmurs as she messes with the pleats. We decided on a mermaid style dress with a sweetheart necklace, made entirely of silk, with gorgeous hand beading. It looks even more beautiful in person than it did in my imagination, and it'll be wasted on Xavier.

My heart twists painfully as I look into the mirror. I was supposed to get my own happily ever after, just like in the romance novels I love so much. My story has played out in my head a thousand times — grandma would choose the perfect man for me, just like she's found perfect partners for each of my brothers. We'd be awkward around each other for a while, but we'd soon find out that we have a lot in common, and that we enjoy spending time together. Of course, there'd be crazy chemistry between us...

Just like that, Xavier hijacks my mind again. *Chemistry*. At least we have that in spades. I bite down on my lip as I think back to each time we've danced together, each time he whispered the word *Kitten* in my ear. And then there are the two kisses we shared, and the way his body feels against mine. I'm having a hard time seeing the good in this situation, but I suppose the chemistry between us is something to be grateful for. It could certainly have been worse — not that I plan to ever sleep with him.

"He'll make you happy," Grandma says, her voice soft, almost like she's trying to convince herself as much as she's trying to convince me.

"Why him, Grams? You do realize he only agreed to this marriage because it's the only way he can grow his company even further, right? This is just a glorified business deal for him. I don't know what you think you see in him, but I promise you that you're wrong."

She leans back in her seat, her expression shrewd. "It isn't really about what I see in him, it's about what I see in *you* — and you, my sweetheart, have never had eyes for anyone but him."

"W-what?"

"Just how many times have you regaled us all with stories of things he'd done to you, week after week, year after year? We both know you could've put a stop to that ridiculous feud of yours easily — it'd have taken but one phone call to Silas. But instead, you grew more lax, left him loopholes and made silly mistakes whenever you wanted to lose to him, to keep the score even."

"That's not true," I say weakly, my cheeks blazing.

"Isn't it?" Raven says as she fiddles with the buttons on my back.

"Rave!" I whisper-shout, shocked at the way she's siding with Grandma on this one. Normally she's completely unresponsive when she's tailoring a dress, entirely in a world of her own, but today she's clearly got enough of an attention span to call me out.

Grandma chuckles, and my heart softens. Every time I've tried to talk to her about my engagement, she's just seemed so happy with the thought of me marrying Xavier that I don't have the heart to tell her the truth — that he's not at all what he seems. If she keeps smiling like that, I'll play my part, even if Xavier's promise of fidelity turns out to be false.

My stomach twists at the thought of being Xavier's wife. For as long as I can remember, I wanted to be the love of my husband's life, the centre of his universe. I've always dreamt of being with someone that could break down my walls, someone that'd stay with me no matter what. I won't be any of those things to Xavier, and having to mourn the loss of my dreams while smiling for my grandmother is proving to be harder than I expected.

"That dress over there," Grams says, drawing my attention to a beautiful emerald evening gown on a hanger. "Wear that to the annual real estate gala. It's this month, isn't it?"

"Oh, I wasn't planning on—"

"He's going to be your husband, Sierra. There's no point in avoiding him. If anything, I'd advise that you start attending the same events again. You might as well get used to being around him, because you'll be seeing a lot of him."

Nineteen

SIERRA

I sigh as I stare at the mirror, taking in the emerald dress Raven helped me into. The last thing I want to do today is attend the annual real estate gala, but there's no getting out of it if my grandmother demands that I go.

"You look stunning," Raven says, her smile bittersweet. None of us have managed a real smile since we learned about grandma's illness. Not even work and my sudden engagement to Xavier have been able to distract me from it.

I'm acutely aware that I only have a few more months left with my sweet grandmother, and I don't want to spend them fighting with her. It's clear he's not willing to walk away, and if marrying Xavier is what'll make her happy, then I'll play my part. I just hope he does too.

"Since you're both going to the gala, you should've just attended together," Raven says carefully.

She's tried to talk to me about Xavier and our engagement a few times, and each time, I've shut her down. For so long, I'd imagined what it'd be like to find out who I'd marry. Raven and I would cyber stalk him first, and then we'd tail him the way we did to Celeste, to make sure he's a good person and not some kind of whacko, and it'd be this whole experience. But since it's Xavier, I don't need to do any of those things. I *know* he's not meant for me, and I can't keep up a pretense when I'm facing my best friend, who knows about all my romantic dreams that'll never come true.

"It'd just start rumors, and I don't want anyone to know. I plan to keep our marriage a secret, and the second I can, I'll divorce him."

Raven looks at me with twinkling, knowing eyes. "We'll see."

I huff and mess with the fabric of my dress. "I *will*."

"Windsors don't divorce, Sierra," she says, smirking. "Not because it isn't possible, but because the matches are always right — even if grandma has to scheme and trick us into thinking we were making our own choices."

"There's an exception to every rule," I tell her, shrugging.

She laughs. "Perhaps, but you won't be it."

I glare at her. "Honestly, what's gotten into you? I thought you'd be on my side, and you just haven't been."

She reaches for me and gently pushes my hair out of my face. "I'm always on your side, babe," she says, sincerity oozing off her. "But what I won't do is pretend I don't see what grandma sees. He's a perfect match for you, and deep down, you know it too. You're just too scared to admit it, to put your heart on the line."

I stare at my best friend, my heart aching. "Forget it," I mutter, defeated. "There's no talking to you when you're like this."

She knows how hard it is for me to let someone in. For as long as I can remember, I've been too scared of the eventual pain that comes with loving someone, the inevitable abandonment. Raven has always been my only real friend, the only one I've let in that wasn't already essentially family. Even Celeste was already Zane's girlfriend when I first befriended her, and every other friendship I've ever had has been shallow, never growing beyond pleasantries. I can't even imagine opening up to Xavier.

"Sierra?" Raven says as she walks me to the door. "It takes time to learn how to communicate with your partner, especially if you have history. Give him the benefit of the doubt, okay?"

I purse my lips and nod, but I can't help the tinge of vulnerability I feel. The thought of trusting him, only to have him betray my trust... I'm not sure I'd be able to take that.

My sense of foreboding follows me all the way into the annual real estate charity auction, and just as I've decided that coming tonight was a mistake, I spot Xavier across the room. He looks incredible in that tuxedo, and for a few moments, I just stare at him, struggling to comprehend that Xavier Kingston is about to become my husband — in no less than three weeks, if my grandmother gets her way.

He looks up, and then he takes a second look at me, his eyes lighting up with equal parts surprise and appreciation. He smiles when he notices I'm wearing one of the Laurier pieces he sent me, and I hesitantly take a step toward him, only for Valeria to appear by his side.

My heart twists painfully, and I turn around, not wanting to see him with her. I'm on autopilot as I walk into the restrooms, and I stare at myself in the mirror without really seeing myself — all I can see is the way Valeria just grabbed his arm, and the way he instantly turned to look at her with pure tenderness in his eyes.

A small part of me had hoped that he meant what he said when he told me he's mine, that things would've changed, and he'd have come here alone. If I'm truly honest with myself, that's why I'm here, to see for myself what my marriage to Xavier would look like, what his word is worth.

"Sierra?"

I blink in surprise when Valeria walks in, her long, dark, wavy hair cascading down to her waist, enhancing the way she looks in that deep crimson evening gown. I've never seen her up close, and it pains me to admit that she's even more beautiful than I thought she was. She's a natural kind of beauty, the kind that barely needs to wear any makeup to look perfect, like Raven.

"It's Sierra, isn't it? We've never formally met, but I'm Valeria."

She wrings her hands, seemingly growing more nervous by the second. She gives off a sweet and innocent kind of vibe, kind of like Faye, and I can easily see why Xavier is so protective of her. For years, I've caught glimpses of her, built an opinion of her based on nothing but my own perception, and now that I'm facing her, I don't know what to make of her.

"I saw the way you looked at Xavier when you walked in, and the way your expression fell when you saw *me*, and I wanted to make sure you aren't misunderstanding anything." Had I been that obvious? Insecurity unlike anything I've ever felt before renders me speechless, and Valeria smiles shakily. "You know what Xavier is like," she continues. "He loves to hide behind that facade he's crafted. It's all my fault, but he tends to be scared to say the wrong thing, so unless he loses his temper, he just doesn't really say anything at all."

I tense and look away, something akin to jealousy putting its claws in me. "I don't need you to make excuses for my fiancé," I tell her, my tone more hostile than I'd intended. "Nor is it necessary for you to show off just how well you know him, or how close you are. I've had the pleasure of witnessing that for myself over the last few years."

I study her for a moment, my heart aching. She's my polar opposite. I'm much taller than her, curvier, and I'm most certainly not soft-spoken, like she is. Disappointment blends with helplessness as I step away from her, my mood souring further.

"No, please," she says. "That's not... Oh god, I didn't mean to... I just thought..."

I look over my shoulder and raise a brow, uncertain whether that desperate look in her eyes is all an act. "I suggest you think twice the next time you decide to educate me on anything related to my fiancé. If there's anything Xavier wants me to know, he'll tell me himself. It's not your place to do so in his stead."

My entire body is tense when I walk out, and my steps falter when I find Xavier waiting just outside the restrooms. For a second, it crosses my mind that he might have come looking for me, but then his gaze moves past me, pausing on the door. "She's inside," I tell him, my voice carrying a hint of bitterness.

He looks at me in a way he has never before — with suspicion and blame. "What did you do to her?" he asks, his tone threatening. He's never spoken to me that way before, and it hurts more than I care to admit.

My heart twists painfully, and I step closer to him. No woman has ever been able to inspire that kind of reaction from him — until her. Is this what I'll have to contend with throughout our marriage? I'm standing right in front of him, but it's her his eyes seek. "Xavier, if this is what fidelity looks like for you, I don't want it." My voice breaks on the last few words, and I hate myself for it.

Twenty

XAVIER

I trace a finger over the tuxedo Raven sent me, and I can't help but wonder what Sierra would say if she found out her best friend has secretly been helping me match my outfits to hers for longer than she could possibly imagine. Would her eyes flash in that beautiful way they do whenever I get on her nerves?

I sigh as I think back to my last conversation with her. I haven't had a chance to speak to Sierra since the charity auction, and even if I did, what would I say? One wrong word spoken to the wrong person, and Valeria's life could be in danger, and she's only just regained it.

My thoughts are interrupted by the sound of the ringtone Elijah set for security breaches, and I frown as I pick up. "What's wrong?" I ask as I begin to walk to my weapons cabinet.

Elijah chuckles, and I instantly relax. "You will not believe this," he says.

"What?" I say dryly, irritated he used this emergency line for something that clearly isn't an emergency. "The Windsor brothers just tried to breach our system. From what I can tell, Lexington is trying to shut your security system down from just outside our gates, so I can only assume they're planning to break in."

"No," I mutter. "They're planning something far worse."

"Oh?"

"They're going to take me. Let them."

"*Let them?*" Elijah repeats, incredulous. "What do you mean, *let them?*"

"Come on," I mutter as I walk into my living room. "Like you wouldn't want to have a *chat* with the man Valeria will someday marry. They're just trying to prove a point, making sure that I'm aware they can get to me at any time if I don't treat their sister right, so yes, let them in."

"Just so you know — I won't come save your ass if you turn out to be wrong about them."

I chuckle, unable to help it. "When have I ever needed saving?"

He sighs and ends the call, and I sit down on my sofa in anticipation. Six minutes later, my doors open, followed by loud, rushed footsteps. I have to give it to them, they're efficient and quick, because I don't quite get a glimpse of them before they put a fabric bag over my head and bind my hands behind my back. I pretend to struggle, trying my best to fight my instincts lest I accidentally hurt my future brothers-in-law, and they drag me away.

They don't say a word as they throw me in a vehicle, and on instinct, I begin to map out the route, carefully counting the time since we left and each turn I can feel them take. I smirk to myself when I realize they're likely taking me to one of my own damn warehouses.

"Don't bother," I hear Dion say as I'm pulled out of a car and directed into the warehouse, before I'm shoved in a chair. "He knows it's us. I told you guys this was a stupid idea."

"How do you know?" I hear Luca ask.

"He hasn't asked a single question, and though he has a black belt in jiujitsu and Krav Maga, he hasn't used any of his signature moves — which is a good thing, because he'd have broken several of our bones."

Shit. Dion knows me far too well. I should've resisted harder and shouted or some shit. Lex pulls the bag off my head, and I force myself to keep my expression neutral. "Boys," I murmur, leaning back in my seat.

This warehouse might look abandoned, but it isn't, and I just know that Elijah is watching us on the cameras. By now he's probably called Hunter and Zach, and hell, maybe even Mom and Dad too. Hunter would've likely made popcorn by now, and Zach would be providing a running commentary on every single thing that happens. I just know they're going to turn this footage into memes that'll haunt me for the rest of my life, but what can I do? I can't disappoint my future in-laws either. I just hope Mom won't let them replay this at our next meeting — I'm not sure I'll survive the embarrassment.

"Let's have a chat," Ares says, dragging a chair closer. The sound would've been eerie to anyone but me, and judging by the look on Dion's face, he knows I'm not exactly intimidated. I crouch a little, trying to play the part. I don't want them to feel like I'm cocky, or like I don't take their concerns and love for their sister seriously. "My grandmother will lay down some rules, but so will we. Just because we supported you in asking for her hand doesn't mean we're handing over our sister without keeping an eye on her. We do not trust you unconditionally — we don't trust *anyone* unconditionally when it comes to Sierra's happiness."

"I would expect no less of you," I reply earnestly, though I can't help but admit that I'm a little concerned about the rules they're referring to. Sierra already seems intent on making things more difficult than they need to be, and I don't particularly want the Windsor brothers interfering in my marriage, but the least I can do is hear them out.

Zane rummages through the tools I have on site and grabs a wrench, and I only just about keep from sighing. He doesn't have a bad bone in his body, so the sight he's presenting me with is honestly more endearing than anything else. I have no doubt these men would hurt me severely if I were to mistreat their sister, but right now, there's no need for me to fear them.

"You'll respect her autonomy," Ares says. "That includes her bodily autonomy."

My eyes widen, and I look away, unable to face them at the mere insinuation of me sleeping with Sierra. "Of course," I reply instantly, trying not to take offense. I'd never touch her against her will, and they don't need to know just how much she *does* want me.

"You'll be faithful to her," Luca says. "I don't know who that girl is you're often with, but if you cheat on Sierra, you'll never sleep with a woman again."

My eyes meet Dion's, and he throws me a sympathetic look. He's the only person I've ever told about Valeria, and even he didn't know until about a year ago. "I don't think that'll be an issue," he says, amusement crossing his face. "He hasn't slept with anyone in years. I doubt he's going to start messing around now."

My eyes fall closed in embarrassment. "Fucking hell, Dion," I mutter. I sigh as I glance back at the Windsor brothers, surprised to find such palpable relief on their faces. Had they actually been worried about that, even remotely?

"Be patient with her," Dion says, his voice soft. "She'll need time to adjust, and though we think you might just be perfect for her, she won't see it that way. It'll be hard for her to leave her family, to suddenly not be a Windsor anymore when she's always taken such pride in being part of our family. Make sure she feels welcome in your home, and help her connect with your family. Sierra would never admit it to you, but she always hoped to have in-laws that would love her, since we lost our parents so young."

Lex nods. "Don't resent her for not reciprocating your feelings, or for not responding the way you might want. She's a romantic, but she's slow to trust, and she might not let you in easily. If you can win her over, she'll love you for the rest of your lives. She doesn't love easily, but she loves deeply."

"Don't give up on her," Zane adds, his voice sounding pained. "Marriage isn't easy, Xavier, especially not when it's arranged. If you're going to marry her, *commit* to her, even at times when it's hard. Promise me that even if she shatters your heart into pieces, all those broken shards will still belong to her, and you'll give her a chance to put them back together."

I look at them and nod, my expression earnest. "I promise," I tell them. "I'm going to do everything in my power to make her happy, no matter what it takes. You have absolutely nothing to worry about. I will always respect her and her decisions, in every single way." They hear the unspoken implication — I'll place her happiness above mine, always, no matter what.

Lex grabs a bag and pulls out a bottle of whiskey. "Honestly, just release him," he says, sounding defeated. "Dion was right. He's fucking smitten with her. What were we even thinking?"

Twenty-One

SIERRA

I stare at the framed photo of my parents on their own wedding day, wishing they could see me in my wedding dress today. Would Mom have given me any marital advice, and would Dad have had tears in his eyes as he walked me down the aisle? Would he have given Xavier a stern warning, and told me I could always come home to him if I wanted to?

I draw a shaky breath, teetering on the verge of tears. I miss them more than ever before, and I wish they could've been here with me today. Perhaps my heart wouldn't ache as much if they were.

"Sierra?"

I look up at the sound of Celeste's voice, and the edges of my lips turn up when I see my five sisters-in-law entering the room in matching bespoke emerald Raven Windsor Couture gowns. Celeste holds up the hairpin I gave her when she married Zane, and tears fill my eyes. It was my mother's.

"You once told me that this would bring the wearer happiness," she says as she approaches me, her touch gentle as she slides it into my elaborate hairdo. "And it did, Sierra. It brought me happiness beyond anything I ever could've dreamed of, and now it's your turn."

"I also told you that I'd ask for it back when I was ready. Today isn't... this isn't real."

My sisters-in-law all smile and exchange glances. It's clear they believe I'll be like them, and this union will result in the happily ever after they've all found, and I don't know how to explain to them that it's different for me. Xavier and I are different.

"Even if you have a second wedding ceremony someday, you'll always remember this one as the day you legally became Mrs. Kingston. Besides, I'd argue that you need the hairpin a lot more today than you will in the future."

"On that note," Val says, stepping forward with a set of documents. "Together with your brothers, we have all decided to gift you 15% of our companies. That way, you'll never lose your ties to us, and even if everything goes to hell and you choose to walk away from the company you'll now share with Xavier, you will have this."

I stare at them in disbelief. They're giving me *millions* that they've all worked so incredibly hard for. How could they possibly have known that I've been feeling anxious about no longer being a Windsor? The closer we got to the wedding, the more I began to feel like everything would change, and I'd lose a part of myself forever. I tried to suggest that I keep the Windsor name, but Grandma absolutely wouldn't have it.

Faye gently wraps her hand over my shoulder. "Of course we all hope things will work out," she says carefully. "But that doesn't mean we won't do everything in our power to ensure you maintain a certain level of independence from Xavier."

Raven smiles shakily. "You will always have us, Sierra, but we all know that you'd never ask for our help, so we hope you'll at least accept this — the means to always jump back on your own two feet, until you're stable enough to reach out your hand and take mine."

"I think he might pleasantly surprise us," Raya says, handing me a jewelry box with the illustrious Laurier logo on it. "Xavier asked me to give this to you, and it came with a note."

I raise a brow when I open up the box to find a stunning and priceless diamond choker inside, the clasp set with tiny blue diamonds. My hand trembles as I unfold the note, my heart racing.

Dear Kitten,

I deeply regret to inform you that I have decided not to leave you at the altar, much to your disappointment, I'm sure.

Time for your first act — pretending you're overjoyed with this gift. It's the first of many I'll shower you with throughout our marriage, and nothing will bring me greater joy than seeing you wear it as you walk down the aisle toward me. I picked the best diamonds I could find, and yet, they don't shine as brightly as you do.

I'll be waiting at the altar; a million years and a day, if that's what it takes.

Forever yours,
Xavier

Forever yours? Is that a threat? I don't even realize I'm smiling until I hear my sisters-in-law chuckling, their tones teasing as they begin to question the contents of the note. I pull it to my chest as Faye leans in to take a look, my cheeks blazing. There isn't anything particularly intimate about it, but it still feels private.

"There is more," Raven says, the sweetest smile on her face as she hands me another box, a note stuck on top of it. "This is from Xavier's mother."

I pause, startled. His *mother*? I've only ever seen her in passing, and she's always looked formidable and intimidating. She has a certain kind of aura that makes her feel entirely unapproachable, and she's always struck me as someone you don't want to mess with. My hand trembles as I reach for the note. It hadn't yet occurred to me that the Kingstons haven't taken an interest in this wedding, and I should've wondered why.

Dear Sierra,

By the end of the day, you will be my daughter-in-law, and I couldn't be more thrilled to welcome you into our family. I hope you aren't upset I haven't reached out before — Xavier made me promise not to.

In the box you'll find a bracelet my mother gave me on my wedding day. I was hoping you'd wear it as your 'something borrowed', but please know that you don't have to.

I can't wait to finally get to know you, Sierra, and above all else, thank you.

Thank you for marrying my fool of a son.

All my love,
Gabriela (though I'd love it if you'd call me mom)

"Wow," I whisper, feeling far more touched by her note than I expected to be. I'm shaking as Faye helps me put on the simple silver chain, one single tiny pendant on it that looks a little like a blue eye.

"It's to ward off evil," Raya explains, smiling. "She's likely hoping it'll shield you from any negativity or ill-wishes."

My heart warms, and I smile when the door opens, and Grandma walks in. She pauses by the door, her eyes filling with tears. "Oh, my little girl," she says, her voice trembling. "You look beautiful."

"So do you, Grandma."

"Are you ready, honey?"

No. "Yes," I reply, happy to see her looking so radiant today. This is the healthiest I've seen her look since I found out about her diagnosis, and in part, I have Xavier to thank for it.

My sisters-in-law walk out of the cabin my brothers built inside the maze, through the secret doors disguised as hedges, and I smile at the thought of Xavier having to find his way through.

As if Grandma knows what I'm thinking, she leans in, her shoulder brushing against mine. "Xavier and his family arrived by helicopter," she tells me, her tone amused.

"He *what*?"

She bursts out laughing and takes my hand. "You've met your match, sweet girl, and I'm beyond grateful I get to live to see you marry him."

Twenty-Two

XAVIER

I nervously adjust my bowtie as I take a look at our wedding guests. There are only a handful of chairs, and they're taken up by the Windsor boys, my parents, and Valeria. Sierra has made it clear she doesn't want anyone to know about us, and I fucking hate it. If Dion hadn't reminded me that it'd be easier to give our marriage a real chance when no one is watching our every move, I'd have invited every damn person I know. Instead of that, I'm following Sierra's lead, trying by best to remain as patient as I have been for years.

A violin begins to play, and Sierra's sisters-in-law walk down the aisle, reassuring smiles on their faces. Nerves instantly assault me, and I shift my weight from one foot to the other. She hasn't changed her mind, has she? "Chill," Zach whispers. "She'll be here." I take a deep breath, hoping he's right. I wouldn't put it past her to just run off and leave me standing here, waiting for her in vain.

The girls all take their places, and at last, she appears at the end of the aisle, on her grandmother's arm. She looks like my wildest dreams come to life, and my entire body reacts at the sight of her.

Fuck. I can't believe she's about to become *my wife*. In what world does someone like me get to marry *Sierra Windsor?*

Our eyes lock, and she looks as nervous as I feel, a tinge of heartbreak in her eyes. Today is a dream come true for me, but it's clear to her this is nothing but a nightmare she's trying to live through. Her grandmother places Sierra's trembling hand in mine, her eyes on her granddaughter. "I love you," Anne says, her voice breaking.

"I love you more," Sierra replies, her voice soft, pained. When she turns to face me, all of that love drains away, until there's nothing but resentment in her beautiful eyes. It hurts, but all that matters is that she's here with me. "Put away those claws, Kitten," I murmur, teasing her. "You don't want to accidentally damage your new toy, do you?"

She rolls her eyes and leans in. "There'd be nothing accidental about it, Xavier," she whispers. "You'll be lucky if you survive the night."

I can't help but laugh, my heart racing at the thought of having her in my bed. It's crazy to think that this beautiful woman is about to become mine.

"We have gathered here today to witness the marriage of Xavier Kingston and Sierra Windsor," Zach says, stepping forward to officiate for us.

I tighten my grip on Sierra's hand, and she raises her head to look into my eyes. "You look ethereal," I whisper. "That necklace looks as gorgeous on you as I imagined."

The compliment catches her off guard, and my heart skips a beat when she blushes beautifully. She looks at me like she's finally really seeing me, and I can't help but smirk when her gaze roams over my body in appreciation. Her eyes lock with mine, and I chuckle softly, pleased with the desire I see in them. I'm so taken with her that I don't snap out of my daze until I hear Zach say my name.

"Do you, Xavier, take Sierra to be your lawfully wedded wife, to have and to hold, to love and to cherish, from this day forward, for better or for worse, for richer or poorer, in sickness and in health?"

Her breath hitches, and I smile, my heart overflowing with tenderness. "I do." There's not a beat of hesitation in my voice. I've waited long enough to say these words.

Elijah grins and steps forward with our rings, and I note the surprise on Sierra's face when I take the diamond eternity ring and slip it onto her finger. It isn't the kind of ring you could mistake for anything but a wedding ring, and seeing it on her hand brings me a strange kind of satisfaction.

Zach turns to Sierra, and I watch her as panic begins to cross her face. "Do you, Sierra, take Xavier to be your lawfully wedded husband, to have and to hold, to love and to cherish, from this day forward, for better or for worse, for richer or poorer, in sickness and in health?"

Her eyes widen a fraction, something akin to regret clouding those beautiful emeralds. She lowers her eyes and draws a shaky breath. "I do." She doesn't say it with as much conviction, but fuck, just hearing her say the words is such a relief. Her hand trembles as she takes the thick gold wedding band from Elijah and slides it onto my finger.

"It is my honor to pronounce you husband and wife. Welcome to the family, Sierra," Zach says, earning himself a sweet smile from my wife. "Xavier, you may now kiss your beautiful bride."

I grin and gently reach for her, my hand slipping around the back of her neck as I tilt my head, my lips hovering over hers for a moment. Sierra's breath hitches, and her eyes fall closed when my lips meet hers. I'd planned to make it a quick peck, but one touch, and all my willpower fades away. I pull her flush against me, deepening our kiss, and my beautiful wife responds by rising to her tiptoes, her hand wrapping into my hair as she parts her lips for me.

It isn't until I become aware of my brothers' chuckles that I pull away, my heart racing and my body thrumming with desire. Sierra looks just as flustered, and I can't help but smile happily. She can pretend all she'd like, but it's clear she wants me. It isn't much, but it's enough for now.

"Mr. and Mrs. Kingston, everyone!" Zach announces, and

Sierra smiles back at me shyly before we turn to face our families, and all the while, I can't take my eyes off her.

I watch as her smile slips, shock mingling with betrayal when she finds Valeria sitting next to our mother, and it kills me to know that I'm the reason she looks so hurt. I've tried to think about how to tell her about what happened to Valeria and why there's so much secrecy around her, but my words continue to fail me, and I just don't know where to start. My wife looks down, her shoulders slumping, and my heart wrenches as I silently vow to fix my mistakes.

Twenty-Three

SIERRA

My heart feels heavy as we walk into Zane and Celeste's rose garden, where we're holding a small reception. Faye begins to play the piano as we walk in, and I try my best to force a smile.

"Those papers you just signed?" Xavier says, reaching for my hand and holding on tightly. "They included a non-disclosure agreement."

"I'm aware," I tell him, trying to pull my hand out of his. "*My* lawyers drew that up."

He just smiles cryptically and keeps hold of my hand. "I thought you said you wanted to put on a good act for your grandmother?"

I instantly cease my attempts to break free from him and sigh, throwing him a veiled glare that he pretends not to notice. Xavier chuckles and leans in, his lips brushing over my ear. "How will you make it through the photos and the cake cutting, let alone our first dance? You're a terrible actress, Mrs. Kingston." My heart skips a beat at the way he addresses me. "What?" Xavier whispers, before sneakily pressing a kiss just below my ear. "Do you like the sound of that, Mrs. Kingston?"

I place my hand against his chest, noting the way his heart is racing just as fast as mine as I rise to my tiptoes and brush my lips against his ear. "Not at all. If I look even remotely excited, it's because I was planning how to kill you in your sleep. Do you have a preferred way to go? Poison, perhaps?"

He laughs and grabs the back of my neck, his gaze heated. "I do, actually," he says, pulling my body flush against his, a mere inch between our lips. "I'd love to suffocate between your thighs."

I gasp, and my reaction only makes him laugh harder, his forehead pressed against mine. "Fuck," he murmurs. "I'm going to enjoy finding ways to make you all flustered. I didn't think you could get more beautiful than the way you look when you glare at me, your gorgeous eyes sparkling and your cheeks all flushed... but this? Yeah, this'll become my new favorite pastime."

"You're crazy," I tell him, pulling away a little.

"Oh baby, you don't know the half of it." I raise a brow, and he straightens a little, pulling away. "That craziness? I get it from my mom, who is walking toward us right now."

Nerves suddenly rush through me, and I find myself squeezing Xavier's hand. He smiles at me endearingly and lets go of my hand, opting to wrap his arm around me instead. "Mom," he says, his tone carrying a hint of warning. "Dad."

"Sierra," Xavier's mom says, instantly enveloping me in a tight hug. "It's so good to finally meet you. I've heard so much about you throughout the years."

"All lies, I'm sure," I tell her, smiling nervously as she pulls back.

"So you're telling me you didn't slash all of Xavier's tires recently?" Xavier's dad asks.

I throw him my most innocent look. "His tires? How would one even go about slashing those?"

Xavier's mother bursts out laughing and grabs my hand, her expression filled with approval when she notices the bracelet I'm wearing. "I have a feeling you're going to fit into our family just fine," she says, and my heart warms instantly. I'd never admit it to Xavier, but one thing I always wanted out of my marriage was loving in-laws that treated me like their own daughter. I always wanted to know what it'd be like to have a mom, and the way Gabriela is smiling at me makes me wonder if maybe I'll have that with her, even if it's only for a few years.

Our family members form a little line behind Xavier's parents, and I grin as each of my brothers hug me tightly, before turning to Xavier and shaking his hand with entirely too much force. Before long, it's his brothers that are congratulating us, and they each take delight in hugging me just a little too long, clearly in an attempt to get on Xavier's nerves.

"Stop being a dick, Hunter," a soft female voice says, and I raise a brow when I spot Valeria behind him. Hunter lets go of me, and I stare at her in disbelief as she steps forward. It's one thing for Xavier to invite her. It's something else for her to actually show up on his wedding day. The mere sight of her, here, in my brother's observatory, fills me with a new kind of rage.

"Welcome to the family, Sierra," she says, smiling nervously. I raise a brow in confusion, and she pushes her hair behind her ear with a trembling hand. "I've always wanted a sister, and I'm honestly so excited to have a sister-in-law. My mother and I are always outnumbered at dinner, but I have a feeling we may just be able to shift the tides with you on our side."

I stare at her in pure disbelief. "You're Xavier's *sister*?" I glance at my husband then, unable to comprehend what she's saying. "But you don't have a sister."

He reaches for my hand and squeezes tightly, his expression unreadable. "I do," he says, his voice soft. "You just didn't know about her. Very few people do."

"I tried to tell you that time in the bathroom, but I didn't handle it well, and I'm really sorry," Valeria says. "I'd love to make it up to you, if you'll give me a chance. Xavier told me you love cookies, and I love baking..."

"It's a date," I tell her, feeling incredibly awkward as I begin to think back to what she actually said. I'd been so jealous that I wasn't really listening, and I only have myself to blame for it.

Valeria grins happily, seemingly not holding my past behavior against me, and Xavier raises our joined hands to his lips. "Care to dance with me, Mrs. Kingston?" he asks.

I nod, grateful for the reprieve. "Look at me," he says as our song begins to play, his voice soft, pleading. I lift my face as we take our positions for the tango. "There's a reason why we keep Valeria so well-protected and out of the media. No one knows she's my sister, Kitten. I'll... I'll tell you everything someday, I promise."

I'm quiet as we follow our usual steps, my mind whirling. I accused him of being romantically involved with his *sister*. No wonder he told me the mere insinuation was sickening. I just wasn't listening. My leg hooks around Xavier's thigh, our eyes locking. "I'm sorry," I tell him, my voice quiet. "You should've told me the truth sooner, but I should've listened more carefully to what you did tell me too."

He merely smiles at me without a hint of blame. "You don't have a thing to be sorry about — except maybe my poor tires."

I grin at him. "Says the man that *stole* my design plans. They were worth a lot more than your stupid tires."

He laughs as he twirls me around and dips me, his gaze heated. "About as much as your jewelry, I suppose."

"Don't be ridiculous. My jewelry is priceless. Your tires were replaceable."

His eyes twinkle, something I can't quite read in them. "I suppose it's time I return your jewelry, hmm?"

"I thought you said you wouldn't return it until you got what you wanted?"

He pulls me against him, both of us straightening. "I did. I got exactly what I wanted, Sierra. You."

Twenty-Four

XAVIER

Sierra can barely look me in the eye as we walk out of the observatory together, toward the limousine that's waiting for us. She blushes so beautifully when I open the door for her, only to tense slightly, her smile withering away as she sits down. It isn't until I join her that I realize why.

Opposite my wife sit her grandmother and both of my parents, cryptic smiles on their faces. "What is the meaning of this?" I ask, irritated. Sierra finally seemed to let her guard down by the end of the night, only for these three to ruin everything.

"Congratulations on your wedding, kids," Anne says, smiling tightly.

Mom nods. "Welcome to the Kingston family, Sierra. Roger and I are both beyond thrilled to have you."

"Indeed," he says. "However, as you're well aware, this is an arranged marriage and a business merger. As such, it comes with a set of rules."

Rules? They must be joking. So far, I've had to listen to rules from Sierra, and then her brothers, and now this? "They are meant to ensure you give your marriage a true chance," Anne explains, smiling sweetly. "Though the merger is mutually benefi-cial, we wouldn't want to do it at the expense of your happiness. Your parents and I firmly believe you can have both — your happiness and a thriving business, provided you're willing to work for it."

"We'll only give you a few rules to abide by," Dad says. "First of all, you must be faithful to each other. Should one of you stray, you both lose everything, and your company will fall into the hands of your siblings."

I clench my jaw and nod, irritated. The mere insinuation that I'd ever cheat on Sierra is ridiculous. I know she doesn't like me all that much, but I know her, and she'd never cheat either.

"Secondly," Sierra's grandmother says. "You must share a bed every night, and you can't be apart for more than two weeks over a six month period. You cannot have separate lives or bedrooms."

Sierra tenses, but personally, that's a rule I can get behind. I hadn't been sure what to expect of our marriage, and Sierra has pointedly refused to talk to me privately since I saw her at the charity gala. I figured I'd have quite the battle ahead of me, but this might just make things easier.

"Third and final rule," Mom says. "You must remain married for a period of three years. If, after that time, either of you wishes for a divorce, you'll be granted one with your assets being split per the pre-nuptial agreement you both signed."

Three years... is that enough time to make her fall for me? "Understood," I tell them, uneasy.

Sierra nods too, seemingly just as uncertain about our situation as I am. "Sierra," her grandmother says. "You'll start off your marriage at Xavier's residence, and I expect you to live there for at least six months. If, after that, you both would like to spend some time in your old home, you can. Raven has already arranged for your things to be moved to Xavier's house. You should find every-thing you need."

I breathe a sigh of relief. If her grandmother had allowed us to stay on the Windsor Estate, she'd find countless reasons to never be around me.

"What?" She looks out the window and realizes we've left the Windsor Estate. "But I thought..."

She thought we'd spend our wedding night at her house? I suppose it would've made sense, since our wedding took place on the Windsor Estate, but I'd much rather have her in my own bed tonight.

"For the first three months, you're exempt from attending family events. I'd like you both to focus on your marriage, and give each other a real chance," Mom says.

"Promise me," Anne says. "Both of you. Promise me that you'll actively try to make this marriage work."

Sierra tenses, clearly not comfortable with lying to her grandmother. I reach for her hand, and she looks into my eyes as I entwine our fingers. "I promise," I say, my eyes never leaving hers. She takes a shaky breath and nods. "Me too," she replies, her voice barely above a whisper.

I squeeze her hand as my parents and her grandmother begin to discuss the merger, and Sierra holds onto my hand tightly. She watches the scenery pass by, and I watch her, my heart beating faster the closer we get to my house.

"We will proceed with the merger within the following months, but considering the complexity of the deal, it will take several months just to get the paperwork done," Mom explains as we drive through our gates, and I nod, trying my best not to let on that I couldn't care less about the merger.

"Remember your promise," my dad says as we pull up in front of my house, and I nod as I step out of the car and offer Sierra my hand. She takes it hesitantly, her expression conflicted. Her eyes narrow when I smirk at her, and she gasps when I sweep her off my feet and into my arms.

"What are you doing?" she asks, outraged.

I chuckle as I carry her to my front door. "Putting on an act. Isn't that what you told me to do?"

She relaxes in my arms, seemingly placated by my lie. Truth is, I just want to carry my wife over the threshold and into my home, but there's no way she'd let me if I told her that. The door swings open automatically as I approach, courtesy of my security team, and I grin as I carry her straight through the house and into my bedroom.

"Put me down," she says, her voice filled with the same venom I've gotten used to.

"I don't want to."

"Xavier, I swear, I'll bite you," she warns, shifting in my arms to brush her lips over my neck.

I swallow down a needy moan at the feel of her lips on such a sensitive part of my throat. "Don't threaten me with a good time, Kitten."

She stiffens, almost like she's only just realized what she's doing, and I laugh as I gently lower her to the floor, loving how beautifully she's blushing. "You're fucking breathtaking, you know that?"

She looks at me like she isn't sure if she should believe me, and I sigh as I reach for her. Sierra steps back and turns around, seemingly flustered. I watch her as she walks through my room, her curious gaze roaming over every little detail.

"You act like you've never been here before, but I know for a fact that you've snuck into my bedroom several times." She looks up sharply, surprised I'd know that. "I always wondered, you know? The camera in the hallway showed you sneaking into my room, but nothing was ever amiss. So what did you do in here?"

"I have no idea what you're talking about," she denies, her voice pitched higher than usual. I smirk as she walks into my walk-in wardrobe, only to pause in shock. "*Raven*," she mutters, sounding aggrieved.

I follow her in and bite back a smile when I realize half the room is now filled with Sierra's clothes, some I've seen her wearing before, and some that look brand new. My wife rummages through her things and blushes fiercely when she pulls out some scraps of red lace that I think are supposed to be pajamas. "How could she?"

Sierra grumbles. I peek over her shoulder and read the note Raven left.

> *You once bought something similar for me, and you were right, so the very least I can do is reciprocate. Thank me later! Love you!*
>
> *PS. Good luck getting your wedding gown off without Xavier's help. I made the buttons at the back too tiny and too numerous for you to do it yourself.*

I can't help but laugh, and she pulls the note to her chest as she glares at me, her eyes sparkling absolutely beautifully. "Need some help, Kitten?"

Twenty-Five

SIERRA

"Need some help, Kitten?" Xavier asks, his voice a unique blend of seduction and amusement. I crumple up Raven's note, shocked I didn't see this coming. After all, she learned all of that cunning behavior of hers from *me*.

I glare at my husband, unwilling to admit that I do, in fact, need his help. Instead, I throw the note in a drawer and walk over to the mirror, my heart pounding wildly. I'd given Raven a few racy sets of lingerie and nightgowns when she was forced to marry Ares in her older sister's place. She'd always been in love with him, and I was just so certain the feelings were mutual, so for *her*, it was a perfect plan. For me, on the other hand, it's a *disastrous*, terrible plan.

I sigh as I assess my dress. She'd been shockingly gleeful as she helped me into my dress, but I'd been so preoccupied with the thought of marrying *Xavier Kingston* that I completely missed the signs. There's absolutely no way I can get these buttons undone, not unless I rip my dress apart, and she knows I'd never do that to one of her precious creations.

Xavier appears behind me and places his hands on my shoulders, his expression unreadable. "Let me help you," he says, his voice soft. For once, his tone isn't mocking, nor does he appear to be teasing me.

I nod almost imperceptibly, and he smiles at me sweetly as he places his hands at the top of the long row of buttons. He works quietly, taking his time to undo them one by one, his fingers softly caressing my spine as more and more of my skin is revealed. His touch elicits a soft shiver, and I blush fiercely, scared he'll mock me for being so affected by such simple actions.

I lift my head to look in the mirror, and my heart begins to beat wildly when I notice that his sharp cheekbones seem a little flushed, his gaze heated. I bite down on my lip when my dress comes undone and hold it up at my chest, our eyes meeting in the mirror. Xavier leans in and presses a soft kiss to the back of my neck, his touch featherlight. I gasp, and he steps back, the edges of his lips turned up, like he's suppressing a smile.

I rush past him and reach for one of his t-shirts instead of the red lacy nightgown Raven left me, and Xavier chuckles as I disappear into his bathroom. My heart pounds so wildly I'm certain I can hear it, and the thought of walking out in nothing but a pair of panties and this t-shirt that smells so much like him has me feeling far more flustered than I could've imagined. I've joined Raven's fashion campaigns a few times, and nudity doesn't really bother me, but somehow, I'm feeling a little shy tonight.

"Sierra," Xavier says when I walk back out with my dress in my hands. "How about a glass of champagne?"

I drape my gown over an armchair in the corner and raise a brow. "Champagne?" I ask, noting he's already taken off his bow tie, suit jacket, and cufflinks. His gaze roams over my body, and I'm hyperaware of the fact that he can probably see the outline of my nipples through his ridiculously soft t-shirt. Considering the countless pins in my updo, there's no easy way for me to hide behind my hair either.

"I could do with a drink. What about you?"

I nod hesitantly. I'm far too nervous to even look at his bed, and

I'm not too sure how to behave, what to do or say. He smiles and tips his head toward his kitchen, and I follow him hesitantly. Xavier glances at my bare feet and frowns before leaning in and sweeping me into his arms. "You shouldn't walk on the cold marble floor barefoot," he says, holding me tightly. "I'll buy you some slippers tomorrow."

I stare at him in disbelief, unsure what to make of him. He seems different tonight — sweeter, more thoughtful, and I hate how much hope it gives me. Xavier gently places me on top of his kitchen counter and rummages through his wine fridge, until he pulls out an expensive looking bottle of champagne that just so happens to be my favorite kind, a blanc de noir.

He hands me a glass and holds up his own. "To new beginnings," he says, his eyes on mine.

I nod and tap my glass against his, my heart racing. "You have good taste," I murmur, surprised how good the champagne is.

"Of course I do," he remarks, without missing a beat. "I married *you*, didn't I?"

I blink at the cheesy line and burst out laughing, unable to help it. "That was... that was kind of cute."

He smiles sheepishly and places his glass down before moving to stand in front of me, his hands on either side of me. "I can be cute," he says, his voice soft. "There are a lot of sides of me you've never seen before, Sierra. You don't know me as well as you think you do."

I instinctively reach for him and wrap my hand around the back of his neck. "No," I whisper. "I guess I don't."

His expression falls, and he sighs as he reaches for my hair, surprising me when he begins to pull out my hair pins carefully. My hand slides to his chest, and I keep it there as he moves closer, parting my legs to stand between them. "Why didn't you tell me she was your sister?" I ask as my hair slowly begins to come undone. "How is it even possible for you to have a sister that no one knows about?"

He caresses my hair and carefully frames it around my face, his touch so tender that I hardly recognize him. "It isn't my story to tell,

Kitten. Valeria left home when she was twenty and disappeared. She didn't come back until five years later, and life hasn't been the same since, for any of us. Not even Dion knew about her until about a year ago."

"I wish you'd told me," I whisper. It hurts that they waited to tell me until I signed a non-disclosure agreement this morning, but I understand wanting to protect your family. I just wish I knew why they've gone to such lengths. Even when Valeria attends events with Xavier, he ensures there are no photographers on site, and she's never been mentioned by name in any of the papers. That kind of silence from such vicious media outlets comes at a high cost.

He cups my face, his eyes darkening. "I'm a little glad I didn't. If not for that, I'd never have gotten to see you acting jealous."

"Jealous?" I repeat, outraged. "I was *never* jealous."

"No?" he asks, placing his index finger underneath my chin. "Sure could've fooled me."

Twenty-Six

XAVIER

I pull my wife a little closer, loving the way she's snuggled up to me in her sleep, her head on my chest and her leg wrapped around my hip. I bite down on my lip and softly caress her thigh, my need for her overwhelming. My cock twitches when she shifts a little as she stirs, a soft sigh escaping her lips as she brushes her nose against my neck. I keep my eyes closed and my body still as she begins to wake up, her entire body tensing when she realizes what position we're in.

She gasps and sits up, the sheets falling away from me. I can feel her eyes on me, and just as I'm about to tease her for staring, I feel the tip of her finger lightly touch my abs. She holds still, almost like she's trying to see if it'll wake me up, before she explores my body further. It takes all of me to keep my eyes closed as she moves her hand to my chest and slowly drags her fingers down, taking her time to tease me with her featherlight touches. My heart is pounding wildly by the time she reaches the waistband of my boxer shorts, and I hear her breath hitch as she hesitantly touches the contours of my rock hard cock. I involuntarily moan softly, my head falling back just a touch, and just like that, her hand is gone. I hear the sheets rustle, followed by her soft footsteps as she escapes into the bathroom.

I smirk as my eyes flutter open, the room empty. It'd be pretty safe to assume that my wife quite likes my body. It hadn't occurred to me that I could use my body to tempt her with. If I'd known, I'd have taken off my shirt last night, long before she fell asleep on the sofa after a few too many glasses of champagne. Our evening wasn't exactly what I wish it'd been, but it was nice to sit with her and throw little jabs back and forth, neither of us quite sure where we stood with the other.

I sigh as I get up and walk over to my guest bathroom, not wanting to lose a moment with her. I know her well enough to know she'll be back at the office bright and early tomorrow morning, which only gives me today with her before she'll begin to hide behind work.

I smirk when I find Sierra in our kitchen wearing yet another one of my t-shirts, and she looks over her shoulder when I walk in, only to do a double take, her eyes slowly roaming over my bare chest and settling on my gray sweats. "Morning, my darling wife."

Her eyes shoot up to mine, and she blushes so fiercely that I can't help but chuckle. "Good morning," she says, sounding a little breathless. A drop of water runs from my wet hair, over my neck, and down my abs, and she follows its journey with wide eyes. "Your, um... your hair is wet."

I run a hand through it, loving the way she's looking at me. I've never seen her look at me that way before, and fuck if it isn't the most thrilling thing I've experienced in years. I hum noncommittally as I walk up to her and stand behind her, my fingers brushing over the hem of my t-shirt. "I see you've taken a liking to my t-shirts."

I place my hand on her waist and look over her shoulder at what she's doing. My sweet wife seems to have assembled all the cheese varieties I bought for her, along with some kind of weird contraption that definitely isn't mine.

"It's Raven's fault," she says, her tone disgruntled. "She didn't give me any comfortable clothes at all. Everything she sent over is either highly inappropriate, or it's workwear." She turns to face me, her back against the counter and her eyes on mine. "I should've asked first, I'm sorry. Is it... um, is it okay for me to wear this?"

I place my hands on either side of her, caging her in. "If I say no, will you wear something inappropriate for me?"

"Xavier," she warns. My sweet kitten places her hand against my chest, like she often does when I get a little too close to her, but this time, her breath hitches, and she pulls her hand off me in a rush.

I chuckle and place her palm back on my chest, before slowly dragging it down to my abs, my fingers between hers. "Touch me all you like," I tell her, my tone teasing. "You're my wife, Sierra. I'm all yours."

"I guess I should stop wearing your t-shirts," she says, pulling her hand away with a hint of reluctance. "There clearly aren't enough for us both."

She turns around to face her cheeses again and I smile to myself as I place my chin on her shoulder. "I certainly won't object if you take that t-shirt off."

She gasps, and I chuckle, pleased she hasn't stepped away or told me to fuck off. It isn't much, but she's letting me be near her, and that's a lot more than she'd have given me just a few days ago.

"What is that, Kitten?" I ask, intrigued. "Is that a fucking guillotine?"

She laughs, and the sound is like music to my ears. "Lex made it for me," she explains, sounding a little giddy about it. "It's a cheese slicer in the shape of a guillotine."

"How sharp is it?" I ask, concerned about how close her fingers are getting to it.

"Why don't you put your hand in it, and you'll find out."

I reach for the device and Sierra instantly grabs my hand, bringing it to her chest as she turns back around to face me. "Are you insane?" she snaps. "What the hell, Xavier? That's a *blade*."

I cup her face, noting the way she's trembling. "Be careful what you ask for, Kitten. There isn't much I won't do for you."

She looks into my eyes like she's only just realizing how completely fucking unhinged I can be. Sierra thinks she's seen the worst of me, but she has no fucking idea who I was when I was younger, what I've done. She thinks she knows me well, but it seems she's forgotten that the city we live in was named after us because we founded and ran it with an iron fist. Zach might be the mayor now, but we've always run this town, and it wasn't always through legitimate means.

"Don't ever get hurt on my behalf," she says, her voice barely above a whisper.

"Then I suggest you handle me with care, Mrs. Kingston."

Twenty-Seven

SIERRA

"Come on," Xavier says as soon as we've finished the cheese toasties I made for us. "Let me show you around. You'll be living here, after all."

I bite down on my lip in an attempt to keep from telling him that I know this place *far better* than he could possibly imagine. I've broken in countless times to wreak havoc, and each time I did, I lingered a little longer than I should have, trying my best to learn more about him.

"Let's start here," he says as he leads me to his home office. "Not that you really need an introduction to this specific room," he adds, throwing me a knowing look.

I blush and try to look as innocent as possible, and he grins at me as he grabs my hand and leads me to his desk. He presses my thumb against a near-invisible scanner at the edge of his desk, and the top drawer that I've never been able to get into springs open. I gasp in surprise, my curiosity nearly getting the best of me. I've always wanted to know what he hides in there, since there aren't many hidden spots in his home.

"Everything I own is yours now too," he says, his voice soft. "Nothing is off-limits to you anymore."

Xavier lets go of my hand and reaches for the documents inside, his movements a little hesitant as he spreads them on his desk. "Your new passport, driver's license, and bank cards," he says, his expression unreadable. "That black card there is a duplicate of my own credit card, and it has no limit." I part my lips to object, and he grins. "I'm well aware that you don't need my money, but I still want you to have access to it. Perhaps it sounds strange to you, but I always imagined my wife buying whatever she wants with my card."

I reach for the card, my heart skipping a beat when I realize it says Sierra *Kingston*. It suddenly feels so real, so official, and I can't help but feel a little conflicted. "But you never imagined your wife to be *me*. You should save these kinds of things for the woman you'll eventually marry, after me. That way, it'll still be special."

The thought of him with someone else fills me with unexplained rage, and I try my best to school my features as I place the card back down on his desk. Xavier searches my face, his eyes twinkling with something I can't quite read. "Didn't I?"

"What?" I ask, confused.

He just shakes his head and smiles cryptically as he reaches for my hand and pulls me along. Xavier shows me his gym, the guest bedrooms, his pool and spa, the media room, and the gardens, but all the while, I can't really focus on anything but the fact that he's entwined our fingers, and he hasn't let go once. I should probably object, but oddly enough, I don't want to. His hand feels huge against mine, but in some kind of strange way, it's reassuring too.

"Let me show you my favorite room," he says, side-eyeing me as we walk toward his garage. "Though I'm well aware you're *very* well acquainted with it."

My eyes widen innocently and I wisely keep my retorts to myself, earning myself a husky chuckle. "I'd tell you where to find all the keys," he adds as he reaches for the cupboard that holds his keys, his eyes narrowed. "But you already know where they are."

He lets go of my hand and reaches for one specific key that seems to be shaped like a cat, and I frown when he hands it over. "This is yours," he says, before grabbing my free hand and pulling me to the bespoke matte black supercar on the round platform — the one that nearly got me caught last time. Xavier tips his head toward the new numberplate on it, and I stare at it wide-eyed. MRS. KINGSTON, it reads. "Lexington made it for you. It doesn't have the Windsor Motors branding on it because it's meant to truly be a one-of-a-kind car, so instead, it has an entwined S and K as its logo. It's armored and bulletproof."

I frown in confusion, mentally doing the math. Our engagement was announced two months ago, but I know my brother and his work better than most, and it would've taken him at least a year to build this kind of car. I suppose it's not impossible for him to have done it quicker if he prioritized it above all his other work, but still. It doesn't really add up.

"I can't drive that," I murmur, my face blazing hot. "The media would lose its mind."

Xavier looks at the numberplate and sighs. "Someday," he says, his voice barely above a whisper. He clears his throat and runs a hand through his hair. "Come on, there are two more rooms I have to show you."

I frown in surprise, certain this is all of it. I've spent many hours sneaking through his house in the last couple of years, and I know for a fact that there aren't any more rooms. Xavier turns and heads toward the exit, and I instinctively grab his hand. He looks down in surprise, and I quickly pull my hand out of his again, realizing what I just did. The way he smiles as he grabs my hand and holds on tightly makes my heart skip a beat, and I look away, unable to face him.

"I think you'll like this, though not as much as you'll like the last room," he says as he leads me back toward our dressing room.

I gasp when he pushes against one of the panels against the wall, and it slides open, revealing a walk-in vault similar to my own. "No wonder you were able to find mine," I grumble, and he chuckles as his hand wraps around my shoulder, and I try my best not to notice how delicious he smells, and how incredible his abs look up close. I secretly touched them this morning, and it was almost like I was in some kind of trance. I didn't even fully realize what I was doing until he groaned, and I've been wanting to touch him again ever since, certain that I imagined how his body felt.

"Here we go," he says, pausing in front of countless jewelry sets that have been put on display beautifully. "I promised I'd return this to you when I got what I wanted."

I step closer, my fingers trailing over the heirloom piece my grandmother gave me, before I take a moment to really take in everything else. All the pieces he gifted me are here, right along with everything he stole. "You commissioned those pieces from Laurier long before we got engaged," I begin to say, unable to comprehend his thought process. "Why?"

He simply shrugs. "You like Laurier jewelry, and I wanted you to wear something that you'd love, but that'd make you think of me. Nothing else I did seemed to get to you, so I thought this might."

I narrow my eyes at him. "So you were trying to ruin my favorite jewelry brand for me."

He barks out a laugh and runs a hand through his hair, not realizing how incredibly sexy he looks when he does that, his entire torso on display, and his sweats hanging low on his hips.

I glance back at the jewelry on display as he tips his head toward the end of the room. He supposedly commissioned ten pieces, but he's only given me eight so far. Who were the other two for? His mother perhaps, or Valeria? I know my wedding ring was made by Laurier too, but he couldn't have ordered it back then, since we weren't engaged yet.

"I think this might become your favorite room," he says, his tone teasing. "It's at the back of the house, so it's not exactly super hidden, but it isn't accessible any other way."

I raise a brow when he grabs my hand and presses my palm against the wall at the back, and it slides open. Xavier pulls me through, and I gasp in disbelief when I find myself standing in the most gorgeous library I've ever seen. It's got two floors, a gorgeous spiral staircase, and more books than I can count. I'm in a daze as I gently touch the spines of some of the books, my surprise mounting when I realize that at least some of them are romance books — and not just any, but special or first editions of most of my favorites.

"How do you have these?" I ask, turning around to face Xavier, not realizing how close he's standing.

"I've read them," he says, leaning in and resting his forearm against the shelf, right next to my head. "They were very informative."

My heart begins to race as I lean back and look into his eyes. "W-were they?" I stammer.

"Yeah," he replies, cupping my face, his thumb brushing over my bottom lip.

I reach for him, fully intending to push him away, but somehow, my hand ends up wrapped around the back of his neck, my eyes on his lips. "What did you learn from them?" I ask, my voice tinged with desire.

Xavier leans in and tilts his head, his mouth inches from mine. "This." His lips come crashing against mine, and I groan when he pushes me flush against the bookcase, my hand threading into his hair. This kiss is different to all the ones before it — it's filled with unbridled desperation that I meet beat for beat.

"I can't believe you're mine," he murmurs before nipping at my bottom lip, only to run his tongue over the seam of my lips in a silent demand to open up for him. Xavier deepens our kiss, his hands roaming over my body hungrily as he grabs my hips and lifts me up, my legs instantly wrapping around him. I moan against his mouth when I feel how hard he is, and he rolls his hips, his hands slipping underneath the t-shirt I'm wearing.

"Wait," I whisper, pulling back when I feel his hands wrap underneath my breasts, his thumbs caressing the underside of it. "Stop." I'm breathing hard, my thoughts a mess.

Xavier carefully lowers me to the floor, his gaze roaming over my face. His hand trembles as he carefully pushes my hair out of my face, and I look into his eyes, feeling more conflicted than ever. I thought I knew what I was getting into when I married him — I was convinced I knew him better than anyone else... but this version of Xavier is one I don't recognize.

Twenty-Eight

SIERRA

I hesitate as I park my car in front of Xavier's garage at nearly ten in the evening, having stayed at the office far longer than I needed to. The thought of facing him makes me nervous in a way it never did before, and it's got everything to do with how weird Xavier's been acting lately, and the way he kissed me in his beautiful library.

He's been so unlike himself that I'm not sure what to make of him. I've taken to avoiding him as best as I can, and much to my surprise, he hasn't said anything about it. It's almost like he expected it. Part of me thought he'd make a fuss and would inconvenience me unnecessarily, but he's merely kept to himself. Most days, it's easy to forget we're married at all, until I get home and find him in our bed without a shirt on, his expression conveying something I could swear is *longing*.

My mornings with him are even worse. He holds me so tightly every morning, and the way his body feels against mine leaves me desperate for him. In a matter of days, he's managed to completely confuse me, and I hate it. I was so certain I knew what I was getting into by marrying him, but I couldn't have been more wrong.

I take a deep breath as I step out of the car, my heart racing as I walk into the house. It's surreal that I live here now, in the same home I've broken into so many times, and I'm not sure I'll ever get used to it. My steps falter as I reach the doorway to Xavier's bedroom and find him sitting in bed, the sheets bunched around his naked torso and his laptop on his lap. He looks up and smiles, and my heart goes wild. "Kitten," he drawls.

"What is with your personal vendetta against tops?" I snap, unable to keep myself from sneaking a few looks at his wide chest and strong arms.

He chuckles and drops his head back against the headboard, looking up at me from lowered lashes. "I wear shirts and ties every day, wifey. Why would I want to wear them at home too?"

Wifey? My face heats at the sound of that word on his lips, and I tear my gaze off him as I rush into the bathroom. I take my time in the shower, trying my best to calm my nerves and failing. He keeps making my heart race, and it's driving me crazy.

Xavier's eyes light up when he spots me walking in wearing one of his t-shirts, and he smirks. "Those look infinitely better on you than they do on me," he remarks when I get into bed with him, his voice soft.

My gaze cuts to his, and I try my best to determine whether or not he's joking, mocking me somehow, but he seems earnest, and it just doesn't make any sense. I narrow my eyes at him and reach for my own laptop, determined to work for another hour and absolutely refusing to let him distract me with his stupid abs and that lazy smirk.

"Place a small coffeeshop there to increase foot traffic," Xavier says, leaning in to look at my screen.

My first instinct is to snap my laptop closed, but I resist and reluctantly acknowledge that he's right. "How did you know I'd been wondering how to increase foot traffic?"

He chuckles and moves closer, throwing his arm around the back of my pillow, not quite close enough to touch my shoulders, but close enough for me to instantly be hyperaware of him. A thrill runs down my spine when he leans in further to take a better look at my screen, giving me a perfect view of his abs as his side presses against my arm. It's unfair how perfect his body is, and I hate that I can't help but notice it.

"I know you," he says, his voice filled with something I can't quite define. Possessiveness, perhaps? "Actually, I think you might just have enough space to put in a food court."

I raise a brow and turn to face him, only to freeze in place when I realize how close he is. My breath hitches, and his gaze drops to my mouth. "This is weird," I whisper. He tenses almost imperceptibly, and I instantly feel compelled to finish my thought, not wanting him to misunderstand. "I'm so used to protecting my projects from your prying eyes and hands that this is a little weird. You're usually trying to steal my projects from me, and I honestly kind of hate to admit that your input is helpful."

Xavier grins and reaches for me, making the butterflies in my stomach go wild. He wraps a strand of my hair around his finger, his gaze roaming over my face. "I've never stolen any of your projects," he denies, grinning in a way I can't quite resist.

"What?" I ask, my voice a lot more husky than I intended. "You've never stolen projects from me? You're kidding me, right?"

He lets go of my hair and lightly caresses my cheek with the tip of his fingers. "Nope. Not a single one."

I stare at him wide-eyed, fury slowly taking hold of me. "You damn liar," I snap. "*Artemis* was mine," I tell him, reminding him of the theatre he stole from me, right along with its design plans. "And don't get me started on how your two best restaurants, *The Siren* and *Renegade,* were both supposed to be mine too." I glare at him as I rack my brain, trying to recall every major project he's stolen from me over the years.

"Didn't steal them," he says, shrugging as his gaze roams over my face, a hint of glee in his irritatingly sexy eyes. "It was simply meant to be. Not even you can fight fate, can you?"

"You absolutely insane bullheaded piece of —" I'm tempted to scream into a pillow, but instead, I turn my head and bite down on the arm he's got wrapped around me.

Xavier tenses his muscles and bursts out laughing as he wraps his hand into my hair. I pull back to look at him, wishing I'd had the heart to actually bite him hard enough to hurt. "You think this is funny?" I all but growl.

He tightens his grip on my hair, his breathing a little uneven as he smiles at me. "Aren't you cute, my sweet little Kitten?" He brings my face closer to his, the feel of his fingers against my scalp doing something funny to me. His gaze moves from my eyes to my lips, and my heart begins to pound wildly. "I don't know what I love more, your cute little fangs, or those claws of yours that you won't show anyone but me."

His nose brushes against mine, and I whimper involuntarily, my entire body flooding with desire. "If you want to bite something," he murmurs, his forehead dropping to mine. "Might I suggest my lips?"

"You think I won't?" I ask, moving just a touch closer, my body buzzing with equal parts adrenaline and desire.

"I dare you to," my husband whispers against my mouth, and I give in, trapping his bottom lip between my teeth. He tightens his grip on my hair and groans as he kisses me, rapidly taking control.

His movements are both slow and determined as he deepens our kiss and pulls me on top of him, letting me feel just how hard he is. The thought of him wanting me that desperately only fuels my own desire, and I can't help but moan as he moves his tongue against mine just right.

"You drive me crazy," he whispers against my mouth. He starts to move his hips, and the way he feels between my legs is maddening. I gasp when a jolt of desire rushes through me, one hand wrapping in his hair as the other begins to roam over his chest and abs, my inhibitions fading away. My breath hitches when his hands move underneath my t-shirt, his thumb brushing over my panties. My hips involuntarily move against his hands, my need for him taking on a life of its own.

Xavier groans and kisses me harder. "You're wet," he groans against my mouth as he pushes the fabric aside and brushes his thumb over my clit.

I moan loudly, unable to help myself. "Xavier," I beg, my grip on his hair tightening as I pull his mouth back on mine. He circles my clit, slowly pushing me toward an orgasm, and I moan against his lips, unable to take it. "Please," I whisper, my legs trembling.

Xavier pulls back to look at me, forcing me to face him as he keeps me on the edge. "Please what?" he asks, toying with me. "You want to come for me, don't you?" he says, smirking as his touch becomes rougher, faster. "I'll give you what you want if you ask nicely."

"You're insufferable," I tell him, pushing my hips against his fingers harder, riding his hand desperately. I'm so close, and he knows it.

"And you're beautiful," he whispers, just as my muscles begin to contract, my moans becoming incoherent. "*Yes*," he groans, his eyes filled with desire. "Come for your husband, Kitten."

My forehead drops to his shoulder, my breathing erratic as wave after wave of pleasure rushes through me, making me lightheaded. Xavier turns his head to kiss my cheek, his arms wrapping around me as he hugs me tightly, keeping reality at bay for a few more moments.

He gently strokes my back as my breathing evens out, and all of a sudden, I'm too scared to lift my head, when I'd been so bold moments ago. "You've got some work to finish, don't you?" he whispers, almost like he's giving me an out, like he knows how vulnerable I suddenly feel. Xavier presses another kiss to my cheek, and I pull back a little, keeping my gaze downcast.

He chuckles and pinches my chin, lifting my face before he leans in and kisses me, slowly, leisurely, before pulling away. Our eyes lock, and he smiles so sweetly that I can't help but blush as I scramble off him and grab my laptop. I thought he'd taunt me, but he just moves onto his side and watches me as I pretend to work for over an hour, until eventually, his breathing deepens, and he falls asleep.

Xavier has always confused me, but never as much as he does these days. I thought I'd be intensely unhappy being married to him, but instead, he's slowly filling me with hope that I absolutely shouldn't be feeling — hope that maybe, just maybe, Grandma was right about him.

Twenty-Nine

XAVIER

I lean back in my seat in my own damn conference room as my wife laughs at something Graham said, and all the while, I quietly plot his demise. It'd only take me a few days to sabotage his business and tank his share price, at which point I could swoop in and facilitate a hostile takeover. I can't remove him as a shareholder altogether, but if I can get my hands on enough shares, I can force him off this project and make sure he stays far away from my wife.

"You can't still remember that," Sierra says, her eyes filled with glee. "I was six!"

Maybe blackmail would be faster. Surely there's something I can find on him? No one has a clean slate — not even the kindest souls. A hostile takeover could take months, but his reputation? That could be ruined in a matter of days. So could his bones.

"Of course I remember," he replies. "My mom has pictures of that day framed. Me and you in that tiny kiddie pool, down right brawling over that stupid bath duck."

Our meeting ended twenty minutes ago, and they're both still sitting here, reminiscing about memories I don't share with Sierra, and it fucking destroys me. I've known her for nearly two decades, but he's known her longer.

I breathe a sigh of relief when Graham finally rises to his feet and gathers his documents. Things seemed so perfect last night, but Sierra has barely looked at me today, and it fucking hurts. It's like I don't even fucking exist when *he's* in the room.

"There's a new bistro around the corner," Graham says softly, his words clearly meant only for her. "Shall we go check it out if you haven't had lunch yet?"

"Sierra," I snap, my voice betraying my mounting anger. "Do you have a moment?"

Her eyes meet mine, and I hold her gaze, drinking her in. Graham's shoulder brushes against hers, and he leans in, his mouth far too fucking close to her ear. "Want me to wait for you?"

She turns to face him and smiles up at him in a way that straight up cuts through my heart, slicing it into pieces. "No, it's okay," she says, her tone soft and sweet. "We'll catch up later."

She stares after him as he walks out, and I walk up to her, placing my index finger under her chin, lifting her face to mine. "What the fuck was that, Mrs. Kingston?"

Surprise crosses her face, and for a few moments, she looks entirely disarmed. "What was *what*?" she asks, her tone a little uncertain.

I take a step forward, and she stumbles back, until she's perched at the edge of my conference table. Sierra's eyes flash when I cage her in, placing my hands on either side of her. "You know damn well what I'm talking about," I warn her. "You're fucking insane if you think I'm going to let you get away with flirting with another man right in front of me."

She grabs my tie and yanks on it, catching me by surprise when she pulls me closer. It's clear she's not the least intimidated, and that look in her eyes takes the edge off my anger. "You're insane if you think that was *flirting*." She sounds furious, indignant.

I part her legs to stand between them, making her skirt ride up, and Sierra's cheeks flush beautifully when I grab her hips and pull her against me. "Then what was it? Explain it to me, because I vividly recall you promising me loyalty and fidelity."

My wife surprises me further when she wraps her legs around me and balls my tie in her fist. "It's called *reminiscing*, Xavier. It's something you do with *friends* — not that you'd know."

"You're right," I tell her, placing my hand around the back of her neck. "I clearly *don't* know." My gaze drops to her lips, and her breath hitches. When my eyes meet hers again, they're filled with barely disguised longing. "What I do know is that you're my *wife*, Sierra Kingston. You're *mine*, and it looks like you need another reminder of that little fact."

Her breathing quickens when she feels me harden against her, and she tilts her head almost imperceptibly. "The last thing I need is a *reminder*," she says, her voice different now, huskier, despite her best attempts to inject venom into it. "I've been trying my best to forget."

Sierra inhales sharply when I rotate my hips, driving my cock into her harder. The desire that flashes through her eyes is unmistakable, but she'll deny it with her last breath, I just know it. I tilt my head, my lips a mere inch from hers. "You fucking infuriate me, you know that?"

"The feeling is mutual," she murmurs against my mouth, before tightening her grip on my tie and pulling me closer, until my lips are on hers. I moan when she kisses me, her hand wrapping into my hair while mine runs over her body, only to settle on her thighs. My tongue brushes over her lips, and she opens up for me, deepening our kiss as one of her hands roams over my chest.

My wife gasps when I slip my fingers between her legs and she pulls away just a touch to look at me just as brush against her panties. "Wet," I murmur, loving the way she's looking at me. "Just like last night. At least your body remembers who it belongs to, hmm?"

"I don't belong to you," she retorts, even as she tilts her hips forward just a touch, pushing against my hand harder. I smirk as I push the silky fabric aside, the feel of my bare finger against her soaking wet, smooth pussy nearly undoing me. *Fuck*. It feels like I've waited an eternity to have the mere chance to experience this with her.

I bite down on my lip just as she moans, her eyes darkening. "What was that, baby?" I ask, taunting. "I can't hear your lies over the sound of your desire."

She grabs the lapels of my suit, her breathing ragged. "God, I hate you," she claims, and I look into her eyes as I slip a finger into her, curling it inside her as I press my thumb against her swollen clit. She moans so fucking beautifully that my cock begins to throb, my mind hazy with pure lust. She's the only woman who can do this to me, the only one I've ever lost my cool over.

"Yeah?" I murmur, torturing her by circling her clit and never quite touching it. "You might hate me, but your pussy fucking loves me. You want to come for me, don't you?"

She balls her hand in my hair and pulls my mouth back to hers, until there's only an inch between us. "Shut up," she whispers.

I grin as I slip another finger into her, my thumb finally caressing her where she needs it most. "Make me," I growl.

Sierra kisses me, her hips moving with my fingers as I push her toward the brink of an orgasm. I swallow down all her moans as I increase the pace, my touch becoming rougher. My beautiful wife comes for me, and the fucking sounds she makes... they'll feature in my fantasies for the rest of my life.

"He can't give you that kind of pleasure," I tell her once her inner muscles stop contracting. "For as long as we're married, I'm the only man that's touching you." She blushes fiercely when I pull out my fingers and bring them to my lips, savoring her taste. "You're *mine*, Sierra Kingston. Whether you like it or not."

She pushes against my chest and slips off the conference table, only for her knees to buckle. I grin as I wrap my hand around her waist and pull her against me, holding her in my embrace. Sierra places her hand against my chest, her eyes on mine. For once, there's no venom in her gorgeous emeralds — this time, there's only shyness and something I can only describe as vulnerability.

"I was about to say no to his request to have lunch together," she murmurs.

My heart skips a beat as I gently brush her hair out of her face. Does she realize how much of a relief it is to hear that? I doubt she has any idea just how much every little action she takes affects me, how much power she holds over me. "Don't wait up," I tell her, pressing a lingering kiss to her forehead. "I have meetings until late."

She pulls away, seemingly snapping out of the sweet daze she'd been in. "As if I would," she says as she straightens her skirt, the blush on her face diminishing the effect she was going for.

I chuckle, and she glares at me as she storms out of my conference room, leaving me staring after her. What has she done to me? I think I've finally well and truly lost my mind.

Thirty

SIERRA

"Where is your husband?" Grandma asks when I walk into her house for our weekly family dinner. "I told you that you're exempt from attending family events, but I also told you that if you wanted to come tonight anyway, you had to bring Xavier with you."

A hush falls over the room, and I blush involuntarily as I walk over to my usual seat, my brows rising when I realize there's an extra seat at the table now. "He's too busy with work to make it," I reply, grinning brightly.

Raven leans in, her shoulder brushing against mine. "You never even told him about tonight's dinner, did you?"

"Nope," I whisper, before pouring myself a glass of wine. The last couple of weeks have been a whirlwind, and though I wouldn't admit it, I really just needed to come home and be around my siblings for an evening. I've never felt quite this confused, and I haven't really felt like myself since I got married. I blame Xavier, of course. If he hadn't kept touching me like he truly wanted me, I wouldn't be second guessing everything I thought I knew.

"I am so sorry I'm late," I hear a familiar voice call from behind me, and I stare in shock as my husband walks into the room holding a giant bouquet of sunflowers that he hands to Grandma with the sweetest smile on his face.

"Oh, that's okay, sweetie," she replies, gently taking his hand. "I'm glad you could make it after all. Sierra said you were too busy with work."

He looks at me then, our eyes locking. My heart skips a beat when he smirks, before tearing his gaze off me. "I wouldn't miss it for the world. You invited me yourself, after all." One of our household employees takes the bouquet from him, and my brothers all snicker to themselves as they exchange money, clearly having made bets that I'm not privy to.

Xavier sits down opposite me, and my face heats when I feel his foot against mine. I kick him, and he smirks as he traps my ankle between his. I try my best to break free without letting on what's going on, and he continues to talk to grandma happily, pretending to be none the wiser.

"So, how has it been?" Raven asks quietly when the starters are served.

I glare at her. "I'm not telling you anything, you traitor."

She chuckles as she wraps her arm around my shoulder and leans in, her head dropping against mine. "So there is something to tell, then? Spill." I can hardly hear her voice over all the noise my siblings are making, and for once, I'm grateful for it.

I hesitate for a moment, before telling her everything — the kiss in the library, the way I bit him, and even everything that happened in his office. She smirks as she listens to me, a knowing look in her eyes.

When we got married, I'd been so determined that our marriage would be on paper only, and that we wouldn't really have anything to do with each other outside of our obligations to our families, but he's impossible to ignore — impossible to *resist*. "I don't know what to make of him, but I do know myself, and I'm not capable of being physically intimate with someone without there being an emotional attachment too."

She looks at me like she understands, but she couldn't possibly. "Why do you assume there is no emotional attachment on his part?" she asks.

I smile wryly, acutely aware of the way Xavier is still keeping my ankle trapped, and I try my best not to look at him. "I just know him," I murmur, unsure how else to explain. I've been watching him for years, and other than when I thought he was dating Valeria, he's never even remotely given me any indication that there was a woman in his life he cared about romantically, and I doubt I'll be the first.

"Has it ever occurred to you that you only know one side of him, and that maybe, there's more to him than the parts you've gotten to know?" I begin to object, but she smiles at me in that way that shuts me up. "I thought I knew Ares when we got married," she says, her tone subdued. "But you don't really know someone until you've lived with them, until you've seen them at both their best and worst. So far, all you've seen of Xavier is what he's shown you, and maybe that's only one small piece of the puzzle."

She looks at me like she knows something I don't, and I'm tempted to believe her. It's true that the way he's been behaving since the wedding has been a little different, and more than once, I've felt like I didn't know him as well as I thought I did.

"Give him a chance, Sierra. Give *yourself* a chance to be happy. We both know no man has ever come close to knocking down your walls — except for him. Deny it all you want, but there has always been something between you two, so why not take this chance to figure out what that could become? Stop lettings your fears dictate your thoughts and actions."

Her words still reverberate through my mind as I walk onto Grandma's patio after dinner, my eyes on the starry sky above me. For as long as I can remember, I've wanted a happy marriage of my own — a partner I'd truly connect with, someone that'd be my best friend *and* my husband. Could I have that with Xavier? The thought of putting my heart on the line terrifies me, and though I'd never admit it, I know he holds the power to destroy me in a way no one else ever could. So far, he hasn't given me any indication that he wants anything more than my body, and I'm terrified of the way he's been making me feel each time he touches me. He leaves me wanting more than I think he's willing to give, and I'm not sure how to handle that.

I startle when someone drapes a suit jacket over my shoulders, and I whirl around, coming face to face with Xavier. He sighs as he reaches for me and gently pushes my hair out of my face.

"What are you doing?" I ask, my eyes roaming over him. Xavier looks incredible in a suit, but he looks even better at the end of the day, with his sleeves rolled up and his tie long gone, his top buttons undone. Raven is right — there are so many parts of him I've yet to discover, and I'm scared of what I'll find.

"Waiting for you to stop running," he answers, his expression unreadable. "I told you, didn't I? I'll wait a million years and a day, if that's what it takes."

Thirty-One

Xavier

I lean back in my chair as I listen to the proposal brought forward by a well-known property hedge fund manager, and he smiles at me reassuringly as he presents his figures.

"I'd like a better look at *how* you came up with those projected figures," I tell him, and he nods as he instantly begins to dive into it.

He has my full attention, until I notice a security alert on my phone, notifying me that Sierra just got home — at six in the evening, when she usually doesn't come home until closer to ten.

"Apologies," I say, rising to my feet. "I need to go. Something has come up." I reach for my jacket and throw it on in a rush. "Sam will be in touch to reschedule," I tell him as I walk out the door.

"Is there an emergency?" Sam asks, concern written all over his face as he follows me out of the conference room, and I shake my head.

"No. My priorities just changed."

Sam raises a brow and stares at me like I've lost my mind. "That deal you just walked out of is worth millions."

I shrug as I grab my briefcase from my office and press the

button that takes me down to my garage. "I don't need more money," I tell him. "I just need a chance with my wife."

"You're kiddi—" he shouts as the elevator doors close, and I grin on my way out, my entire body thrumming with excitement as I rush home.

My heart is still beating just as wildly by the time I walk into my kitchen to find my beautiful wife standing behind the stove, still in her work clothes, and at least ten different cheese varieties on the counter.

"Kitten," I murmur as I walk up to her, feeling oddly nervous. She's never been home early, and I'm not too sure how to behave around her now.

Sierra looks over her shoulder and smiles, her cheeks instantly becoming perfectly rosy. "Hi," she says, a hint of shyness in her gorgeous eyes.

"Hi," I repeat, my hand wrapping around her waist from behind as I look over her shoulder at the dish she's making.

"It's macaroni cheese," she explains. "It sounds simple, but it's a recipe Zane created for me, and it's honestly just really delicious. I think you'll like it."

Pure elation rushes through me at the insinuation. "You're making enough for me, too?"

She nods and turns around to face me, her gaze roaming over my face. "I thought that maybe, I don't know, maybe it would be nice to have dinner together?"

I smile as I gently caress her cheek with the back of my hand. "I'd love that," I tell her. "Let me go set the table."

She nods and returns to her dish while I begin to set the table and light some candles, before choosing a wine that might go well with her pasta. Sierra looks a little flustered as she carefully carries a serving plate to the table, and I smile at her as I pull out her chair for her.

"Here, try this," I tell her as I pour her a glass of wine, and she nods as she serves me some pasta. I've heard Zane brag about how much she loves this specific version of macaroni cheese, so to have her make it for me is a little surreal — not that I could ever admit that, since it's not something I'm supposed to know about.

"How come you decided to cook today?" I ask carefully. "You know you can just request any dish from the housekeeper via our app, right?"

She nods and looks away. "Is it not good? I'm sorry... I forgot that not everyone loves cheese as much as I do. I should've—"

I reach for her hand and squeeze gently. "It's perfect," I reassure her, annoyed with myself for phrasing that wrongly. "It's actually my new favorite food. Let's have it every single day."

My gorgeous wife laughs, and I grin back at her. "I just wanted you to know that there are plenty of employees around if you want anything, even if you don't necessarily see them around."

She nods, and we both eat quietly for a little while. "You know, having this dish with you reminds me of something. Do you remember when I'd just started working for Windsor Real Estate? My grandmother was training me, and I'd been working on my first big project with—"

"—with Realiance," I recall, my mood instantly souring.

Sierra's eyes widen, and she nods slowly. "Right," she murmurs. "You know why I remember that project so vividly? I'd been pretty addicted to cheese sandwiches with smoked cheddar that Ares had flown in for me, but there was this one time that you'd dropped by the Realiance office for some reason, and you'd just taken a huge bite of my whole block of cheddar that I'd kept in the fridge there. I still haven't forgiven you for it."

I can't help but laugh as I recall how petty I'd felt as I looked her in the eye and did it. I'd never in a million years admit it, but I'd done it because I'd overheard her telling the heir of Realiance that she'd make him a cheese sandwich too. He'd clearly been flirting with her throughout that project that I helped fund, and she didn't even realize it. "You were pretty much fresh out of college then, and you'd been working so hard. I don't think anyone on that project worked more hours than you did."

I remember those days all too well. The first time I saw her after she returned from college was at a conference not long before the cheese incident, and I was left reeling for days, trying to convince myself that I couldn't possibly find my best friend's little sister that beautiful. I hadn't seen her in years, and I don't think I ever looked away from the moment she returned, not while she was even remotely in my field of vision.

"Come to think of it, that isn't the only time you stole my food. The cheese was pretty unforgivable, but there was one time you really crossed a line."

I bite back a smile and look away, my cheeks suddenly feeling awfully hot. "The cookie," I mutter, still ashamed of my actions. I'd found her standing in a corridor by herself before a meeting. She'd seemed nervous, and then she reached into her bag and pulled out a cookie. The way she moaned when she took a bite played a significant role in my fantasies for years to come, and what I'd done after certainly wasn't one of my finer moment.

"I'd just been peacefully eating one of the cookies my grandma had made especially for me while I waited for my meeting to start, and you just walked up to me, grabbed my wrist, and took a bite of my cookie. I think that's the moment I realized we would always be enemies."

I chuckle, wondering what she'd do if she knew what was going through my mind then. "Yet here you are, Sierra Kingston. I don't know about you, but personally, there's nowhere I'd rather be."

Her eyes widen a fraction, and the way she blushes completely messes me up. "Here I am, sharing my favorite dish with you voluntarily."

"What do I have to do to make that happen again?"

She chuckles and pushes her hair behind her ear. "You just have to ask, Xavier. While I don't have time to cook every day, occasionally making something you love isn't much to ask of your wife, provided you're willing to return the favor."

I stare at her in disbelief, my heart racing wildly. "I love the sound of that," I admit.

"Of me cooking?"

"Of you calling yourself my wife."

She looks away and rises to her feet in a rush, but the smile she tries to hide speaks volumes. "Leave it," I tell her as she reaches for our plates, rising from my seat. She looks up at me, and I smirk as I grab her wrist and pull her against me. "Tell me, Kitten... this dinner date, is this you deciding to stop running?"

She places her hand against my chest, her expression betraying a hint of insecurity. "What if it is?"

I look into her eyes as I thread my hand into her hair and tilt her face. "Then I'm going to kiss you, Sierra. No provocation, no tempting you into biting me just so I can feel your lips against mine—"

Sierra rises to her tiptoes and cuts me off with a kiss, and I moan as I pull her closer, my hands roaming over her body as I step forward, forcing her back, until I've got her pressed against the wall. "God, you have no idea how long I've waited for this."

She moves her hand up from my nape, until the tips of her fingers lightly thread over my scalp. "No more waiting," she breathes against me, her body moving against mine sinfully.

"No more waiting," I agree as I lift her up against the wall, and her skirt rides up as she wraps her legs around me. She moans when I drive my cock into her, her grip on my hair tightening as her lips find mine again.

"Xavier," she whispers, only for my blood to run cold when an alarm sounds through our house. I pull away from my wife and slowly lower her to the floor, my stomach turning. "What's that?" she asks, looking around.

I brush her hair out of her face gently, regret unlike anything I've ever known rushing through me. Is this a reminder that someone like me doesn't get to be with someone like her? Is it fate intervening to show me that my past will never loosen its hold on me?

"I need to go," I whisper. "I'm sorry."

Thirty-Two

XAVIER

"I took care of it," I tell Elijah as I pull up in front of my house, my clothes and hands stained with blood that isn't mine, my mind numb.

"You made a mess," he complains, the sound of keystrokes in the background telling me he's already dealing with the aftermath. "Couldn't you have handled matters in a cleaner way?"

I walk into my house, weary to the bone. Images of everything that transpired keep rushing through my head, and I almost wish I could go back for another round, that I hadn't permanently put an end to that asshole's suffering.

"I didn't have the patience for it." I've yet to tell Elijah what exactly happened, and it's best he never finds out. "You would've been a lot more brutal."

"I wouldn't have left evidence everywhere," he retorts. "This is going to require one hell of a cleanup crew."

"I don't care, Elijah. It was worth it, trust me."

I pause when I notice Sierra standing in the doorway to our dressing room, pure horror written all over her face as she takes in the blood I'm drenched in. "I need to go," I tell Elijah, before ending the call.

Sierra takes a step toward me, but I walk past her and into the bathroom, my stomach turning. Why is she still awake at four in the morning? *Fuck.* She was never supposed to see me like this. My sweet wife was never supposed to find out that I'm not just the businessman she thinks I am, but there's no way of undoing what she just saw.

I stand underneath the shower until the water finally runs clear and try my best to scrub off every last drop of blood, but there's no washing away the darkness of my soul. I knew I wasn't good enough for her, that she was too pure for me, too innocent, and for years, that knowledge was sufficient to keep me away from her. When did that change? When did I become so selfish that I pulled someone like her into the shadows?

I'm coated in self-loathing as I walk back into our dressing room wearing nothing but a towel, and Sierra tightens her grip on the first aid kit she's holding. "Are you hurt?" she asks, her voice soft.

I wish I were. At least then, it wouldn't have been so obvious that the blood on my clothes wasn't mine. "No."

She steps forward and kneels in front of me, her eyes zeroing in on my bruised knuckles. "Go to bed, Sierra," I tell her when she reaches for my hand. "I'm not myself tonight. You shouldn't be around me right now."

I don't have it in me to pretend tonight. I'm tired, broken, and desperate for just a fraction of her affection. I'd lose myself in her if I could, even if it's only for a few moments.

"No," she says as she begins to disinfect and bandage my knuckles. "I'm your wife, Xavier. Let me help you. We said we'd stop running, didn't we?"

I thread my hand through her hair and stare at her, taking in her angelic beauty, her gorgeous emerald eyes. She's a fucking vision, and I'm not even remotely worthy of her. I'd forgotten, over the years. Our rivalry allowed me to escape my reality, gave me purpose, pushed me to be better — but for what? At the end of the day, I'm still a thug dressed up in expensive suits, and she's damn near royalty.

I wish I could steal away some of her light, until we're both cast in shadows, until we're the same, she and I. Would she finally really see me then? My wife ignores my words and reaches for my other hand, disinfecting that too. "You never fucking listen, do you?" I murmur.

She looks up with those bright deviant eyes of hers, and pure need rushes through me, my thoughts becoming hazy. "Just let me help you," she repeats, her voice soft. "Please, Xavier."

"You want to help?" I whisper, cupping her face, my thumb brushing over her lips. "Then put your mouth to good use. Make me forget about everything but you."

She tenses, almost like she's only just become aware how close her face is to my cock, and how the mere sight of her affects me. A storm brews in her eyes as she stares up at me, and I begin to wonder, will what she saw tonight forever change the way she looks at me? I suppose I deserve it for pretending to be a better man than I am, for tricking her into believing she'd married someone honorable. "Just go," I tell her as I rub my face, my heart aching. "Get out. I won't warn you again."

I feel her gaze on me, but she doesn't move. Instead, she reaches for my towel and yanks it off, startling me as her soft, trembling hand wraps around my cock. I groan and ball my hand in her hair. "Which is it?" she asks, her voice tinged with anger, even as she licks her lips, her eyes taking in my cock with a hint of intimidation. "Do you want me to get out?" she asks, before leaning in and dragging her tongue up from the base, drawing a needy moan from my throat. "Or do you want me to put my mouth to good use?"

I lean back against the drawers behind me, my eyes on her while hers roam over my body appreciatively. Our eyes lock when she opens her mouth and puts the tip of my cock on her tongue, before sucking down on it and exploring the sensitive ridges. She hums, the vibration fucking driving me crazy as she takes me deeper.

"Fuck," I groan, rocking my hips involuntarily. "*Sierra*," I moan, my tone meant to be a warning instead of the plea it clearly is.

She pulls back a little, letting me slip out of her mouth with a pop. "Use me," she says, her eyes burning with longing. My wife looks at me like she understands how desperately I need an escape tonight, like she wants to be the one I turn to, and I almost let myself believe it. "Show me how you like it."

"You don't know what you're asking for, Kitten," I warn her, even as I grab my cock and pull her head closer, my body and mind at odds.

"I do," she promises, when she shouldn't possibly. She has no idea how many times I've fantasized about having her on her knees for me, how desperately I need this, need her.

I clench my jaws for a moment, and then I nod against better judgement. "Open your mouth."

My precious wife does as she's told, and I look into her eager eyes as I slowly push in, until she recoils a little, only to do it all over again, slowly fucking her face. She sucks down on me, her tongue fucking perfection as my thrusts rapidly becoming more uncontrolled, faster, harder, *deeper*.

"That's my girl," I groan, my residual anger draining away as I focus on nothing but her. "You're sucking your husband's cock *perfectly*, Sierra."

I let myself live this fantasy in which she truly wants me for who I am, desires me despite the blood I've spilled. I delude myself into thinking I'm worthy of her affection, her devotion. "Such a good fucking girl," I murmur as she begins to suck harder, her tongue teasing me endlessly.

All of my thoughts fade away, until there's nothing but her and how fucking amazing she's making me feel. Sierra is the only one in this world that can make me forget about my worst nightmares. My moans fill up the room as I begin to lose control, and she whimpers on my cock like I'm the one giving her pleasure.

"Fuck," I grunt, lightheaded. "Sierra, baby, I can't take much more...*fuck.*"

I pull out, but she instantly bends forward, our eyes locking. "No. Give it to me," she demands, before taking me back into her mouth as deeply as she can.

I moan as I push as far down her throat as possible without making her gag, only to pull back almost all the way. "You're such a good wife," I whisper, knowing full well we're on the cusp of everything we've got unraveling. She hums as I set a rhythm that keeps me on the edge, trying to savor this moment with her.

I can't help but feel like this is the only time I'll ever get to experience this with her, and she watches me as every last shred of composure melts away. "Sierra," I groan as I come deep in her throat, and she swallows it all down like the good girl she is.

She's panting when I pull out of her mouth, her eyes dark with desire. "Face that way," I order, pointing toward the full-length mirror on the wall. "On your hands and knees."

She hesitates for a split second before complying, and I smile when she positions herself the way I told her to. "Good girl," I murmur as I move behind her and slowly push the t-shirt she's wearing up. She has no idea what it does to me to see her in my clothes. She thinks she's hiding more of her body that way, but all it does is turn me on. Sierra gasps when my hands begin to caress her ass, kneading, squeezing, before I grip the straps of her panties and pull them down her thighs, leaving them just above her knees. I chuckle when I notice how wet she is, how swollen and sexy her pussy looks. "All of this, just from sucking my cock?"

I watch her face flush in the mirror and smirk, fucking ecstatic that this is all for me, that she's mine. "Such a perfect, pretty pussy," I whisper, before leaning in and dragging my tongue right down it, needing a taste. She moans as I lap at her clit, and her hips begin to move as she gives in to desire. "Xavier," she begs as I toy with her, taking my time to tease her and never quite giving her what she wants. She sounds desperate — for *me*. "Oh god," she moans when I suck down on her clit hard, and just like that, she comes all over my tongue, her legs shaking.

I grin at her when her eyes meet mine in the mirror, desire

ruling my every thought. I wish she'd always look at me that way, like there's no one but me, like I'm all she cares about. Sierra gasps when I push my cock against her pussy and drag it back and forth a few times, before pushing in just slightly.

She tenses, and I look up in the mirror at her wide eyes. Realization dawns, and I pull away. What the fuck was I just about to do to my wife? She thinks I don't know, but I'm well aware she's still a virgin. She's been waiting for her husband her whole life, and here I am, almost about to fuck her on the goddamn *floor* like some kind of fucking animal.

"Xavier?" she whispers, her voice tinged with confusion as I pull away and grab a pair of sweats, getting dressed in a rush. My stomach turns at the thought of how selfish I continue to be with her, and it sickens me.

Sierra turns and kneels on the floor, facing me with those innocent eyes of hers. I take a long hard look at her and walk away, before I do something I'll regret for the rest of my life.

Thirty-Three

XAVIER

I pull up in front of my house and stare at my front door, feeling conflicted. For the third time this week, I've driven home only to find myself unable to enter. By now, Sierra would've had enough time to process what happened, and she's smart enough to understand that I must've killed someone to justify the amount of blood I was coated in. I can't bear the thought of facing her and finding nothing but horror and fear in her eyes. I'm desperately clinging to this space filled with unknowns I've been existing in. It's ironic how I've become Schrödinger's fucking *kitten*.

I sigh as I reverse back out and continue to drive around aimlessly, like I have every night for the past two weeks, only to end up in front of my best friend's house without even realizing it. *Again*. I take a deep breath and place my arms on my steering wheel, before resting my head on top. What the fuck am I going to do? How am I supposed to look my wife in the eye knowing that I've forever ruined the image she had of me? I've always known I'm a rotten apple, but fuck, when it comes to her, I just so desperately wanted to be good, *deserving*. I never wanted her to know about the evil that resides in me, the things I've done to protect my family. She'd never understand — she wasn't raised like I was, wasn't taught to shoot instead of learning to ride a bike.

I startle when my car door opens, my eyes widening when Dion steps into my car. "I didn't say anything the last three nights you parked in front of my house," he says, leaning back. "I get what it's like to not want to talk, and to not really be sure where to go, but you can't keep this up. Tell me why you're here looking like someone ran over your fucking pet when you should be at home with Sierra."

I sigh and pinch the bridge of my nose. "I fucked up," I admit.

He tenses, clearly trying his best not to let his concern show, but I know him too well. "What did you do?"

I lean back in my seat and stare out the window, feeling conflicted. Dion has always been the only person I could talk to, the only one I could say anything to without fear of judgment, but it's different now. I can't tell him the full story. I can't tell him that I spoke to Sierra harshly, and that I fucked her face ruthlessly, instead of treating her with the care and patience she deserves. She told me to use her, and I fucking did.

I lost myself in her, forgot about everything but her for a few moments. I was so far gone that I nearly took her virginity on the goddamn floor in our dressing room. She didn't even say anything, didn't stop me, but I know she'd always have resented me if our first time was wrapped in a haze of anger.

"Just tell me," Dion says, his voice soft. "You know me, Xave. There's nothing you could say that I'll take the wrong way."

I look down at my hands, regret settling deep in my chest as I try to determine which parts of the story I can tell him, and which parts I must keep to myself. "An anonymous source reached out and sent me a photo of Valeria that no brother should ever have to see." My stomach recoils, and I grit my teeth. "They had her chained to a bed. It was... it was fucking gruesome. She's never told me what happened to her, but it wasn't hard to guess. Seeing it, though? It tore me apart. I can't believe how strong my sister is, how much she's endured so quietly, and how well she's done since coming home."

I bend forward and drop my head back to my steering wheel as I take a deep, steadying breath. I needed to get this off my chest, and I didn't even realize it. "They tried to blackmail me, told me they'd send the photo to the media and every other source that might be looking for her, and there is no way I was going to let anyone ruin all that progress she's so painstakingly made. I found the asshole and made sure he'd never talk again, and then I found every single person in the photo." I sigh and squeeze my eyes closed, restless. "Sierra saw me come home drenched in blood."

Dion is silent for a moment. "I would have done the same, Xavier. If that had been Sierra, they'd be finding body parts all over the country for months."

I smile humorlessly, my breathing easing just a touch. "I showed Sierra parts of me I wish didn't exist, and now I don't know how to face her. She'll have questions I can't answer, and I'm scared I'll go home and find her looking at me like I walked right out of her worst nightmare, like I'm someone she fears."

He falls silent for a moment. "She wasn't scared, was she? Even when you walked in with blood on your hands, she didn't fear *you*."

"How do you know that?"

Dion smiles and shakes his head. "She knows you better than you think, Xave, and so do I. I'd never have let you marry my sister if I thought you'd ever be a threat to her, so stop beating yourself up over doing what needed to be done. Did you forget that you helped me capture Faye's father when I found out he'd been physically abusing her all her life? I would've done the same had I been in your shoes, and that doesn't necessarily make me a bad person, does it?"

"It's different," I try to tell him. I'm not even sure why I'm here. I should've known my best friend wouldn't just let me be without trying to talk to me. He refuses to accept that I'm beyond helping, beyond saving.

Dion squeezes my shoulder, and I turn my face to look at him. "Xave, you were depriving her of an opportunity to truly get to know you, to love you, by only showing her what you thought she wanted to see. Maybe this is for the best. She was bound to find out, and it's best for her to learn this kind of thing sooner than later."

"Dion, if I showed her all of me, she'd fucking run, and you know it. She only needs to see the person I'm trying to become, and nothing else."

"Give her some credit," he says, his tone reassuring. "She never wanted the jokester you pretend to be, Xavier. The parts of you she's always liked were the parts you inadvertently revealed when she got on your nerves and made you lose your temper. Besides, I suspect my sister has always known exactly who you are. Every misconception, every misunderstanding she's got, stems from *her own* insecurities, her inability to believe someone could truly want her and put her first. She's doubted herself countless times, but never you, not when it mattered. She looks for excuses sometimes, reasons to push you away so she doesn't have to put herself out there and face rejection, and she doesn't even realize she does it. Don't give her more excuses."

I stare at him in surprise. Just how long has he known about my feelings for her? How long has he been watching us both, and how could I not have realized it?

"What am I supposed to tell her when she asks me whose blood I had on me?" I haven't even told her about my family's past, and Valeria's disappearance. I never wanted her to know, never wanted her to see my murky past when I've worked so hard to build a future in which we could be together.

"You'll tell her that you can't give her answers right now, but you will when you're ready. She's your wife, Xavier. Someday, you're going to have to let her in, or you'll always wonder if she truly loves you, or if she'd walk away if she really knew you. Trust me, I know."

I stare at him, the mere thought of truly letting Sierra in fucking terrifying me, and he smiles like he gets it. "Xavier, you didn't scheme for years to have the mere chance to marry my sister, only to give up at the first hurdle. Stop letting your fears cloud your judgment and keep walking the road you chose. No one else can do it for you."

"I didn't sch—"

"Oh, shut up," he cuts me off. "Lie to yourself all you want, but don't bother lying to me." I stare at him in surprise, and he smirks. "Go home," he says, his tone filled with kindness despite his choice of words, "and don't fucking come back. I don't want to see you for at least another week. Your presence is keeping me from my wife."

I smile involuntarily as he opens my car door. "I'm going to tell Faye you threw me out."

He laughs as he steps out of the car, and I sigh, his words echoing in my mind long after he closes his front door.

Thirty-Four

SIERRA

I sigh as I wrap up my work, not particularly looking forward to being alone. Not even our beautiful library can entice me to go home when I know I'll just spend all evening wondering where Xavier is. He's barely been home since that time he came back with blood on his clothes, and I know he's avoiding me, but I don't know what to do about it.

Our roles seem to have been reversed, and I'm learning the hard way that karma is a bitch. I should've appreciated every moment of him being sweet and kind, because now that things have changed, I keep wishing we could go back to a time when he'd lay in bed half-naked, waiting for me as he worked on his laptop. He felt like my *husband* then, and now we're even less than the rivals we used to be — we're strangers that share a home. I hate it, but he won't give me a chance to so much as speak to him. I've tried to wait up for him countless times, but he's never home before three in the morning, and he's gone by six.

My heart skips a beat when my phone buzzes, only for disappointment to wash over me when I realize it isn't Xavier. I instantly beat myself up over my expectations — if not for the way his side of the bed looks in the mornings, I wouldn't even know if he came home at all, so why would he suddenly be texting me?

GRAHAM

> Wanna grab dinner after tomorrow's meeting? I found a new restaurant I want to try

I bite down on my lip as I think back to the way I falsely insinuated that something was going on between Graham and me. How would Xavier respond if I went out for dinner with Graham? Would he care at all? Would he stop avoiding me?

I sigh as I grab my purse and head out, my thoughts a mess on the drive home. Several times, I've come close to calling my family's head of security, Silas Sinclair, to ask if he'd find Xavier for me. It's a thought I haven't entirely given up on, but I'm trying my best to be patient. Maybe it's silly, but I'd like to believe that I know him well, and I'm certain that whatever happened just caused him to need some space. I can give him that, so long as he comes back home to me eventually.

I'm restless as I walk into the house, my longing for him beginning to become overwhelming. "Damn you to hell and back, Xavier," I mutter, only to pause in the doorway to his bedroom, a soft gasp escaping my lips when I find him sitting in bed, the sheets bunched around his waist and his laptop on his lap.

He looks up and smiles, and my heart goes wild. "Kitten," he drawls.

"You're home," I murmur, the butterflies in my stomach going wild.

He drops his head back against the headboard, looking up at me from lowered lashes, and my heart skips a beat as I take in his wide chest and strong arms. How many times have I imagined him sitting in bed just like that, only to find our bedroom empty? "I'm home," he repeats, his words sounding like a quiet promise that I hope he'll keep.

Xavier glances back at his laptop, and I stare at him for a few moments before I snap out of it and rush into the bathroom. I have so many questions, but I know I can't ask them, not without pushing him away all over again. Maybe I'm crazy, but I know he'd never hurt anyone who didn't deserve it, and it's not like I hadn't heard the rumors about his family. Throughout the years, I noticed that people who threaten the Kingston family simply disappear, and I'm not so naïve to believe that every instance of that was mere coincidence. He thinks I don't know, but I'm well aware of who I married.

I take my time in the shower, trying my best not to let my thoughts spiral. I'm terrified of doing or saying something that'll make him shut me out. He might not have said the words, but I know he doesn't want to talk about why he came home with blood on his clothes. I suspect it's at least part of the reason he's stayed away, and I don't want to risk saying anything that'll make him disappear again.

I clutch my towel as I walk into Xavier's dressing room, my eyes zeroing in on the nightgowns Raven sent me. Before I can overthink it, I slip into the red one. I regret it almost immediately — it's far too revealing. It's entirely made from lace and silk, and it clings to the contours of my body. Not to mention, the lace that covers my breasts doesn't actually cover all that much. Instead of lamenting on them, I push my insecurities aside and take a deep breath.

I try my hardest to act casual as I walk back into Xavier's bedroom and run a hand through my hair. My husband looks up, his gaze heated and his cheekbones a little flushed. He swallows hard, his breathing uneven. God, I've missed that. I've missed the way he looks at me, and everything we'd only just begun to give in to.

"What's wrong?" I ask innocently as I place my knee on my side of the bed, relief surging through me when I recognize the desire in his eyes. I don't know how else to reassure him, to quietly tell him that nothing changed for me.

Xavier's eyes run over my body hungrily, and I try my best to calm my racing heart. "Nothing," he says, sounding calmer now. His eyes move to mine, and he does something I absolutely hate — he smiles *politely*. It drives me completely crazy, because I know what his real smiles look like, and this isn't it.

He looks back at his laptop, and my heart sinks as a vague sense of rejection and humiliation washes over me. He's home, but he's still pushing me away — it's just a bit more subtle now.

I bite down on my lip as I sit next to him and stare at the wall, unable to comprehend why my heart is aching so much. I'd foolishly thought that we'd both just pretend nothing happened, and we'd go back to the way we used to be once he came home, like we so often did whenever we took our feud too far. "I'm having dinner with Graham tomorrow after our meeting with him," I lie, something dark unfurling deep in my stomach.

Xavier slams his laptop closed and puts it aside before turning to me. "What did you just say?" he asks, his tone carrying a hint of danger.

"I'm having—" He pulls me on top of him in one smooth move, his hands on my waist as he makes me straddle him. I instantly blush fiercely at the feel of his erection between my legs, his boxer shorts doing absolutely nothing to hide it.

"Need I remind you that you're married?" he asks, his voice strained. "Or that you vowed to be faithful?"

I place my hands on his shoulders, our eyes locking. "Need I remind you that this isn't a real marriage? If it were, you'd have been home with me every night for the last two weeks, instead of god knows where."

His hands slide from my waist to my ass, and he squeezes gently. "Oh, it's very real," he says, his voice soft. "Don't do anything you'll regret, and trust me, if you go on a date with another man, you'll regret it."

I rise to my knees, not realizing that it just puts my boobs at eye level for him. He clenches his jaws and slips his hands underneath my nightgown, his hands moving to my waist. "Don't be so foolish as to forget who I am, Xavier. No one gets away with threatening a Windsor. Not even you."

He rolls us over, and I fall back onto the bed, his body on top of mine. "Perhaps so, but you're no longer a Windsor, Sierra *Kingston*."

Thirty-Five

SIERRA

RAVEN

Xavier just tried to place an order for ten more nightgowns for you, so I take it he likes them?

I stare at my phone in shock and blush fiercely as I put my phone away, uncertain how to reply to her. He seemed genuinely angry last night, and after he told me I'm a Kingston now, he pushed off me and left me in bed all by myself. I fell asleep alone, and his side of the bed was still empty by the time I woke up. I was so certain that I'd messed up and increased the distance between us even more, but maybe I haven't. Maybe I was right to provoke him. For reasons I can't quite explain, I want him to show me the parts of himself he keeps hidden. I don't want his patience. I want to be the one he loses his cool over.

I glance at the clock and touch up my cherry red lipstick, a hint of nerves running down my spine at the thought of my monthly meeting with Graham and Xavier. I'm not sure what it'll be like to face Xavier after last night's argument, especially since Graham will be there too, but somehow, I'm quite looking forward to it. I'd rather be at odds with him than not have him around at all.

"Sierra?" Claire says, a hint of panic in her voice.

I look up to find my sweet assistant hovering by the door, concern written all over her face. "What's wrong?"

She steps forward and gulps. "You may want to look out the window."

I rise to my feet, my silk skirt swaying as I walk to the floor-to-ceiling windows in the corner of my office, only to find my own face on a large billboard opposite my office.

"They're everywhere," Claire says, her voice trembling. "I've been informed they went up in the last twenty minutes, *everywhere*."

I stare at the image in shock — it's a photo of me on our wedding day, my cheeks flushed and a surprisingly happy look in my eyes. "When you say everywhere..."

"Every billboard in the country. They're all photos of just you, but in all of them, you're clearly wearing a wedding dress. There are dozens of reporters in the lobby, and I'm not sure what to say to them."

"Tell them it's a campaign for Raven Windsor Couture," I tell her, unable to keep from smiling. I should be mad at the stunt he pulled, but instead, I just feel oddly giddy. From the moment we got married, Xavier subtly made it clear he wanted me, that this marriage was more than the merger he claimed it was. Just as I'd begun to realize that, everything changed, and I was worried things had changed forever. I've missed him, missed *this*.

I lean against the window as I stare at the billboard, Xavier's hand on my shoulder just about visible, his wedding ring the only identifiable clue. I should frame the full version of that photo and put it in our bedroom.

"Kitten."

I whirl around at the sound of my husband's voice, and he walks into my office, a smug expression on his face. He looks at me, really looks at me, for the first time in weeks, and I struggle to keep up my peeved facade. Right now, what he needs is the crazy, petty rival he's gotten used to over the years, and the unspoken rules that came with our rivalry. It provided a level of comfort, and I get that like no other. I'm happy to give him whatever he needs so long as keeps looking at me just like that.

Xavier tips his head toward the billboard behind him and chuckles, like he's mighty pleased with himself. "Seemed like you needed to be reminded that you're *my wife*," he says.

The edges of my lips turn up, and I try my best to resist smiling. Like I could ever forget that I'm his. "Did you forget that we agreed to keep our marriage a secret?" I ask, crossing my arms.

He mimics my body language, but it just makes his muscles that much more apparent. My gaze roams over his suit, and my silly mind can't help but think about what is underneath it. He has no idea that I've replayed the way he feels against me a thousand times, or that I wish he hadn't stopped that night in front of the mirror.

Xavier smirks and raises a brow. "I never agreed to that, Sierra. Did you ever hear me say those words? Did you see it listed in our non-disclosure agreement?"

"W-what? I definitely asked my lawyers to include it." I frown, genuinely confused.

"You should probably have read the papers one final time before signing them, because that sure as hell wasn't in there."

He reaches for me, his gold wedding band reflecting the light. Something that feels a lot like possessiveness unfurls in my chest at the sight of it. Unlike me, he never takes his ring off, and I secretly love seeing him wear it.

Xavier cups my face, his thumb brushing over the edge of my bottom lip. "If I were you, I'd keep my distance from Graham. I'd never hurt you, Kitten. Graham, on the other hand..."

"Are you threatening me?" I ask, fury rushing through me.

He smiles humorlessly. "Make of my words what you will, so long as you stay away from him."

I part my lips to argue with him, but before I can get a word out, my office doors opens, and Graham walks in. I step away from

Xavier instantly and paste on a polite smile. "Graham," I say, walking toward him. "Let's head to one of the conference rooms. It'll be easier for us to look at slides there."

Graham looks from me to Xavier and nods slowly before he follows me out, his expression unreadable. Did he realize he walked in on something? I need to find a way to tell him about Xavier, but there's just too much going on — the merger, our tumultuous marriage, grandma's illness. Talking about any of it feels impossible.

Graham seems oddly quiet as he plugs in his laptop, his gaze roaming over my face every few seconds, before moving to Xavier, who decided to sit right next to me, pulling his chair closer than necessary. He thinks he's getting on my nerves, but his behavior is reassuring. He seems much more like himself now, and I'm glad I gambled and tried to provoke him.

"We've begun to set the foundation," Graham explains, running us both through the progress and Lena's notes.

I tense when I feel Xavier's hand on my thigh. He slowly pulls my silk skirt up, until he's got his hand on my bare skin, his thumb drawing circles lazily. I glance at him, but he stares straight ahead.

"What are your thoughts on that, Sierra?" Graham asks.

I blink in confusion, entirely clueless what he's talking about. Xavier squeezes my thigh reassuringly. "We agree," he replies. "It makes sense to switch out the materials considering the rising cost and higher demand, especially since the new materials are far more sustainable."

Graham's eyes flash with irritation, and he stares at me for a few moments, but I merely nod in agreement. I might have my qualms about Xavier, but he never makes bad business decisions. I'd never admit it to him, but when it comes to our business, I trust him blindly.

"I'm pretty sure Sierra is fully capable of answering for herself," Graham ends up saying.

Xavier smirks at him. "Sierra and I are merging our companies. Our decisions are joint decisions going forward, so I do, in fact, speak for us both."

Graham stares at me wide-eyed, and I nod slightly. His expression falls, and he takes a step back. "A Windsor merger is never just a merger," he says, his tone pained. "I suppose congratulations are in order?"

Xavier smirks, his hand slipping off my thigh to wrap around my shoulder instead. Graham stares at where he's touching me, and his eyes flutter closed for a few moments. He takes a deep breath and shakes his head as he grabs his laptop and walks out.

"Graham!" I call, rising from my seat in a rush.

I take a step toward him in an attempt to follow him, but Xavier rises from his seat too, his eyes blazing with anger. "Don't," he says, grabbing my hand. "Don't go after him, Sierra."

Thirty-Six

I'm so furious I can barely think straight as Sierra and I make our way home, my mind endlessly replaying the way she just looked at Graham. Neither of us says a word as my driver pulls up in front of our house, the tension palpable.

"Why are *you* so mad?" Sierra snaps, slamming the door closed behind her. "I'm the one that should be mad, Xavier."

I whirl around to face my wife and pull my tie loose. "You can't be serious," I retort. "How the fuck am I supposed to feel if not fucking mad, Sierra? I just sat there as my *wife* nearly fucking ran after another man."

"He's a friend!" she shouts, throwing her purse on the console table in the foyer. "I wanted to follow him because that wasn't how I wanted him to find out."

"No," I say mockingly. "Had it been up to you, he'd never have found out at all. Tell me, Sierra. Would you have kept it from him forever if you could?"

"Why the hell are you suddenly acting like my husband when

164

we've barely spoken in two weeks? Just who do you think you are? You can't just touch me the way you did and then treat me like I don't even exist!"

I sigh and stare up at the ceiling for a moment. She's right, of course, but she's also evading my question, and we're arguing about two entirely different things. "That's not an answer and you damn well know it," I tell her, my voice losing all fight. "You know what? Fuck it, Sierra. Fuck this."

I turn my back to her and walk away, heading straight for our dressing room. I figured she wouldn't want to be around me right now, but much to my surprise, she follows me. "You want an answer?" she asks, her voice faltering when she notices I've unbuttoned half my shirt.

"Actually," I tell her. "No. I don't care, because it doesn't make a fucking difference. It never does."

"Yeah, you've made it abundantly clear that you don't care," she says, her tone filled with bitterness.

My shirt falls open, and I raise a brow. "What is that supposed to mean?"

Her eyes flash, and she takes a step toward me. The vulnerability she shows me knocks me off my feet, and I take a steadying breath. Sierra hesitates, and then she shakes her head. "Forget it," she tells me, her voice soft. "You're right. It doesn't matter."

She sighs and turns to walk away, but I grab her and pull her back to me. "What do you want from me?" I ask, pained. "Just tell me, and I'll fucking do it."

She rises to her tiptoes, her lips so close to mine I can almost taste her. "Nothing," she whispers. "Everything."

I groan and tighten my grip on her hair before I kiss her, losing myself in her. She whimpers softly and opens up for me, and I instantly deepen our kiss, my tongue tangling with hers. She tastes like chocolate and cinnamon, and it drives me completely wild.

My wife gasps when I push her up against the wall, but she doesn't take her lips off mine for even a second as she wraps her legs around my hips. "Fuck," I groan, kissing her like my life fucking depends on it, like this is the only time I'll ever get to kiss her. Hell, it might just be. Every moment with her is precious, and I'll never take even one single second of her wanting me for granted. It won't last, after all.

"Xavier," she moans, her hands pushing at my shirt as I move my lips to her neck, needing more. I shrug out of my shirt and tug at her top, pushing it up. She helps me get it over her head, and I take a second to look at my wife in that sexy black lace bra. "I need to see you," I whisper, before reaching behind her and unhooking her bra.

Sierra blushes fiercely and threads her hand into my hair, pulling my lips back to hers and I oblige happily, kissing her as I carry her to our bed. My beautiful wife gasps when I lay her down and move on top of her, holding myself up on my forearm.

She looks so vulnerable as she lets me pull her bra away, and it's a mystery why, because she's the most beautiful woman alive. "Fucking gorgeous," I murmur as I lower my mouth to her skin, loving the way her nipple hardens against my tongue. She squirms underneath me, her hand moving over my arms, like she can't get enough of my body either. I'm in a daze as she squirms underneath me, my thoughts revolving solely around her. She does that to me — keeps me in the moment, makes me unable to remember anything else.

"Xave," she says, sounding desperate. I smirk as I move my lips back to hers, loving the way she moans against my mouth when I slip a hand underneath her skirt, the back of my fingers brushing over her lace panties. "Wet," I murmur gleefully, pushing the fabric aside. "Look at how wet you are for your husband." I've fucking missed her, missed the way she feels in my arm, the way she tastes. I didn't even realize that I've felt *incomplete* for the last two weeks, right until this moment.

I pull back to look at her, committing this image of her to memory. She looks like a fucking goddess lying here with her skirt around her waist, her dark nipples hard and pure desire dancing in her eyes. Sierra bites down on her lip when I push my middle finger into her, my thumb swiping over her clit. "You're so fucking tight, baby," I groan, my lips brushing over hers.

She balls her hand in my hair and kisses me, and fuck if it doesn't drive me completely insane. Sierra tangles her tongue with mine leisurely, her hips moving against my hand as I slip another finger into her, teasing her g-spot while my thumb presses against her clit. I need her desperate for me, her pussy dripping and silently begging for me.

"Xavier," she pleads, repeating my name over and over again as I increase the pace, my touch becoming rougher.

"You want to come for me, don't you?" I murmur, smirking as I keep her on the edge. God, she has no idea how many times I've fantasized about this exact moment, how thoughts of her kept me sane at the worst of times.

She nods, soft little pants escaping her lips. "*Please.*"

I bury my free hand in her hair and push a third finger into her, noting how incredibly tight she is. "Tell me you're mine," I beg, needing to hear the words. I know I don't deserve her, but fuck, I *need* her.

"I'm yours," she moans. "I'm all yours, Xavier."

Something swells in my chest, and I smile at my wife as I give her what she wants, making her come. Her muscles contract around my fingers, and the way her eyes flutter closed as she moans my name will forever be ingrained in my mind.

Her body relaxes, and I pull her into my arms, holding her tightly. I've missed her so fucking much. She doesn't know how how badly the thought of her looking at me in fear or disgust has haunted me, how much of a relief it is that she still wants me.

I turn us onto our side when her breathing evens out, my gaze roaming over her face as she slowly caresses my back. "Don't ever, for even a single second, think I don't care about you, Sierra. You're always on my mind. *Always.*"

"I lied," she says, her voice breaking. She cups my face, vulnerability sparkling in her eyes. "When I told you that I wouldn't pretend I'd stay away from Graham, I was just trying to provoke you. There has never been anything going on between Graham and me, and I never agreed to go out for dinner with him today. He truly is just a friend, and I've never wanted anyone but you..."

Relief unlike anything I've ever felt rushes through me, and I bury my hand in my wife's hair as I pull her face to mine and kiss her.

Thirty-Seven

SIERRA

Xavier balls his hand into my hair, our eyes locked as his free hand roams over my body. "Now tell me, Kitten... how should I punish you for your lies?"

I gasp when his hand disappears between my legs again, and I whimper involuntarily. "Xavier," I plead, uncertain what I'm asking for. I'm so sensitive, but I don't want him to stop touching me. My thoughts are hazy, clouded by desire and that look in his eyes. I've missed him so much. Every time I fell asleep alone, I'd find him looking at me this way in my dreams — like I'm all he could ever want.

"Was it fun, making me jealous?"

My head falls back as he draws circles around my clit, not quite touching it, but still bringing me closer to another orgasm. It's excruciating, intoxicating. "Yes," I tell him. "I loved it."

He laughs and slips a finger into me, entirely unaware how captivating his laughter is, what it does to my heart. "Bad kitten," he murmurs, pressing against my g-spot hard. I moan and pull on his hair, trying to make my restlessness known, but it just makes him chuckle in that sexy, irresistible way.

"Bad husband," I retort. "It's not right to tease your wife like that."

His hand stops moving, something that looks a whole lot like vulnerability crossing his face. "What did you call me?"

He looks at me pleadingly, and I just know that in this moment, it's just me and him. No pretenses, no games. I cup his face, my thumb brushing over his bottom lip. "My husband," I repeat, my voice trembling. "Isn't that what you are?"

He draws a shaky breath and drops his forehead to mine, his eyes fluttering closed for a moment, before he tilts his head and kisses me. This kiss is different to the ones before it — it's slow, intentional, almost like there's a hidden message his body is trying to convey.

When he kneels between my legs and reaches for my skirt, I don't resist. His breath hitches when I lift my hips for him, and within seconds, I'm lying in his bed naked. I never thought I'd find myself here — married to Xavier Kingston and desperate for him, but nothing has ever felt quite this right.

I reach for his pants, and he groans when I undo them, my hands trembling with anticipation. He rises to his knees when I push his pants down, his dark eyes filled with desire and disbelief. "What about this?" he asks, placing my hand on the waistband of his boxer shorts. "Take it off for me, baby."

I do as I'm told and undress my husband. "So obedient," he says as he helps me push both his trousers and boxers off entirely. I bite down on my lip when he grabs my hand and wraps it around his cock, his hand covering mine. "You're such a good girl," he tells me, and my cheeks flush instantly. "Why can't you always be this good?"

He moves my hand back and forth, and I watch him, desire pooling between my legs. Xavier is the one moving my hand, but it's clear he's at my mercy. He looks at me like I'm a goddess, and he's my devout worshiper. "If I were, your life would be far too boring."

He releases my hand, but I keep up my movements, earning

myself a delighted expression as he starts to caress my nipples, his movements making my spine arch. "But perhaps I'd have a shred of sanity left."

"I like you just the way you are," I say without thinking.

Xavier's eyes widen, and he looks at me like he wants to believe me but can't. He leans over me, covering my body with his. "Is that so?" he whispers, his lips hovering over mine.

I move my hands to his hair and tilt my face in a silent plea for a kiss, one he instantly fulfills. I moan when I feel his cock pressed against me, and I involuntarily begin to shift my hips, needing him closer. Xavier groans against my mouth, his hand reaching between us to align himself.

"Tell me you want this," he says, his forehead dropping to mine. "If you want me to stop, I need you to tell me clearly."

I tilt my face a little, and he pulls back a fraction to look at me. "Don't stop," I tell my husband. "I want you, Xavier."

"God, you have no idea how long I've waited to hear you say those words." My head falls back when he begins to slide against me, the tip pushing in with every move. It's a maddening rhythm, and the way he rubs against my clit with each shallow thrust distracts me from the fact that the way he's stretching me feels a little uncomfortable, even though he's barely even inside me.

Xavier kisses me, his tongue tangling with mine, his movements filled with barely restrained desire. "How does this feel?" he asks, pushing into me a bit further.

I whimper, reluctant to admit that I can't take it. I don't want him to know I'm inexperienced, and that I'm a little scared. "Fine," I tell him.

Xavier pulls back to look at me, his gaze searching. He presses a sweet lingering kiss to my forehead before pushing off me, and I tense, but he smiles reassuringly as he kneels between my legs and grabs my hips. "My sweet little liar," he whispers as he lifts my hips and pushes the tip of his cock into me, leaving it in place as his hand moves between my legs, his touch leisurely as he begins to stroke my clit, our eyes locked. "I won't hurt you, Sierra. Not if I can help it."

My breath hitches when he pushes in another fraction, his thumb caressing my clit in a way that should be criminal. His movements are slow but intentional, his eyes taking in every single shift in my expression as he slowly builds me up again, his hips rocking back and forth slightly — just enough to slowly inch his way further into me.

"I'm... I'm so close," I whimper.

He grins, his touch becoming rougher. "Then come for me, my beautiful wife. Let me hear you."

My spine arches as an orgasm even more intense than the previous one rocks through me, his name on my lips.

"Good girl," he whispers, looking pleased — *proud*. "You can be such a good girl when you want to be."

He pulls almost all the way out of me before thrusting halfway in, and I moan as my head falls back, my muscles tensing around him. It's too much, too deep. "Xave," I plead. "I can't."

"You can," he promises, his thumb back on my clit. "You can take all of me, baby. You were made for me, Sierra."

I reach for him, my hand wrapping around the back of his neck as I pull him closer, needing his lips on mine. He gives me what I want, kissing me slowly as he continues to thrust into me shallowly, pulling out almost all the way before thrusting into me, sliding just a little deeper into me each time.

"You're doing so good," he promises, his words a soft whisper between kisses. "Almost there, baby."

His forehead drops to mine as he pulls back and pushes all the way into me. "*Fuck. Sierra*," he moans, sounding delirious. The way he says my name makes the discomfort bearable, and I hold him tightly, my hands roaming over his back.

He brushes his nose against mine, once, twice. "You okay?" he asks, his tone filled with tenderness.

"Yeah," I whisper. I thought he'd start to move immediately, and he has no idea how grateful I am that he's giving me a few moments to adjust to the sensation of him inside me. I've never felt so stretched out, and it doesn't hurt per se, but it also doesn't feel as good as it's always described in my romance novels.

Xavier holds himself up on his forearm, his eyes on mine as he reaches between us and presses his fingers against my clit. "Can you give me one more, baby? Just focus on my fingers."

"I can't," I murmur, feeling so sensitive that I can barely take it.

"You can," he says as he traps my clit between two fingers, stroking back and forth gently. The indirect touch drives me wild, and he grins when I begin to rock my hips, beginning to love the way he feels inside me. Each of my little movements just adds to my mounting desire, and the way Xavier watches me doesn't help. He looks at me like I'm the sexiest thing he's ever seen, like nothing exists but me and him.

"That's it," he whispers when I begin to moan incoherently, his gaze heated. "That's my girl."

"Xavier," I moan, overwhelmed by the way he's made me feel. I can't think straight, my thoughts clouded by desire, by him.

"Come for me, baby," he demands. "Come for your husband, Sierra."

He pushes me over the edge, and the moment I come, he pulls back almost all the way, before thrusting fully back into me. It doesn't hurt this time, and he grins when I moan, my legs hooking around his hips.

"You like that, huh?"

I thread my hand through his hair, a mere inch between our faces as he begins to take me with deep and slow thrusts. "Your turn," I tell him, my voice thick with lust. "I want to see you come for me."

He grunts, his eyes falling closed briefly. "You'll be the death of me, Sierra Kingston."

Thirty-Eight

SIERRA

"You've been suspiciously quiet about Xavier lately," Raven says as I put on my hairnet ahead of our shift at the soup kitchen Grandma founded.

I can't help but blush, and Raven instantly begins to giggle. "Tell me everything," she demands as we begin to prep our ingredients. I glance over at Grandma, who is happily chatting away with a few of the people her charity employs, and my heart warms at the sight of her. She seems to be doing well, considering.

"There isn't much to tell," I lie when Raven knocks her shoulder against mine.

"Right," she says, her tone teasing. "That definitely explains the silk scarf you're wearing when it's blazing hot today."

"*Fine.*" I don't know why I even bothered trying to keep anything from Raven at all. "The last couple of weeks have been... unexpected."

"Is that good or bad?" she asks as she begins to chop the vegetables I'm cleaning.

"I don't know," I admit, my tone filled with uncertainty. "We slept together after an argument, and almost every night since. The way he treats me in bed is unreal, but other than that? It's like nothing has changed."

I haven't told her about the way he distanced himself from me after he came home with blood all over his clothes, and I can't, not until I know why. Things are much better now, and he hasn't stayed away from home ever since we first slept together, but it still feels like there's an invisible wall between us, and I don't know how to get past it. I'm starting to worry he'll never let me in.

"I don't feel like I'm getting to know him better, and when I try to ask about his childhood, he seems to shut down and evade my questions. It's like the only things he wants are my body and our business deal, and I guess... I don't know. I'm just kind of at a loss. I just... I really want to be closer to him, but I don't think he wants that." I look away and grab a new batch of veggies. "Before we got married, we agreed to part ways once our three years are up," I admit. "So I guess it shouldn't be surprising that he's just having fun with me until our time is up."

Raven chuckles. "Yeah, right," she says. "There is no way in hell that Xavier Kingston is ever letting you go. That man is playing the longest con I've ever witnessed."

"What are you even talking about?" I mutter.

She throws me an amused look. "Stop focusing on what he says and start paying closer attention to the things he does. Not everyone expresses their affection with words, but that doesn't mean it isn't there. You just need to know where to look."

I sigh, wishing she'd understand. It isn't like I'm expecting him to declare his undying love for me. I just want to have long conversations about more than work. It's clear he's got secrets, and I understand he isn't ready to let me in on those, but I want to know more about him than the things I've learned throughout the years. I want him to *tell me* about the things that shaped him, his hopes, his dreams.

"See?" she says, grinning as she tips her head toward the door.

I look up to find Xavier and Ares walking in together, and my heart skips a beat at the sight of my husband in that navy three-piece suit. Our eyes lock, and he smiles as he makes a beeline for me.

"Kitten," he says, his arm wrapping around my waist. He leans in to kiss me, only for my brother to clear his throat. Xavier tenses and presses a kiss on my cheek instead, and I can't help but chuckle.

"What are you doing here?" I ask awkwardly, my heart racing.

"I heard Zane and Celeste couldn't make it tonight, so Ares and I are filling in for them."

I raise a brow. "I didn't realize you'd grown close enough to my brothers to know that."

His expression shutters closed, and he pulls back to put on a hairnet and gloves. "Put me to work, Mrs. Kingston," he says.

My eyes roam over his face, searching, though what for, I'm not sure. I can't help but feel like I'm missing something, because that carefully blank expression he's got on his face is the same one he wears every time I ask him a question that's even remotely personal. "You can help me cut these carrots for our soup, and then those pieces of chicken breast are next."

He nods and immediately gets to work, and I frown in surprise when I realize he's far better with a knife than I am. "Is this okay?" he asks, and I stare at the perfectly cut pieces in shock. Everything is the exact same width, and he cut that up far faster than I ever could have.

"That's incredible," I tell him, earning myself a sweet smile. "Where did you learn to cut veggies like *that*?"

I notice his eyes widening just a fraction, before he pastes on that smile I've come to hate — the one he's always shown the world, but never me. "Maybe I'm just innately talented," he says, his tone light.

The way he evades questions is so smooth that I wouldn't have noticed it if he hadn't been doing it so often. Until we got married, I didn't realize he'd been doing it for years, every single time I asked him a question he didn't want to answer. He seems fine talking about work, but everything else appears to be off-limits, and I just don't understand *why*. Why does he go to such lengths to shut me out, only to pull me close at night?

We work in silence for a while, the sounds of Ares and Raven's laughter taunting me. I've never been jealous of the happiness they found together, but today I find myself desperately wishing I could have what they have.

"Are you free on Friday?" Xavier asks hesitantly. "It's my mom's birthday next week, and we usually have dinner together. I think she'd really like it if you came."

My eyes shoot to his, and he smiles tightly, almost like he doesn't really want to ask me, but his mother told him to. "This Friday?" Her birthday is so soon, and he's only just mentioning it?

He nods. "It'll just be our immediate family, but she loves The Siren, so I reserve the whole restaurant for her every year."

I turn to face my husband, nerves rushing through me. "Do you want me there?"

He looks pained, but after a few moments of silence, he nods. "I think it would be nice if you came."

It's not exactly an answer to what should've been an easy yes or no question, but I'll take it. I sigh and rise to my tiptoes to kiss his cheek, catching him off-guard. "Then I'll be there, Xavier."

Thirty-Nine

SIERRA

I pace back and forth in the living room before pressing dial, my heart racing wildly. Is this a bad idea? Maybe I should wait for Xavier to get home from work and ask him instead.

"Hello?"

"Hi! This is Sierra. Your, um, your sister-in-law?"

Valeria chuckles softly. "Hi Sierra," she says, sounding amused. "It's so good to hear from you, and thank you for not murdering my brother in the months since you've been married."

It's my turn to laugh, and my cheeks flush. "Well, don't thank me just yet," I mutter, unable to help myself. My words earn me a giggle from Valeria, and I relax, pleased she doesn't seem to dislike me after the coldness I treated her with when she tried to speak to me before I got married.

"I was... well, I'm trying to choose a birthday gift for your mom, and I just wanted to ask you if you knew what I should buy her. Is there anything she likes?"

"Hmm," she ponders. "There is one thing she's really been wanting from you specifically."

I tense involuntarily. "Oh?" I inquire nervously.

"She wants cookies! Ever since she found out about your obsession with cookies a few years ago, she's been making remarks about eating a cookie that meets your standards."

Years ago? How could that be possible? "Do you think she'd like it if I baked her some cookies myself? It isn't much of a present, but—"

"Yes!" Valeria says instantly. "Nothing would make her happier!"

I grin to myself, feeling oddly shy. "Okay, I'll do my best. If I start now, I should be able to make enough for everyone."

"Sierra?" Valeria says hesitantly.

"Yes?"

"Would it be okay if I came over and helped you?"

I blink in surprise, my heart warming. "Of course," I tell her, my voice soft. "I'd love that."

"Alright, I'll be there in ten minutes or so."

I nod dazedly as she ends the call and walk into the kitchen to check that Xavier actually has everything I need. I frown in surprise when I find all my favorite appliances, something dark and ugly unfurling deep in my chest. Xavier doesn't like anything that's sweet, so there's no way he bakes, and Valeria has her own home on the Kingston compound, so why would he have all of this? It hadn't occurred to me that he would've dated women in the past, and he'd have brought some of those women here. I'd been so fixated on Valeria that I completely dismissed all the other rumors about him and some of his brand ambassadors and business partners.

I'm snapped out of my thoughts when one of Xavier's security guards leads Valeria into the kitchen. "Hi!" she says, her smile dropping as her gaze roams over my face. "What's wrong?"

I shake my head and force a smile. "Oh, no, nothing at all!" I say as I begin to pull out appliances and ingredients. He's got high grade vanilla extract, but it's completely sealed and brand new. It doesn't make sense.

"Xavier lamented so much about which things to buy for you,"

Valeria tells me, a knowing look in her eyes. "He forced me to accompany him to ten different stores to make sure you wouldn't want for anything, and his staff have all been instructed to regularly replace anything you might need."

I stare at her wide-eyed and blush fiercely as I tuck a strand of my hair behind my ear. "Am I that obvious?"

She hoists herself up on the kitchen counter and shakes her head. "No, you're just very similar to Xavier. Possessive. Crazy. Hopelessly in love."

"I'm not—" I almost deny being in love with Xavier but then think better of it. We're supposed to act like a couple in front of his family, and I really should be trying to make a good impression on my sister-in-law.

"Tell me how I can help," Valeria says, a sweet smile on her face.

I nod and gather our ingredients. "My grandmother taught me this recipe," I explain. "But somehow, my cookies never taste quite as good as hers. I haven't figured out what the secret ingredient is, but my cookies come pretty close. We'll have to work in batches to make enough for everyone."

Valeria nods, and we work together quietly for a while. I normally don't like having people in the kitchen with me, but she never gets in the way and somehow seems to anticipate what I might need before I even ask for it.

"Valeria?" I say, my voice carrying a hint of uncertainty. "I wanted to apologize for treating you so coldly that day in the restroom."

She grins. "No need to apologize. If anything, it's exactly what I was hoping to see. Sierra Windsor, filled with jealousy and throwing the words *my fiancé* around like they truly meant something to you."

I look down, unable to refute her words. I really was jealous, and I'd felt so possessive, when I really had no right to feel that way. I still don't.

"I also need to apologize, for taking so long to tell you that I'm Xavier's sister when I knew my presence around Xavier upset you."

"I'm sure you had your reasons," I tell her quietly as I knead the dough. Truthfully, telling me that wasn't her responsibility. It was Xavier's.

"I do, and I think it's important you understand them," she says, her voice trembling. "If I tell you my story, will you listen?"

I look into her eyes, noting how they're a perfect replica of Xavier's. How did I miss that? "Of course."

"Not even my brothers know as much as I'm about to tell you, but I think it's important for you to know, because it'll explain why Xavier is the way he is, why he struggles to express himself and holds back his emotions, until they boil over. Somehow, you're the only person that's ever been able to draw his old self out, but around everyone else, he's a shell of the person he used to be."

I watch her as she prepares an oven tray for me. "Most people either don't know or pretend to have forgotten, but my family founded this town."

I nod and look away, having heard the stories. I tried looking it up online, but there is no information about the Kingstons dating back more than eight years ago. They've always been here, but it's like they didn't truly exist until about a decade ago. It bothered me when Dion first brought Xavier home, but I dismissed my concerns as I got to know Xavier.

"It wasn't uncommon for my brothers to come home with bruises and blood on their clothes when they were far too young to even be involved in any of it, but that was just our life. We had a reputation to uphold and a town to protect, so when our rule was questioned, it was up to my brothers and my father to rectify that. I didn't want to be involved in any of it, so when I was twenty, I ran away from home."

I stare at her wide-eyed, my heart bleeding for her. I can't even imagine growing up with that much violence and fear. "I would have too," I murmur.

She throws me a shaky smile. "Right?" She tucks a strand of hair behind her ear and draws a shaky breath. "Xavier was the last person I spoke to before I left, and we had a recurring argument about loyalty to our family versus having the honorable kind of future we envisioned. We both said things we didn't mean, as we usually did, but this time, we didn't get the opportunity to apologize and make up." She pushes the tray aside and stares at it for a few moments. "I left, and within an hour, I was captured by a human trafficking organization my brothers had tried to chase out of our territory and take down. They kept me captive for five years, and for five years, I tried my best to dismantle them from the inside out — and I did."

She takes the dough from me and begins to form little balls for the next batch of cookies, like we're just having a normal conversation, and I try my best not to stare at her, not to let my emotions show. My heart aches at the mere thought of everything she's been through, and all of a sudden, I understand exactly why Xavier has always been so protective of her.

"My disappearance made my family go legit in an attempt to honor my wishes. They thought I was dead, but on the off chance I'd truly just run off, they'd hoped that I'd come home if they became the kind of family I'd wanted. They had no idea where I was, but they never stopped looking and came close to finding me a few times. Each time they did, I was moved to a new location and punished for all the damage my brothers did to the organization."

"I don't know what to say," I tell her honestly.

She shakes her head. "You don't need to say anything at all," she replies. "I just wanted you to know that because of this, my family and I agreed that I'd stay hidden. I've done things I'm not proud of in my attempts to escape, and until I've taken care of every last loose end, I'd like to keep my identity hidden from anyone who might come after me. I made a lot of enemies in the time I was there, and not all of them knew my name, since it was a well kept secret." She smiles at me shakily, and I try my best not to imagine how they must've kept her from telling people who she was. "That's why my brothers let me come to some parties where the guest list is highly exclusive and security is very tight, but they won't let me be photographed. They want me to live and be out in society, but only in places they can control, where they believe they can keep me safe."

She smiles shakily. "That's why Xavier seems to have two personas: the joker, and the person underneath it. He'd never admit it, but he's scared he'll say the wrong thing again, and someone else will get hurt. It's not that he didn't trust you back then, or even now. It's himself he struggles to trust. No matter what I do or say, he can't accept that what happened wasn't his fault."

She grabs my hand and squeezes tightly. "So if it ever seems like he doesn't care, or he isn't saying the words you need to hear, please be patient with him. He needs you more than you could possibly know. You're the only person he's let in since then, the only one that can bring out the man we all thought we lost."

Forty

XAVIER

I stare at my wife in the mirror as she puts on her dress, and I can't believe she's mine. Sierra gasps when I wrap my hands around her waist and lean in to kiss her neck. "Xave," she murmurs admonishingly, even as she tilts her neck to give me better access.

"You look far too beautiful." These last couple of weeks with have has been the closest to happiness I've ever been, and it terrifies me. Every time she moans my name, her eyes filled with nothing but me, I wonder if I've asked for too much, if I should've just walked away when I realized she was ready to start chasing her own happiness.

Every time I watch her read her romance novels all curled up on the sofa in her library, the sweetest giggles leaving her lips randomly, I wonder how long I'll get to have her, how long it'll take for me to say the wrong thing and push her away, or put her in harm's way.

I always knew she wasn't meant for me, that she's too good for me, but I've never been able to contain my selfishness when it comes to her. I've always craved her attention in whatever way I could get it, and even now that she's my wife, I can't get enough.

Sierra giggles when I unzip her dress, and her eyes sparkle with desire as it pools on the floor. She turns to face me and buries a hand in my hair, our eyes locking. "What do you think you're doing?"

"You, if I'm lucky."

She laughs, and fuck if it isn't the best sound in the world, followed only by the way I'm about to make her moan my name. "We'll be late," my wife says, even as she unbuttons my shirt, her hand roaming over my skin hungrily.

"I don't care," I murmur as I turn her around and bend her over her dressing table, our eyes locking in the mirror. She gasps when I part her legs and slip my fingers between them, my cock instantly beginning to throb when I find her wet. "This..." I murmur, before bringing my fingers to my lips for a taste. "This is all I care about."

She moans when I circle her clit, teasing her ruthlessly. "Xavier," she warns. "Are you going to mess around, or are you going to fuck your wife?"

I smirk, a deep kind of pleasure washing over me at the way she's referring to herself. I fucking love it when she calls herself my *wife*. I groan as I undo my trousers in a rush, loving the way she moans when I slide my cock against her pussy. "You want this, baby?"

"Yes," she whimpers, rocking her hips in an attempt to get me closer.

I push the tip in and reach for her hair, tangling my hand into it. She looks fucking magnificent in the mirror. That lustful expression, the way her tits are pushed up against the wooden table, and that beautiful flushed face. "How the fuck are you mine?" I ask, slipping into her an inch.

"More," she demands.

I smirk as I reach around her and begin to draw lazy circles around her clit. "Not until you come for me, Kitten."

She pants, soft little moans escaping her sexy lips as I push her closer to an orgasm while fucking her in the most excruciating shallow way. "Xavier," she begs.

"Yes, my love?"

"*Please.*"

I smile and give her what she wants, my fingers moving faster, rougher. There's nothing more thrilling than watching Sierra come for me and knowing I earned each and every one of those delicious moans.

Her legs begin to tremble, and I bite down on my lip as I push into her fully just as her pussy begins to contract, her body losing strength. I pull her against me and hold her up with my forearm against her stomach. She rests her head against my shoulder as I take her slowly, her breathing uneven and her eyes on me through the mirror. I've never experienced anything this intimate, and it's messing with my mind, makes me feel things that can't be real.

She tilts her head and kisses me, and just like that, she's got me losing myself in her. I take her with hard, slow thrusts, and she moans against my mouth. "What are you doing to me?" I murmur against her mouth, certain she's bewitched me.

Sierra smiles and reaches behind her, her hand wrapping into my hair as she brings my lips back to hers, demanding that I kiss her. I oblige happily, and the way she tangles her tongue with mine pushes me over the edge. She swallows down my moans and tightens her grip on my hair when I come, and it's the most unreal experience. I'll never get enough of her, not in a million years.

"We really are going to be late," she tells me when I pull out of her, and I smile sheepishly. I'd better not tell her that my mother actually really hates it when I'm late. Instead, I just help my wife get cleaned up and dressed, taking every opportunity to touch her.

"Don't forget this," I murmur, slipping her wedding ring onto her finger. I hate that she rarely wears it, that I'm someone she wants to hide. Even if it's only for tonight, I want to feel like she's truly mine.

Sierra surprises me when she places her hand on my thigh as I drive us to the restaurant, and I grab her hand, entwining our fingers as I steal a glance at her. I've never wanted and feared something in equal parts, but that's exactly how I feel about her. I'm terrified of fucking things up with her, but I also can't let her go.

"You're late," Hunter says when we walk in, before reaching for my wife. I pull her back before he can hug her and glare at him, but she just laughs and pushes me aside to hug my brother.

"Hunter!" she says excitedly, and I watch the two of then through narrowed eyes. Much to my surprise, Sierra moves on to Elijah, and then Zach, before finally hugging Valeria tightly, treating them all like they're her own siblings. I thought she'd be reserved around them, wary of our reputation, but instead, she's treating them with unexpected kindness.

My heart feels a little funny as I watch her with my family, noting the way she seems to get a little nervous as she approaches Mom. "I'm so happy you're here," Mom says, grabbing her hand.

Sierra smiles shyly and holds up the small bag she brought. "It isn't much, but I baked you some cookies for your birthday."

Mom's eyes widen, and she takes the bag carefully. "You did? For me?"

"I can see why you love her so much," Dad says. I tense, unable to refute his words yet not quite ready to admit it either. "You look at her the way I look at your mother, Xavier. It's okay to love her, you know? It's okay to be happy."

I keep trying to remind myself of that, but it's near impossible to silence that little voice in my head that tells me that everything we have will disappear when she finally asks me the questions I know she has, and she'll never look at me the same again.

Forty-One

SIERRA

"Are you sure you don't mind spending the evening with my grandmother?" I ask as we pull up in front of her house.

Xavier smiles and leans in, his lips brushing against mine. "I'm sure," he murmurs, before threading his hand into my hair and kissing me. I melt against him, and he sighs as he drops his forehead to mine. "Actually," he says. "I changed my mind. We should go home and spend the evening in bed."

I laugh and pull back. "Absolutely not."

He pouts as he follows me to Grandma's front door, and I pause in front of it, turning back to face him. "Xavier," I say hesitantly. "Grandma hasn't said it outright, but every time I speak to her she makes it clear she's pretty worried about us. I just wanted to ask if... well, um..."

"I'll be on my best behavior," he promises instantly, placing his index finger underneath my chin. "I'll pretend to be the perfect husband."

I cup his face, our eyes locked. "You don't need to pretend," I whisper, letting the insinuation hang in the air between us. His eyes widen a fraction, and the vulnerability that crosses his face catches me off guard. I don't want to look for things that aren't there and drive myself crazy by reading too much into things, but maybe Raven was right, and I need to pay more attention to little cues, instead of focusing so much on everything he isn't saying. "Come on," I tell him, entwining our hands as we walk in and head straight for Grandma's kitchen.

"Sierra, sweetheart," Grandma says, grinning from ear to ear. She's become so thin that she's swimming in her beloved apron, and my heart wrenches painfully as I hug her. She's never felt more fragile, and I'm acutely aware that my time with her is dwindling.

She sighs when I hug her a little too long, not wanting to let her go. "Shall we bake some cookies?" she asks. "I've been wanting to teach Xavier my recipe."

I pull back and stare at her, wide-eyed. "Him?" I ask, pointing at my husband. "You want to teach him when I'm the one that's been begging to learn your recipe? What did he do to deserve that?"

She grins as she reaches for Xavier, and he gently brings her hand to his lips to kiss the back of her hand. "Are you doing okay?" she asks him, sounding concerned. "It must be hard to live with my granddaughter."

I gape at the two of them in disbelief when he nods. "I've never been more tired," he replies, sounding aggrieved.

I throw him the filthiest glare I can manage. He's never been more tired because *he* never lets *me* sleep. "You..."

Grandma wraps her arm around his waist and stares me down, and I press my lips together, not daring to curse out my husband when she looks at me that way. "This is so unfair," I mutter, before stalking to the sink to wash my hands.

Xavier chuckles and follows me. He reaches around me, my back pressed against his chest as he grabs my soapy hands and massages them, using the residue to wash his own hands. I tilt my head to look at him, my heart racing, and he grins as he presses a soft kiss to the tip of my nose before pulling back, leaving me standing there with blazing cheeks. Was that all just a show for Grandma, or was it more?

"Where do we start?" he asks Grandma, who immediately puts him to work.

"I've told her a thousand times that I'm not keeping the recipe from her," she grumbles, complaining to my husband. "It's not my fault they don't taste the same when she makes them, is it? Let's see if they're any better when you make them."

I cross my arms and stare at them in disbelief when they begin to discuss whether to make sugar cookies or chocolate chip cookies today, only to decide that they'll make both. I thought Xavier would be as awkward around Grandma as I've been around his family, but that isn't the case at all.

I've just begun to make pink icing when Grandma looks at Xavier and grins. "That reminds me," she says. "I bought those Medjool dates we were talking about last time, and you were right. They were so much better than the dates I'd been using."

Xavier smiles sweetly at her, but I notice the way his shoulder tense just slightly, the way he looks at me furtively for a moment, like he hadn't expected Grams to bring this up.

"Dates?" I ask. "What are you talking about?"

"Oh, I mentioned wanting to make healthier brownies for you, and Xavier suggested I try Medjool dates," Grandma says.

I tilt my head, still not quite comprehending what she's telling me. "When did he suggest this?"

"Last week, wasn't it?" she asks Xavier.

He nods, his expression guarded.

"You spoke to him last week?"

Grandma looks at me like I've lost the plot and nods. "Yes, Sierra. He's been taking me out for lunch once every two weeks ever since you got married."

What? I look at my husband, but he's avoiding my gaze. "Why didn't I know about this?"

"Well, I'm his grandmother now too," Grams says, seemingly

defending Xavier. "I see almost all of my grandkids at least once a week."

"I know," I tell her, smiling. "I just wish I'd known, so I could've joined too."

He looks up then, his shoulders relaxing. "I should've mentioned it," he says, his voice soft. "I'm sorry."

We both fall silent as grandma puts the cookies in the oven. "Call me when the timer goes off, alright?" she says. "I just going to make a call in the meantime."

I nod as she walks away, no doubt just wanting to give us space. "Why didn't you tell me?" I ask, my voice soft.

"I wanted to get to know the woman that raised you while I still could, and I didn't want you to feel like I was using her to force you to spend time with me — nor did I want to encroach on your time with her."

"Xavier," I murmur, my voice breaking. "Why won't you just talk to me? Why don't you tell me these kinds of things? I'm so tired of trying to figure out what you're thinking, of feeling like you're shutting me out. I just... it *hurts*. I won't ask you questions you clearly don't want to answer, but please, don't shut me out entirely."

He reaches for me, and I stare at him as he brushes my hair out of my face, my heart bleeding. "Sierra," he says, sounding pained. "The last thing I ever want to do is hurt you. I'm not great at expressing myself, but I promise you, I only ever have good intentions when it comes to you."

"Try," I plead. "Can't you try to communicate with me, Xavier? *Please.*"

He looks away, his expression tormented. "You don't know what you're asking for. You don't want to know what's going on in my deprived mind, Kitten."

I brush the back of my hand over his cheek in a soft caress. "I'll be the judge of that."

Forty-Two

XAVIER

I'm feeling uneasy as I walk into Graham's office building for our meeting. Every time I see Graham, I'm instantly reminded of the way Sierra looked at him when he found out about us. I have no doubt that she'd never have told him had it been up to her, and it doesn't sit well with me. She told me he called and apologized for his reaction, claiming he was just caught off-guard, but there was more to it. He's been acting professional in all of our meetings since, but it's clear he's got a thing for my wife, and I don't like it one bit.

"Mr. Thorne's last meeting is running late by about thirty minutes, Mr. Kingston," his assistant tells me as she leads me to a conference room. Every month we rotate our meeting location between our offices, and it's his turn to host this time. "Ms. Windsor is already here."

Mrs. Kingston, I mentally correct, irritated that I can't say the words out loud. Sierra rises to her feet when I walk in, and pure possessiveness rushes through me as I take in that navy dress she's wearing. She looks fucking incredible with her long hair draped over her chest like that, her dress clinging to her curves beautifully. My wife smiles at me and then looks past me, answering a question Graham's assistant must've asked — something about coffee or tea, but all I can focus on is how fucking gorgeous my wife is. Damn. I can't even blame Graham for wanting her. How could anyone look at her and not be mesmerized?

She walks up to me when the door clicks closed behind me, her hand instantly wrapping around the back of my neck. "What are you looking at?" she asks in that playful fake mad tone of hers, the one she uses when she says things she would've done back when we were mere rivals.

I wrap my hand around her waist and pull her flush against me. "My *wife*," I answer, earning myself a sweet little smile as she rises to her tiptoes and brushes her lips against mine, once, twice, before she kisses me fully. I groan as I step forward, until the back of her thighs hit the conference table behind her.

"Xave," she says, pulling away. "Graham should be here soon."

I smirk as I grab her waist and lift her onto the table, positioning her so her back is facing the door. "Didn't you hear? Graham is running thirty minutes late," I tell her, before parting her legs to stand between them, my lips finding hers.

She threads her hand through my hair and pulls back a little, only to give in and kiss me, almost like she can't quite resist me either. "Still," she says in between kisses. "Maybe he'll be done sooner."

"What?" I ask, a tinge of insecurity taking root deep in my chest. "Scared Graham will see you kissing your *husband*?" I pull away from her and step back, running a hand through my hair in frustration. I never quite feel like myself around Sierra, and that hasn't changed since we got married. I can't think straight, can't be as detached as I am in every other area of life. She makes me want and do things I shouldn't, and it's fucking maddening.

She looks at me that way she does sometimes, like she sees straight through every wall I put up, every facade I craft. "Come here," my wife says, her tone assertive.

I raise a brow as I walk back to her, and she catches me off guard when she reaches for my tie and pulls me closer, her lips crashing against mine. I groan as I grab her hips and pull her flush against me, kissing her harder than before, my movements a little less controlled.

She moans when I move my lips to her neck, her head falling back. "You're cute when you're jealous," she tells me, and I pull back to throw her a glare, my hands moving to her thighs.

"Baby, you don't want to see what happens when I truly get jealous."

She's smiles, her eyes hooded. "I forgot to tell you that Graham asked me out for a drink after this meeting."

I clench my jaw and look into her eyes as I slide my hands up her legs, my thumbs brushing against her tights, loving the fact that I can feel how wet she is straight through it. "Yeah? What did you tell him?"

"I told him I'd love to go."

My hand freeze in place as my gaze cuts to hers, and I stare at my wife, my heart wrenching painfully. That was not what I was expecting her to say — at all. Does she still want him? If I hadn't intervened when I did, she would have started dated him, and I'd have lost my chance with her forever. Does she regret missing out on him and what they could've had?

"He's taking me to The Renegade."

My blood begins to boil as I envision her laughing with him over cocktails in a restaurant I fucking own — one that serves all her favorite dishes and drinks all because I made it so. It hurts to know that he's exactly the kind of man she should've been with, the kind of man I could never be — someone with strong morals, a good reputation that isn't built on fear and intimidation, a long-standing reputable family history. No man has ever made me feel as insecure and threatened as Graham Throne does.

Sierra grins at me in a way I know all too well, and just like that, every bit of anger drains away. She only smiles at me that way when she's trying to get under my skin. "Little liar," I murmur. My wife looks shocked that I saw through her lies, and her expression just adds to my relief. "Now, how am I going to punish you for provoking me?" I ask as I reach for her tights and rip them at her crotch.

Sierra's breath hitches when I sit down in the chair in front of her and pull her to the edge of the table, putting her pussy on eye level for me. "Tell me why you lied," I demand as I kiss her inner thigh, slowly inching my way forward.

Sierra buries her hand in my hair, her breathing shallow. "You said I didn't want to see what happens when you're truly jealous. Turns out, I do."

I chuckle, unable to help myself. Of course she does. My wife lives to provoke me. "You're about to find out," I warn, before pushing her panties aside and darting my tongue out for a taste.

The way she moans is like fucking music to my ears, and I groan against her pussy as I grab her legs and throw them over my shoulders, my hands gripping her thighs tightly. "Xavier," she pants, and I grin as I torture her clit, lapping it up with harsh, punishing strokes. "Oh *God*."

"Not even God can save you now," I warn her, before pushing two fingers into her to tease her further, bringing her to the brink of an orgasm with my tongue. Her grip on my hair tightens, and she begins to fuck my face, her hips moving on their own accord as she chases her orgasm, not giving a fuck that we're in Graham Thorne's conference room. It resolves every bit of lingering bit of insecurity I felt, and she doesn't even know it.

"Please," she begs. "*Please*."

I use the tip of my tongue to give her exactly what she wants, and my gorgeous wife comes all over my tongue, her moans unbridled. I did that to her, and it's the best fucking feeling in the world.

"I'm not done with you," I murmur as I rise to my feet and begin to unbuckle my belt.

Sierra bites down on her lip when I take my cock out, the sexiest moan leaving her lips when I drag it over her pussy. "I'm going to fuck you on this conference table, and every damn time you see Graham, you're going to be reminded of the way you took your husband's cock in his office. I'm going to ruin the mere sight of him for you."

She gasps when I push the head in, her gaze heated. "You see that, baby? See the way your hungry pussy is fucking swallowing my cock?" I grab her hair and ball my fist as I thrust all the way into her, needing her with a ferocity I've never felt before. "Such a perfect fucking pussy, and it's all *mine*." I pull back, my eyes on hers as I thrust back into her, hard. She moans loudly, her gaze hazy, like she can't think straight, like her mind is filled with nothing but me — just the way I like it. "Every goddamn inch of you is mine, Sierra Kingston," I warn her as I fuck her with fast, hard strokes, and she takes it all.

"*Yes*," she moans, pulling on the lapels of my suit jacket, her legs tightening around my hips. "But you're mine too, Xavier. Don't you ever dare forget it."

I groan, my forehead falling to hers as I take her harder, not caring that the entire table is moving. "Fuck, baby. When you say shit like that..."

As if she isn't torturing me enough, she begins to squeeze her inner muscles, and I know I'm a lost cause. "*Fuck*," I groan, unable to hold on for even a second longer as her pussy squeezes the life out of my cock. My head drops to her shoulder as I come deep inside my gorgeous wife, and she holds me tightly, not realizing just how much comfort it brings me when she hugs me like that.

I sigh happily as I pull out of her, her eyes widening when I move my hands between her legs and push my cum deeper inside her. "I want you to sit in that chair with your ripped tights and my cum dripping out of your pussy, down your thighs," I tell her, aware of the voices I hear in the hallway near us. "Smile at Graham all you want, baby, but you'll do it remembering who you belong to."

Much to my surprise, my wife merely smirks at me in a way that can only be described as *victorious* as she helps me buckle up. She sits down moments before Graham walks in, and I take my seat next to her, my body still thrumming with lingering desire.

He takes a long, hard look at us both, his gaze lingering on

Sierra's bright red face, and I smirk as I open up my laptop, following my wife's lead. I can barely focus on a thing Graham says as he starts the meeting, his expression clearly crestfallen, and judging by the new email in my inbox, it appears I'm not the only one.

From: Sierra Windsor
Subject: I'm yours

I would never do anything that'd make you uncomfortable, Xavier. I'd never go out for drinks with a guy that seems even remotely interested in me. I'm a lot of things, but unfaithful and disloyal don't make that list.

I'm sorry for provoking you, but I've learned that it's the only way you'll be honest with me. It took me a while to realize why I loved our rivalry so much, why I still enjoy provoking you — it's because you put up this strange facade any other time, refusing to speak your mind or show me how you really feel.

I don't want you to be patient with me or choose your words carefully. The man that just fucked me on this conference table? That's the man I want.

I want your raw unfiltered truth, your insecurities, your jealousy. I want every single thing you dislike about yourself, every single thing you try to hide. I want all of you — all the little things that make you who you are, not who you pretend to be.

. . .

Love,

Your wife

I stare at her over my screen, and her eyes meet mine, a hint of uncertainty in them, like she isn't quite sure how her email will go over. I need to try harder to meet her needs. She shouldn't have to resort to her little schemes just to get her emotional needs fulfilled, and I'm clearly fucking up, letting her down. I sigh as I reach for her hand and lift it to my lip, kissing the back gently, and she smiles at me like she doesn't give a single damn that Graham is watching.

Forty-Three

SIERRA

"Xavier?" He looks up from the sofa, his expression conflicted as he stares at what appears to be a box in his hands. Normally, he'd have met me halfway when I come home from work, and he'd have kissed me until I'm breathless. He's been acting even more distant than usual for a couple of days now, and I suspect it has everything to do with me admitting that I want him to let me in. I should've known I was asking for too much, that I overstepped.

"Kitten," he says, rising to his feet, the box in his hand. He seems hesitant as he walks up to me, and nerves rush through me. "I'm sorry, I didn't hear you come in."

I nod and rise to my tiptoes to kiss him, my eyes dropping to the box he's holding when I pull away. "What's that, and why is it stealing your attention away from me?"

Xavier throws me an amused smile and looks down. "I've been thinking about what you said to me, about not wanting to guess what I'm thinking, and wanting more than the carefully curated version of myself I've been showing you."

I nod, my heart in my throat. "That... honestly, just forget I said anything," I murmur, looking away.

He gently places his index finger underneath my chin and forces me to face him. "Don't do that," he says, his tone pleading. "Don't dismiss your needs simply because I failed to meet them."

I stare at him in surprise, caught off guard by his words. "I'm not —"

"This is for you," he says, handing me the box. "Someday, I'm going to tell you all about why I'm not as good with words as you'd like me to be, but until then, I'm going to find little ways to bridge the gap between us. I know it's not enough, but please know that I heard your concerns, and I'm working on it."

"Xavier, you don't have to do anything you're not comfortable with. I spoke without thinking, and I've regretted those words ever since."

He cups my face and brushes his thumb over my lip. "The things we say often are a cause for regret," he says, his tone bittersweet, "but I'm learning the hard way that though words can hurt, the words we leave unspoken can cut just as deep. There are so many things I want to say but can't, things you need to hear, and because of it, you're hurting." He pulls his hand back, and I glance at the box he handed me. "Open it."

Xavier watches me as I pull the bow loose, his expression tormented. He's right — if Valeria hadn't told me about their past, I wouldn't have understood, and I'd have let my own fears and insecurities keep us apart. It would've hurt even more than it does.

"This..." I stare at the book he gifted me wide-eyed. "This is a signed and personalized special edition hardback," I whisper, in awe. "This version isn't even out yet." I gasp when I realize it has sprayed edges, only for my heart to drop when I open it. "It's annotated," I say, trying my best to mask my outrage when I recognize his handwriting. I hold up the book and raise a brow. "What is this? A declaration of war?"

"What?" he asks, confused. "I... I thought you'd like this."

I bite down on my lip and take a calming breath before forcing a smile for my husband. He *defiled* a special edition, and he has no idea.

"Maybe this isn't a good idea," he says, trying to take it back, and I step away, holding it to my chest.

"It's mine," I tell him, a little panicked. "You gave it to me, so can't have it back." He smiles and shakes his head as I throw him a suspicious look before carefully taking another look at my new book. "It's gorgeous," I tell him, my voice shaking. His eyes roam over my face, and I grin at him, genuinely this time. "So you actually read this?"

He nods. "I initially started reading it because I wanted to know why you loved it, and as I was reading it, I highlighted all the passages that reminded me of you. I added some notes in the margins to let you know why something made me think of you, when it might not be obvious from the text."

I flick through my brand new edition of *A Curse of Shadows and Ice*, my heart soaring when I look at it again, seeing it with new eyes. The thought of Xavier reading a beauty and the beast roman-tasy is endlessly amusing, and I can't help but grin when I realize he's highlighted one of my favorite parts — the part where the heroine says *I only promised to be with you until death do us part. I was just expediting the death part*, right before she stabs the emperor in the heart, on their wedding night no less, not realizing he's immortal.

In the margins, it reads:

> *I think I know what he saw in her, even that early in their story; it's the same thing I see in you. It's rare to find someone who isn't intimidated by me, but you never have been. My fears are the same as Felix's, someday you'll see the monster inside me, and you'll run like everyone else does.*

I look up at him, but he's looking away. "I know it isn't the same as me spontaneously telling you what's on my mind, or learning to communicate the way I need to, but it's ..."

"It's perfect," I tell him, trying my best to blink back the tears in my eyes. I can't believe how thoughtful this is, how much effort this must've been. But even more so, I can't believe he sees himself that way. I place the book on our coffee table and reach for him. "Xavier, you are no monster."

"I wish I weren't," he says, burying his hands in my hair. "If I could wash my hands clean, I would, Sierra. There's nothing I wouldn't do to become the kind of man you want."

"I only want you," I admit. "It's only ever been you."

He drops his forehead to mine and draws a shaky breath. "You can't mean that."

I rise to my tiptoes and kiss him, loving the way he makes the softest sound in the back of his throat before pulling my body flush against his. He kisses me hungrily, desperately, and I step forward, making him step back, until we both tumble onto the sofa. He groans when I straddle him, his gaze caressing my body. "I want you, Xavier Kingston. The good, the bad, and everything in between." My hands roam over his shirt, and I smile as I pull begin to unbutton it. "Let me show you just how much."

Forty-Four

XAVIER

I stare out my office window and smile at the torrential rain outside. "Free up my schedule for the rest of the day," I tell Sam. "I'm going home."

"W-what?" he stammers, clenching his tablet. "You can't! You have an acquisition meeting that's been scheduled for months and a critical site inspection."

I smile and shake my head. "I have something more important to do today."

Sam stares at me in disbelief as I grab my things and walk out of my office, my heart at ease with my decision to prioritize myself for just one single day. I've hidden behind my work for so long, but I can't keep walking the same road and expect my destination to change.

I'm oddly nervous as I walk into my house, wondering whether any of the steps I've taken lately were the right ones, or if they'll lead me astray. My heart is racing as I change into gray sweats, leaving my torso bare — just the way my sweet wife likes.

My mind is filled with nothing but thoughts of her as I walk into her home library and light the fire in our marble fireplace, before grabbing a cosy blanket and placing it over the large armchair in the corner. I look around the room and pause for a moment, deciding to add a few candles too.

Just as I've made a hot chocolate with Sierra's favorite white chocolate, the door opens, and I smile to myself. "Oh!" she says, shocked when I meet her halfway. "You're home early!"

I grin as I walk up to her and place my index finger underneath her chin, tipping her face up to kiss her. She sighs happily and rises to her tiptoes, her hand roaming over my chest, her fingers lingering on my abs. "I had a feeling you'd rush home to read by the fireplace," I murmur, taking her hand as I lead her into our home library. "So I thought I'd work on my laptop as you read. I won't bother you, baby. I just want to sit with you."

Sierra gasps when she realizes I've already lit the fire for her, and she turns to face me. That look in her eyes... it's more than affection, more than I'd ever have dared dreamed of, more than I deserve. "Xavier..."

"Here," I tell her, handing her a travel mug and cutting her off. "I made you a hot chocolate." I noticed that Sierra doesn't like using normal mugs near her books, and I think it's because she's scared she'll spill something.

She takes it from me with trembling hands, and it pains me that she appreciates these little things this much. It means I haven't been treating her well enough. She should be used to this, and I've failed her. "Actually, can you hold this for me while I get changed?"

I nod and tip my head toward the little electric coaster I asked Lex to make for her. "I got you this," I tell her, showing it to her. "It'll keep your drink warm. I know you hate it when your drink gets cold because you forget about it while reading, so I thought you might like this."

She brushes the back of her fingers over my cheek, her eyes filled with longing. "You're incredible." Sierra rises to her tiptoes and presses a soft kiss to my cheek before rushing off, and I smile to myself as I sit down in her favorite massive chair, her cup safely locked into her electric coaster.

I glance at the hardback I gave her, still every bit as nervous at the thought of her reading everything I wrote in the margins. She hasn't said much about any of it, but the way she looks at me and the way she behaves around me has changed. My wife has somehow become even sweeter, and I suspect it's because even though I can't say the words she wants to hear, they're still reaching her. I never quite understood the power of the written word until now, and I've never been more grateful for it.

"Kitten," I growl when she walks in wearing the sexiest damn nightgown I've ever seen — one of the new ones Raven sent over. It's mostly white, with small pink flowers embroidered on it, and my wife looks absolutely enchanting in it.

"What?" she asks innocently, knowing full well what she's doing to me. She places her knee on our lounge chair and reaches over to grab her book, giving me a clear view of her cleavage, and it takes all of me not to grab her and bend her over.

She climbs on and spreads my legs, making herself comfortable against my chest, and I wrap my arms around her, hugging her to me. She sighs happily and tilts her head to kiss my neck, once, twice, before she faces forward and opens up her book. Looks like she got about halfway through, and the idea of sitting here with her as she reads all the little notes I left her is a little nerve-racking.

I place my chin on her shoulder and smirk when I realize the next chapter she's about to read is a steamy one. My heart instantly begins to race when I remember the notes I left in the margins...

I imagined this to be us when I read this, and I wonder... do you do the same thing? Is it my face you see when you imagine your heroes? Don't ever tell me if it's not. I don't think I could take it.

"Yes," she whispers, grinding her ass against my rock hard cock subtly. "It's always your face I imagine. It always has been."

I smile, pleased with her words, though I doubt it's true. She squirms a little when my hands begin to roam over her body, my touches slow and leisurely. I bite back a smile when her nipples harden for me easily, the sheer fabric likely only adding to the sensations. "Xave," she says, her voice filled with desperation.

I glance over her shoulder and read along with her as the emperor uses his magical shadows to bring the heroine to the brink of an orgasm. I might not have magical powers, but I don't need them to have the same effect on my wife.

I keep teasing her nipples as my other hand slips between her legs, and I chuckle when I realize she isn't wearing panties. "Were you hoping I'd do this?" I whisper into her ear as I slip my middle finger into her and coat it in her wetness before I circle her clit.

She whimpers, and I can't help but be a little jealous of her book. She got this wet just from some words on a page? Sierra moans as she turns the page, and pure desire rushes through me as I slip two fingers into her and press against her g-spot, using the heel of my hand to caress her clit at the same time.

"Xavier," she moans.

I nip at her ear before kissing her just below it. "That's right, baby," I whisper. "Your book might have made you wet, but it's me that's touching you. It's *me* that'll make you come." She begins to pant, but she doesn't put her book away, so I increase my pace, outright torturing her as I bring her to the edge and keep her there. "This pussy belongs to me, you hear me?"

"Yes," she replies. "*Yes*. I'm yours, Xavier, as much as you're mine."

I grab her hair and kiss her as I give her what she wants, loving the way her pussy contracts around my fingers, her moans silenced by our kiss. My wife collapses against me, breathless, and I smile to myself. *Take that, Felix Osiris.* Fictional asshole. How fucking dare he make my wife wet when he isn't even real? Fucking prick.

"I thought you said you were going to work while I read?"

"I am working," I retort lazily. "Being married is hard work." I tense involuntarily when I realize what I just said and shake my head. "No, I mean— I don't mean that being married to you is hard work, Sierra. I—"

My wife cuts me off by pushing her book aside and turning to straddle me. She looks into my eyes as she shoves my sweats aside and grabs my cock. "*Fuck*," I moan when she aligns it and lowers herself on top of me, taking all of me in one smooth move.

I grab her ass as she begins to ride me, a beautiful blush on her face as she buries her hands in my hair. "It *is* hard work," she says, "but you make it look easy, Xave." Sierra lifts herself almost entirely off my cock, before coming down on me hard, drawing a helpless moan from my throat. "You're mine, Xavier," she says, her eyes never leaving mine. "Every thought you second-guess, every word you think is misspoken. I want it all — no exceptions."

I grab her hair and pull her mouth to mine, drowning myself in her. How the fuck did I get to be this lucky? This kind of luck... it can't last, can it?

Forty-Five

SIERRA

I frown at my architectural drawings and sharpen my pencil, annoyed that I can't quite get it right. "Damn it," I mutter, leaning back in my seat at our dining table.

"Let me see," Xavier says as he puts down a cheese platter before sitting down next to me. I stare at it wide-eyed and grab the whole platter with both hands while he reaches for my drawing.

Xavier chuckles when I take a bite of some smoked cheddar and moan in delight. "I've never before been jealous of cheese that I bought myself," he says, shaking his head as he grabs my pencil. "You do the weirdest things to me, Mrs. Kingston."

"You did this to yourself," I murmur as I grab a cracker and slather it in brie. "You married me, weird quirks and all."

He laughs and leans in to press a kiss to my cheek. "Best thing I've ever done," he replies, before he turns back to my drawing. I watch him as he analyses my work and very quickly makes it better, like it comes easy to him, and I can't help but be a little jealous of how talented he is. It's no wonder we were rivals for so long — we're both far too competitive.

I do a happy little shimmy in my seat as I take another bite of cheese, and Xavier rests his head on his fist, his elbow on the table as he watches me with that enraptured expression. "I may just need to take you to the restaurant in Paris that I flew this in from. I haven't been in years, but I think you'll like it. It's small and quaint, but it has a gorgeous view of the Eiffel Tower, impeccable service, and the absolute best food I've ever had."

I raise a brow, jealousy slowly unfurling in my chest. "Sounds romantic," I murmur, instantly wondering who he went with. It's clear the memory is a good one, judging by the way he's smiling.

Xavier raises a brow, and then he chuckles. "There's no need to look at me that way," he tells me, seemingly amused. "I went with a good friend of mine, a *male* friend. His family owns that restaurant chain, along with many other things in Europe."

I look up in surprise, suddenly realizing that he's never mentioned any friends, or even things he's done in the past that I wasn't already aware of, such as visiting France. "Are you still friends with him?" I ask carefully.

Xavier tenses just a touch, but then he sighs and nods. "I'd say that Dion and Enzo are my only two real friends. I'll introduce you someday. I think he'd love to meet you."

He still seems to think long and hard before he tells me things, but he *has* started to share snippets of his past with me. Only ever good memories, and I suspect they're heavily redacted, but I don't really mind. I don't need to know every single thing about him, I just want to feel like he's letting me in, like I'm someone he trusts and wants to share his life with.

In recent months we've both grown a lot as a couple, and we've slowly started to take baby steps toward each other. Each time I tell him funny stories about my childhood, he emails me a day later with a story of his own, and we've just been going back and forth like that, slowly getting to know each other in ways we didn't before. He leaves me little notes around the house and sends me little gifts almost every day, just things that reminded him of me with a story attached.

Yesterday he sent licorice to my office with an accompanying note reminding me how I once ground up licorice and put it in his coffee machine at home and at his office, because we'd been competing for a candy factory acquisition, and he'd graciously bowed out after my little prank, stating I'd ruined licorice for him forever. His note told me that ever since, he thought of me every single time he saw licorice anywhere, and it made him smile every single time. He told me I'd infiltrated his life in more way than he could count, more ways than I could possibly know.

That new kind of intimacy between us and the vulnerability we've shown each other has brought us closer, and though I'm scared to admit it to him, I've started to see a real future with him, and I wonder if he does too.

"I never asked you, you know?" Xavier says eventually, looking up from my drawing again. "Why did you decide to go into real estate?"

"Because of my dad," I admit, my heart constricting painfully. I rarely talk about my parents, because unlike my older brothers, I don't really have any memories with them. All I have is countless regrets, memories I wish I'd made, photos I wish we'd taken together, and questions I wish I could've asked. "Remember the observatory that we held our reception in?"

"Zane's observatory?"

I nod. "My dad had that built for my mom. It was one of Windsor Real Estate's first projects. Before me, the company had an external CEO, with my grandmother being the chairwoman, but I always knew that I wanted to manage it myself one day. The idea of building places that people set their roots in, that they make memories in... that was what appealed to me. What about you?"

He smiles, but it doesn't quite reach his eyes. "There was a time when things were incredibly tough for my family, and I felt like I was drowning. I needed a lifeline, and Enzo, the friend I just mentioned, gave me one. He asked me to manage his property acquisitions for him, and when it became clear I had a knack for it, he pushed me go into real estate myself. Dion wholeheartedly agreed, and the two of them helped me set things up and got me going. They both taught me a lot of practical things that I simply couldn't have learned at school, and I fell in love with the process of watching things be built up from scratch. It reminded me that it's possible to build almost anything, if you're patient enough — even something as elusive as a better future."

He smirks at me then. "Then eventually, this girl came along that challenged me at every step, and I fell in love even more, harder than ever before. I became obsessed with competing with her, and she inadvertently helped me grow my company into more than what I ever thought possible. *She* became my lifeline. This incredibly beautiful, batshit crazy girl, became the highlight of my entire damn life. She gave me purpose, and she doesn't even know it."

I stare at him, scared to ask him the one question on my mind. Did he fall in love with the girl in his story, with *me*, or did he fall further in love with real estate? I know better than to ask questions I might not like the answer to, so instead, I reach for him, my hand cupping his face. "Maybe that girl was falling in love with *you* the whole time, through every battle, every prank, every single thing you did that ensured you'd be on her mind as much as she was on yours, and maybe she just didn't realize it."

He grins as his nose brushes against mine. "Maybe I did it on purpose. Maybe I just *wanted* her to think of me, even though I knew I didn't deserve her attention."

"I think she disagrees," I tell him, my lips brushing against his and my hand wrapping into his hair. "I think you might just be uniquely perfect for that crazy girl."

He groans when I tighten my grip on his hair and kiss him, losing myself in him, in this moment. God, I'm so in love with him, and I'm starting to think he feels the same way. We've come so far from where we started, all in a matter of months, and I just know... this story we're writing together, it's my favorite one of all time.

Forty-Six

SIERRA

I sigh as I check my phone for the hundredth time today, only to *still* find no new text messages waiting for me. Xavier and I have begun to text each other throughout the day in the last couple of weeks, and the effort he's been putting into our marriage has far exceeded my expectations. He now joins me for lunch with my grandma every week, and he even helped me out with a family incident involving Lex and Raya, no questions asked. Things have just been perfect, except, perhaps, for that one time when I found out the hard way that my brothers are all traitors.

I'd caught Xavier sneaking out of the house one night, and he'd been acting so incredibly suspicious that I thought he might've been cheating on me, so I followed him instead of hanging out with my sisters-in-law, like I'd planned to, only to find out he'd been going to poker night with my brothers for longer than I could've imagined. They all tried to deny he was there, only for all their lies to unravel when I walked into Lex's house. I've forgiven my husband for secretly gathering intel on me throughout the years, but I'm definitely not going to make it easy for my brothers to earn my forgiveness. I'm going to milk that *forever* and make them suffer.

I sigh as I put my phone down, only to pick it back up straight away. Xavier has become someone I've come to rely and depend on, to the point where him not replying to his text messages for a few hours completely unsettles me.

I know he had a meeting today that required him to take his jet early in the morning, but he told me he'd be back in time for tonight's charity fundraiser, and I can't help but worry. I hesitate before ringing my Head of Security, and a dear friend of mine.

"Hi, sweetheart," he says, picking up on the first ring. "Tell me. What can I do for you?"

I smile involuntarily. "Hi, Silas," I reply, a little nervous. Xavier has his own robust security team, ran by Elijah, and I know that they're on par with Silas, but it's worth a try. It's better than calling my brother-in-law with a ridiculous request. "I was just wondering... would you be able to tell me where my husband is?"

He laughs, and I can't help but blush. "I can find out for you. Xavier recently consented to sharing some of his data with me, for your comfort, so it shouldn't take me long to find out."

I raise a brow. He did? The Kingstons are notoriously private, and now that I've married into the family, I understand why. Their security is far tighter than what I'm used to, and though Xavier has tried his best to ensure I don't notice it, it's hard to miss the cars that tail me everywhere I go, and the bodyguards that desperately try to blend in but fail miserably by virtue of their size.

"His jet is en route," Silas tells me. "Should be another hour or so before he lands."

I sigh as I thank Silas before ending the call, my eyes on my reflection in the mirror. I'm wearing a formfitting cream dress that I really wanted Xavier to see, and I paired it with one of the diamond Laurier necklaces he gave me when he stole mine. If he isn't landing until an hour from now, he might be too tired to attend at all.

I'm a lot more crestfallen than I'd like to admit as I head to the fundraiser by myself thirty minutes later. I only attend a handful of them a year, and this is the first one I'd genuinely been looking forward to, because it's the first one I thought Xavier and I would attend together as a couple.

I bite down on my lip as I walk into the ballroom, my thoughts beginning to take control of me. Did he schedule his meeting the way he did so he wouldn't have to attend with me? Our marriage is still a secret, after all. It was my decision to keep it to ourselves, but the longer we're married, the more I'm beginning to regret that choice.

"Sierra?"

I look up and smile when Graham walks toward me, a glass of champagne in his hands. "Graham!"

He wraps his arm around my waist in a quick side hug, and I swipe a glass of champagne off a tray as we stand together. "I'm surprised you're alone," he says.

"Xavier had a meeting that couldn't be postponed," I tell him, my mood souring all over again.

He nods and smirks. "You don't hear me complaining. I never get to hang out with you anymore. I've missed you, you know?"

"We see each other every month," I tell him, laughing. "We literally have a standing meeting."

His smile wavers, and he nods. "Yeah, but it isn't the same. We used to hang out together and grab dinner."

I look away, remembering the way he walked out of my office when he realized Xavier and I were together. He called me the next day and apologized for reacting the way he did, and we never spoke of it again, but I still find it a little awkward to be alone with him now.

"The three of us should grab dinner together sometime," I say carefully. I tried not to notice, but I've come to realize that he doesn't see me as just a friend, and I'm not comfortable having dinner with him alone. It doesn't feel right.

"And risk the wrath of your husband for intruding on even a second of your time together? I know better than to get on Xavier Kingston's bad side."

I roll my eyes. "Xavier is just one big teddybear. It's hard to get on his bad side — trust me, I've tried."

"You're just as delusional as he is," Graham says, laughing. "You could never get on his bad side, because he's always been *on* your side. You just never realized it, and those of us who did never understood just how deep his affection for you ran."

I stare at him wide-eyed, and he chuckles as he takes my champagne glass and puts it away before taking my hand. "Come on," he says. "Let's dance. Who knows if I'll ever get another chance to dance with you."

I smile as I take his hand, only to freeze when I spot my husband walking into the room, a beautiful woman on his arm that I vaguely recognize. Isn't she an up and coming singer? I stare at him in shock as the brunette lets go of his arm to take his hand, throwing him one of those spoiled expressions as she drags him to the dance floor. He smiles indulgently as he *lets* her, and fury and heartache battle for dominance as I begin to see red.

Did he think I wouldn't have come without him? Did he think I wouldn't have heard if he brought a *date* to an event I expected to attend with him? I stare at them shell-shocked, my eyes roaming over that tux he's wearing, before moving to the beautiful brunette in her dazzling black dress. He must've changed on the plane, and come straight here, and he didn't even call me to let me know.

His hand wraps around her waist, and I take a step forward. "Excuse me," I tell Graham, my body thrumming with indignation. He says something that doesn't quite register, my focus solely on my husband.

I can feel countless eyes on me as the crowd parts, until I'm only a few steps away from Xavier. He looks up, surprise flickering through his eyes when I place my hand on his arm. "Apologies for cutting in," I tell his date. "I've really been looking forward to dancing with my *husband*, and I don't think I can wait a moment longer."

She smiles sweetly and steps away, seemingly not taking offense at all, nor does she seem surprised by the way I referred to him.

Xavier, on the other hand, looks at me with fiery eyes. "Kitten," he murmurs as he takes me in his arms. "You look a little murderous. I think I like that look on you."

I glare at him and wrap my arms around his neck, my body pressed flush against his. This isn't a civil dance — not in the slightest. "Who is she?" I ask, my voice breaking.

He looks at me in confusion, like the idea of him being with her is preposterous, and then he chuckles. "Sierra, that's Calliope, my brother's best friend. Hunter is very much in love with her, though he'd never admit it, and I don't have the least bit of interest in her. I am, however, very interested in your reaction." My shoulders sag in relief, and he stares at me in wonder, something akin to hope sparkling in his eyes. "I thought you wanted to keep me hidden, that you wouldn't want me to approach you so openly the second I walked in."

"I don't," I tell him, and his expression falls. He puts a little bit of space between us, but I bridge it and thread my hand through his hair. "I don't want to keep you hidden, Xavier."

His eyes widen in shock, and I smile as I lean in to kiss him, ignoring the gasps I hear around us. He groans and instantly deepens our kiss, my body melting into his. We're both breathing hard by the time I pull away, and he looks at me like he's trying commit this moment to memory. "You're mine, Xavier Kingston," I tell him. "And I want the world to know it."

Forty-Seven

SIERRA

I stare at all the articles about Xavier and me, each of them having captured a slightly different moment of the lead-up to me grabbing Xavier and kissing him. I blush fiercely as I look at all the comments and the outrageous speculative headlines.

SIERRA WINDSOR SABOTAGES XAVIER KINGSTON'S DATE

SIERRA WINDSOR JEALOUS OF MORE THAN JUST HER RIVAL'S SUCCESS

SIERRA AND XAVIER CLASH AT FUNDRAISER— BUT NOT THE WAY WE EXPECTED

"For god's sake," I mutter, my heart racing. The way I look at him in these photos leaves very little guesswork, in my opinion, and they still can't quite get it right. Honestly, at this rate, the headlines should've just read SIERRA KISSES XAVIER IN A JEALOUS FIT. Even SIERRA AND XAVIER REVEAL THEIR RELATIONSHIP would've made more sense than this.

"Kitten?"

I gasp and jump up in surprise when Xavier walks into my office holding a giant bouquet of pale pink Juliet roses — my favorite. It shouldn't surprise me that he knows such little details about me. He shows his affection in unexpected ways, and I've learnt that it often comes in this shape — it's him proving that he pays attention to every little thing I do or say, and remembering little remarks that anyone else would've forgotten.

"These are gorgeous," I whisper as I take them from him, suddenly feeling incredibly shy. He doesn't know how meaningful these kinds of things are to me. These are all things I've been reading about for years but never got to experience for myself, until him.

"Not quite as gorgeous as you are," he says, leaning in for a kiss. My eyes flutter closed, and I rise to my tiptoes, deepening our kiss.

Xavier is breathing hard when he pulls back, his forehead dropping to mine. "It's six," he whispers. "And I was wondering if you'd have dinner with me? I can wait for you if you're still busy with work."

He pulls back to look at me, his expression a little uncertain, and I nod. "Let's go," I tell him, oddly nervous. He's asking me out on a date, isn't he? We've been spending so much time together in the last couple of months, but we haven't gone *out* on dates, and I'm oddly excited about it.

Xavier grabs my hand and entwines our fingers as he leads me through my office building, toward his car, and I grin to myself as I squeeze his hand. I hear the whispers around us, but I couldn't care less.

"Wow," I whisper to myself when we walk onto the rooftop of The Siren. Everywhere I look, there are planters with Juliet rose bushes and countless candles. There is only one table, and Xavier grins at me as he leads me to it. He pulls out my chair for me, and I sit down hesitantly. "What is all this?"

He reaches for my hand over the table. "There's something that I wanted to talk to you about."

His words instantly make me nervous, and I panic inwardly when he pulls out a set of documents. Is he trying to tell me that he took offense to the way I publicly kissed him last night? Is he going to sue me for it? He can't, can he? He's the one who said that keeping our marriage a secret wasn't part of our NDA.

"You look like there's something crazy going on in your mind," he says, chuckling lightly as he slides to documents toward me, and I frown when I realize they're property deeds. "I've been meaning to give this to you since the day we got married, but I couldn't really find the right words, and I was worried that you'd take it the wrong way."

"What is this?" I ask, my cheeks rosy.

How could he possibly have known I was thinking something crazy? It's becoming more and more common for him to know what I'm thinking without me even saying anything at all, and each time he seems to read my mind, I just fall deeper in love with him.

"I've thought long and hard about how to say this, and which words I'd choose, but now that I'm sitting here with you, I can't remember a single one of them," he says, his voice trembling just a touch. Xavier is always confident, and I'm not quite sure what to make of him tonight.

I reach for the documents hesitantly, my heart racing. "You're giving me every single major acquisition we've fought about over the years?" I ask, looking the documents over. "All six of them?" I frown as I read through the documents carefully. Indus, The Renegade, The Siren, Renaissance, Everest and even Artemis. He's giving me every project that I thought I'd won, only for him to swoop in and steal it away. Each of these I'd designed right down to the last detail, and he copied every single thing I'd wanted.

Xavier nods, his expression unreadable. "You know how I once told you I never stole any projects from you, and you were so mad you bit my arm?"I laugh, unable to help it. He smiles back at me, his gaze filled with adoration. "What I didn't tell you then is that they were always meant for you. I always planned to give them to you, because it was never the properties I was after."

"Then what *were* you after?"

His gaze roams over my face. "You."

I bite back a smile as my heart thunders in my chest. "You want *me*?" I repeat. "What will you give me in return?" I ask nervously, in an attempt to play off his words in case I'm misunderstanding what he's saying.

He looks into my eyes, nothing but sincerity in them. "*Everything.*"

"Are you sure?" I ask, my voice breaking as insecurity shines through. "What if my demands are too high?"

"There's nothing you could ask for that I won't give you."

"What if I want your heart?"

I thought my words would surprise him, but he merely smiles, his eyes overflowing with affection. "It's already yours. My heart has *always* has been yours, Sierra. I am *madly* in love with you, and I have been for far longer than you could possibly imagine." Xavier reaches for my hand and squeezes gently.

"Always?" I repeat, my heart filled with hope.

He glances at the property deeds and smiles. "In order of acquisition, what do these six projects spell?"

I frown as I think back to the last eight years or so, when these properties were acquired. In order of when he stole each of these, it'd be...

The Siren
Indus
Everest
The Renegade
Renaissance
Artemis

"SIERRA," I whisper in disbelief when I recognize the pattern the first letters form.

My husband looks down, his cheekbones flushed. "When I say *always*, I truly mean it. It's always been you for me. I never dared tell you how I feel, especially not when I couldn't tell you the truth about myself, and my past."

"You don't have to tell me," I tell him, my heart aching. "It was never about knowing everything about you, Xavier. I just didn't want to feel like an outsider. I wanted to feel closer to you, and I do now."

He shakes his head. "Dion said something to me a while ago that stuck with me, and he's right. He told me that if I didn't tell you the truth, I wasn't ever really giving you a honest chance to love me, and I'd always fear that you'd leave me when you found out that there were parts of me I'd hidden from you — and it's true." Xavier runs a hand through his hair and sighs, his expression sorrowful. "Those properties? I want you to have them regardless of what you think of me when I'm done telling you everything I need to say to you, but that isn't what I wanted to talk to you about today."

I nod, my heart beating wildly, nerves rushing down my spine. "I'm listening," I tell him, my voice soft.

Xavier's eyes fall closed for a few moments, before he looks at me with pure resignation written all over his face. "The night I came home with blood on my clothes, I'd cut out a man's tongue, and I'd dismembered several others."

My stomach turns, and I take a deep breath. "Did they deserve it?"

His eyes widen, like that isn't at all the response he was expecting. "Yes," he says, sounding a little confused.

"Tell me why."

"It's a long story," he replies, "but it's one you deserve to hear."

I nod, and he begins to tell me about his family's criminal roots, and I listen raptly. "I wanted out," he admits, "and I wasn't the only one — Valeria did too. We argued about it often, because she'd actually been gathering the courage to leave, but I didn't dare disappoint our parents. One particular night our usual argument blew over, and I told her to just leave instead of always talking about it." He looks away, pure heartbreak in his eyes. "She walked out the door, and I watched her go, even though my instincts were telling me to stop her. That was the same night she disappeared, and I didn't find out until recently what happened to her in the time she was missing. My foolish words cost her everything, and she hasn't been the same since."

Xavier can barely look at me as he continues to tell me about his past, and eventually the photo he received, and the way he responded to that attempted blackmail. "I wish I could tell you that was all in the past, and that I'm a better man now, but the truth is, I don't regret it, and I'd do it all over again if I needed to." He clasps his hands and slowly raises his eyes. "I understand that this changes everything, Sierra. I thought of keeping this from you for the rest of our lives, but then I realized that it'd just hurt you so much more if you eventually found out we built our love on a bed of lies, and I love you too much to do that to you."

"You're right," I murmur. "It changes everything."

He looks heartbroken as I rise from my seat, only for his brows to furrow as I walk up to him. He pulls his chair back, his eyes widening when I place my knee between his legs and my hands on his shoulders.

Xavier reaches for me, only to pull his hands back as he looks into my eyes, his expression one I haven't seen on him before. He looks uncertain, hopeful, and *mesmerized* — all at once. "Let's announce our marriage," I tell him, my voice trembling. "I love you, Xavier. I love every single part of you, including the parts you wish never saw the light of day. Every experience, every regret made you who you are, and I wouldn't change a thing about you. I love you just as you are, Xavier Kingston, and I always will."

Forty-Eight

SIERRA

I lean against my husband on the sofa and smile to myself as I post a photo on my social media channels with one simple caption: **Mrs. Kingston**. It's the same photo that Xavier put on a billboard outside my office, except this time, he hasn't been cut out of it.

Xavier looks up at me with the sweetest smile after he posts his own photo, and I rush to take a look at it, curious what he chose. A blush spreads across my cheeks when I navigate to his account and find that he's posted a photo of us kissing, moments after we were pronounced husband and wife. His caption is just as simple as mine, but far more romantic: **Mine. Always & Forever.**

Pure giddiness rushes through me as I watch everyone's shocked reactions coming in, and I can just about imagine the countless requests for comments Ares must be getting right about now. "Oh wow," I whisper when just minutes later, Xavier and I are both tagged in individual posts each of my siblings and sisters-in-law posted, all of them featuring wedding photos of us with them, and cute captions.

RavenWindsor: There isn't anyone else I'd ever be willing to share my bestie with! Love you both endlessly.

ValentinaWindsor: This story has been in the making longer than anyone could possibly imagine, and I've loved watching it unfold. Couldn't wish for a better ending.

FayeWindsor: These two are a perfect symphony, and I'm lucky to call them my family.

CelesteWindsor: What's meant to be always will be, and Xavier and Sierra were definitely meant to be.

RayaWindsor: These two are amazing individually, but the way they complement each other? Magical.

AresWindsor: Congratulations, both of you. Honored to have an extra brother.

LucaWindsor: about damn time.

DionWindsor: Pleased to officially welcome you into our family, brother.

ZaneWindsor: called it.

LexingtonWindsor: Best of luck, mate. You'll need it.

I bite down on my lip, moving from tears to laughter as I read all the captions, and Xavier wraps his arm around me as he shows me posts from Hunter and Zachary.

HunterKing: Congratulations, both of you. Your happiness has the sweetest melody.

MayorZach: Officiating for my brother and sister-in-law was the greatest honor I've ever been bestowed. Welcome to the family, little sis.

"My parents, Elijah, and Valeria don't have social media presences," he explains, and I nod, pressing a kiss to his cheek, unable to get a word out. I've never felt so loved, so welcomed, and it leaves me feeling far more emotional than I'd imagined.

I take a shaky breath as I navigate to my settings and change both my name and my username, and I can't help but grin at the words Sierra Kingston. "Fuck," Xavier groans, pulling me onto his lap, my back against his chest and his arms wrapped around me. "Do you have any idea how long I've waited for this?"

I lean back against him, my heart overflowing with happiness. "How do you feel about going on a honeymoon?" I ask, a little scared to suggest it. Neither of us can afford to take much time off considering our current workload, but I want to be alone with him for a little while. "I always imagined going on a honeymoon someday, and now seems like the perfect time to escape. The media is no doubt going to double down on us for a bit, so we might as well hide out somewhere together."

"I think I have an idea," he murmurs, nuzzling my neck. Xavier pulls away a little to look at me, his expression a little uncertain. "Remember when I mentioned Enzo? He got engaged a few days ago, and his fiancee is throwing a party in Malta to celebrate. I was going to decline the invitation, but—"

"I'd love that," I tell him immediately. I didn't actually think he'd ever introduce me to Enzo, and there's no way I'm going to let this chance slip away. Xavier has told me a lot about himself, but I know it was an abbreviated version of his story, and I can't wait to learn more about all the experiences and people that shaped him.

"I'll get the jet ready," he says, before lightly pinching my chin and leaning in for a kiss. I sigh as I cup his face, feeling more secure in our marriage than ever before. I don't think I've ever felt this happy.

I giggle as Xavier grabs me and turns us over, so I'm lying flat on the sofa, his body on top of mine. He studies me that way he does sometimes, like he wants to remember every single thing about me, and I gently touch his soft hair. "This is real, isn't it?" he whispers.

I nod. "The realest thing I've ever felt."

He draws a shaky breath and leans in to kiss me, his knee parting my legs. My arms wrap around him, and I moan as his body moves against mine as he kisses me slowly, leisurely, every touch part of his slow seduction. "Xave," I plead when his hand moves underneath my dress, and he smirks at me as he begins to raise it, only for the doorbell to startle us both.

He pulls away and helps me tidy my clothes, his expression instantly stormy. "Must be my family," he says, sounding far from pleased as footsteps soon follow.

"Xavier! Sierra!"

I rise to my feet and smile when my mother-in-law walks in, followed by Valeria, who throws me an apologetic smile. "I told her not to bother you," Valeria says, "but she saw the wedding announcement, and she has decided that it means she no longer has to stay away from you."

My mother-in-law grabs my hands, her eyes brimming with excitement. "Xavier nagged and nagged, telling me not to over-whelm you in the first few months of your marriage, so I begrudg-ingly agreed to stay away until you'd adjusted, and it seems like you have."

"*Mom*," he groans, and I smile to myself. His whole demeanor changes when his mother is near, and it's so endearing.

"I have," I promise, squeezing her hand. "And there's absolutely no need to stay away." It's much more likely that Xavier was scared she'd say something he didn't want me knowing about, but he doesn't look the least bit worried anymore.

"Wonderful! There are so many things I've been wanting to do with you. Would you let me take you out sometime this week? I'd love to take you shopping."

My husband runs a hand through his hair, and Valeria shoots him an amused look. "Maybe next week," he says, pulling me closer, his arm wrapping around my shoulders. "I'm taking her to Malta for Enzo and Tiffany's engagement party this week. We're staying a couple of days after too."

I notice Valeria tense, and her eyes widen as she stares at her brother in shock. "What?" she says, her voice breaking.

He looks her over and frowns. "I thought you knew," he says, his voice soft.

Valeria runs a shaking hand through her hair, her expression lost. "Can I... can I come?" Xavier falls silent, and she takes a deep breath. "I never told them, Xave. I never reached out to anyone once I got back, not even them."

"Valeria," he says, his tone carrying a hint of reluctance. "It isn't safe. There'll be too many people, and it's a foreign territory."

"Please," she begs, and Xavier sighs, giving in. "I won't attend the party. I just want to see them afterwards and congratulate them myself."

"Fine, but you're being escorted straight back onto the jet within twenty-four hours."

Forty-Nine

SIERRA

I'm entirely unnerved as I board the plane with Valeria and Xavier, a dozen bodyguards accompanying us. "Surely this is unnecessary," I murmur, having gotten used to my own family's security measures that aren't quite this visible.

"She's right," Valeria tells her brother, even as her trembling hand slips into mine. "You're overdoing it, Xave."

He glances at us, his expression tormented, and I sigh as I squeeze V's hand, silently urging her to let it go. He looks the way he does sometimes, like he's battling demons he refuses to admit exist.

"The world just found out that you're my wife," he eventually says as he kneels in front of my seat and helps me buckle in. "That puts an even bigger target on your back than before. The Windsors are frequently targeted by paparazzi and business competitors aiming for an advantage, but it's different for us. We're targeted by people that want us dead. Things will never be the same again, Sierra. I'm sorry. I know it seems excessive, but I promise you, it is necessary."

I nod and reach for him, my hand wrapping around the back of his neck as I lean in and brush my lips against his softly. "I understand," I tell him, grateful he told me the full truth himself. I was able to infer most of it from bits and pieces Valeria told me each time she came over to hang out with me following that time we baked cookies together, but that wasn't the same as my husband sitting me down and telling me everything I needed to know, every reason behind the increased security, and the concern currently etched into his face.

Xavier pulls away from me when V takes her seat next to me, and she sighs when her brother turns to face her. "I still don't think you should come," he says. "If you insist on it, you need to understand that we'll no longer be able to keep your identity under wraps. There's a chance you'll be photographed, and the media will find out who you are. Anyone who may have been looking for you will be alerted to your survival when they see your face, and the tactile peace you found, the events I've taken you to? That all ends. I'll no longer be able to keep you safe in crowds, no matter how well curated the guest list is."

"I'm aware," she says, her tone resolute. "I've spent years hiding, working with Elijah behind the scenes to tie up the loose ends I left, but I'm done moving in the shadows, Xavier. I want my life back. I didn't fight so hard to survive only to not really live the life I nearly lost."

His expression shutters closed, but something akin to guilt flickers through his eyes, and I just about keep from reaching for him when every single cell in my body longs to wrap my arms around him and tell him that it wasn't his fault.

Xavier takes the seat opposite me, and V reaches for my hand as we get ready for takeoff. I entwine our fingers, and she drops her head on my shoulder. We've gotten close over the last few months, and at least once every two weeks or so, she comes over to borrow books or beg for a new batch of cookies, promising to help bake them only to just eat half my cookie dough before it even makes it into the oven.

I doubt she'd ever admit it, but I know she's been doing all she can to make sure things work out between Xavier and me, offering me stories about their childhood that I didn't think he'd ever tell me and generally making me feel welcome and included. It wasn't until she started doing it that I realized how badly I'd missed the kind of sisterhood I'd gotten used to with my own sisters-in-law. "Does flying make you nervous?" I ask, tightening my grip on her hand.

She shakes her head and sighs. "It's not that. It's just..." She looks at her brother, who seems engrossed in his work, his noise canceling headphones covering his ears. "What did Xavier tell you about Enzo?"

I study her, surprised to find so much torment in her eyes. "I know that Enzo comes from a long line of oil magnates, and that your family always helped them maintain their wealth and position, through whatever means necessary. Xave told me that it was always a symbiotic relationship, but things changed with Enzo and Xavier. From what I understand, they became real friends, and Enzo wanted more for all of you than the future that laid ahead of you."

"Did he tell you anything else?"

I raise a brow and think back to every mention of Enzo. "He told me that even before you disappeared, Enzo was the one who pushed for you guys to go legit, and he helped your Dad start and manage his corporation, setting down the roots for everything the business grew into. After you were gone, he seemed to have really taken the reins and pulled your family out of the shadows they previously operated in, pushing Xavier into real estate and helping your other brothers find their footing too."

V looks down. "So he doesn't know then. That's good, I guess."

"Doesn't know *what*?"

She looks into my eyes and draws a shaky breath. "If I tell you, will you promise to never tell Xavier?"

I nod and gently squeeze her hand. "Of course. I have five sisters-in-law — six, now that I have you. I'm used to keeping secrets, V."

"Enzo and I had secretly been dating for a little over two years when I was taken." My eyes widen, and she glances at her brother, her expression tormented. "He'd asked me to elope with him a few weeks prior, on our two-year anniversary, and I'd told him no because I didn't think my family would ever forgive me. It's the one decision I've always regretted, even more than storming out of the house after my argument with Xavier. I should've said yes, and if I could ever go back in time, *that's* the one thing I'd change."

I stare at her in shock, not quite comprehending her words. "*What*? Then why didn't you tell him when you came back? You clearly still care about him, V. If you had, then maybe —"

She shakes her head. "I was going to, but by then, he'd already been dating Tiffany for over a year, and I'd just been so mad. I just... why did it have to be her?" V clenches her jaws much in the same way Xavier does when he's mad, and I bite down on my lip to keep from reacting, giving her space to finish her story and get this off her chest. "Tiff was my best friend, growing up. She was the sister I always wished I had, but she was also the only person who knew about Enzo and me, the only one who knew just how much I loved him. The betrayal stung and destroyed all the hope I'd held onto so desperately. It wrecked me even more than everything I'd endured."

She takes a shaky breath, her expression pensive. "I thought about confronting them, played out the scenario in my head every night for a year straight, but they seemed happy together in all the photos I'd seen of them, and I knew they were better off without me. I was broken, damaged, and she'd clearly become a shining light in his life. I know Enzo, and I know that he'd feel obligated to be there for me, but that isn't what I wanted. Besides, how could I walk back into their lives and put them at risk? Especially after how hard Enzo worked to help my family step out of the shadows. I couldn't do that to him."

Valeria looks out the window, her gaze forlorn. "Honestly, I have no idea what I'm doing right now, but I just... I just wanted to see them together for myself and wish them well, so I can finally let go and move on. I don't want to keep wondering what would happen if he found out I'm still alive, or lie awake at night and wonder if he still thinks of me."

I sigh as I wrap my arm around her. Just like I've always held onto my idea of a happily ever after, she has too, and hers has Enzo's name written all over it.

Fifty

SIERRA

Xavier takes my hand, and I smile at him as I entwine our fingers. It hadn't occurred to me that this is our first public appearance since we announced our marriage, and it's at an event that actually matters to him. "Do I look okay?" I ask, trying not to let my insecurities show. The last thing I want to do is embarrass him when he's introducing me to somehow he really cares about.

"You look perfect," he says, his eyes roaming over my body. "I can't wait to put Valeria back on a plane tonight, so we can be completely alone together."

I wrap my arms around his neck and rise to my tiptoes to press a soft kiss to his cheek. "We could let her stay a bit longer," I murmur. "I don't mind."

He narrows his eyes at me as we leave our villa and walk along the beach, toward the party's venue. "Don't even try it. I know you two are in cahoots these days — she needs to get on that plane, Kitten. It's for her own safety, and you know it. There are far too many people here, too many threats."

I pout but nod nonetheless. "Fine," I mutter. "I'm taking her to

Zane's private island for her birthday, though, and you're not invited."

He chuckles and throws me a sweet look. "Fine by me so long as you take adequate security with you," he says, and the way he looks at me makes my heart skip a beat.

"You're nervous," he remarks, seemingly amused as we walk into the gorgeous beachside venue. "It's been years since I last saw you get nervous. You're always fearless, certainty in every step you take."

I look up at him and blush fiercely. "I *am* nervous," I admit. "How could I not be? I'm scared I'll do or say something weird, and I'll make a bad first impression. I don't want your friends to hate me, or think that I'm not good enough for you."

He stares at me in disbelief and raises a brow. "*You*? Not good enough for *me*?" I watch as the edges of my husband's lips pull up, a smile slowly transforming his face. "Sierra, that is the most ridiculous thing I have ever heard. If anyone is unworthy, it's clearly me. There's not a chance that my friends would think badly of you."

I turn to face him and gently caress his emerald tie. It matches my dress perfectly, and it's one of those little things that I secretly really love about him. He always makes sure our outfits match. "You genuinely don't realize, do you?"

"Realize what?"

"That you're the man of my dreams."

He freezes, almost like the words don't quite register, and then he looks away, his cheekbones flushing. I can't help but giggle at his response, and he grins as he wraps his arm around my waist and pulls me closer.

"Xavier Kingston — *smiling*?"

I look up at the sound of an incredulous voice and find an unfamiliar man looking at us both with something that can only be described as affection.

"Vincenzo Rossi — *engaged*," Xavier responds, letting go of me to give his friend one of those weird side hugs that men tend to do. "It was about damn time." I've never seen him look so animated around anyone but me, and my heart overflows with happiness at the sight of him looking so happy.

"I know," he says, looking down. "I kept Tiff waiting too long, hence the massive party." So this is Enzo. He isn't quite as handsome as Xavier, in my opinion, but I can understand why V is so smitten. He looks like a Roman statue, with his half-long wavy hair and his chiseled jawline.

"Meet my wife," Xavier says, wrapping his hand around my shoulder. "Sierra Kingston."

The butterflies in my stomach go wild at the way he addresses me, and I can't help but smile shyly. "It's lovely to meet you, Enzo. I've heard so much about you."

He narrows his eyes at Xavier. "You haven't been telling your lovely wife any lies about me, have you?"

"Do you really think I'd do that?" Xave asks, laughing.

Enzo looks at me with an expression that clearly says — *yes, your husband would definitely do that to m*e, and I burst out laughing.

"Xavier! Oh my gosh, I didn't think you'd come!" My eyes widen when a blonde woman rushes into my husband's arms, hugging him tightly, and I raise a brow when she looks him over, her hands wrapped around his biceps.

"Tiffany," he says, smiling. "Congratulations on getting engaged, and thank you so much for inviting me."

He isn't quite as warm to her, and it's petty, but I find it reassuring when he steps away from her and pulls me against him, before he proceeds to introduce me all over again. Tiffany smiles and congratulates us on our marriage, but it's clear she's curious about us, and I probably should've expected it. We never got engaged the way they did, and we didn't have a big wedding with lots of guests. I never gave it much thought, but in hindsight, I wish I'd gotten to experience all of those things.

I study Tiffany as she talks to Xavier and mostly ignores me, and I can't help but dislike her. I'm not sure if it's because of what I know, or because of the way she seems to be dismissing me. I just can't imagine doing what she did, and not just because my best friend is married to my brother. Maybe it's irrational and petty, but I just can't forgive her for hurting my sister-in-law, even if she did it unknowingly.

"Dance with me," Xavier says suddenly, cutting off his conversation with her mid sentence when the band begins to play a slow romantic song.

I look into his eyes as he pulls me onto the dance floor, my heart beating wildly. "I love you," I whisper, the words bursting from my lips.

My husband smiles and slides his hand up from my nape, into my hair. "I love you more," he tells me, before leaning in to kiss me, the ocean breeze and the music creating a scene right out of my favorite romance novels.

"This is it, you know?" I murmur, my breathing unsteady. "I think this is our real life happily ever after."

Xavier chuckles and presses a soft kiss to my forehead, before kissing the tip of my nose. "No, baby," he murmurs. "This is only just the beginning."

We're in a world of our own as we dance and drink more champagne than we really should, and I wish things could always be like this. We stay on the dance floor until the last song comes on, and he never once takes his eyes off me. I wasn't sure it was the right move when I asked him to take me on a honeymoon, but I'm glad I did. We needed this — time in isolation, without work and our families there to distract us.

Almost like he knows what I'm thinking, he drops his forehead against mine and sighs. "We better keep our word," he says, sounding reluctant.

I glance over my shoulder and find Enzo standing in one corner with his friends, while Tiff is laughing with her own friends. Xavier's hand wraps into mine as he nods at his bodyguards, and two of them instantly approach Enzo and Tiffany. They glance at us simultaneously, and Xavier grins as he tips his head toward the beach, where more of our staff should be escorting V to right now.

"I hear you've got a surprise for me?" Enzo says, throwing his arm around Xavier and stealing my husband away. "What did you do? Did you buy me this island?"

I laugh, unable to help myself. It actually is something I could see Xavier doing. "Unfortunately, it isn't really possible to buy a country," I tell him, "but I'd argue that this surprise is better than that."

Enzo smirks at me. "Better than an island of my own? That's quite a grand promise, Mrs. Kingston."

"You already have several islands anyway," Tiff reminds him.

"You do," Xave agrees, "and don't smile at my wife like that. Actually, don't even look at her."

Tiff laughs and lightly punches his arm as we walk onto the beach. "Never thought I'd witness you being jealous or possessive, Xavier, over a man whose engagement party you just attended, no less."

"If it isn't an island, what could it be?" Enzo asks, his voice playful. It's clear he enjoys winding Xavier up, and I have a feeling we're going to get along really well.

"See for yourself," I tell him, my voice faltering when I spot Valeria stepping out from behind her bodyguard, her long blue dress flowing with the wind.

Enzo follows my gaze and freezes in place, his expression fracturing as disbelief and longing fight for dominance in his eyes. "Valeria," he whispers, before he takes off running, bridging the distance between them until he's cupping her cheek with one hand, his other hand buried in her hair. "It's you," he says, his voice breaking. "It's really you."

Enzo drops his forehead to hers, and her arms wrap around his neck as she bursts into tears. Xavier tightens his grip on my hand, almost painfully so. "That's the first time she's cried since—"

"She's back," Tiff whispers, staring ahead in shock. Something that looks a whole lot like heartbreak crosses her face as she watches Enzo hold Valeria, but then she seems to snap out of it and rushes up to them, wrapping her arms around them both. Even so, Enzo doesn't loosen his grip on Valeria at all, not even for a moment.

Fifty-One

XAVIER

"Where are you taking me?" my beautiful wife asks as I lead her onto the yacht I bought for Enzo's birthday a year ago.

"To one of the islands Enzo owns," I reply, grinning at her. "It's a private spa and resort that he spent years building, only to then never use it."

Sierra falls silent, her gaze pensive. "Maybe he just didn't have anyone he wanted to bring to his island."

I look away, hoping she won't say more than that. I'm not blind. I saw the way Enzo hugged my sister, and it didn't exactly seem friendly and innocent to me. He looked at her like all of his wishes had come true — like she was a mirage, one he was clutching to in fear of it fading away. It would explain the way Valeria responded when she learned of his engagement, and her sudden decision to come when I usually have to coerce her to join me at events.

"Come on," I murmur, leading her toward the yacht's deck, where chocolate coated strawberries and champagne are waiting for us.

My gorgeous wife gasps and whirls around to face me, the

238

brightest smile lighting up her face. "God, I fucking love you," I say without thinking, and her eyes widen a fraction.

She sighs happily as she wraps her arms around my neck. "I love you more, Xavier."

Sierra giggles when I lift her into my arms and carry her to the thick cushions at the front. I lay her down gently and move to lie next to her, both of us turning on our sides to face each other. "Do you really?" I ask, studying her face. "Love me, that is."

She follows the curve of my brow with the tip of my fingers, before sliding her fingers down to my cheekbone. "More than anything," she says, cupping my face. "If there's one thing you should never doubt, it's my love for you, Xavier. No one but you has ever even been able to capture my attention, let alone more than that. No one ever will."

I wrap my hand over hers and sigh. "I guess I'm just having a hard time believing you could love me after everything I told you. I was certain it'd be the end of us, and to be honest, I'm scared you'll change your mind."

"Xave... Valeria had already told me enough for me to have a reasonable understanding of your family's background, and the things she'd gone through. I knew, and I'd never blame you for protecting your family and doing whatever it takes to accomplish that. What mattered to me was *trust*, and you gave me that when you told me the truth. I knew who you were when I married you, Xavier. I'd heard the rumors, and I knew there was at least some truth to it, but I married you anyway."

I stare at her in surprise, and she smiles sweetly. She knew. Of course she did. There isn't much my kitten misses, and I should've realized, shouldn't have underestimated her intelligence. "Not by choice."

She laughs. "Perhaps so, but loving you certainly is a choice. Asking you to let me in, admitting that it hurt when you kept things from me, those were choices. That was my attempt to fight for what I thought we could have, and you stepped up to fulfill my needs, even when it was hard, even when it required you to step out of your comfort zone. Falling in love with you was a choice, Xavier. One that I'll never regret."

I lean in, my lips brushing against hers, and she sighs happily as she kisses me, pulling me closer. My gorgeous wife giggles when I move on top of her, and her hands begin to roam over my body. "If not for the risk of reporters catching us on camera with their damn telescopic lenses, I'd have taken you right here, right now."

She looks up at me with so much love in her eyes, and I can hardly believe that she's mine. I don't know what I've done to deserve her, but I'll never be any less grateful to have her. "I've always wanted to do it on the beach," she says, blushing fiercely. "So I was pretty excited when you told me you were taking me to a private island."

I smirk as I pull her up with me. "We should be there in about ten minutes," I tell her, trying not to let on just how hard my cock is. The mere thought of laying her down on the beach, her long hair spread out around her and a soft breeze caressing our skin... *fuck.*

Sierra looks at me in a way that can only be described as seductive, and I swallow hard when she reaches for a strawberry and bites into it. "You live to torment me, don't you?" I ask, pained.

She grins. "Yes," she replies instantly. "Surely you didn't think marrying me would save you from my schemes? No, Xave. That just made you my prime target. You're in for a *lifetime* of torture."

My sweet kitten squeals when I reach for her and throw her over my shoulders moments before we've even docked. "Torture, you say?" I tell her as I carry her off the yacht and onto the wooden dock. "Two can play that game, baby. Since you're being sassy, I'm going to torture you three times — three times, I'm going to get you close to coming, only to pull away and leave you begging."

My wife gasps. "I'll never forgive you," she claims, and I laugh as I step off the dock and onto the beach. "Did you forget I'm petty? If you do that to me, I'll pay it back a thousandfold."

I tighten my grip on her before laying her down on the perfectly white sandy beach. I don't have enough patience to go to our mansion and unpack. I need her now. "You're so cute when you lie," I whisper, loving the way her eyes spark angrily. "We both know you can't resist my cock."

She narrows her eyes at me and wraps her arms around me. "Shut up," she snaps, pulling me closer.

"Make me," I challenge, and she tries her best to fight a smile as she threads her hand into my hair and kisses me. I'll never get enough of her, not in a million years. My beautiful wife moans when I slip my hand underneath her dress, and she tugs at my shirt, our movements urgent, unrestraint.

"*Fuck*," I groan when I realize she isn't wearing panties, and she smiles at me shyly as she unzips my pants. Her hand wraps around my cock just as I coat my fingers in her wetness, and I watch her, enraptured as he head falls back the moment my fingers brush over her clit. I'm so fucking in love with her, and while I don't think it's possible to fall any deeper, I know she'll somehow make it happen by the time our week here is over.

Fifty-Two

SIERRA

I smile happily as I stare at my computer screen, my mind elsewhere. I haven't been able to focus on anything at all since Xavier and I got back from our honeymoon, my mind constantly replaying the way we were all over each other on the beach, in the jacuzzi, the sauna, and pretty much every flat surface we could find. We spent our nights lying on the beach and watching the stars, trying our best to find constellations when truthfully, neither of us knew what we were looking for. We talked about anything and everything, and it truly was all I'd hoped for and more. I've never felt more loved, never felt more certain that Xavier is the one for me.

My heart skips a beat when my phone lights up with an incoming call from my husband, and I smile as I pick up. "Hi, Xave."

"Hi, Kitten," he says, sighing. "I have a question for you."

"Tell me."

"How would you feel about me retiring? It's just... I've finally found my real passion in life, and I just don't think I should be in real estate anymore."

I raise a brow. "And what, pray tell, is your real passion in life?"

He sighs again, dramatically. "Figuring out how long I can keep you on the edge with my tongue, and how many times I can make you come once I've decided to stop torturing you."

"Xavier!" I whisper-shout, even though my office is empty.

My husband laughs in that sexy way that makes my heart race, and I blush fiercely. "God, what I wouldn't do to see the look on your face right now," he murmurs. "I should've just come see you."

"You have an important meeting in ten minutes, and your mom is picking me up from my office in fifteen. I can't believe you'd call me just to tease me when you *knew* I'd be out with your mother all afternoon! Now I'm going to be all..."

"All turned on? Thinking of me every second of the day, until you get home, where I'll spread you out on your favorite chair in your library?"

"God, I hate you," I groan, squeezing my thighs.

He chuckles, and the sound makes my heart skip a beat. "There's a thin line between love and hate. I think you're mistaking which side you're on."

I've always read about love in books, but never in a million years did I think the real thing would be even better. I was so certain that the books I read were idealized versions of reality, mere fragments of real life, but I was wrong. Life with Xavier is better than any romance novel I've ever read, and not even my favorite fictional book boyfriends can compete.

"Oh, what I wouldn't do to shut up that smart mouth of yours."

"If it involves you sitting on my face, I'm all for it."

"If you don't stop teasing me right now, I'm going to suffocate you. *Death by pussy* is what I'll put on your tombstone, don't even try me."

He bursts out laughing, the sound warming my heart. "God, I love you so fucking much," he tells me, and I melt, right there and then. The words never cease to affect me.

"I love you more," I tell him, my voice softer now. "I miss you," I admit. "I know I saw you this morning, but—"

"— I miss you too. Spending a week together got me hooked on you even more than I already was, baby. I'm having withdrawal symptoms for sure."

"Really? Tell me about the symptoms, because I think I might be suffering from the same thing."

He laughs. "It involves endlessly thinking of your spouse, daydreaming about the memories you made, counting down the seconds until you see them again, thinking of any excuse to call or text them, and wondering if your spouse would be willing to cancel their planned shopping spree with your mom."

I giggle, I can't help it. "I tick most of those boxes, but not the last one. You see, my husband gave me a credit card that supposedly doesn't have a limit, and I have every intention of checking if it's true."

"Hmm, I do love the sound of that. Go spoil yourself, Kitten. I'll be at home, waiting for you. In bed. Naked."

I laugh again, only for the sound of a helicopter to startle me. "Ugh, reporters. I can't believe they've resorted to using a helicopter," I tell Xavier as I walk up to the window to close the blinds. "They did that when the news about Raven and Ares's wedding broke too."

"No!" Xavier shouts, startling me. "Stay away from the windows, Sierra. Zach issued a ban on helicopters near your office. Those are *not* reporters."

An alarm goes off in my office just as my windows are kicked in. "Two men," I begin to say, my voice panicked. "Army green clothing. Black masks. Army style black boots." My words flow out of me on autopilot, courtesy of the kidnapping training Lex forced me to go to for years. "I love you," I add, knowing there's every chance I'll never get another chance to speak to him again.

Xavier shouts my name, and I just about manage to shout back that he shouldn't let Lexington or my grandmother find out before I'm grabbed and pulled out of the window and into the helicopter. I try my best to scramble out of my captors' grip, but they're too fast, too strong, and the last thing I see before I'm knocked out is dozens of bodyguards storming into my office, my mother-in-law not far behind them, a gun in her hands and clear panic in her eyes.

By the time I come to, I'm bound to a chair in an empty warehouse, my head pounding and my vision swimming. I blink rapidly as I try to focus on the man walking toward me. My heart sinks when I realize he isn't wearing a mask. He thinks I won't walk out of here alive, or he'd never have shown me his face. I take note of his brown eyes and graying gray, the thick scar on his forehead and his pale skin, along with his ill-fitting black t-shirt, his bloodstained jeans, and the faded tattoos on his neck. I try my best to memorize every single thing in an attempt to slip a clue into any ransom videos they ask me to make, but the fact that he's shown me his face scares me.

"Let me guess?" I croak out. "An abandoned warehouse? What a cliche."

I'd braced myself to be hit, but he merely laughs, catching me off guard. I'd expected him to lose his temper and inadvertently give me a clue as to where I am, or how many men there are. "Feisty. It's clear what he sees in you."

I take a deep breath, realization dawning. This isn't a normal kidnapping. He isn't after me because I'm a Windsor and able to pay a hefty ransom, which explains why he isn't wearing a mask. It's not money he's after. This is revenge — on Xavier. This will devastate my husband, and there isn't a single thing I can do to keep it from happening.

He sits down in an empty chair in front of me and smiles in the eeriest way, his eyes cold and dead as he opens the folder he was carrying. "You're going to sit here, and I'm going to tell you about every single crime your husband has ever committed, and I'm going to film it all. Your precious husband will get to see the growing disgust in your eyes, your dimming love and respect for him, and then he's going to watch you die knowing that in your final moments, you regretted ever being with a monster like him."

I try my best not to panic and force an innocent smile. He's a storyteller, and I'll get to live for as long as I keep him talking. I only have to stay alive long enough for my family to find me, and the creep sitting opposite me has no idea whose wrath he's invoking. It isn't just the Kingstons he'll have to contend with. It's the Windsors too, the Sinclairs no doubt not far behind them. He has no idea how big of a mistake he made when he targeted me. I'm so much more than just Xavier's wife, and he's about to find out the hard way.

"Crimes?" I question in my most innocent baby voice, putting on an act, just like I was taught. "Oh no, I t-think... m-maybe there's b-been a misunderstanding? My husband is t-the sweetest m-man."

He laughs as he grabs a roll of tape, and my heart sinks when he tapes my mouth shut, depriving me of an opportunity to needle him and gather clues. "Now, where were we?" he asks, before he holds up a photo, his eyes sparkling crazily as he begins to tell me about a guy whose dick Xavier apparently cut off. I can only guess why, and that man is lucky I didn't get to him first.

Fifty-Three

XAVIER

"Breathe," Zach tells me as I stare at the live feed of Sierra being told about every gruesome thing I've ever done, her captor's voice scrambled. There isn't a single identifiable clue in the video — just a clear white backdrop, and Sierra bound to a metal chair, her mouth taped shut. "Every police officer in the city is looking for her."

Dion wraps his arm around me and holds me up while Silas and his wife both type furiously, trying to figure out where the live stream is coming from.

"So far, she's given signs for abandoned warehouse, three men, bound with rope, guns, windows, and a breeze. She indicated that she was knocked out for a while, so we have no timing data to create a radius with," Valeria says, watching Sierra's every move. Both of their abilities to stay perfectly calm despite the situation is both awe-inspiring and terrifying. "They have no idea who they're messing with," she says when Sierra flinches just slightly as she's told about a guy I threw off the same bridge he'd thrown his pregnant ex-girlfriend off, "or what I'll do to them when I find them."

It wasn't until an hour ago that I found out Valeria has been working a lot more closely with Elijah than I thought, going on missions with him to wipe out the list of people she memorized while she was taken captive. Neither of them told me that keeping her from being photographed mattered more for her safety than I could've possibly imagined.

"That's another one that's empty," Ares growls, despair written all over his face as he and his wife tick of warehouses we think could meet the descriptions Sierra is trying to give us, the two of them directing joint teams of Silas Sinclair's security personnel and ours.

Every single person that loves Sierra is here, except for Lex, Raya, and her grandmother, who aren't aware she's missing. It would be too triggering for Lex, and Sierra was right to demand I hide it from him, but I can't help but wonder if maybe he could figure out where the fuck they're keeping my wife.

"This was a gruesome one," her captor says, his voice distorted. "Your beloved husband shot him in the stomach and watched him bleed to death."

I can feel bile rising up my throat and take a calming breath, trying my best not to focus on the fact that all of my brothers-in-law are listening to everything that's being said too. It isn't just Sierra that won't look at me the same anymore. I bury my hands in my hair, feeling fucking helpless.

"Sierra is doing well. She's staying calm," Luca says, his voice grim. "Her breathing looks even, and her eyes are clear."

Zane throws me a reassuring glance, despite the pain in his eyes. "Her attention hasn't slipped once. She's given us clues letting us know she's okay and repeating the same information steadily, in case we missed anything. You need to stay calm and get out of your head, because she's going to need you when we find her."

Raven gently squeezes my arm, her eyes red. "He's right," she tells me, her voice hoarse from her endless tears. "Right now, I'd just be grateful for how long that list is, and how well she's keeping calm."

I pinch the bridge of my nose as I stare at the screen. "She's given us a sign to say there's sunlight, so she's clearly not underground. Where the fuck could she be, and why the fuck can't we find her?"

I glance at Elijah, my emotions boiling over. "Try to undo that voice scrambling bullshit. None of this shit these guys are doing is working — they haven't figured out where the feed is coming from, haven't figured out what this guy's source of information could be, and we can't just sit here and expect to find her by checking abandoned warehouses without a fucking radius."

"On it," Elijah says instantly.

Hunter paces back and forth and pulls a hand through his hair. "Should we consider a social media appeal? Between my audience, Raven's, and Faye's, I think we might just be able to utilize the masses to find her."

I shake my head. "I can't risk that lunatic hearing about it and deciding to end his game early."

"Zach, tell me you're getting closer to finding something," I ask as I glance over the list of people Sierra's been told about so far. Zach has been helping Elijah find a link between them, but they're both coming up empty. Most of them are people I've taken out in my quest to find or avenge Valeria, but a few of them are random thugs from years ago. There's no discernible pattern.

"Your list of enemies is too long," Faye says, her usually sweet voice filled with uncertainty. I know they're trying not to, but they all blame me, rightfully so. She's been trying to figure out which of my known enemies could've taken her, but we aren't getting anywhere with that either. "We're going down them one by one, checking all properties they own and their recent movements, but so far, nothing is flagging."

"We've been checking all their financials," Valentina adds, "but I can't find anything worth digging into."

I nod, and Celeste looks up at me. "Come take a look at this," she tells me. She's been reviewing the footage we were able to gain access to from surrounding blocks, tracking the helicopter to an open field, where it seems to have disappeared. "In this reflection, there's a fraction of a tattoo visible."

The image is so pixelated that it's hard to tell, and I stare at it as our systems attempt to sharpen the image. "I've got his voice, I think," Elijah shouts. He presses play just as the image of the tattoo sharpens, and my stomach drops when I recognize both the tattooed skull and the man's voice.

"I know where she is," I shout as I take off running toward my helicopter, my pilot already on standby, Dion and Elijah on my heels.

Dion really fears flying, even more so in helicopters than planes, but he doesn't even flinch as he straps himself in next to me. My heart is in my throat as we approach the warehouse I think she's being kept at, the same one where I shot the cleaner that I'd learned had been abusing his daughter.

He'd been one of many that had been in charge of cleaning up our messes, and one day, his teenage daughter had come to me, begging for help. I shot him in the head the next time he showed up at a site, and I should've just made sure he was actually dead before walking away.

I don't know how he's still alive, but I do know I'm to blame for what happened to Sierra. My past came back to haunt me, and she paid the price. "Hover over that field there," I instruct as I begin to load my gun. "We'll be shot down if we get too close. Lower me, and I'll be able to run through the fields undetected."

The pilot does as told, and both Elijah and Dion join me. We've only just made it halfway though the field when the warehouse in the distance goes up in flames, and all I can think about as I run as fast as I can is my wife strapped to that metal seat.

Fifty-Four

SIERRA

I wake to the sound of beeping and loud voices, my head pounding painfully as I try to open my eyes. "She's awake," I can eventually make out, along with a lot of crying and rejoicing.

Relief rushes through me when I recognize the feeling of my husband's hand in mine. "Xavier," I whisper, turning my face to look at him.

Our eyes lock, and he stares at me like he can't quite believe what he's seeing. "Thank God," he murmurs, his voice breaking.

"I knew you'd find me," I whisper, my throat burning.

"You've inhaled a lot of smoke," Raven tells me. "Xavier carried you out just in time."

My father-in-law places his hand on Xavier's arm, his eyes filled with just as much relief. "She's awake now," he says gently. "You promised us you'd get your wounds looked at once she woke up."

"You're hurt?" I ask, trying to sit up and failing. My entire body hurts, and I'm not sure why. All I remember was that creep panicking and knocking over barrels with oil, before lighting the whole place up.

"No," he lies, his face a little too pale, his pupils blown. "I'm fine."

"He nearly got crushed by rubble as he tried to get you out," Dion tells me, his tone grim.

I look back at my husband, before looking at my brothers-in-law. "Hunter, Elijah, Zach, get him checked out."

They nod and jump into action, and Xavier struggles when they reach for him. "No," he says, panicking. "I can't leave my wife right now. She just woke up, and—"

"We're with her," my mother-in-law says, reaching for the hand Xavier had been holding, and I hold on tightly.

"We won't go anywhere until you get back," my father-in-law promises, and I nod reassuringly as his brothers all but drag him out of the room, his eyes on mine until the very last second.

"How is he?" I ask, turning my head to face Ares.

"You're the one that was kidnapped," Raven says, sounding furious and worried out of her mind. "You're lying in a hospital bed, Sierra."

"Yes, but Rave, that means *I've* been checked out and treated," I tell her, looking at Val instead. I get where she's coming from, but it isn't myself I'm worried about right now. "How is my husband?"

"It's hard to say," Val admits, giving me the truth I needed. "He was running on pure adrenaline, so I don't think he's even started to feel any pain yet, but the doctors think he broke his forearm, several ribs, and his leg, all on the same side. He needs x-rays, though."

"He's not doing great mentally," Celeste tells me. "He's worried sick about you."

"He thinks he failed you because he couldn't protect you from being taken, despite all of his security measures," Faye says, her voice soft. "They outsmarted everyone, including Silas and Elijah, but Xavier can't seem to accept that."

Dion gently pushes my hair out of my face and sighs. "This is his worst fear come true, Sierra. That man just lived his worst nightmare, and I don't think he's snapped out of it yet. He'll be okay once he realizes you're okay."

I nod, unable to focus on anything but the seconds ticking by as I wait for my husband to come back, and it strikes me then — he's just a few doors down the hallway, and I'm this concerned. I can't even imagine what he must've gone through in the hours I was missing.

"Have some soup," my mother-in-law tells me, holding up a canister with what is no doubt homemade chicken soup, the kind Xavier told me his mom always makes for him when he's sick.

"Thank you, Mom," I murmur when she spoon feeds me with all the patience in the world. Her eyes widen a fraction, and she smiles at me so sweetly that my heart warms instantly. I know she's wanted to hear me say it for a while now, but for so long, I'd felt like an imposter, like I didn't have the right to call her mom, when our marriage felt so temporary.

Xavier's dad grumbles, seemingly unhappy as he throws his wife a dirty look, and I glance at him. "Everything okay, Dad?"

He melts — there's no other way to describe the way his shoulder relax as his expression lights up. "Yes, sweetie," he says, brushing my hair out of my face like Dion did earlier. "I'm really proud of you, you know? You stayed so calm and gave us so many clues."

I smile shakily and continue to sip my soup, my heart uneasy without Xavier here. That look in his eyes worried me, and I need to see him. I need to know he's okay.

"We'll be back tomorrow," Raven tells me when a doctor walks in and demands they clear the room, but I shake my head.

"I want to go home," I tell her.

Raven nods. "I'll make it happen," she promises. "We'll get you whatever you need to be treated at home, if necessary."

She leans in and presses a kiss to my cheek, and I smile at her. "I'm sorry for snapping at you earlier."

Raven merely chuckles and shakes her head. "I would've done the same had our roles been reversed. I'd have wanted to know about Ares before worrying about my own health too, so I get it. Just promise me you'll focus on getting better now."

"I promise," I tell her, and she nods as she leads all of our family members out moments before Xavier is wheeled into the room, severals casts covering his body. His parents rise when they see him, throwing us both sweet smiles before they walk out too, leaving us alone.

"Hi, Kitten," Xavier says, hoisting himself up on my bed with me, seemingly not caring about the pain he must be in. He lies on his uninjured side, facing me, and I gently press my head against his chest as I burst into tears, the shock finally wearing off.

"I'm sorry," he says, repeating the words over and over again as he holds me, my entire body rocking from the force of my sobs.

"I'm j-just so glad you f-found me," I tell him. "I w-was so scared, Xave."

"Me too," he whispers, his lips pressed to my forehead. "God, baby. I was fucking terrified that what happened to Valeria would happen to you too, and I'd lost you for years, or forever."

"But I'm here," I tell him, trying to control my sobs. "I'm here, Xavier, and I'm fine. We're fine."

"No," he says, his voice breaking. "You aren't fine at all, Kitten. You barely survived a traumatic event you would never have had to experience if you hadn't been married to me. I nearly fucking lost you, Sierra."

"But you didn't," I whisper. "I'm right here, Xave. You won't ever lose me."

He holds me tightly, his breathing uneven and his heart beating steadily against the palm of my hand. His expression tells me he doesn't believe me, and I don't know how to convince him otherwise.

Fifty-Five

XAVIER

I run as fast as I can, yet the warehouse never gets closer, forcing me to watch as the flames and thick, dark smoke spread. "Please," I whisper, wishing I could escape from this lucid recurring nightmare. I try to get closer with all my might, Sierra's screams ringing through the air as I shout her name desperately, over and over again.

The sky darkens with smoke, and slowly but surely, I begin to get a little closer, only for the ceiling to collapse the moment I make it into the warehouse, thick metal shards piercing my legs and arms. I don't let it stop me and leave a trail of blood behind me as I forge ahead, toward my wife, who is still desperately screaming for help, for me.

"Sierra," I call out, struggling to find her through the rubble and thick smoke, my lungs burning and my vision swimming.

"Xavier!" she shouts, and I can just about make out her red dress. When I reach her, she's still bound to a chair that's buried almost entirely in rubble, and she looks at me with pure hatred in her eyes. "You're too late," she says, blood running down her forehead. "How could you do this to me, Xavier?"

"I'm sorry," I tell her, desperately trying to remove the pieces of

rubble covering her, only for more to fall. "I'm going to save you, Sierra. Just hold on for me, okay, Kitten?"

It's a hopeless task, and all the while, she stares at me without a single ounce of love in her cold eyes, resignation written all of her face. "You let them take me," she says, her voice filled with blame. "This is all your fault, Xavier. You're the reason I'm dying, and I will never forgive you for stealing the life I should've had."

"You're not dying," I tell her, my words a desperate plea. "You're fine, baby. You're going to be fine."

"You should have protected me," she says as I've just about managed to remove enough rubble to carry her out, chair and all, only for a new batch to fall. "I trusted you, Xavier."

"I'm sorry," I repeat, over and over again. Sierra smiles humorlessly and looks me in the eye as a metal shard drops from the ceiling and pierces her heart, and I scream, my own heart breaking. She coughs up blood as the life drains out of her while I desperately shout her name, cutting my hands on the sharp metal in an attempt to take it out, to undo what happened. "You did this to me," she says, coughing up more blood. "This is on you."

"Xavier! Wake up!"

I gasp and sit up in bed, on the verge of a panic attack, until I see my wife kneeling next to me, wearing one of my black t-shirts instead of the red dress she was wearing in my dream. "You're alive," I whisper, reaching for her.

She instantly moves closer and straddles me. "I'm very much alive and well," she says, cupping my face. "Look at me, Xavier." I do as I'm told, unable to regulate my breathing, my nightmare still holding me in its clutches. "I'm alive, I'm unharmed, and I'm here with you."

I nod and run my hands over her body, needing to determine for myself that she's really here with me, and she isn't bleeding. "You're okay," I say, my voice breaking.

She nods, her forehead dropping to mine. "I'm more than okay," she repeats, her own breathing shallow. "Are *you* okay?"

"I don't know," I admit, scooting back to lean against our headboard. She moves with me, and I bury a hand in her hair, holding onto her tightly. "It felt so fucking real, baby. I watched you *die*." I've had different variations of the same nightmare for over a week now, but most nights I don't wake her up, my screams rarely leaving my dream world. Tonight was a particularly bad one, and I'm still struggling to distinguish what's real and what isn't. My memories of that day are becoming distorted, parts of it now replaced by the things that keep happening in my nightmares, and it's fucking with me more than I care to admit.

"I'm right here," Sierra says, pulling back a little to look at me. "You saved me, Xavier."

I slide my hands under the t-shirt she's wearing and grab her waist, the feel of her soft, warm skin reassuring. There are no scars on her, no blood, just endless concern she shouldn't have to deal with. "I love you," I whisper, the words leaving my lips like a compulsion, my need to say it unmanageable.

Sierra wraps her hand around the back of my neck, her eyes on mine. "I love you more," she says, before leaning in and brushing her lips against mine.

My breath hitches, my eyes falling closed as I ball my fist in her hair and kiss her, needing her with a new kind of desperation. It's never felt this way. I've never felt so desperate to feel *alive*. Sierra groans when I part her lips, my tongue caressing hers slowly, seductively, until she begins to move her hips, her hands running down my bare chest. "Xavier," she breathes, pushing her hand into my hair as she tilts my neck and grazes my skin with her teeth.

I moan and let my head fall back against the headboard, my broken ribs protesting against my movements painfully. My wife sucks down on my skin, marking me, and my cock begins to throb. "I need you," I admit, feeling oddly vulnerable in a way I never have before.

"You have me," she says, reaching between us to free my cock. "You will always have me, Xavier. Forever and always."

I groan when she roughly pushes her panties aside, not even bothering to take them off as she lines me up, her hips rocking back and forth gently, until the tip slips in. Her head falls back when I reach for her and begin to circle her clit, needing to touch her as much as I need to see her. She lowers her hips slowly, taking me inch by inch, until she drops her weight fully, and I bottom out inside her, a needy moan escaping my throat.

Sierra's eyes never leave mine as she begins to ride me, one of her hands in my hair, the other on my chest, almost like she needs to feel my heartbeat. "I love you," she says, and I lean in to kiss her, losing myself in her.

"I love you too," I whisper against her lips as I reach for her hips and lift her nearly all the way off me, before lowering her hard, fast, taking control. She moans fucking beautifully, and I smile for the first time in days, before I do it all over again.

Fifty-Six

SIERRA

I pace back and forth in our library, my eyes on the clock instead of the book in my hands. Every day for the last two weeks, Xavier has been coming home just a little later, his behavior slowly becoming more like it used to be, before he started to communicate with me, and it's worrying.

My eyes light up when a soft chime sounds through the speakers we have all over the house, notifying me he's finally home. I put my book down on our armchair before rushing over, expecting him to meet me halfway like he usually does, only to find him in our dressing room, his hands on his tie. "You're home," I murmur, walking up to him.

He smiles, but it doesn't reach his eyes. "I'm home," he says, his voice soft. I grin up at him and rise to my tiptoes to kiss him, but for the first time in as long as I can remember, he doesn't instantly grab me to kiss me back.

"Is everything okay?" I ask, reaching for his tie to take it off for him.

"Just tired," he says, not quite looking me in the eye. For several

259

weeks now, he's had nightmares every single night, and I can't imagine the effect it's had on him.

"I think you should consider speaking to a psychologist about what happened. I did, and I think it could help." It was one of the first things that Celeste insisted on when I'd recovered, and she drove me there every single day for a week straight, accompanied by armed bodyguards that my mother-in-law won't let me leave the house without anymore. Xavier's mom has done all she can to make sure I feel safe, and I haven't had the heart to tell her that it's overkill, and that I'm truly fine. As a Windsor, I was trained to survive an attempted or successful kidnapping, and as far as I'm concerned, I walked away unscathed. I know Xavier doesn't see it that way, though.

"It's not something I can risk," he says. "I can't admit to crimes I've committed, not even in therapy. It wouldn't just implicate me, but my family too."

I nod and look down. Admittedly, I couldn't really say much during my own sessions either, and I mostly went to reassure Celeste. "Then talk to me," I tell him, my voice soft, my hands pressed against his chest. "I feel like you're slowly distancing yourself from me, Xave. I'm terrified that I'm losing you, that you'll let that man undo all the hard work we put into our marriage. I can't tell what you're thinking, because you've stopped talking to me, and now you're coming home later than usual too..."

He sighs as I push off his suit jacket before moving my fingers to the buttons on his shirt next. Xavier gently cups my face, his thumb brushing over my lips. "I guess reality just caught up with me," he says, and I look up as his shirt falls open. "I thought that because I'd changed, my past didn't matter anymore. I fooled myself into believing that the blood on my hands didn't count, because everyone whose blood I've ever spilled deserved it. If hell exists, that's where I've sent them to, and the world is a better place for it. That's what I told myself, Sierra, day after day, until I believed it."

He brushes my hair out of my face, his hand trailing down to my chin. Xavier lifts my head so I'm facing him, our eyes locking. "I failed to protect my own sister, failed to find her when she was taken, yet somehow, I deluded myself into believing I could keep you safe. I wanted you so badly that I lied to myself, to *you* — about who I am, and the risks that come with being my wife. There's a reason I stayed away from you back when I was stealing those projects from you, quietly hoping that our future would play out the way I wished it would. At least back then, I had the good sense to keep my feelings for you hidden, because I'd known, deep down, that you belong in the light, and my life will always be cast in shadows."

"I belong with *you*," I tell him as I push his shirt off his shoulders. "I've told you this before, and I'll say it again: I chose to love you, Xavier Kingston. The good, the bad, and everything in between. I know exactly who you are, now more than ever before, and I'd still choose you."

He cups the back of my head and brings me closer, his expression conveying pure torment. "How could you love someone like me, Sierra? You don't need to pretend for me, Kitten. You don't need to act like sitting there and being forced to listen to every fucking crime I've ever committed didn't change the way you see me, nor do you have to act like you don't blame me, when we both know I was the reason you nearly burned to death."

I reach for him and hold his face, keeping his eyes on mine. "It didn't change a thing for me," I tell him truthfully. "I've always known who you are, Xavier. I might not have been certain the rumors were true, but I knew chances were high that they were, and it still never stopped me from messing with you every which way — because I know you, and I knew there wasn't a single thing you wouldn't let me get away with." I slide my hand around the back of his neck, my eyes never leaving his. "I don't blame you for the actions of another man, one who clearly deserved what you'd done to him. Hearing about your past and the things you've done didn't change how I see you, Xavier."

He drops his forehead to mine, his breathing shallow. "My nightmares have started to change," he admits. "Every goddamn night, I'm completely fucking helpless as as another person on the long list you were told about takes you from me, brutally murdering you in the same way I ended their life. I can't look at you anymore without fearing the future, without regretting everything you've had to endure purely because I was too selfish to let you chase your own happiness. I stole the future you should've had, Sierra, and it's the most unforgivable crime I've ever committed."

My heart twists painfully as I take in the pain in his eyes, the undeserved self-loathing. "The only thing I'd find truly unforgivable is you giving up on us just as we've found happiness together. I don't want a future with anyone but you, Xavier. I never did, and I never will."

Fifty-Seven

SIERRA

I try my best to control my temper as I park the bespoke car Xavier gave me when we got married right in front of his office building, not bothering to park it in his garage. Two armored vehicles accompany me, courtesy of my mother-in-law, who has become overly concerned about me and will no longer let me go anywhere without my dedicated security team driving in front and behind me, every single person on it vetted and appointed personally by my father-in-law.

Becky, my new personal bodyguard, opens the door for me, and I step out of my car, my stilettos clicking against the pavement as I walk into Xavier's office building, heads turning as I make my way through the lobby, my bodyguard in tow.

Sam jumps out of his seat when the elevator doors open on the top floor, nerves written all over his face. "Ms. Windsor," he says, the way he usually does. "Mr. Kingston is currently in a meeting. I do apologize." The first few times he told me that, I'd left, not wanting to bother Xavier and unable to wait around for long due to my own work schedule. It hadn't even occurred to me that he was lying to my face.

I pause in front of him and raise a brow. "Would you like to try that again?" I ask, smiling without an ounce of amusement. "I suggest you start by addressing me by the right name. It's *Mrs. Kingston* to you."

His eyes widen. "Mrs. Kingston, plea—"

I tap his arm and smile, cutting him off. "That's better. Good job, Sam. Now, you *will* get out of my way. The question is, are you going to do it voluntarily, or will you require Becky's assistance?"

He looks past me, at my bodyguard, and steps aside, his head lowered. I glance over my shoulder, silently communicating to Becky that I want her to guard the door, and she nods sharply.

My hair sways as I turn around and walk into my husband's office, finding him seated behind his desk, decidedly *not* in a meeting. "Hello, Xavier," I say in a sugary sweet voice, taking in his guarded expression as I slam his door closed and walk up to him. He turns his chair toward me when I walk around his desk, and I place my shoe between his thighs, at the edge of his seat. "Remember me?" I ask, sliding my foot forward, right up to his crotch. "I'm your *wife* — Sierra Kingston."

He leans back in his seat, unfazed. "What exactly are you doing, Kitten?" he asks, his brows raised.

"Oh, so you do remember who I am? Funny. I was certain you must've had a concussion I didn't know about, a lapse in memory. How else do you intend to explain why you've been forgetting to come home to me for nearly two weeks now?"

I have it on good authority that he's been staying at a highly secure place owned by Enzo, which I'm not authorized to enter. We both know he couldn't have kept me away at any property owned by the Kingstons, and it's clear he's intentionally avoiding me. His actions hurt far more than I'm letting on, and I just don't understand why he's distancing himself from me to this extent.

Xavier's eyes flash the way they used to, back when he used to love my crazy behavior and returned it with a level of madness I always enjoyed, but then that light dims, and he looks away. "I'm just busy with work," he says, seemingly not caring that it doesn't even remotely sound like a good excuse.

He hasn't been himself since I was captured, and for the first three weeks, he woke up screaming my name nearly every night, his nightmares refusing to loosen their hold over him until I pulled him into my arms, reassuring him I was fine. In hindsight, that was the part that was manageable. What came after it was far, far worse.

As the weeks passed, he became unable to look me in the eye, and unless I touched him first, he wouldn't show me any of the affection I'd gotten used to. He stopped meeting me halfway when I came home, seemingly no longer excited to see me, like he used to be, and he stopped kissing me good night. There were no text messages anymore, no phone calls, no holding hands, until eventually, he just stopped coming home. I've been losing him slowly, over the course of two months, and there isn't a single thing I've been able to do about it. No amount of talking to him about it has helped, and I don't know what to do anymore. The more time passes, the more this situation infuriates me.

"Fine," I tell him. "Let's sell the company. If you're so busy that it's keeping you from me, it's not worth having. Sell it."

His expression cracks just a smidge, something akin to amusement flickering through his eyes for a brief moment, and my heart skips a beat. If there's anything I excel at, it's getting a reaction out of him, and I need it now more than ever before.

I sigh when my husband just doesn't give me a response. Instead, he merely stares at me, almost like he's waiting to see how long it'll take to wear me down and chase me away, without him even having to say a thing.

Each time I try to talk to him, he just shuts down, leaving me feeling like I'm talking to a wall. It's infuriating, and I have no idea how to get through to him. I know him, and I know he loves me more than anything. Xavier spent years acquiring companies I wanted, naming them so an acronym of them spelled my name by the time he gifted them to me. Those are not the actions of a man that's anything but deeply committed, and I'm trying my best to remember that.

"Don't want to sell?" I ask, not expecting a response. He's refusing to play my games, but I know he can't resist forever. I have years of experience taunting him. I excel at it more than I do my actual job. "That's okay. I'll just help you out with your workload."

I throw him a sweet smile as I seat myself on the edge of his desk and face him, placing my hands behind me as I lean back, knowing full well that he should be able to see the contours of my nipples as the fabric of my dress stretches over my breasts. I dressed up for him today, making sure not to wear any underwear under the tight, short black dress I'm wearing. At the start of our marriage all we had was our physical connection, and it led us to everything else. If I can remind him of that, at least, maybe I can have one small part of him back. "Just tell me what I can help you with, Xave, and I'll do it," I tell him. "I can be *very* helpful if you ask nicely."

Xavier's eyes zero in on my chest, and I watch as he clenches his jaws before looking out the window instead. The bitter sting of rejection hits me hard, and I look down, my confidence wavering for a split second. I've never tried to seduce a man before, and it's clear I'm failing at it. I have no idea what I'm doing, but I'm desperate for his attention and unwilling to give up, even if it means making a fool of myself. Nothing else has worked so far.

I bite down on my lip and decide to change tactics as I slip off his desk and turn my back to him, bending over his desk to reach for his mouse. My movements make my dress ride up, and my heart begins to hammer in my chest at the thought of exposing myself. I've put myself at an angle where my ass is pretty much right in his face, and if I bend over even a little more, he'll realize that I'm not wearing a single thing under this dress.

"What are you working on that's keeping you so busy?" I ask, my voice trembling as I click through his documents without actually registering anything I'm seeing. I'm too nervous, too far out of my depth, and the longer he stays silent, the more I lose the confidence I barged in with. I really thought my actions today would make him snap out of his daze, but all I'm accomplishing is humiliating myself. I draw a shaky breath, beginning to accept that I'm going to have to walk out of here with my pride in tatters.

When we first got married he wouldn't let me in either, but at least then, he let his body do the talking. I thought that if I tried to seduce him, maybe it'd be like that again, but I was wrong. I overestimated my own appeal.

I begin to straighten, defeat washing over me, when his voice fills the air between us. "The Stanley project," he growls, placing his hand on my lower back as he pushes me back down. I lean forward on my elbows, my heart pounding wildly as he grabs my thigh with his free hand, his thumb caressing the curve of my ass.

I gasp when he forces my legs apart with his feet, making my dress ride up further. His sharp intake of breath makes a thrill run down my spine, and I arch my spine when he grabs my ass, his thumbs so close to where I want them that I can't help but squirm. I whimper when I feel his hot breath on my skin, and he chuckles before kissing my pussy softly before dragging his tongue down it.

I moan his name when he uses the tip of his tongue to circle my clit, using every single thing he's learned about my body to get me close. "Please," I beg. "I need you, Xavier." I think we both know it isn't just his body I'm talking about, and I've never felt more vulnerable. He responds to my words by pushing two fingers into me and curling them as he laps at me harder, his movements rougher. My moans fill his office as I begin to become lightheaded, and he groans when I come, my legs shaking and my forehead pressed to his hard wooden desk.

I'm still panting and trying to catch my breath when he pulls my dress back down. "You got what you wanted," he says, his voice rough, devoid of the passion I'd expected. "So leave, Sierra. I've got work to do."

My heart twists painfully as I push off his desk, taking a moment to lick my wounds before I straighten and turn to face him. "So have you," I tell him, my voice breaking. "You wanted to hurt me, and you have. You didn't have to go this far, Xavier. Just look me in the eye and tell me you don't want me anymore."

He doesn't refute my words, and I draw a shaky breath, a lone tear running down my cheek. I'm learning the hard way that his silence cuts deeper than anything he could say to me, and God, it *hurts*. "I'll be at home, waiting," I tell him, my voice barely above a whisper as I step away from him. "I'll wait a million years and a day, Xavier, if that's what it takes."

I look over my shoulder when I reach his door, only to find him staring out the window, like I'm not even worth looking at. "I'll wait, because I still want you, and I still love you. Not even the way you're treating me right now will change that."

Fifty-Eight

SIERRA

I sigh as I pull up in front of Xavier's parents' house, my heart aching as I sit in my car for a few moments, trying my best to pull myself together when all I can think about is the interview Xavier did this morning, announcing our merger and heavily insinuating that it's the only reason he married me. I've watched it over and over again, and each time, it hurts just a little more. I get why he did it — he's sending a signal, telling the world he doesn't care enough about me for me to be a viable target that can be used to get to him, but that doesn't make it sting any less.

I draw a shaky breath and lean back, trying to convince myself to smile and put up an act, only to startle when the passenger door opens. My father-in-law smiles as he gets in, his three-piece suit vaguely familiar. "Mom liked the suit you bought for Xavier," he explains when he finds me staring at it. "So she got matching ones for me, Elijah, Hunter, and Zach. I haven't been able to tell her that the boys are all too old for matching outfits."

I smile shakily. "What are you doing, Dad?"

"Sitting with my little girl," he replies. "We don't have to go in if you don't want to, but I don't want you to sit here by yourself."

Tears begin to fill my eyes, and I bite down on my lip harshly as I try to suppress them. "I'm just so tired of hurting," I tell him, burying my face in my hands. I've been coming over for dinner a few times a week, just so I wouldn't have to be home alone in a house that used to be filled with happy memories — memories that are all slowly being replaced by loneliness and disappointment.

I've been wanting to go home to my siblings, but I know I can't suddenly go back more often than I used to, or they'd just worry about me, and I haven't been able to admit to anyone that my marriage is falling apart, and nothing I've tried is helping me keep it together.

Dad offers me a handkerchief that's far too nice to actually use, and I just begin to cry even harder at the thought of everything I stand to lose. It isn't just the love of my life, it's the parents I never thought I'd have too. "Oh, Sierra," he says, his voice soft, pained. "Tell me what you want to do, sweetheart. Should we just track that stupid son of mine down and force him to listen?"

"I've tried that," I tell him, bawling. I tried talking to him a dozen times at home, before he left. Then again at his office, and countless times after meetings I knew he would never miss. I've told him that I miss him, that I'm hurting, and it's like he just isn't hearing me. "He needs help, Dad. I can't get through to him, but maybe someone else can."

The way he looks at me tells me he's tried too, and I avert my gaze, trying my best to compose myself. "Sweetheart, if I could force him to get help, I would. I'm not above locking him into a room with a psychologist, but that won't make him talk."

I wipe away my tears and draw a steadying breath, trying my best to stop my tears. I haven't felt like myself in so long, and I'm tired of feeling weak, breakable. "Let's go in," I say eventually, my voice hoarse.

Dad simply smiles. "Are you sure? If you want to, I can make

Elijah set up a big screen and a projector, so we can watch a movie from the car. We can sit here for as long as you need to, Sierra."

"Would you actually do that for me?"

He grins and gently tucks a strand of my hair behind my ear. "Mom and I have done that countless times with Valeria, and we'll happily do it for you too. For a long time, she'd get ready, determined to go somewhere, only to sit in the car, too overwhelmed to leave. So we'd just sit right here with her."

I stare at my hands. "Can we do that someday?" I ask him.

"Of course," he replies instantly. "Whenever you want, sweetie." For as long as I can remember, I've wondered what it'd have been like if I still had my parents, and now I no longer have to wonder. Now I know what it's like to be consoled by a father when a boy breaks my heart, even if the boy in this scenario is his son.

"Let's go," I say, sounding a little more determined, a little less broken.

"I actually came outside to pre-warn you," he says as we walk to the front door together. "Mom prepared a little surprise for you. Something that I think is not exactly normal, but that she insists is going to make you feel better." I raise a brow as I press my hand to the scanner at the front door, and the door swings open. "I... well, I don't really know how to explain. You'll have to see for yourself."

I frown when I follow him to the kitchen, where Valeria is hand making fresh pasta, and my mother-in-law is cutting fresh herbs for the pasta I've come to love so much that she now makes it for me once a week. "Oh, Sierra, honey, there you are," Mom says, smiling at me, before she grabs a handful of finely chopped parsley and throws it on the floor. She glances at the ground then, and I walk around the kitchen island to figure out what she's doing, only to find Hannah, Raven's older sister, on her hands and knees, a toothbrush in her hands. "You missed several spots," Mom says, her tone much harsher than I'm used to. "Clean that up."

I watch in shock as the woman who tormented Ares and Raven for years brushes the floor with a toothbrush, and I'd be lying if I said that it didn't make me feel a whole lot better. Ares had mentioned that he forced her to work as a maid in retaliation for what she'd done to them, but I'd completely forgotten that it was the Kingstons she'd been sent to.

I very rarely see any staff at any of our houses, and things always just seem to get done when I'm not looking, so it hadn't occurred to me that I could've been making Hannah pay for what she put my brother and my sweet Raven through. If not for her, Ares and Raven wouldn't have missed out on so many years of happiness, and Raven wouldn't have had to watch her designs burn in the streets, when she never did anything to deserve that. "Just can't find competent staff these days," Mom says, smiling at me sweetly.

A streak of pure viciousness washes over me as I glance at some of the leftover flour on the counter and swipe it off, making an even worse mess of the floor. "Indeed," I reply. Hannah doesn't even look up, clearly unable to face me, and she doesn't realize that it just brings me more joy to find all her haughtiness gone. She used to be one of the most famous actresses alive, and now she can't even lift her face to look me in the eye.

Mom doesn't say a thing as I continue to throw things on the floor throughout dinner, and neither do Valeria nor Dad. They do, however, join me in throwing stuff on the floor, until eventually, I feel a little better, some of the venom disappearing from my heart.

"Come on," Valeria says after dinner. "There's something I want to show you."

I raise a brow and follow her upstairs, my curiosity getting the best of me. I've been here so often in the last couple of weeks, but I've never gone upstairs. There's never been any need for it. "We all grew up here, and even though we've all moved out, Mom kept our bedrooms intact in case we ever want to stay over. I lived here for a while when I first came back home and ended up doing a lot of snooping."

She opens one of the doors and I follow her in, only to freeze at the sight of the framed photo on the wall, in which Xavier is smiling back at me, Dion standing on his left, and Enzo on his right. "This is Xavier's bedroom."

She nods and grabs my hand, pulling me to the bed, completely ignoring my reluctance. Valeria climbs onto Xavier's bed and yanks on my hand, until I'm seated next to her, her expression telling me that there's no point resisting. I blink in confusion when she bends forward and reaches for something underneath the bed, pulling out an old battered cardboard box.

"V," I murmur. "That looks like something that's private." The last thing I need is to find out about all the girls that came before me, or worse, the one that got away, the one he'd never have shut out and abandoned.

"Just look," she says, turning it upside down, letting the contents fall all over the bed. "Please, Sierra."

My heart skips a beat when I recognize every single thing in front of me, and my hands tremble when I reach for an old crumpled ticket to a real estate conference that I attended when I was fresh out of college. I remember seeing him there and feeling so intimidated by the thought of saying hi to him, because I didn't think he'd even remember his best friend's little sister, since I hadn't seen him in nearly five years. I hovered around the stage after watching his presentation, and he grinned, greeting me by name, telling me he was looking forward to witnessing everything I'd accomplish, and that he had no doubt I'd become a worthy competitor.

I bite down on my lip when I pick up a pink pen that Valentina had once given me, remembering that I'd thrown it at him because he'd told me that my presentation for a small project he shouldn't even have been interested in sucked. It was just a few months after the conference, and he'd told me everything that was wrong with it in his scathing tone. I hated him for it, but I did take his words to heart, and because of it, I won the next project I was vying for.

"How does he have all this?" I ask, reaching for several little pieces of torn paper with hateful things written on it that we'd passed back and forth, each time we found ourselves seated next to each other at a meeting or conference throughout the years. I laugh as I read the messages, each of them from different years.

Your tie is ugly.

— Not as ugly as that neon color on your slide deck.

— Love those bands around your thighs. Do they keep up your stockings?

You can see them?

— Every damn time you reach up to point at things in your slides, as can every other man in this room. Use a laser pointer or put on my suit jacket. Pull up the sleeves if you must and call it fashion.

If you ever, EVER, touch my cookies again, I will kill you.

— I'm keeping this as evidence of premeditated murder.

I'm serious, Xavier. This isn't funny.

— Okay, I'm sorry, Kitten. ^-^

Kitten?????

— Is your coffee as bitter as the look on your face when you lost that project?

Screw you.

— *Hopefully someday, Kitten.*

?????

You suck.

— *Are you offering me a taste, Kitten?*

What?

— *Never mind.*

— *That guy is an idiot. Why he is looking at you like that?*

Who, Tim? I think he's sweet.

— *His jokes are painful to listen to. Fucking kill me now.*

Wdym? I think he's super funny.

— *He's not even a little funny. Fuck him and his dumb jokes.*

Should I?

— *Idk, let me ask your brother.*

Don't!! I'm just kidding.

— *I'm not. Don't let me catch you anywhere near him.*

God, I hate you.

— Don't really like you right now either, Kitten.

You look uncomfortable. I love that look on you. Wear it more often.

— That's because the woman next to me keeps touching my leg.

I bite down on my lip as I recall the last one. I didn't realize it until much later, but I must've lost my mind when I blatantly reached over and looked her in the eye as I grabbed her arm under the table, squeezed with more force than necessary, and threw it off Xavier's leg.

He'd chuckled and grabbed my wrist, placing my palm flat on his strong thigh, his hand covering mine throughout the rest of the presentation we were sitting through. That was the first time I'd reluctantly admitted to myself that Xavier is far too handsome for his own good, and not even I was immune.

"Why would he have kept these things?"

"Because for a really long time, he thought this was all he'd ever have of you, all he deserved to have." Valeria takes a deep breath and reaches for my hands. "I know I don't have the right to ask this of you, but please, Sierra. Please don't give up on my brother."

I sigh as I squeeze her hand. "I wasn't planning on it."

Fifty-Nine

SIERRA

My entire body tenses when I pull up in front of my grandmother's house and find Xavier leaning against the hood of his car, his arms crossed. He's wearing one of the suits I bought for him, and it's unfair how good it looks on him. My heart races wildly as I step out of my car, and he straightens when I walk up to him, his arms falling to his side.

"You're here."

He nods. "You asked me to come."

"I also asked you to come home."

Xavier looks away and sighs. "I think this might not be the time or place to discuss that."

I nod, my heart wrenching. "Right. When is it ever?" I smile humorlessly and take a step away from him, but he grabs my waist and pulls me flush against him.

"What are you doing?" I ask, trying not to notice how good he smells, how amazing he feels against me.

Xavier wraps his hand into my hair, and I instinctively place my palm against his chest, noting how fast it's beating. "Your grandmother is standing by the window," he says, dropping his forehead to mine.

Disappointment washes over me, and I let my eyes flutter closed in an attempt to hide the pain. "Thank you for putting up an act for her," I tell him, my breathing uneven. It's been so long since we've been close enough to kiss each other, and I've missed it even more than I realized. "She's been worried about you. I told her that you broke a few bones on a skiing trip, but when you didn't join me for a few weeks straight, she grew suspicious. I didn't realize you'd still been going to see her every other week, without me, and I ended up misspeaking. I apologize for the inconvenience."

It hurts to know that he kept seeing Grandma without me. He couldn't have made it clearer that it's just me he doesn't want anymore. "No inconvenience at all," he says, cupping my face. I lean into his touch without thinking and tense when I realize what I just did, but he tightens his grip on my hair before I have a chance to pull away. "Pretend for me, Kitten. There's no need to worry your grandmother. Our issues are ours, and they shouldn't affect her, especially not given her health."

I sigh and wrap my arms around his neck, laying my head on his chest the way I used to. He hugs me tightly, and for a few moments, it's easy to pretend nothing has changed between us.

I've barely seen him since that day in his office, and every phone conversation or meeting we've had since felt cold and impersonal. Every time I even remotely gave him any indication that I was treating him as my husband at work, and not just a business partner, his expression would fall, and eventually, I stopped trying, unable to bear feeling like I was pushing unwanted affections on him.

We've been around either his family or mine a handful of times since, but each time, he conveniently found ways to be on the other side of the room, as far away from me as he could be without drawing suspicion. I've learned to fake bright smiles and hide red eyes, and slowly but surely, I've gotten used to sleeping alone.

"Let's go in," I say, pushing off him, my eyes on my feet as I turn toward Grandma's front door, only to startle when he grabs my hand and entwines our fingers. I glance at our joined hands, my heart throbbing painfully as he pulls me along.

I smile at my grandmother when we walk in, and she seems relieved to see us together, her gaze moving between us. "Hi Grams!" I murmur, injecting as much excitement into my voice as I can before rushing up to her and enveloping her in a tight hug. I try my best not to notice how thin she is these days, how sickly she looks. I remember when she seemed invincible, an immovable boulder in my life, and I took it for granted. I thought she'd always be there, her arms providing me with shelter during the toughest storms. When did our roles reverse?

"Xavier," she says, tutting. "I'd begun to worry about you both, you know? Seems like it was for naught, judging by how indecently you behaved with my sweet little girl right in front of my house."

He chuckles, the sound having become so foreign to me that I can't help but sneak a look at him as he approaches us. "I do apologize," he tells Grams, pressing a kiss to her cheek before offering her his arm.

She takes it like she's used to him offering her assistance, and I watch them together, noting how close they are, how much he seems to care. Xavier helps her onto her chair at the kitchen island, and it pains me to see how easily she tires these days. "I'm glad I wasn't wrong about you," she says, cupping his face. Xavier tenses, his eyes widening, and I frown, surprised by his reaction. "When you came to me, all but begging me to let you marry Sierra, I almost said no, since you'd thrown a wrench in my plans. If not for my grandsons telling me they stood by your decision, I would've sent you away."

"What?"

Grandma smiles at me, that same old cunning look in her eyes. It's faded now, and she looks worn out, but it's still there. "Will you do something for me, my sweet girl?"

I nod and reach for her hand, well aware she just evaded my question. "Of course."

"Spend the night here, both of you. I don't think I have many nights left, Sierra. I'd like to spend one more under the same roof with you both, just to put my own heart at ease. Let me sit with you for a few hours tonight, and let me make you two breakfast tomorrow. I'd like to see with my own two eyes that you're happy, that you'll be okay without me."

"I won't be," I tell her, my voice breaking. "You can't leave me, Grandma. I won't be okay without you." Tears fill my eyes, and Xavier pulls me into his arms as I try my best not to cry. I cling to him, and he cups the back of my head, my nose pressed to his neck.

"We'll spend the night," he tells grandma, hugging me tightly. "But only if you promise not to say things like that. You're breaking my heart, Grams."

"Fine," she says, and I pull away from Xavier a little, acutely aware she's watching us. He must be too, because he cups my face, his gaze roaming over me like he's really seeing me, for the first time in months. I look into his eyes as he leans in and presses a soft kiss to my forehead, and it takes all my strength not to burst into tears all over again.

Sixty

XAVIER

Sierra is quiet as she kisses her grandmother goodnight, and we both watch as one of her live-in nurses escorts her to bed. "Thank you for tonight," Sierra says, turning toward me when her grandmother's bedroom door falls closed. "I really appreciate it."

She sounds so polite, so distant. It's more than I deserve, and I know it. "Like I said, it was no inconvenience at all." If anything, it was as close to perfect as it gets these days, because our attempts to put up an act also allowed me to quieten my recurring invasive thoughts.

Sierra nods and gestures toward the staircase, and I follow her silently, my heart constricting painfully. She looks tired, and I wish I could pull her back into my arms the way I did before we walked into the house. Having her lay her head on my chest like that rebuilt hopes that had slowly crumbled with each nightmare, each attempt to look at her and see our current reality, and not the potential futures my mind keeps pushing on me.

The edges of my lips tug up when we walk into what can only be described as a princess's room, and she seems bashful as she looks around, seemingly seeing it through fresh eyes. "It's not really what you're used to, I'm sure, but it's only for a night."

I look around, taking in the plush carpets, the shades of lilac and pink, and the white four-poster that's far smaller than I'm used to. "It's cute," I tell her, pulling my tie loose.

"I'll grab you some of my brothers' clothes. I think you're probably most similar to Ares in size, right? Raven likes being prepared for any scenario, so she keeps enough clothes here for us all, most of it brand new. I should be able to find you something."

I nod and throw her a grateful smile that she doesn't return, and I watch her walk away, my heart in tatters. It's fucking killing me to stand here, knowing I lost the best thing that ever happened to me. She has no idea how badly I want to see her smile, how much I miss the smell of her hair. Every time I try to tell her how I feel, I'm overcome with visions of her bound to that chair, bleeding, *dying*, and the words just fade away.

I run a hand through my hair and turn to take a look at her bedroom, only to pause by her dresser. My heart twists painfully when I find photos of her with Graham scattered all over it. In some of them, they're kids, and in others, they look like teenagers that were dating. I bite down on my lip harshly as I pick up one that looks to be a prom photo, the two of them dressed up in matching outfits. I tried not to pay attention to them getting closer again during meetings, and I tried not to notice when he made her laugh, telling myself I was overthinking it, but maybe I wasn't. Maybe she got tired of waiting for someone who never deserved her in the first place.

"Here you go," Sierra says, and I turn around, the photo slipping out of my hand. She glances at it, her expression unreadable as she hands me a towel and a change of clothes still in its plastic wrapping. I'm not sure what I expected, but I didn't think she'd pick the picture up, only to stare at it with a nostalgic smile before hiding her photos away in a drawer with a sigh. She makes no excuses, gives me no explanations, and it fucking hurts to know I'm not entitled to them anymore.

I knew she'd fall out of love with me if I couldn't give her what she needs, and I thought I'd braced myself for it, made peace with it, so why does it hurt so fucking much? I draw a shaky breath and walk toward her bathroom, my thoughts a mess.

Sierra's bedroom is empty when I walk out wearing a pair of brand new boxers that are far too tight for me, and I sigh as I pull on the waistband before getting into her bed. She looks surprised when she walks in wearing a large black t-shirt that isn't mine, clearly having used a different bathroom. Her eyes roam over my chest and abs, and I'm reminded of the countless times I've waited for her in bed like this in an attempt to seduce her.

"I guess the pajamas didn't fit," she says, looking away. There was a time when her eyes would linger without her even realizing, and her cheeks would flush so fucking beautifully, her reluctant desire written all over her face. To be wanted by her was one of the highlights of my life, and I wish I'd savored the experience more.

Sierra gets into bed with me, her body tensing when her arm brushes against mine. "Oh, sorry," she says, trying to create a bit of space between us and failing, when I wish she'd just roll over and lay her head on my chest, like she always used to. "I always thought this was such a huge bed, but you're—" She snaps her lips shut and sighs. "I'll try to stay on my own side of the bed, but just wake me up if I do anything in my sleep that makes you uncomfortable."

"Like what?" I ask, turning onto my side to face her.

Her eyes roams over my face, lingering on my mouth, before they travel down. "Like if I accidentally hug you in my sleep, or if I touch you anywhere that—" She clears her throat, her expression pained. "I just don't want you to think that I'm taking advantage of this situation. I know you don't want to be here."

There's so much she doesn't know, so much she'll never know. "I do want to be here," I tell her, my voice soft, my words springing forth without conscious thought.

"Right," she says, studying me for a moment before she turns and reaches over, switching off the lights.

I lie back, taking comfort in the feeling of her shoulder pressing against mine, the sound of her steady breathing, and the sweet scent of her shampoo. Sierra shifts away a little, clearly trying to find a way to get comfortable without touching me, and I desperately wish things hadn't changed between us.

"Come here," I tell her, wrapping my arm around her and pulling her half on top of me, the way she always used to sleep. She gasps when I move a little, until her head lies on my chest, and fuck if it isn't the biggest thrill to have her so close again.

"Is this... is this okay?" she whispers.

I hum and wrap my hand around her waist, my heart skipping a beat when I realize her t-shirt has ridden up. "It's a small bed, Sierra. Let's just sleep the way we always do." She shifts a little more, moving a little closer, and I bite down on my lip when she throws her leg over me, the way she used to. I notice the exact moment the realizes that I'm rock hard, and she becomes impossibly still, but she doesn't move her leg away. I hesitate for a split second, before grabbing her thigh and holding her the way I've been dreaming of, before my nightmares took over.

She squirms just a little, her nose brushing against my throat, and I draw a shaky breath. "This t-shirt," I murmur, sliding my hand further up her back, underneath it. "Whose is it?" It's an odd thing to be upset about, given our circumstances, but her wearing my t-shirts has always been our thing, and the thought of her wearing another man's t-shirt while she's lying in my arms hurts more than I expected — even if it is one of her brothers's.

I expected her to throw some snark my way or refuse to answer, but she merely sighs. "It's Dion's."

"The fabric feels rough. You should take it off," I say without thinking, and I instantly berate myself for my inability to just keep my goddamn mouth shut and my jealousy at bay. Just as I'm sure she's chosen to ignore my words, she pushes against my chest and kneels, before grabbing my hand and placing it on the hem of Dion's t-shirt. She looks at me, and there is no way in hell I could possibly ignore the quiet plea in her eyes, the *hope*.

She bites down on her lip when I sit up, our eyes locking as I push the fabric up. Sierra raises her arms for me, and my breath hitches when I pull her t-shirt over her head, my eyes roaming over her perfect body. My wife looks at me with so much vulnerability in her eyes, and it's too much for me to take, too much to resist.

I groan as I thread my hand into her hair and grab her, covering her body with mine as I push her down. She gasps in the moments before my lips meet hers, and then she's kissing me back, one of her hands wrapping into my hair while the other roams over my back.

"God, Sierra," I groan, moving my lips to her neck, unable to hold back. She moans when I suck down on her sensitive skin, marking her as mine. It's juvenile, but I can't fucking help myself as I move down to her breast and do it all over again, leaving clear evidence of tonight.

"Missed this," she breathes when I suck down on her nipple, her spine arching as he pushes against my mouth harder. I'm impatient, desperate, and she lifts her hips for me eagerly when I reach for her panties, needing them off.

"Tell me this is still mine," I whisper as I move back on top of her and reach between us, my fingers trailing over her pussy.

"Always," she moans, and I reward her by teasing her clit, loving how quickly she got wet, how she's soaking my hand. She moves her hips against my hand, her movements tinged with desperation, and it drives me completely fucking wild. I get her close, and then I pull away, earning myself the neediest little whimper.

I push down my boxers in a rush, and her head falls back when I drag my cock against her pussy, the feel of her nearly undoing me. "*Yes,*" she urges, and my lips find hers as I push in a fraction, only to pull out again, dragging my cock over her clit in the process. I continue to tease her like that, pushing slightly deeper in every time, and within minutes I've got her panting, her muscles flexing around my throbbing cock. "Please," she begs. "*Please.*"

I groan and kiss her as I increase the pace, pushing against her clit harder, taking her deeper, until her breathing begins to accelerate, and her legs begin to tremble. "That's it, baby," I whisper against her mouth, not letting up. "Come for your husband, Kitten."

She moans loudly as I push her over the edge. "*Xavier,*" she begs, and I fuck her with hard, deep strokes, my control slipping as her bed slams against the wall, over and over again, her name on my lips when I come deep, *deep* inside her. "*Fuck,*" I groan, lightheaded as I collapse on top of her, my body coated in sweat. The moment I stop moving, distorted memories begin to flash through my head, and I bite down on my lip in an attempt to chase them away, to stay in the moment with her.

Sierra wraps her arms around me and holds me tightly, and I press my lips against her neck, my heart racing. We lie together like that for longer than I'd intended, not a single part of me ready to let her go, not even as the screams I hear in my nightmares every night begin to echo through my head.

"Xavier?" she says eventually, her voice sounding sleepy. "Is it true that you asked my grandmother for my hand in marriage?"

I take a deep, steadying breath as I contemplate my answer, before settling on the truth. "Yes."

"Do you regret it?"

Sixty-One

SIERRA

I stare at my computer screen, unable to focus on anything but my memories of last weekend. Xavier never answered my question when I asked him if he regretted marrying me, but he way he touched me renewed the hope I'd lost, and my heart begins to race as I reach for the silk scarf around my neck.

My face had been beet red by the time we sat down for breakfast with Grams, my thighs bruised and my pussy sore from the countless time we did it, his intensity unmatched. It was like he was scared he'd never get to touch me again, like he knew he shouldn't be indulging, and it made one thing very clear to me. He still loves me. I'd begun to wonder if maybe I was just misunderstanding why he was distancing himself from me, and maybe he'd simply started to fall out of love with me, but that night we spent together proved me wrong.

Grandma took one look at us and smirked, her eyes lighting up in a way they hadn't in months. She thanked us for staying over and told me it was a relief to see how happy we were together, and I'd wondered what she saw that I didn't, because I'd started to forget what it felt like to truly be happy. I'd grown tired of being the only one that still wanted to make this marriage work, of waiting for him to put me above his fears.

I sigh as I reach for my phone and click on my text messages. I haven't spoken to him since last weekend, and every text message I sent went unanswered, every call ignored, and God, it hurts. I almost wish he hadn't kissed me that night, hadn't touched me, so I wouldn't have gotten my hopes up only to find that nothing has changed.

Where do we go from here? I thought that I'd just have to be patient, that he needed to heal both his body and mind after what happened. I knew it triggered him, that it reminded him of losing Valeria, and I genuinely thought all he needed was time, but I'm not sure how much more my heart can take.

"Mrs. Kingston?"

I look up in surprise when Becky walks into my office, concern etched into her usually expressionless face. "What's wrong?" I ask, instantly on high alert.

Following what happened, Elijah had the glass on all properties I frequent changed to a type that's near impossible to destroy, and the only car I've been driving is the armored one Xavier gave me. Silas gave me a new bracelet that can't be removed, and I'm certain I'm now as safe as humanly possible, but that doesn't mean all my loved ones are too.

"I... I need to take you to the hospital at once, ma'am."

I rise to my feet in a rush, my stomach turning. "What happened?" I ask as I grab my bag and begin to move on autopilot, my body shaking.

"It's your grandmother," she says, her voice soft. "She was admitted urgently."

I bite down on my lip harshly as Becky escorts me out of the building and into a car that's waiting for us. "Mayor Kingston cleared the roads for us. We'll be there soon," Becky tells me before closing the door.

I try my best to control my breathing, to keep from panicking as

I call Xavier, only for my call to go to voicemail after a few rings. I try again, and again, and again, until the hospital comes into view just as my call goes to voicemail again. "Please, Xavier. Can you please come to the hospital? It's Grandma, and I need you. I don't know what happened, but I'm scared, Xave. I can just feel it. Something is wrong, and I... God, I just really need you. I can't do this alone. Please. *Please*."

I take a deep breath and end the call when Becky opens the door for me, several bodyguards already waiting by the entrance. I'd give the world to have Xavier's hand in mine right now, to hear his soothing, reassuring voice, telling me everything is going to be okay.

My heart drops when I find Ares and Raven standing in the hallway, in front of the room Grandma has been assigned. "Sierra," Ares says, his voice breaking, and I freeze in place when he swallows hard, tears in his eyes. I bite down on my lip harshly, drawing blood, and he looks down, his eyes falling closed. "She's gone."

I shake my head, my legs losing strength as I stumble. Raven catches me and wraps her arms around me, holding me tightly as I fall apart, a sob tearing through my throat. "I'm sorry," she whispers. "H-her organs began to f-fail, and it all happened s-so quickly," she tells me through her tears. "We d-didn't get here in time either."

I cling to my best friend, my heart shattering into a million pieces as she gently directs me toward the room, but I'm not ready. I can't see her, can't accept this. "I saw her last w-weekend," I cry. "She's fine. She's *fine*."

Ares wraps his arms around us both and holds on tightly. "She was in pain, Sierra," he says, his voice hoarse. "She's at peace now."

I look up when Dion, Faye, Lex, and Raya arrive. They take one look at us, and their expressions fall the way mine must have, disbelief crossing their faces. "Zane, Celeste, Luca, and Val are in the room," Ares says. "We'll go in next, to say our goodbyes."

I feel sick when Raven squeezes my hand and leads me into the room, my head pounding painfully and my vision swimming. I try my best to breathe, but there isn't enough air in the room, and I drop to my knees by Grandma's bed, my hand gently covering hers as I cry my heart out. She looks like she's sleeping, but her hand is just a little colder than I'm used to, and she doesn't look quite like herself, though I can't figure out why.

It isn't until much later that I understand why she felt like a stranger. Her soul was long gone, and she took my heart right along with me.

Sixty-Two

XAVIER

"Please say something," I beg as I watch my wife stare at her reflection in the mirror in our dressing room, her eyes roaming over the black mourning dress that was delivered to her this morning.

She ignores me, like she has from the moment I stepped off my jet and listened to her voicemail, calling her back immediately as I turned the plane back around and rushed home to her. I got there too late, and she'd already left the hospital. I found her in our library, staring at the fireplace wordlessly, her eyes glazed over.

Sierra reaches for her lipstick with trembling hands and touches up her makeup, but her grief is evident in the redness of her eyes, and the bags underneath them. She hasn't let me hug her as she cried herself to sleep next to me, night after night, hasn't even let me hold her hand. If not for my mother, she wouldn't have eaten anything in days, and it's Raven that helped her into the shower. No matter what I do or say, she won't lean on me, and I only have myself to blame for it.

"We need to leave," she says eventually. "Grandma doesn't like it when I'm late."

I reach for her hand, but she wraps her arms around herself as she walks out, and I follow behind her, my heart in turmoil. Sierra looks up in surprise when she finds my parents and all of my siblings, including Valeria, parked outside our house. They all opted for black cars today, and they're all patiently standing in front of them, waiting for Sierra. My wife buries her face in her hands for a few moments, and I draw a steadying breath as she tries her best to straighten her shoulders and regain her composure. This time, she doesn't pull away when I wrap my arm around her and guide her to our car.

"Your siblings will be just behind our own security and the police escort," I explain as we drive to the Windsor Estate, where the procession starts. Anne Windsor's funeral is one of the most secure yet high risk events of the year. Many politicians, royalty, and almost every business tycoon across industries flew in for it, to honor the woman that we all deeply respected. Most brought their own private security, but the city was fully shut down for it too, police and armed forces on high alert.

Sierra stares out the window as she watches the hearse drive through the Windsor gates, Windsor household staff standing on either side of the open gates, tears in their eyes as they watch Anne leave one final time. The hearse is followed by Ares and Raven's car, then Luca and Valentina's, Dion and Faye's, Zane and Celeste's, Lexington and Raya's, and then us, followed by my parents and siblings. Every part of today has been carefully orchestrated, security acutely aware of who is which car, and even what speed we should all be driving at. Much to my surprise, the roads leading up to the graveyard are lined with people in black mourning clothes.

"I recognize some of these people from the charities Grandma founded or supported, but most are Windsor employees," Sierra says, her voice breaking. The Windsors gave all of their employees a day off today, but I know for a fact that none of them asked their employees to be there today, so to see them all here warms my heart.

"She was so loved," I tell Sierra as our driver stops the car, and our security personnel approach to open the door for us. I step out and offer my wife my hand, and she hesitates before taking it. It hurts to know that even now, when she needs consolation more than anything, it isn't me she wants anymore.

I wrap my arm around my wife as we're escorted to our seats on the front row, hundreds of people are already waiting in the open air. We're seated with her sisters-in-law, and she draws a shaky breath when her brothers carry the casket in. Raven wraps her arm around Sierra, and my wife places her head on Raven's shoulder as the ceremony starts.

Almost like the gods are weeping too, rain begins to fall, and black umbrellas are raised everywhere as we sit back and listen as Ares addresses the crowd, thanking them before regaling us all with stories about Grandma Anne — their version, not the one the world knew. He tells them about growing up with her after they lost their parents in a plane crash, and how she tried her best to never make them feel their loss. Some of Sierra's somberness lifts when he begins to talk about about heated fights for cookies, and how their close-knit family is a testament of Grandma's love and values, and that they'll never take it for granted. All the while, I watch my wife, wishing I could take away her grief and carry it all by myself.

Ares is trembling as a priest takes his place, and I draw a steadying breath, my own chest aching. I'll miss our lunches, and the way she'd pry for information about our marriage in far from subtle ways. I'll miss her cookies, and the advise she always had ready for me when she realized that I was so busy with work that I couldn't get my mind off it.

In the last few weeks, especially, she kept reminding me that there's always sunshine after rain, eventually, and to hold on to memories of better days. I'm not sure how, but she knew I'd been struggling, yet she never forced me to talk, nor did she seem angry at me for not being okay and in turn, hurting Sierra. The last thing she ever said to me was that she didn't regret entrusting me with her granddaughter's happiness, and as the priest asks us all to rise, I silently vow that I'll ensure she'll *never* regret it, if it's the last thing I do. I'll find a way to make her happy again, to make her smile again, no matter the cost.

"No, *please*," Sierra says, when the casket is being lowered, and she tenses when we're all asked to drop flowers on top.

"Come on, Kitten," I murmur, wrapping my arm around her as we follow her siblings. Sierra is shaking as she clenches a red rose so tightly that her palms begin to bleed from the thorns, blood running down her fingers.

I watch her as she holds her hand over the casket, her expression crumpling when she loosens her grip on the rose. Her legs tremble, and I catch her as she falls to her knees, a sob tearing through her throat for the first time today. I pull her close and hold her as she cries her heart out, and all the while, I wish I had the power to undo what happened — her being taken, her grandmother's death, all of it. There's nothing I wouldn't do to turn back time to when she was happy.

Sixty-Three

XAVIER

"What are you doing?" I ask, panicked as Sierra calmly pulls her clothes off hangers and folds them, before placing the stack in an open suitcase.

I drove us home after the funeral, and she sat in her favorite chair in her library for hours, before suddenly reaching for her phone and rising to her feet. Moments later, she walked into our dressing room, her expression unreadable. "I'm leaving," she says, her tone devoid of any emotion.

"What do you mean?" I ask, panic coursing through me as I grab her hands and hold them in mine. "This is your home, Sierra. *Our* home."

She raises a brow and smiles humorlessly. "Is it? Could've fooled me."

My wife pulls her hands out of my grip and continues to pack, so I reach for her suitcase and begin to unpack everything she's put in it, my mind a mess. I don't know what to do, how to stop her from leaving when I know I don't have the right to. She stayed for her grandmother, and now she has no reason to put up with me anymore. I can't even blame her for it. My stomach turns, and my head begins to pound as visions I don't want to see rush through my mind, reminding me why I should let her go, even as my heart protests.

"Stop it," she tells me when I empty her suitcase, her tone filled with resignation. "Just stop, Xavier."

I kneel in front of her, going down on both knees as I reach for her hands, feeling sick. "Don't leave me," I plead, just as a soft chime sounds through our house, alerting me to my parents' presence. Nonetheless, I don't look away from my wife, nor do I rise to my feet. "I love you, Sierra. More than anything," I tell her, my voice breaking. "I know it hasn't felt that way, but I swear it's true. I know I fucked up, Kitten. I know I failed you, and I know you're disappointed in me, but please, please let me fix this. Please let me be there for you."

"It's too late," she replies, her voice soft. "You *haven't* been there for me, Xavier, and I... I'm tired. I'm just so tired. I don't have it in me to wonder if you're only here because you pity me, and I can't handle the pain I feel every time I look at you, on top of the grief I'm drowning in."

She looks over my shoulder and sighs as she pulls her hands out of mine just as Raven and Celeste walk into our dressing room, my mother and Valeria in tow. Raven looks at me, a hint of compassion in her eyes as she reaches for the suitcase I'd just emptied.

"Don't do this," I beg as the girls begin to help Sierra pack while she and I stare at each other. "Please, Sierra," I whisper, my voice breaking.

She kneels in front of me, her hand trembling as she cups my face. My eyes flutter closed, and my breath hitches when she presses a soft kiss to my cheek. "I'm sorry," she murmurs. "I just can't be alone right now, Xavier... and that's how I feel when I'm with you, even when you're here."

She rises to her feet when the girls begin to carry her things out, taking one last look at me before she walks away, leaving me sitting here in a room filled with regret.

My mom sighs as she puts her hand on my shoulder, and I look up at her, my heart aching. "Mom," I murmur, my voice breaking. "What do I do?"

"You need to think long and hard about the way you've treated her, Xavier, and what you've been telling her with your actions every single time you didn't show up for her. She stood by you and fought for you and your marriage, and you repaid her by pushing her away instead of confiding in her and working with her to overcome what had happened. It was a horrible experience for you both, and I understand why it triggered the fears and traumas you thought you'd put behind you, but here's the thing, Xavier... you don't get to decide what Sierra needs. Not then, and not now. Only she can determine that. Pushing her away served *you*, not her, and the sooner you realize it, the sooner you can start fixing the damage you've done, if it isn't already too late."

Valeria kicks one of t-shirts that fell to the floor as I tried to unpack what Sierra was packing, and I look at her to find her staring at me with pure loathing in her eyes. "You should've respected her choices when she decided to be with you even after it nearly cost her her life. She's the one that should've been running away, scared of who she'd married, but she stood by you, and you didn't deserve it."

"Valeria," Mom scolds, but she shakes her head.

"No," she snaps. "Someone needs to say it, and it might as well be me. I'm deeply disappointed in you, Xavier. I will never, ever, forgive you if your actions lead me to lose my sister-in-law. She never wavered, no matter what you put her through, but I was the one who sat with her as she chose sad movies to watch, just so she'd have an excuse to cry when you didn't come at night. I'm the one that dragged her to Mom and Dad's house for dinner until she felt comfortable going by herself, so she'd eat something instead of working and starving herself to death in your absence. Did you know that I begged her not to give up on you after you told the press that your marriage was a business deal? I held her hands and pleaded with her, when I should've just punched you in the face for the way you were hurting her. I should've just slapped some sense into you."

She takes a step toward me, and mom grabs her arm, throwing her a warning look. "We do not solve our problems with violence. Not anymore," she reminds my sister, who stares at me like she despises me, like she's the one I've wronged.

"I will fix this," I promise, praying to God that I can, that Sierra will give me a chance to right my wrongs. "I'll do whatever it takes, I swear it."

Sixty-Four

SIERRA

I look up at the sound of a security notification from one of the robots Lex gifted me, its weird little face turning into a video feed that shows me Xavier sitting on the hood of his car, in front of my house.

He's been showing up every single day, and though I've been refusing to let him in, he hasn't stopped showing up. Every day, he leaves me little gifts — more annotated books that I haven't had the heart to open, countless Juliet roses, a nicely packaged cheese platter from the French place I've grown to love, and an endless amount of little notes with short messages telling me that he misses me and loves me.

Somehow he seems to know that I'm watching him, because he looks up and smiles right at the camera in that devastatingly hand-some way as he holds up a clear bag filled with what appear to be homemade chocolate chip cookies, followed by a large sign that reads:

MADE THESE FOR YOU. I'LL TRADE THEM FOR A MINUTE OF YOUR TIME PER COOKIE.

I watch in absolute disbelief as he reaches for another sign and holds it up:

I'LL EAT THEM IF YOU DON'T WANT THEM.

I frown when he reaches into the bag and holds up a cookie, before biting off a big chunk, making it clear he isn't going to leave them for me like he has with all the other things he's been giving me. I sigh as I watch him, oddly grateful he seems to have turned back into the man I fell in love with while simultaneously feeling bitter about it. I can't help but feel like he's only doing this because I left, and I can't go back to someone that doesn't appreciate what he's got until it's gone. He'll just take me for granted again the moment this all blows over, and I won't survive the heartache next time. It destroyed me to feel like I wasn't enough, and it left my self-esteem shaken, my heart broken.

Xavier looks up in surprise when I open the front door, and his expression moves my numb heart, makes it beat again, even if it's only for a moment. He looks at me like he can't quite believe what he's seeing, like the mere sight of me captivates him. I've gotten so used to him averting his face whenever our eyes lock that I just stare at him for a few seconds, caught in the moment. "Come in," I tell him, stepping back. "We need to talk."

He hesitates before pushing off his car and following me in, his gaze searching as he studies my face. "Sierra," he says when we walk into the living room, and the way he says my name makes me turn to face him. It's been so long since I heard him say my name like that, like I mean something to him, like I'm not just an inconvenience. "For you."

I take the cookies from him and stare at them, my heart aching. My grandmother taught him how to make these, and his always tasted more like hers than mine do, even though we make them the exact same way. Just seeing them soothes my aching heart.

It's clear he's trying to be there for me, but it feels like too little, too late. "Xavier," I say, my voice lacking the usual affection I used to say his name with. I've never felt so tired, so filled with regret. I wish we'd never gotten married, never fallen in love. At least then, I'd still have had our rivalry to distract me from my grief.

He steps forward, his movements hesitant as he brushes my hair out of my face. He'd stopped touching me like that, and there was a time when I'd wondered how long I'd have to wait to regain that kind of intimacy, but I've learned the hard way that the passing of time is cruel, and that the moments we experience are truly one of a kind. What's lost can't be regained, it can only be replicated, each new moment never quite the same, never quite enough.

I step away, and he pulls his hand to his chest, resignation and regret crossing his face. "What's wrong?" he asks, his voice soft, placating.

I look down and glance at the folder on my coffee table, my heart heavy as I hand it to him. "Let's put an end to this."

His hands tremble as he opens the folder and stares at the divorce papers, disbelief flickering in his eyes as he lifts his head and looks at me. "What?"

"You once told me that I shouldn't lower my standards just because you failed to meet them, and I'm finally taking your words to heart. I'm done expecting better from someone who is more attached to his fears and insecurities than to me. You made me fall for you, only to push me away and show me that my love isn't worth fighting for. You built me up, only to shake the foundations I thought we had, and you didn't even have the decency to watch me fall apart. Even so, I was convinced that you'd snap out of it, that you'd realize that what we have is worth everything — every risk, every nightmare you had to endure just to wake up to me. I was certain, Xavier, because all along, I was willing to risk dying if that's what it took to be with you."

Xavier drops the papers, and I watch them scatter on the floor as he reaches for me, his touch gentle as he cups my face. "You're right," he says, his voice soft. "I failed you, Sierra. I vowed to stand by you, for better or worse, but I ran when things got tough. I shut you out, undoing all the hard work we'd accomplished together, hurting you over and over again when all I've ever wanted to do was love you. I don't deny it, Sierra, nor will I make excuses. You deserve better than that. But I swear to you, I'm done running. Please—"

"—it's too late," I tell him, not wanting to hear his excuses, his empty promises. "I refuse to be with someone who isn't willing to heal from the scars left behind by his past. You're right, Xavier. I deserve better."

His eyes flash with pain, and he steps closer, until his body is flush against mine. "Then I'll be better," he tells me, his gaze unwavering. "I'm not signing those papers. I'm never letting you go, Sierra. I'm going to show you that you're worth fighting for, and I'm going to do everything in my power to earn your forgiveness. I'll try, day in and day out, for a million years and a day if I need to."

Sixty-Five

SIERRA

I raise a brow when I pull up at my house after a meeting that ran far later than I expected and find two cars parked in front — Xavier's, as usual, and his parents' town limousine.

Xavier pushes off the hood of his car, his expression stormy as he reaches for my car door and opens it for me. "Hi, Kitten," he says, smiling, though it doesn't quite reach his eyes today. "You look beautiful."

His eyes roam over my red dress hungrily, and I try my best to ignore the way my heart has started to respond to him again. "You look like you still haven't signed the papers."

He sighs, longing radiating off him as he hands me a bag. "I made you sugar cookies today. Decorated them too. I hope you like them."

I reluctantly take the cookies and step away from him, acutely aware that we seem to have an audience. I've only just turned my back to him when the limousine's door opens, and I look over my shoulder to find all three of Xavier's brothers, Valeria, and his parents step out.

"Sierra!" Valeria says, smiling as she rushes up to me and hugs me tightly, making me stumble back. Zach musses up my hair when V steps away, Hunter kisses my cheek, and Elijah offers me a quick hug, all four of them pretending Xavier isn't standing right there, watching them.

"Hi, honey," Mom says as she hands Dad what appears to be a grocery bag before she hugs me tightly, her arm wrapping around my shoulders as she pulls me toward the front door. Dad at least acknowledges Xavier's presence with a grumble before he walks past him, and they all leave him standing there.

"What are you all doing here?" I ask, confused as I let them in. The boys instantly begin to mess with the robot Lex gave me, asking it to show them to the kitchen.

Dad gasps when my robot, Lola, takes the grocery bag from him and wheels forward with it. "What kind of abomination is that?" he asks, and I bite back a smile at the sheer horror on his face.

"We're here to cook you dinner," Valeria explains.

"Yeah," Hunter says, looking over his shoulder. "You haven't come home in a while, so we weren't sure if maybe your cars were all broken or something."

"You didn't call, that's for sure. Had to check if your phone plan was still active, and it is, so I'm not sure what that's all about," Elijah adds.

Zach just chuckles and throws me a sweet smile. "We all missed you," he says as he helps Dad unpack the groceries they brought, before they all wash their hands and start to divide tasks, while I just look around in shock.

"We're making one of your favorites — Cacio e Pepe," Mom explains.

Zach begins to grate Pecorino, while Elijah tackles the Parmigiana. Dad gathers ingredients to make fresh pasta with, Hunter begins to chop salad ingredients, and Mom appears to have started making Parmigiana di Melanzane, another one of my favorites.

Valeria, on the other hand, just holds up a bottle of red wine that I happen to really love, and she grins at me as she pours glasses for me, Mom, and herself. "How have you been?" she asks as she lifts herself onto my kitchen counter, like she usually does.

I swirl my wine and stare at my glass for a few moments. "I don't know," I admit. Grief comes and goes in waves, and I often forget my grandmother isn't here anymore, until I pick up my phone to call her, or I begin to get ready for our weekly family dinner, only to get to her house and find my family sitting together quietly, none of us willing to let go of the tradition. They haven't said a thing about Xavier's absence, but they know he's been waiting in front of my house every single night, forgoing every other commitment for it, including, apparently, poker night.

I was so sure that I wanted a divorce when I had the papers drawn up, convinced Xavier didn't love me the way he claimed he did. I felt like I'd been going crazy, like my memories of us just weren't quite right, because I struggled to reconcile the man that had distanced himself from me with the man I'd fallen in love with. I'd been certain Xavier would sign the papers in a heartbeat, that he'd just been staying with me for my grandmother's sake, but he's still here, he's still showing up weeks later. Every single night, he waits for hours, never leaving until my bedroom lights turn off. I don't know what to make of him, and I can feel myself being swayed.

"It's okay to not be okay," Valeria says. "Healing takes time, Sierra."

I nod and take a sip of my wine. "I guess that's exactly what I'm doing." I'm trying my best to heal from losing people I lost, in different ways. It's almost easier to mourn the dead, since it's finite, and I get to cling to only the best memories. It's tougher to mourn the loss of a relationship, to face the what-ifs, the endless wondering if it was something I did, and what it was about me that made him give up on me when he promised me forever. I never made him doubt my commitment to him, made it clear his absence was hurting me, and even so, he continued to destroy everything we'd so painstakingly built — our trust, our happiness, the intimacy between us, and even the open communication we'd fought for.

"Dinner is ready," Dad shouts, and I glance over to find that Mom has already set the table. I should've been helping, but instead, I've just been sitting here, lost in my own thoughts.

I'm oddly nervous as I approach the table, my heart hurting as I look at the faces of all the people I thought would be family forever. "This won't change my mind about Xavier," I say carefully. "I don't want him to join for dinner either."

Mom looks surprised. "Good," she says. "He isn't invited, and we aren't here to change your mind, Sierra. We're just here because we love you."

I bite down on my lip to keep it from quivering, but I can't stop the tears gathering in my eyes. Someday, when Xavier eventually remarries, they'll all love another woman this way, and the thought of losing them too breaks what's left of my heart.

Valeria wraps her arm around me and pulls me to her, hugging me tightly. "Don't cry," she pleads. "We're here to make you feel better, not to make you cry."

I smile through my tears and try my best to pull myself together, and they all throw me understanding smiles, proceeding with dinner like they somehow knew that's exactly what I needed. Zach laughs at me as I choke down a big bite of pasta, tears still streaming down my face, and Hunter raises a brow as he looks at my plate. "Do you want some pasta with your cheese?" he asks, and just like that, I'm smiling again.

They don't let me lift a finger as they clean up after dinner, and Mom smirks at me as she walks over with one of the boardgames I keep in the living room, clearly not at all intending to go home just yet, and I'm beyond grateful for it. Somehow, she must've known that I wasn't ready for them to leave so soon.

"What's this?" Elijah asks, holding up the bag of cookies Xavier made me. I watch as he holds up one of them — one that's decorated with an X and a S on it, in pink and white, and he shrugs as he bites it in half. For a moment, I imagine what Xavier's face would look like if he'd seen his brother do that, and I can't help but laugh, my heart feeling a little lighter for the first time in weeks.

Sixty-Six

XAVIER

My heart races as I walk into Sierra's office building, trying to figure out why she hasn't cancelled today's meeting like she has all others. I can't figure out if it's good or bad, and I can't help but fear that it means she's no longer affected by being in a meeting with me.

For two months, I've shown up in front of her door every single day, giving her little handwritten notes and little gifts that reminded me of her and some of our best memories, hoping to thaw her heart, but she still looks at me expressionlessly, and every single day, she reminds me to sign the papers, not offering me any other words.

I'm starting to lose hope, and I'm beginning to worry that I'm harassing her, that my displays of affection are truly unwanted, and she just wants me out of her life. She hasn't banned me from entering the Windsor Estate, but where do I draw the line? Ultimately, all I want is for her to be happy, and I'm beginning to see that my presence in her life has the opposite effect.

I take a deep breath and gather my courage before walking into her conference room, only to freeze when I find her perched at the edge of the table, smiling up at Graham as he looks down at her with an expression that can only be described as intimate. My heart constricts painfully, even as it rejoices at the sight of her smile, something I've missed desperately.

She turns toward the door, and surprise flickers in her eyes when she sees me, like she genuinely didn't expect me to be here, and it strikes me then. She hasn't been cancelling these meetings. It was only me that was uninvited. "Xavier," she says, her face falling as she pushes off the table and nearly stumbles. I watch as Graham wraps his arm around my wife's waist with far too much familiarity, and she smiles up at him as she finds her footing, his touch lingering for a few moments, before it falls away when she takes her seat.

"I hope I'm not late," I tell them, trying my best to rein in my temper as I sit down next to Sierra.

"Not at all," Graham replies as he reaches for his laptop and plugs it in, clearly irritated I'm here. Have they been having these meetings together, just the two of them? Was she with him, every time she came home late? Elijah refused to tell me anything about her and went so far as to cut off my access to any of her security information. Is this why? Was he trying to keep me from seeing something I shouldn't?

I draw a shaky breath as Graham begins to walk us through some of the complications the project manager has run into, and Sierra stares at him throughout his presentation, seemingly enraptured. She doesn't look my way once, and it fucking kills me, because I remember when she used to look at me that way. I remember when we'd both be in the same room, and it'd be like no one else existed, no matter how many other people we were competing or working with.

She watches him, but I watch *her*, my eyes roaming over her face, before moving on to her body. My heart stutters when I recognize the short navy dress she's wearing. Did she even think of me as she put it on? Did she remember that I'd fucked her in it, right on top of Graham's conference table?

I run a hand through my hair as my gaze is drawn to her hands when she opens up her notebook and grabs a pen. She hasn't been wearing her wedding ring for some time now, and that's definitely the kind of thing Graham would have noticed. Did she tell him that we separated? That she left me and moved back into her own home? Does he know she asked me for a divorce?

I'm fucking desperate for her attention as I reach for her pen and pull her notebook closer, but she only glances at me for a moment, dismissing my actions as she looks back at Graham like he's actually saying something of interest, when we both know he's not. These meetings are formalities. This is never where we find out anything we didn't already know.

That dress is one of my favorites. You look gorgeous.

She glances at the note I left on the edge of the page, her gaze lingering. I'd been so sure her reaction would give away whether or not she remembers that day, but her expression is unreadable. I bite down on my lip when she looks away and scribble something else onto the page.

Does he know I fucked you in it on his conference table?

This time her eyes widen, and she finally looks at me. I smirk at her, pleased I finally got her attention, but then she looks down and snaps her notebook closed, something akin to guilt crossing her face before she turns away from me, almost like she can't quite face me. My heart drops as I look down at my hands, at my wedding ring.

That look... what did it mean? My stomach tightens, and I suck in a breath as my mind begins to fuck with me. My hands begin to tremble, and I move them underneath the table before clasping them, my breathing accelerating. Why did she look at me like that?

Was it because she wore that dress for *him* today? It certainly wasn't for me, since she clearly hadn't expected to see me here today.

Was it something far worse than that? Did she sleep with him? At least a handful of times, she didn't come home until nearly midnight, and I'd stupidly assumed she must've been with her siblings or their wives, when I should've considered that she might have gone out for dinner with someone else. She might have gone home with someone else, not returning to her own bed until late at night.

I look at her again, just as she's smiling at something he says, and it fucking kills me that he can do that to her, when I no longer can. I take a steadying breath as my gaze moves between them both, and I'm reminded of something she once said to me, just before I rushed over to her grandmother to ask for her hand in marriage. *"I don't want to wait anymore. I'm going to write my own story and marry a man of my choosing."*

The man of her choosing was never me.

It was him.

I lean back in my seat when the meeting concludes, and she rises to her feet, walking up to him. They murmur among themselves, and my heart twists painfully as I listen to them discussing their dinner plans like I'm not even here, like she isn't still legally my wife.

"Sierra," I say, my voice soft. "Can I talk to you?"

She looks at me, and it hits me then. We've been in a similar situation before, and I'd told her she was crazy if she thought I'd let her flirt with another man right in front of me, before reminding her that she's mine. Today it isn't me she'll kiss. It's not my fingers that'll slip between her legs, taunting her for being wet and needy.

She tells him she'll meet him at the restaurant, and he throws her a sweet smile, their eyes locking for a few moments, like he's trying to quietly ascertain if she's okay, the way I used to. Sierra watches him walk away like she can't bear to see him go, and the pain rapidly becomes unbearable.

"What is it?" she asks, showing me none of the sweetness she just showed him.

I stare at my wife, taking in those beautiful eyes that I've always loved, those lips I fantasized about for years, and the way her nose points up just a touch at the end. "Do I even stand a chance?"

She looks away, her eyes dropping to her notebook, where they linger for some time. "Sign the papers," she says, those gorgeous eyes I've always loved entirely devoid of emotion.

Sixty-Seven

SIERRA

My heart feels heavy when I get home and find my driveway empty after dinner with Graham, his girlfriend, and a few of their friends. I should be relieved that Xavier isn't here tonight, yet I can't help but feel a sense of loss as I get out of my car. I'd wondered how long it'd take for him to stop showing up.

I run a hand through my hair as I walk to my front door, only to pause when I find a black box waiting for me, a gold ribbon on it. My heart begins to ache when I recognize his handwriting, and the way he curls the S in my name.

My hands tremble as I carry it to my living room, my every instinct telling me that the contents will hurt me even more than he already has. I suck in a breath when I pull the ribbon loose and lift the lid, my stomach tightening as I stare at the divorce papers. I'm shaking as I reach for them, my movements slow, reluctant as I flick through them. He signed them. I didn't think he ever would.

I trail a finger over his signature, my heart twisting painfully. This is what I thought I wanted, yet it brings me no joy at all, no relief. It doesn't feel like a clean break, or a fresh start, like I'd hoped it would. It just feels like heartbreak far worse than anything I've ever felt before.

I bite down on my lip as I glance back at the box that was far too big for the documents, my brows rising when I realize there's something else in it. My heart begins to race when I reach for the book in it, a sticky note on the cover.

Read this before you file the papers.
Forever yours,
XK

I pull the note off to take a closer look at the cover, and my eyes widen when I read the title. *The Story of Us.* It looks hand bound, the cover art a painting of Xavier and me, on our wedding day. I frown when I realize the cover is textured, *hand-painted*, in a style I recognize all too well. This was painted by The Muse. How is that even possible? The Muse is an anonymous painter best known for their street art, and I've been a huge fan for years. I once mentioned to Xavier that I wish they did book covers, and he'd laughed, telling me that there wasn't anything in life I couldn't relate back to my love for books.

My heart is racing as I sit down on the sofa and carefully open the book, shock coursing through me when I realize that the endpages at the front also contain stunning art, painted by The Muse. I stare at the depiction of us sitting together at The Siren, surrounded by Juliet roses, the painting spanning two pages. I remember that night all too well, and more than once I've wished I could return to that moment, when we were happy, and the worst we'd ever done to each other was pull stupid pranks and steal projects from each other.

My hand trembles as I turn the page and read the dedication. **For my wife, the love of my life.** My eyes widen when realization dawns, and I turn the page. Xavier *wrote* this. I inhale shakily as I begin to read.

You'd be surprised to learn that I'd never even met you when I first began to love you, but it's true. Granted, I wasn't 'in love' with you, but it was love all the same. It all started with a parcel I opened by mistake, and the sweet handwritten letter it contained, along with one single cookie, both meant for my roommate — Dion Windsor.

You see, his sweet little sister had sent him a letter, telling him she missed him so much that she'd be willing to part with one of her beloved cookies, if he'd just come back home. I'd thought to myself then, Dion Windsor was the luckiest guy alive. If not for that letter, I might have continued to keep my distance, missing out on a friendship that's lasted a lifetime — the very same friendship that would eventually lead me to the love of my life.

I'm enraptured as I read page after page, learning that Dion gave all of his cookies to Xavier throughout their years at boarding school, and each time he received a new cookie, Dion would tell Xavier all about me and the contents of the accompanying letter.

It was the only time the usually gloomy Dion would glow instead, and I loved that unknown girl for having that effect on him, when nothing else did. I think that's when I first realized just how special you are, Sierra.

I read all about how surprised he was when he first met me in person, when Dion brought him home later that year.

I was just a child myself, but you were really little, the same age as my own little sister, and you instantly seemed to dislike me. I remember thinking to myself that you had good judgment. I, on the other hand, thought you were adorable.

I smile to myself, only for my heart to constrict painfully as I keep reading and learn about Dion asking Xavier to look out for me and our brothers after they left college, many years later.

Dion stayed overseas while I came back home, and I did as I was asked, checking up on you and your siblings every few months for years. I'd begun to attend poker night with them occasionally, in part because they made it easier to cope with the

fact that my sweet little sister had gone missing without a trace, and in part to make sure they were okay.

It wasn't until you came home from college that I suddenly became interested in attending every single month. You see, until then, I just had my security team watch out for you — until you walked into that conference hall, and I genuinely didn't know what hit me.

I recognized those emerald eyes of yours, but everything else about you had changed, and you were quite simply the most beautiful woman I'd ever seen in my life. I felt terrible; you were my best friend's little sister, six years my junior, and someone I'd vowed to look out for, so I tried my best to stay away, and God, I've never been more grateful to have failed at something.

It's heartwarming to read about those first few months of my career from his perspective. Everything I thought was mere coincidence, was far from it. I pause on a part that surprises me.

That morning, I'd been informed you had a meeting with a CEO that always creeped me out, and I'd been worried sick, so I made sure to schedule a meeting before yours so I could stick around after. Who could've known that once more, it was a cookie that would seal my fate?

You were standing in the hallway, seemingly nervous as you waited for your meeting, and I'd just been about to walk up to you when you grabbed a cookie from your bag and bit into it. God, the way you moaned, Sierra... It was sinful, and I wasn't thinking straight when I approached you, needing to know how good of a cookie it could possibly be to make you sound like that. I grabbed your wrist and took a bite of your cookie, and just like that, I made it to the top of your most hated list, though it took me years to realize that's how I condemned myself.

I laugh to myself as I think back to that day. I'd been so sure he'd done it on purpose, to annoy me, and he's right — it's what made me think of him as my nemesis. I'd begun to act sassier around him, throwing glares his way each time I saw him, and he'd smile at me every time, which would just anger me further. It didn't help that he'd begun to criticize my work every chance he got, and I didn't realize back then that he'd just been mentoring me, in his own way. I smile to myself as I read about every single interaction we've ever had from his point of view, watching our story unfold differently to how I experienced it.

I couldn't stay away after that. I told myself I was just keeping my promise to your brother each time I teased you, quietly opening corporate doors for you while protecting you from the worst parts of the industry, but we both know I'm lying. I was falling in love with you, with each piece of paper we scribbled on during a meeting, each time we butted heads, and each project we competed for. I knew you weren't meant for me — I wasn't just your brother's best friend, I also had a murky past that I didn't want spilling over into your life, but as the years passed, and I began to reform myself, I began to think that maybe, some-day, I'd become someone you could love.

I pull my legs up underneath me as I continue to read about the projects he stole from me, and the way he'd let me get away with things when I genuinely thought I had the upper hand. I gasp when I read about the way I nearly got caught breaking into his house that very first time.

Thinking back, those were moments that I held so dear. You have no idea how many times I've rewatched videos of you breaking into any of my properties, just to see you smile as you wreaked havoc. It was after that very first time, when you'd nearly gotten caught spraying graffiti on the side of my brand new office that I created the Mrs. Kingston Protocol — a security protocol that allowed you to do absolutely anything you wanted at any Kingston property, at any time.

All of our security staff was trained to recognize you on the cameras that you never knew existed, and every time they spotted you, they'd follow your actions, ensuring you never set off an alarm and were never caught. The protocol only failed twice in over seven years, once because Valentina had been with you, and she didn't have the same clearance you do, and once

because a guard had already been on patrol by the time you acti-vated the protocol, and you'd caught him by surprise. It was hubris, to name the protocol that, and I knew it, but even back then, I just couldn't help myself when it came to you. It wasn't anything I thought you'd ever learn about, so there was no harm in it, right?

The hours pass as I continue to read about him sneaking into poker nights and hiding it from me, so I couldn't force my brothers to un-invite him and thereby cut off his source of inside informa-tion on me. I'm enraptured as I read about the first time we danced the tango together, our first kiss after he bailed me out of jail for breaking into his office with Val, and eventually the way he felt we begun to drift apart involuntarily when Valeria returned home, his focus on her safety and wiping out any threats to her.

I'd remembered then, that I wasn't the kind of guy you would ever be with, but I kept pretending, kept deluding myself into thinking that I could be.

He never even suspected that I was jealous. It didn't even occur to him at all, judging by the several pages he wrote about trying to figure out what he'd done to deserve a stink bomb being sent to his office after the first time I'd seen him with Valeria, and the way he tried to keep me from distancing myself, only to eventually decide that it'd be for the best.

My heart hammers in my chest as I read about the way he approached my grandmother, and eventually our marriage. It's so special to read about the way he couldn't quite believe it when I'd begun to fall for him. It's an unreal experience, and it makes it hurt so much more to read about the fears he couldn't shake off after I was taken, the endless nightmares, and the way he couldn't pull himself out of his head when he woke up, fear reeling him in throughout the day, even when I told him he was breaking my heart.

His writing makes it clear he tried his best to control his mind, only to continuously feel like it was failing him. It hurts to read how much he was suffering, and how his nightmares made him unable to look at me without feeling like he was slowly suffocating me, my life draining away because of him.

I knew it wasn't true, that it was all in my head, but I was too scared and ashamed to tell you just how bad things had gotten, because I was just so sure that if I did, I'd lose you forever. I thought I'd get better eventually, and it'd be like things had never changed.

Ironic, isn't it, that it was that exact thought process that led us here? As if that wasn't bad enough, I'd once again become scared to say the wrong thing and put you at risk like I'd done with Valeria, because that wasn't just an irrational fear anymore, it was a likely possibility, and your life wasn't something I'd ever risk.

I inhale shakily and try my best not to cry as I continue to read about his struggles, my grandmother's funeral, the divorce papers, the way he'd begun to come to my house every day in hopes that we'd work things out while fighting his own fears every single day, until eventually, I find myself reading about today, and the way he felt during the meeting. I'd been trying so hard not to look at him that I couldn't focus, and I hadn't even been looking at Graham. I'd been trying to stare at the screen behind him.

I think back to the guilt he thought he saw on my face, and I sigh when I realize what happened. His note had reminded me of the day he'd mentioned, when Graham wanted go to a bistro nearby and Xavier'd gotten jealous. I'd been been worried my husband would find out about my dinner plans, and he'd misunderstand, which he did.

I'm oddly scared when I finally get to the last page, not wanting the story to end and unsure what I'll find.

This story... it's one I was certain would end in the words, 'and they lived happily ever after', but instead, you'll always be the one that got away. The thing is, I should've tried harder, should never have given up on the only woman I've ever loved... but what else could I do when you'd begun to look at another man the way you used to look at me? Your happiness is all I've

ever wanted, even if it's at the cost of mine. You deserve to be happy with the man of your own choosing, and I should never have gotten in your way. My selfishness cost you so much, and there's nothing I can do to make that right, but this I can do — I'll let you go, even if it's the hardest thing I've ever had to do, even if I'll regret it for a million years and a day.

I love you, Sierra. Thank you for allowing me to experience real happiness for the first time in my life, and for allowing me to live out some of my grandest dreams. I'll never regret you, Kitten. You will always be the best thing that's ever happened to me.

Sixty-Eight

XAVIER

I sigh when I hear heels clicking behind me, expecting my mother to walk into my living room like she's done every day for the last week, just to scold me until I showered and ate. "Saved you the hassle," I say, refusing to get up and face her. "I showered not long ago, and I ate something sometime today. I don't remember what, but I remember doing it, so please, just leave me be today." I've been sitting here ever since I got out the shower, somehow just not having had the energy to get dressed or do anything else.

Everything in my house reminds me of Sierra — especially my soap, and it'd just been too much. I'd stood there as I remembered the times she'd get in the shower with me, and I'd soap up her body, touching her suggestively as I pretended to clean her body thoroughly. She'd giggle, until her laughter turned into moans, and then she'd whisper my name in the moments before she came. Knowing I'd never get the experience that again was too much to bear, and I'd walked out of the shower and sat down on the sofa with nothing but my towel on, my body still dripping wet.

"I can... I can come back another day if now isn't a good time. I'm sorry, I should've called."

I rise to my feet in a rush and turn around, certain my mind is playing tricks on me. "Sierra?"

She smiles shakily, her gaze roaming over my body as she takes in how wet my skin still is, her cheeks flushing. I stand there, frozen as her eyes follow a drop of water running down from my neck, to my chest and abs, until it disappears against my towel.

My wife walks around the sofa, and my eyes drop to the book she's holding, the one I wrote for her. "I came to return this," she says, looking down at it.

My heart wrenches painfully, and I swallow hard as I follow her gaze. There's one part of the story I omitted — just one. I'd started writing it because I'd planned to propose again on our one year wedding anniversary. The last few pages were meant to be all about how I'd give her the book and I'd watch her read it, mentally documenting all her smiles and little squeals as she reads, something I've really come to love doing. I'd sit with her in our library, until she got to the part where she's reading all about how I got down on one knee in front of her, and she'd have frowned, knowing that never happened, and then she'd have gasped as I did it in real life. I'd tell her, 'the way this story currently ends is fictional, but I want nothing more than to make it our reality. I know I don't compare to the heroes you read about, but I will never stop trying to make your wildest dreams come true'. I had it all memorized, spent months working on what I'd say. This was supposed to become her new favorite book, *our story* her favorite of all. Now it's one she doesn't even want to hold on to.

I reach for it wordlessly, but she pulls it to her chest. "The ending sucked," she tells me, and my eyes meet hers. "So I rewrote it."

"What?"

Her hands tremble as she hands it to me, and I stare at it for a few seconds, scared of what I'll find. I'm tempted to stretch out this moment, desperately wishing I could stay here forever, in the unknown, where I don't have to acknowledge that we're truly over. "Read it," she whispers.

I reluctantly flip the book open and navigate to the last few pages, the ones I'd left blank. Underneath my last sentence, in her handwriting, it reads:

> this isn't how The Story of Us ends. It's just one arc of our lives, the first real hardship we had to overcome as a couple. We nearly failed, you and I. We failed to understand each other, failed to communicate despite the promises we made, but we'll learn from it, won't we? This book is proof of it, of how far you and I had come together, before we let our efforts go to waste.
>
> So here I am, offering you an alternate ending. Our story has veered off course, but what if we just rewrite it together? I still love you, Xavier Kingston, and you're still the only man I've ever wanted, the only one I've ever loved. That kind of love is worth fighting for, so here I am, asking you if you're willing to be vulnerable with me, to acknowledge the pain we've both caused and start healing with me.
>
> After all, 'Happily Ever After' isn't a moment, it's a choice, one we must make over and over again, every single day. It's a commitment to each other, a promise to keep working toward happiness, to never take it for granted or forsake it in favor of our fears and insecurities. Let's uphold our vows, Xavier. Let's honor the promises we made. Let's rewrite this ending, together.

"I left some space at the end," she says, her voice breaking. "Maybe someday, we can add a few sentences." My wife looks at me with so much hope in her eyes, and my eyes never leave hers as I put the book down and reach for her.

Her breath hitches when I thread my hand through her hair and pull her closer, my forehead dropping to hers, her arms moving around my neck. "There is nothing I won't do to rewrite our ending," I tell her, my voice breaking. "I love you so much, Sierra. There's *nothing* I won't do for another chance with you."

Her hand moves up my nape, into my hair, and then her lips come crashing against mine. I groan as I pull her against me, savoring her taste, and the feel of her. I'll never take this for granted again. I'll never forsake her. "I'll never let you go again," I whisper against her lips, grateful to have her here in my arms. There's nothing I won't do to ensure her happiness, nothing I won't do to make sure she turns out to be right, and this become just one arc in our story, one we'll learn from and never repeat.

Sixty-Nine

SIERRA

I lean back in my car as I wait for Xavier to finish his therapy session, my eyes glued to my e-reader. I wasn't sure what to expect when I went to his house with *The Story of Us* in hand. Having read his words, I knew we deserved one more chance, but I wasn't sure what it'd mean in practice. Would it be one of those things we say and promise, but don't deliver on? Would things be okay for a little while, only for time to cast its wicked curse, making us forget all about our commitments as we slipped back into our comfort zones?

I'd been scared to trust, and Xavier proved all of my fears wrong. I thought he'd been committed to me before, but the way he's been behaving from the moment I came home has exceeded all of my expectations. He decided to go to therapy to overcome some of the scars from his past, and I've been driving him there once a week, enjoying sitting in the car with my book for an hour, after which he takes me out for lunch.

Though he can't be fully honest during his sessions, therapy has been working better for him than I could've hoped, and it helped him not spiral when Elijah nearly failed to foil an attack on Valeria last month. She stopped hiding after Grandma's funeral, where she was photographed extensively, and as expected, it resulted in an increased amount of attempted violence toward us all. I didn't know until recently, but in the years she stayed hidden, Valeria wiped out every criminal organization she'd learned about during her time in captivity, leaving behind a Queen of Spades playing card every time. Her list of enemies is longer than that of all her brothers combined, but she seems entirely unfazed by it.

My phone rings, and I look up in surprise when I see Valeria's name flash across my screen. "I was just thinking about you," I tell her, grinning to myself.

"Sierra," she says, her tone grim. "You need to help me."

I sit up, instantly on high alert. "What happened?" I ask, running a diagnostic on the tablet I carry everywhere, finding all of our security measures intact.

Xavier has spent months training me, teaching me how to shoot, and making sure my fitness levels and fighting skills stay at a level he's comfortable with. He's going to therapy, but in return, he asked that I make sure I'm never helpless, and that at the very least, I'm able to defend myself beyond what I was taught in my kidnapping prevention classes. It's a task I've taken very seriously in an effort to show my commitment to him, and I've spent months learning about all kinds of security protocols, learning Krav Maga, and becoming comfortable carrying and using a gun.

"Enzo is acquiring half of Kingston Enterprises. I wasn't told until literally ten minutes ago, and they've already drawn up the paperwork. Elijah isn't listening to me and keeps saying that he's more than happy to let go of managing the business so he can focus more on operations. You need to help me, Sierra. You need to talk to Xavier for me. If they sign those papers, Enzo will become my boss, and I...I can't work with him. I just... I can't."

I frown as I listen to her. Kingston Enterprises is our private intelligence firm, and Elijah and Valeria mostly work with government agencies, off the record. Most of the people that work there don't even exist on paper, and I would have been surprised that

Enzo would want to get involved with it — had Valeria not been working there. "I'll talk to Xavier about it, alright?"

She thanks me as Xavier walks up to the car, and I end the call just as he opens the door. "Who was that?" he asks, leaning in for a kiss.

I wrap my hand around the back of his neck and lose myself in our kiss for a few moments, my heart instantly beginning to race. He still gives me butterflies, and he still makes time stop the moment he touches me.

"Valeria," I answer, before pressing another quick peck to his lips. "I'm supposed to talk to you about Enzo trying to acquire a big stake in Kingston Enterprises."

His expression shutters closed, and he looks away. "It's a good partnership," he says. "Enzo is exceptionally skilled at making businesses thrive, and quite frankly, Elijah just isn't interested in that. He wants to be a field agent, but we can't hand the reins over to anyone we don't fully trust. I don't have time for it, and Valeria isn't ready for the position, nor has she ever wanted it."

I nod as I drive us to The Siren, where we go for lunch almost every week. Valeria changed a lot after Enzo's engagement party, and very quickly too. She became much more spirited, and more than once, I've heard Mom remark on how she's herself again. I'm not sure what caused it exactly, but I know it's got something to do with Enzo.

"I think it's a great idea," I murmur. It feels like a betrayal to say it, because I know this isn't what she imagined I'd say when she called me for help, but I think she needs him — more than she knows, more than she cares to admit. Seeing him at his engagement party wasn't closure for her. It was something else, something I can't quite put to words.

Xavier smiles as he steps out of the car and walks around it to open the door for me. "It is," he reassures me, entwining our fingers as we walk in and head straight for our usual table.

"So, how is your book?" he asks as we sit down. I never ask him about his therapy sessions, because I think that's private, and it's enough for me that he's going. So instead, Xavier and I spend our lunch break talking about the books I'm reading, and every week, he asks me about my favorite scenes, only to then find little ways to re-enact them throughout the week. It's thrilling to know he's really listening to me like that, that he cares enough to make my little daydreams come true.

"Okay, so," I begin to tell him, and he leans in, watching me like I'm telling him the most riveting story he's ever heard, and my heart pounds wildly. I'm so in love with this man, and it's absolutely unreal that I get to be his wife.

"So if I'm understanding correctly, the hero bought the apart-ment the heroine was renting when her landlord threatened to evict her? So now she can stay there? But she doesn't know he bought it?"

I nod excitedly, and Xavier frowns. "I don't get it. Why didn't he just buy the whole building? He could've just moved in next door, and then he'd get to see her every day. Plus then she wouldn't have to suffer from all those noise complaints you mentioned earlier, since there'd be no pesky neighbors anymore."

I blink at him. "That's... it's just..." I shake my head and burst out laughing. "You know what? All my life, I'd been scared that no one would ever live up to the heroes I read about, and I guess it's true." He tenses, his expression falling. "You're *better*, Xavier. You're more than my dreams come true — you raised the standard, and I fear I'm forever spoiled."

He lifts my hand to his lips and kisses my knuckles gently. "Good," he tells me, his eyes twinkling. "Because I love spoiling you."

Seventy

XAVIER

"When are you finally going to tell me where we're going?" my wife asks excitedly as she looks out of the window of our private jet.

My heart warms as I watch her, and gratitude rushes through me when she looks at me and smiles. She's so beautiful, so precious, and somehow, she's entirely mine. It's surreal, and even after all this time, I can hardly believe that she's my wife.

"You've been acting kind of weird all day," she adds, narrowing her eyes at me as she crosses her arms and stares me down. "First you wake me up super early, then you drag me onto this plane with a suitcase Raven has allegedly packed for me, and you won't even tell me where we're going. You're up to something. You're being too secretive."

I grin and reach for her hand as the plane begins to descend. "You always see straight through me, don't you?" No one knows me like she does, and it's thrilling to have one person in my life that's just mine, someone who understands what I'm thinking without having to explain. "I'm taking you on a little island retreat."

She gasps and tightens her grip on my hand. "Are we going back to Enzo's island? God, I loved it there."

I shake my head. "I bought us one of our own, since you seemed to really love it. Besides, Enzo is being weird about that particular island anyway. Told me it's meant just for his wife and no one else, when somehow, that wasn't an issue last time. He isn't even married yet, so I don't know why he's being like that."

Sierra's eyes light up, and she laughs. "Probably for the best," she says, her eyes roaming over me. "You're always so stressed out when we go on holiday. I'd much prefer having a place of our own that we know is highly secure, so you can actually rest. You're never fully relaxed in unknown places."

There's no judgment in her eyes, no blame, and I love her for it. "I have a surprise for you," I admit.

"I know," she replies. "Why else would you have been scheming all morning? Not to mention that you bought an *island* and I'm only just finding out, when you usually tell me everything."

I can't help but chuckle, and she grins as she leans in and threads her hand through my hair, pulling my lips onto hers. I groan as I kiss her, loving the feel of her. I don't think I'll ever get enough of kissing her, of being with her. I smile as we both sit back, my eyes on hers as we land. She's the light of my life, the love of my life, and every single day, I fall a little deeper in love.

Sierra gasps when we step off the jet, on our own runway. "This is incredible," she says as she looks around and finds miles and miles of clear blue water around us. She looks so happy as she reaches for my hand and pulls me along, even though she has absolutely no idea where she's going, and I just know I'll follow this woman to the ends of the world if that's where she chooses to lead me to.

"There's something I want to show you," I tell her as we get closer to our holiday mansion. Sierra looks over her shoulder, her eyes filled with curiosity.

I try my best to smile, but I'm just so goddamn nervous as we head toward the beach behind the house, down a trailing stone path. My hands are clammy, and I know she can feel it, but thankfully, she doesn't say anything as she follows me.

Sierra tightens her grip on me, her breathing becoming a little shaky when she spots the giant stone book on the beach, texted carved into it before it was painted over. It's a replica of The Story of Us, opened up to a page that isn't in our version of the book — *yet*.

Sierra has tears in her eyes when she looks at me, and I think she knows what's coming. "I had a more robust plan," I tell her as we pause in front of it. "But then you took my hand and started to look at everything so excitedly, and I just knew I couldn't wait a second longer."

She looks from me to the painting on the background of the left page, in which I'm down on one knee, and tears begin to gather in her eyes when she read the word *Let's Start a New Chapter* written over it in big letters.

"Sierra," I say, reaching for her hand and stealing back her attention. I smile up at her, my heart overflowing with happiness. "Every day, I'm fighting for my life against the romance heroes you love so much." She bursts out laughing, her tears drying. "And it's a worthwhile fight, Kitten. You deserve the world, and nothing makes me happier than trying to give it to you. You changed my whole outlook on life, made me want to be a better person than I ever thought I could be, and in my quest to become worthy of you, I began to learn how to love myself, scars and all — something I didn't think would ever happen. That's what you do, you know? You make everything you touch better. You saved me, a thousand times over, with each little smile, each note scribbled in the margins of a notebook at a meeting. Each little action kept me on the right path — the path that led me here, to you."

I tighten my grip on her hand, my heart pounding wildly. I'm already married to her, and somehow, I'm still terrified. "I don't regret any part of our story, because every single page we've written together made us who we are, and it made us stronger than I ever could've hoped. However, if there is one thing I could do over, it would be this..."

She gasps when I go down on one knee and reach for the ring box I've been hiding from her. She sniffles when I open it clumsily, and I notice the exact moment she recognizes the priceless pink diamond I once bought at an auction because I saw the way she'd looked at it, the one the media has been reporting about for years, pondering who its recipient would be.

I know she's always dreamed of a proposal, and having an engagement ring. I should've proposed to her once I'd gotten her grandmother's approval, so she wouldn't have had to miss out on it. "I hope it's not too late," I say nervously, my heart hammering in my chest. "Sierra, you are the love of my life, and if you'll let me, I'd love to make up for everything we've missed out on. If you'll let me, I'll show you that you've always been the heroine in my story, every single day, starting with this: Sierra Kingston, will you marry me — in a place of our choosing, with our friends and family around us as we make our vows?"

"Yes," she says, a tear running down her face. "Yes. A thousand times, yes. I'd want nothing more, Xavier."

Seventy-One

SIERRA

My heart aches in a bittersweet way as I look into the mirror, taking in my wedding gown. Raven altered it for me, making it strapless, with a much longer, removable train that attaches at the waist. Wearing it feels different this time. It's mostly the same dress, but today, I really feel like a bride. I just wish my grandmother and parents had been here today to see me marry the love of my life.

"You look stunning," Raven says as she walks in. "It was beautiful before, but the alterations just look so... *romantic*."

I grin at her. "I owe it all to you," I tell her earnestly. "Thank you for creating the dress of my dreams, Rave. Twice."

She smiles at me and gently brushes my hair out of my face. I had it up the first time, but today it's loose and wavy. "It's a true honor. Besides, thanks to Xavier's antics with the billboards, my waiting list is now three years long." I laugh as I remember what he'd done, a thrill running down my spine.

Raven looks down for a moment, and I follow her gaze, realizing that she's holding an envelope. "This was delivered just now — by Grandma's attorney. It's for you."

I raise a brow as I take it from her curiously, my eyes widening when I recognize Grandma's handwriting. I'm trembling as I open the envelope and find a letter from Grandma, addressed to me.

Dear Sierra,

If you're reading this letter, you'll have followed in your siblings' footsteps, and you're about to marry Xavier Kingston once again — by choice, this time. I have no doubt that you look incredibly beautiful, and just like last time, Xavier won't be able to take his eyes off you for even a single second.

I never told you this, but your match was determined long before Raven and Ares got married. I knew it'd be Xavier when he first began to meddle in your career, quietly taking an interest in projects that were far too small to warrant his attention. He spent more time than he reasonably should have guiding you, protecting you, without you ever even realizing it.

I knew then — this was the man that would eventually marry my precious granddaughter; someone who never asked for anything in return for everything he did for you, not even recognition. He was always just happy to see you thriving, and he never grew impatient with you, never demanded more than your attention.

I'd just scheduled a meeting with Xavier's parents when he walked into my home, your five brothers in tow, all but begging me to marry you. He'd cloaked his request for your hand in a merger, but even then, there was clear *love and commitment written all over his face, though he was scared to admit it. T*

hat love never wavered — not even when you both desperately pretended you weren't struggling, going to great lengths to put up an act for me. I knew, even then, as I witnessed pain in both of your eyes, that you would find your way back to each other, because he loves you almost as much as I do.

Please be happy together, Sierra. Live a life filled with wonder, devoid of regrets, and overflowing with love. You deserve nothing less, my sweet child.

All my love, always, Grandma

I pull the letter to my chest and draw a steadying breath, something akin to *comfort* washing over me. For so long, the mere thought of Grandma made me cry, but today it brings a bittersweet smile to my face. "You were right, Grams," I whisper, certain that somewhere, somehow, she can hear me. All of a sudden, I'm sure I can smell her perfume, and I sigh happily.

I look up at the sound of knocking, and my father-in-law walks in, only to freeze at the sight of me. My brothers all fought viciously about who would get to walk me down the aisle, but instead of choosing one of them and upsetting the rest, I chose the man I've come to consider my own father, the man that'll be my dad for the rest of my life.

It just felt right to be walked down the aisle by the man that sat in my car with me when his son upset me, the man that walked into my kitchen to make me fresh pasta while he left his son standing outside. He treated me like his own daughter even after I'd asked for a divorce, and I just know that'll never change, no matter what the future brings.

"You look beautiful, sweetie," he says, smiling at me so proudly as he offers me his arm. "Are you ready?"

"What would you do if I say no?"

"Why, I'd get the jet ready, of course. Mom always has an exit plan ready." I burst out laughing, and he narrows his eyes at me. "You'd better not tell Xavier I said that. He's gotten a little testy lately, claiming we're playing favorites and that we like you more than we like him. Mom has sternly advised me *not* to admit that it's true."

"My lips are sealed, I promise," I tell him, feeling so incredibly loved. I've always wondered what my parents would've been like, and I have a feeling they'd treat me the same way. My in-laws filled a void I thought I'd always have to live with, and I'm so incredibly grateful to have them.

My heart overflows with happiness as Dad guides me toward the aisle Celeste created for me on our private island, where we've flown all our loved ones to for our wedding. She transformed the beach into something from a fairytale, turning the stone book on the beach into the backdrop for the ceremony, paperbacks that she saved from being destroyed used as decoration everywhere. It's everything I ever could've dreamed of, and more. I've never felt more loved, and I think I've finally truly found my place in life.

Faye begins to play the piano, and I take a deep breath as we reach the start of the aisle. I can't help but smile when I see Xavier standing at the end of it. He looks at me awestruck, and my smile becomes a little shaky when his expression crumples, and tears gather in his eyes. I don't think I've ever seen him cry before, and I can't help the tears in my own eyes.

He draws a shaky breath as I walk toward him, composing himself, and we both ignore our brothers' snickers, cash being exchanged everywhere, as though they betted on whether or not my sweet husband would cry at the sight of me. They'll pay dearly for that — they just don't know it yet.

"Wow," he whispers when his father places my hand in his. "I can't believe I get to marry you twice. You look... wow."

"I love you," I whisper, my heart racing.

"I love you more," he replies instantly, squeezing my hand, our eyes locked. I wonder if he knows that the lucky one here isn't him. It's *me*. Xavier smiles as Zach starts the ceremony, and as I stand here with him, surrounded by our loved ones, I realize that this is where our happily ever after begins.

Epilogue

XAVIER

"How do you feel?" I ask as we get off the plane on Enzo's island. We're running much later than I would've liked, and I can only hope my sister will never find out that we were nearly late for her wedding.

Sierra glares at me, pure rage written all over her face. "This is all your fault," she snaps, pausing mid-step as she takes a deep, steadying breath.

"I'm sorry, Kitten," I tell her. "I'm the worst. Awful, really."

"You are," she agrees, and I smile at her as I bend down and lift her into my arms. She sighs and rests her head on my shoulder as I carry her to the mansion she needs to be at as Valeria's maid of honor. "I think I'm dying, Xave. I'm going to die any second now."

I try my best not to smile as I gently lower her to the floor a few steps away from the front door. "You're not dying," I promise her, having gotten used to this. "I think you'll be okay."

"I *won't* be okay," she insists, her face pale and her eyes filled with despair. "I can't do this for another seven months."

I grin as I rub her shoulders gently, taking in her beautiful sky blue maid of honor dress, her wavy hair, and that beautiful glow of hers. "The morning sickness won't last forever," I promise her as I hand her one of the ginger candies she likes. I keep them on me at all times now, along with peppermint candy, since I'm never sure which of the two she'll want.

Sierra takes it from me and sighs happily as it hits her tongue, her body relaxing just a little as she brushes her fingers over my tie. It's the same color as her dress, and she smiles as she looks up at me. "I love you," she whispers. "I hope you're looking forward to being a DILF."

I burst out laughing and drop my forehead to hers, still every bit as enamored with her as I've always been, but perhaps even more so now. Our marriage has only grown stronger since our second wedding ceremony, and we've been very intentional about our commitment to each other. We've had our ups and downs, but we've weathered every storm together, learning to lean on each other when times got tough. She's given me so much grace, and she's stood by me as I worked through some of the scars the past left, my burdens feeling a little lighter every day, until one day, the weight was off my shoulders.

Every day, I make sure she knows just how much I appreciate her, how much strength she gives me, and how much better my life is because I get to share it with her, and somehow, she still seems to think she got the better deal out of the two of us. But then again, she's always been a little crazy, so that shouldn't surprise me.

I kiss my wife's forehead before leaving her in front of Valeria's room, my heart aching just a touch at the thought of my sweet little sister getting her own happily ever after. I know we aren't losing her, but still, I can't help but feel a little somber as I make my way to Enzo's room to fulfill my best man duties.

I sigh when I walk in and find him seated, my brothers and my dad standing in front of him, their guns clearly visible in their holsters. Enzo just smiles at them, not the least bit intimidated, and

I shake my head. "That guy chose to marry *Valeria*," I remind them. "He clearly has no sense of fear, nor any self preservation skills. Trying to intimidate him is like throwing a drop of water in the ocean."

He throws me a grateful smile, and I push past Elijah and Dad, who are grumbling to themselves, and pause in front of him. "Honestly, Enzo, if she's forcing you to marry her against your will, blink twice. I'll find a way to save you." He opens his eyes as wide as possible, and I can't help but chuckle.

He rises to his feet, his smile fading a little as he runs a hand through his hair. "I've waited for this moment for well over a decade, yet somehow, now that we've finally made it here, I'm scared that I'm going to fail her, and I won't be able to keep her happy."

I place my hand on his shoulder as I lead him out of the room and toward the altar, trying my best to keep him on schedule, lest my sister murder me. I don't fear much, but I've definitely learned to fear my sister's wrath. "I get it," I admit. "I felt the same way when I married Sierra — both times. It's like you've waited your whole life for this moment, and then you're standing there, suddenly wondering if you're even good enough for everything you have, if you deserve it, and if you've got what it takes to be with women as amazing as ours. I was like that too, Enzo." He looks at me like he's clinging onto my words desperately. "I'll tell you something I wish I'd been told before I got married," I say, pausing for a moment. "You *are* going to fail her at least a few times. It's inevitable when you share a whole lifetime with someone, Enzo. Things aren't always going to be perfect. What matters most is how you handle your mistakes, and whether or not you learn from them. You'll both fuck up occasionally, but each time it happens, you'll become stronger together too."

That's what being with Sierra taught me. I used to think that marriage was an end goal, that I'd get to keep her forever if I could just get her to marry me, and I wish things were that simple. You have to earn the right to be with someone every day, in little ways that show them you care, that you love them, that you still *choose* them, long after you say 'I do'.

He stares at me and nods, nerves written all over her face. "You know there's nothing I won't do to make her happy, right?"

I smile at him as I take my place next to him, my gaze roaming over the crowd. "I'm well aware," I tell him, remembering everything he's done just to end up standing here with Valeria. "You know you're perfect for her, right?"

I watched her slowly turn back into the person she was before she was captured, all because he refused to give up on her. If not for him, I might have lost my sister forever, even though she was right there with us. Enzo looks at me in disbelief, and I smile as music begins to play. He tenses as he stares ahead, and I can't help but mess with him. "Wait, come to think of it... V didn't board my jet this morning. Was she supposed to come with me? I hope she found her way here."

He panics, and I stare ahead expressionlessly, until my wife walks down the aisle, and just like that, I'm mesmerized. Our eyes lock, and I sigh happily, silently praying that my sister will have what we have while simultaneously wondering how I got to be this lucky.

Sierra smiles at me, and a sense of calm washes over me as I stare at the love of my life, still every bit in love with her as I've always been. Somehow, our love just grows stronger every day, and I can't wait to continue writing our story together, our happily ever after never ending.

Want more of Xavier and Sierra? Scan the QR code on the next page or go to my website catharinamaura.com/bonuses to gain access to the following bonus scenes: their first kiss (when he bailed her out of jail years ago!), Sierra catching Xavier at poker night with her brothers, Sierra's bachelorette, Grandma's letter to Xavier on their second wedding day, and more.

. . .

I can't wait to tell you The Muse's story next: Mine for a Moment is a brother's best friend workplace romance filled with angst and spice, and I'm excited for you to read it on 15 October! It's available at all retailers. Preorder by scanning the following QR code:

Xavier's siblings are getting their own series after Mine for a Moment, and the ebook version of Valeria and Enzo's book is already up for preorder too!

More by Catharina Maura

Ares and Raven: The Wrong Bride

The man Raven has always loved is engaged to her sister. But when her sister leaves him at the altar, she's asked to step in and marry him instead.

Luca and Val: The Temporary Wife

When the secretary he thought he hated suddenly quits her job, he realizes he'll stop at nothing to make her his — especially if it means getting out of his arranged marriage by marrying her instead.

Dion and Faye: The Unwanted Marriage

Despite resisting for years, Dion Windsor can't escape his engagement to alluring pianist, Faye. Seeing her with another man makes him realize he's done running. Time is up, and whether she likes it or not, she's his, as long as the secrets he holds don't destroy her...

Zane and Celeste: The Broken Vows

Childhood rivals turn into star-crossed lovers, until tragedy tears them further apart than ever before... Forced back together through an arranged marriage neither wants, they learn that not everything is what it seems.

Lexington and Raya: The Secret Fiancée

Raya never expected that ruining Lex Windsor's shirt would lead to an evening filled with games and laughter. She walks away the next day never expecting to see him again — until he shows up as her professor, offering her class an internship. He knows something she doesn't: none of their meetings were coincidental, and the two are arranged to be married.

Silas and Alanna: Bittersweet Memories

When her boyfriend breaks her heart, Alanna goes after his older brother in a quest for revenge. It would have been simple — if he wasn't also her new boss. As they spend time together, she realizes he knows her better than he should. He knows about the memories she's lost.

Made in the USA
Middletown, DE
31 August 2024

60100030R00210